RECRUITMENT

THE RESISTANCE TRILOGY, BOOK ONE

K. A. RILEY

A NOTE FROM THE AUTHOR

Dearest Fellow Conspirator,

What you have in your hands is one-ninth of what's called an *ennealogy*, a rare and hard-to-pronounce word meaning "a nine-part series." It's basically three sequential, interlocking trilogies. (Think *Star Wars* or *Planet of the Apes*)

Here is the Reading Order for the *Conspiracy Ennealogy*...

#1: **Resistance Trilogy**

Recruitment
Render
Rebellion

#2: **Emergents Trilogy**

Survival
Sacrifice
Synthesis

#3: **Transcendent Trilogy**

Travelers
Transfigured
Terminus

I'm glad you chose to join in the Conspiracy! Enjoy the revolution!

KARiley

To Lucy, L.A., Uncle Nephew, and Little Rain for setting me up and bringing me home.

"'Whether Tempter sent, or whether tempest tossed thee here ashore,
Desolate yet all undaunted, on this desert land enchanted
On this home by Horror haunted—tell me truly, I implore
Is there—*is* there balm in Gilead?—tell me—tell me, I implore!'
Quoth the Raven 'Nevermore.'"

— Edgar Allen Poe, *The Raven*

PROLOGUE

Everyone knows what happens on the day you turn seventeen. But no one knows what happens after that.

Because the day you turn seventeen, the Recruiters come to take you away.

In the Valta, no matter what day or month you were actually born, everyone has the same birthday: November 1st. That's the anniversary of the day, fourteen years ago, when the Eastern Order invaded our country.

Four years into the war, our little town in the mountains caught fire and our whole world went dark. My memory is hazy, but I'm old enough to remember those first attacks. I was a six-year-old girl when our town burned.

One minute, everyone was living perfectly normal lives. The next minute, a fleet of silver drones—no one knows exactly how many—appeared overhead and fired down a coordinated EMP blast that wiped out our power. In one brilliant flash of photoelectric blue, cell phones stopped working. The wi-fi went down. We lost the television stations, satellite feeds, social media, radio, traffic lights, power outlets, car engines, ham radios, even the flashing lights on the restored carousel in Miner's Park…everything. One minute, the world was alive with activity and color. The next minute, there was just…nothing.

The adults seemed dazed by it all, like they were walking around in a fog. As if cutting all those signals and wires disconnected something in them, too. But the next day, when word spread of a second swarm of drones on the horizon, the adults were shaken into action. Led by my father, they hustled all the kids in town into the school and got to work hammering big sheets of plywood up against the windows.

The adults saved us.

But by the time they'd finished, it was too late for most of them to save themselves.

The drones rained down a hail of plasma fusion bombs. Buildings burst into flames. The woods at the far end of town were engulfed. The streets and sidewalks melted. People and animals screamed. The cries were so inhuman that I couldn't tell which sounds were coming from which species.

Somehow, the school survived the attack, so most of us did, too. The adults who were left alive, like my father, did their best to reassure us. They promised us we'd be okay, that help was on its way.

But no help came.

In the aftermath and in my terror, I latched onto my father as he explained how my mother was never coming home. When he said the word "never," I pressed myself deeper into his shoulder, and I sobbed and screamed until my throat burned. As the days passed, I stared at my father and at my older brother Micah as they cried, too, and as they slowly turned into hollowed-out husks before my eyes. It would be another two years before any trace of life reappeared in their faces. A few years after that, the

Recruiters took my brother away. Later that same year, my father disappeared, without a trace or an explanation, in the middle of the night.

After that, I learned to rely on what I had. Instead of friends, I had fellow survivors. Instead of family I had Render, the jet-black raven my father and I raised together and trained. Render became the only living thing in the world I felt connected to.

Otherwise, like my town, I felt alone. Forgotten.

The Valta has always been isolated, but it used to be by choice. The town is tucked away among snowy peaks and has always been hard to access, so we never got too many tourists passing through. The sleepy little town was built on a wooded plateau on the side of a mountain, with impassable summits on three sides and a single steep road snaking down on the other. We liked it that way. We prided ourselves on our inaccessibility.

But after that first wave of attacks, we found ourselves cut off from the world against our will. When the war came to us, the majestic peaks surrounding us on three sides suddenly seemed more like the oppressive walls of a prison.

To add to our natural confinement, the army began to guard us on the fourth side, at the end of the road down at the bottom of our mountain. To this day, no one is allowed to cross, either coming or going. *Government orders,* they tell us. *It's for your own good.*

Beyond the army's outpost is a hundred-mile strip of desert wasteland, lying between them and whatever they're protecting us from on the other side.

The total government lock-down that occurred ten years ago included buried land mines, motion-detector assault drones, electrified fences, and long coils of razor wire around the perimeter of town. In those early days, whenever we asked, the soldiers told us it was to keep us safe.

I still wonder why being kept safe sometimes feels so unbelievably dangerous.

It wasn't long before the soldiers stopped their routine patrols and started coming up the road just once a year on what became known as Recruitment Day. And it wasn't long after *that* when we realized that the remaining adults in town couldn't guarantee their own survival, let alone ours.

With so many dead, no connections and no hope, the town's younger residents did what we had to do: we took over.

We learned to grow food, to make clothing. We learned to fend for ourselves. There were still adults around, but many were either elderly, disabled, injured in the drone strikes, or else too shell-shocked to take care of us the way I know they wanted to. I can't say I blame them. By most estimates, our town's population went from about six hundred to less than one hundred in just under forty-eight hours.

Before the strikes, the most crowded place in town was the Farmer's Market on Main Street.

After the strikes, it was the graveyard.

Word used to go around that there were other towns like ours out there. Contented little prison camps where the government kept people isolated and blissfully ignorant as to what was occurring beyond their borders. We used to get snippets of news from couriers or from the occasional straggler who'd lost their way and somehow made it over the mountain passes to the Valta, trying to get to one place or escape from another.

For a time, we heard tales from the older kids about life out in the rest of the world. Whispers about roving militias. Armed street gangs. Mysterious government training in special facilities in strange little towns that didn't show up on any map. They told us about those who moved from town to town, taking teenagers away for mysterious reasons.

Now, there are exactly twenty broadcast points in the Valta known as *viz-screens,* posted on crumbling walls or rising up from thin metal poles positioned around what's left of our town. The screens are the only source of information coming from the outside world. From the flickering monitors, the polished reporters known as Casters tell us with beaming smiles and impossibly white teeth about the war we're winning. Twenty-four hours a day, seven days a week, we hear about the great life that lies ahead for all of us Sixteens after Recruitment Day comes. We hear about the progress made by our side. We see grainy footage of our soldiers marching through the ruins of cities to engage in battle against the Eastern Order. Other than the soldiers on patrol down at the foot of the mountain, the Casters are our only real connection to life outside the Valta and the only day-to-day confirmation that anyone else is even alive out there.

One year after the attacks, the first of the Recruiters showed up in the Valta. On November 1st, every new seventeen-year-old in town—there were twenty of them that first year—was rounded up and carted off in a convoy of big military trucks to fight for our side against the enemy invaders.

The Recruiters don't talk much. They don't tell us where they're taking the new Seventeens, or what the endgame is. They just show up every year on the same day, square-jawed and armed to the teeth. They used to talk to us more, give us information about the war and about the outside world. Most of the time now, though, they're cold and silent as stone.

Every November 1st, they return to the Valta to escort the willing. They hunt down and drag away the defiant. Then their transport trucks disappear back down the only road out of town, taking the new Cohort of Seventeens with them.

My name is Kress, and I'm sixteen years old.

This is the last day of October.

My last day in the Valta.

My last day of wondering.

1

"I SEE YOUR LUNATIC BIRD'S SHOWING OFF AGAIN," CARDYN SAYS, scrunching his eyebrows together as he sidles up to me and stares at Render.

"He does that," I reply. "He knows he's the most handsome guy around."

"Pfft. He *wishes*."

The raven who's been my companion since I was seven years old is parading around on top of the derelict wooden fence that lines one side of the old parking lot where we sleep on nights when it's too hot in the bombed-out school building we call home. Render is alternating between staring at Cardyn and gawking at his own reflection in a set of wind chimes fashioned out of the jagged pieces of a shattered mirror. Someone decided a few years ago to hang it from the branch of an old tree, and over time, it's become Render's favorite distraction on the school's grounds.

Most of the Valta's buildings were either demolished in the bombings or are too structurally damaged to live in. But aside from the collapsed northeast corner where a few windows were shattered, Shoshone High School managed to escape most of the mayhem. For those of us who survived, it's become our home, our meal hall, and the hub of our lives. The building is also our shelter during drone strikes. Though we haven't had any of those for a while now.

Shoshone High School is where the Sixteens and the older Juvens take on the responsibility of teaching the Neos—that's what we call the younger kids—how to read, write, garden, hunt, and learn about the world. At first, there were no hierarchies or labels. Over time, though, it made sense to organize ourselves. After the first couple of years of the Recruitment, the older kids established the groupings of Neos, Juvens, and of course, the Sixteens. It made it easier to arrange for teaching and training. Plus, every few years, we got to feel like we were graduating. The system works, which is why we've kept it to this day.

Beyond the fence at the far end of the school's weed-covered parking lot is thick forest, overgrown and untended since the last massive bombing by the Eastern Order a couple of years back. A lot of the trees were hardy enough to survive, but others were scorched beyond recovery. That raid was the worst by far. Fortunately, it was also the last.

Now, instead of being afraid during attacks, we just live in fear of the *possibility* of being attacked. To be honest, I'm not sure which is worse.

Everyone knows about the Eastern Order, though no one seems to know where they came from or how they managed to invade our country. We've been told that in the bigger cities out past the mountains, they plant bombs, target schools, derail trains, and fly airplanes into buildings. People say they're religious psychotics who believe that some god or other told them to kill anyone who's not among what they call "the Faithful." All I know is that they're the ones who killed my mother and who might even be responsible for the disappearance of my father. For that reason alone, I hate them more than words can say.

The Casters say that for the Eastern Order, killing is a job, some kind of duty or an obligation. The Order casually mows down men, women, and children, all because some deity told them to. All day long on the viz-screens, we see images of the Order marching through burning cities and down bombed-out highways, killing without mercy. The twenty monitors set up throughout the Valta are the only source of restored power we've been given by the Execs, the remaining leaders of what used to be the American government.

The good news is that after the last raid, things went quiet. Some said the Order didn't return because they figured they'd killed us all. In some ways, I felt like they had. My life had changed forever, and so had everyone else's. Those who survived were left hanging on by a fragile thread, barely able to contain our grief.

In that final attack we lost our supply shed, the water tower, our back-up air-raid shelter, half the woods, and most of the remaining adults. When the smoke cleared, we went from about a hundred people left to just forty. Forty, that is, plus Render. Somehow, he manages to survive everything.

It's part of the reason he's so popular in our sad little town. Most of the population of the Valta knows him far better than they know me.

Not to mention that he's pretty good at pissing my friends off.

"What the heck is he doing *now*?" Cardyn asks, aggravated and clearly trying to hide a feeling of uneasiness. The raven's eyes are locked onto Cardyn's, like he's competing in a staring contest.

To anyone who doesn't know him, Render probably looks threatening and unreadable. That's what happens when the whites of one's eyes disappear. Darkness takes their place. The eyes go from being windows revealing one's soul to bottomless pits of pure mystery. Sometimes I wish I had eyes like his. I'd love to be so unapproachable that I could scare off strangers with one menacing look. Of course, being a five-foot-five, one-hundred-and-twenty-pound teenage girl, I'm the furthest thing from threatening. I'm strong after years of struggling to survive, and sure, I can keep up with some of the other Sixteens when it comes to running or other physical activities. But I'm hardly the athletic star of our Cohort. Whenever I try to appear threatening, Card tells me how I'm more shadow than menace, which usually makes us both laugh.

Cardyn shifts on his feet. "He's really creeping me out."

"He's studying your face," I tell him with a shrug, eyeing his chestnut-brown eyes and disheveled hair. "He's memorizing your features. Mapping you."

"Mapping me? What for? Is he making a note of my gigantic nose?"

I let out a laugh, partly because his nose isn't even remotely large. I'd never say it out loud, but for me, it's always been Card's mouth that stands out. He has almost comically full lips, especially for a guy. Some of the kids used to call him *grouper,* after the fish. But he never seemed to mind. I've heard him call himself worse on a semi-regular basis all our lives. Like me, Card's always known that self-deprecation was the best way to avoid an insult. One time a few years back, he told me his philosophy. "Preemptively tell the world that you suck, and they'll never accuse you of sucking. At the very worst, they'll pity you for your suckiness, and that's way better than having them think you're arrogant."

There was a morbid logic to it.

Now that he's on the verge of adulthood, Card's grown nicely into his odd-ball features. Pale, freckled skin. Fine reddish hair on his arms. Big hands, callused from helping to build the elaborate pulley and bucket systems we use to move water, haul lumber, and transport unsalvageable materials out to the debris field on the edge of town. It doesn't surprise me that some of the other girls are interested in him. To me, though, he's still the same friendly, goofy guy I've known all my life.

And currently, Render's fascinated with his features.

"Anyhow, I don't get why he'd look at me," Card says. "Everyone knows you're the prettiest girl in the Valta. He should be staring at *you*."

I shoot him a look of shock, only to realize his ears have gone red, like he didn't really mean to say the words out loud.

"What are you talking about?" I ask him as I feel my own cheeks flush in a sympathetic show of embarrassment. "I'm not even close to being the prettiest. Kella looks like one of those swimsuit models from the old magazines. Rain has perfect skin and hair, not to mention that she's amazing at everything. I'm just...me."

I catch my reflection in one of the slowly-turning pieces of mirror on the inelegant wind chime hanging to our left. Sigh. There I am. Long, brown hair. Big, almond-shaped eyes that look like my mother's. Olive skin that somehow manages to turn pink at the slightest hint of self-consciousness. A pointy nose that I never much liked. Lips that are neither full nor thin, as if they can't quite make up their mind.

A year or so ago, Rain told me how pretty I was. I was shocked at the compliment. I replied that I didn't have time to worry about whether I was attractive or not. But the truth is that sometimes I want to think about something other than the devastation of the last several years. It feels good to be superficial, to dwell on stuff that shouldn't matter.

Because the truth is that everything else in my life matters so much that it hurts.

I pull my eyes away from my reflection, convinced that Card's gone insane. "Besides, Render's not judging you," I tell him, quickly changing the subject away from my looks. "He's storing your face in his memory banks. His internal hard drive." It was my father who taught me about ravens' intellect, their ability to recognize a face and to pass their knowledge down from generation to generation. Dad had learned it, he said, from some old documentary on television—back when people could watch what they wanted instead of the government-legislated programs on the viz-screens.

Cardyn blows out a rapid, unconvinced puff of air, like I've just told him pigs can now fly and sing opera at the same time. "That's ridiculous, Kress. Okay. He's a pretty smart bird. I'll give you that. But he's not some supercomputer genius."

"Isn't he?" I ask. I look up at Render, who cocks his head to the side, questioning.

Ravens have incredible memories. If a person wrongs them, they hold a grudge for their entire life. About a year ago, a straggler wandered into the Valta and tried to steal some food from the town's supply shack. When I caught him in the act just outside the shack, he grabbed me. "You're a pretty young thing, aren't you?" he said, licking his foul lips as I tried to yank myself away. Not only did Render attack him from above, forcing him to release me from his grip, but when the man tried to return three months later, the raven issued a series of preemptive dive-bombing maneuvers that resulted in some bloody wounds to the would-be thief and guaranteed he would never come near the Valta again.

It also turned Render into the town hero. Ever since then, the Neos rush up to me practically on a daily basis and ask about him. Swarming around me like hungry kittens, they ask if they can feed him or pet him. Somehow, I've become pseudo-famous by association, but the fact is, he's the star.

And I'm pretty sure I know why he's taking stock of Card's features now.

After tomorrow, he'll never lay eyes on Card's face again.

Or mine, for that matter.

I thrust the thought out of my mind and issue a long, sharp whistle, followed by two short ones. "Hey, Render—seek my right shoulder!" I call out.

The onyx-black bird lifts off, circling over my head once before landing exactly where I told him to. He's a large bird, close to six pounds, with shaggy feathers on his neck and an almost purple sheen to his black wings. I have to shift my head to the side to give him room on my narrow shoulder and upper arm.

"Oh, come on," Card replies, clearly unimpressed. "He had a fifty-fifty shot at getting that right."

"So, then, you're admitting that he understands what a shoulder is," I reply, pleased to be able to claim a small victory. Card opens his mouth to spew a retort but closes it again, defeated.

Reaching into a plastic pocket in my small canvas messenger bag, I draw out a fat, wriggling caterpillar and feed it to Render, who gobbles it up with a snap of his sharp black beak. "Good boy," I tell him.

Cardyn yanks his shoulders up in a hard shrug. "I guess it's impressive. But what's the point? Why bother training him at all? He's just a bird, and it's not like he can come with us tomorrow when the Recruiters show up." As he speaks, he reaches out without seeming to realize what he's doing and strokes a finger over the top of Render's smooth, feathered head. I've always known he has a soft spot for the raven. All the Sixteens do. Render's been a sort of mascot for years now, a constant companion, albeit one with a few seriously mischievous habits. He's been known to steal jewelry—rings, necklaces—not to mention that he likes to pull apart abandoned wool sweaters, apparently just for kicks.

"I was sort of hoping the Recruiters would let me bring him with me," I reply. I know it's an impossible wish, but I've been holding onto it all the same, more for my sake than for his. Ever since my brother got recruited and our father disappeared, Render is the only family I have. In fact, he's more than family. He and I are connected in ways that no one but me knows about, and I've never been more acutely aware of our strange bond than I am right now.

I glance down, peeling back the sleeve of my jacket for a

second to peer at the design of black bands and curves that decorate my forearm. The tattoos, as I like to call them, link me to the raven's mind, to his emotions, even to his vision. At first, the connection was just a vague fog in the back of my mind. Recently, though, it's gotten stronger, more detailed. More important. Render is literally part of me, and having him torn away is what I've dreaded most about Recruitment Day. The worst part of all is knowing it will hurt him even more than it'll hurt me. His species bonds for life. I was the first person, the first *anything*, he saw after he was born in the big room Dad set up as a lab in the high school. Back then, Render used to snuggle up against my neck and fall asleep in the evenings while I read by candlelight. He cried the first time I shut him outside for the night.

The fact is, I'm the only other true member of Render's *Conspiracy*, the name for a group of ravens. Without me, he has no one. Although the Neos and Juvens would gladly take care of him when I'm gone, because he imprinted on me so early, our bond is exclusive. He's not likely to connect like this with anyone else over the course of his lifetime.

"I hate to say it, Kress, but there's no way they'll let you keep him," Card says as if he's been reading my mind. "We don't know what the facilities are like, but I can't imagine they're set up to accommodate a bird."

"He's not just a bird. He's my drone," I protest, though I know perfectly well that Card's right. I've known all along that my chances of being allowed to bring Render with me were slim to none, but I haven't wanted to face it. Hearing the words from Card's mouth send a sharp jolt of pain to my heart, a shot of reality punching me hard in the chest. "I guess I thought my training methods might impress the Recruiters. Render's amazing at surveillance. You know how good he is at keeping an eye out—he's better than any guard dog. He could be taught to recognize enemy uniforms and call out warnings. Who knows? Maybe they'd even let me take him on missions."

Card gives me an *Are you kidding me right now* roll of his eyes, which only serves to push me into defense mode.

"He can go where no human can, not to mention do things no drone can do," I insist, realizing as I'm speaking that this is the same argument I might end up desperately trying to use tomorrow while the Recruiters shove me into the back of a truck. "He should come with us."

From his perch on my shoulder, Render lets out a loud, vibrating *kraa* as if to announce his agreement.

Card pulls his hand away from the raven and raises an eyebrow. "Maybe you're right about him being good at surveillance," he says as Render launches himself from my shoulder with a flutter of feathers and a thunderous beating of his powerful wings. He soars above us in a big loop before landing on the roof of the school. "But I'm not sure it's a good idea to tell the Recruiters about him, Kress."

"What do you mean?"

"We don't know much about them. From what we've heard, they need us for our skills, but they *want* us for our obedience."

"So?"

"So you may not want them thinking you're too independent or too smart. Karmine says armies don't like autonomous soldiers—even ones with smart-as-hell birds."

"Karmine doesn't know everything," I mutter. "He may read a lot of books, but it's not like they talk about the protocol of having birds in the military."

"Well, you never know." Card looks away for a moment, like he's having trouble putting his thoughts into words. "The thing is, I can just see you prancing up to the Recruiters tomorrow and asking, 'Can my bird come with me?' You know as well as I do what'll happen then."

I stare at the ground and swallow hard, determined not to let Card see the tears that have just begun welling in my eyes.

He's right. I know he is. A few years ago, a Recruit named Marcy tried to smuggle her cat onto the truck. She got caught right away and ended up with a black eye. Her cat ended up getting shot at by one of the Recruiters. It skittered into the woods, and we never saw it again. I can only imagine what they'd do to a threatening-looking bird.

But I'm not exactly in the mood to face the truth at the moment.

"Look, Kress, I just don't want any strikes against you on the first day," Card adds softly. "I don't want anything to happen to you."

"Aw. You're worried about me," I say, pushing away my emotions and plastering on a fake grin as I lift my face to look at Cardyn again. "That's sweet." I give him a playful shove, which is about the most intimate I'm ever willing to get with him or anyone. To say I've kept to myself since my father and brother disappeared is putting it mildly.

Card returns my gesture, pushing my shoulder with his fingers like he's itching for a low-key brawl. "Screw that! It's *me* I'm worried about. If the Recruiters find out I'm best friends with someone who owns a super-powered bird...well, there's no telling what they might do to *me*."

I pull my eyes up to the roof, where Render is strutting proudly, surveying his territory. "He's *hardly* super-powered. Besides, I don't own him. No one can really own an animal. How many times do I have to tell you that?" I'm trying to sound offended, but my lips betray me by twitching into a smile.

"As many times as it takes before it sinks into my big, ugly head."

"Oh, come on. Your head's not *that* big."

"Oh, so you're saying it's ugly?"

I duck low when Card play-punches at me, but the sparring

ends there when I shoot him a look he always refers to as the *glare of death.*

I lean down and yank a long piece of brown grass out of the ground. When I've straightened up, I take a deep breath, preparing myself to make a confession. "To be honest, I was hoping to have a shot at Special Ops. I guess I was thinking Render could help me get there if they give me a chance to show what he can do."

Card's jaw drops open. "You really think you'd have a shot at the most secret and sought-after division in the military?"

He's right. Special Ops is legendary. They say that only the highest-level Recruits are admitted for the classified missions they assign. Intelligence, spying, all the good stuff. The only problem is that no one ever hears from the Special Ops soldiers once they've been deployed.

So the legend ends with silence and secrecy.

But I'm certain of two things:

One, it's Special Ops that will win the war we've been fighting all these years.

And two: I want to be part of it.

"Why wouldn't I have a shot?" I ask with a frown.

"I didn't mean it like that. Look, you've got more going for you than most of us in the Valta. All this stuff you do with Render…" Card leans in close and whispers, "and the secret tech-training your dad taught you makes you extra-worthy."

The truth is, I haven't let Card in on *everything* my dad taught me about tech. I haven't told him about just how integrated my existence is with Render's or about the true nature of the pattern of black bars, dots, and curves on my forearms that I explain away as leftover marks from one of Dad's failed experiments. I promised my father never to divulge the full extent of the secret to anyone, and I've kept my word all these years.

"Of course, some people still say Special Ops doesn't even really exist."

"Yeah, yeah," I reply with an exasperated sigh. "I know all the rumors. About how they just made up a Special Ops division to inspire Recruits to excel in the other three military deployments, like it's some kind of twisted test to push them to the limits. All I know is what Micah told me when he was here—that some of his year's Recruits got taken away for Special Ops training. He seemed to think it was very real. Told me they were the most talented of the bunch—the really smart ones, the most gifted."

My brother, who's five years older than I am, was recruited along with all the other new Seventeens in his class. As far as I know, he's the only Recruit who's ever made it back to the Valta to tell anyone about the world beyond the mountains and about the ongoing war raging down below. One day, he came out of nowhere and startled me while I was doing a training session with Render in a small clearing deep in the woods about a quarter mile down the mountain. At first I was euphoric to see him, but I quickly realized that my big brother—my role model and my hero—was red-eyed, rail-thin, and barely coherent. He disregarded my joy at seeing him, shrugged off my attempt at a hug, and started rambling rapid-fire about Special Ops and the war. I asked him about some of the other Recruits who'd gone with him, but all he'd wanted to talk about were tests and training...and about how no one should ever have to see what he's seen.

After that, he clammed up and dropped to his knees, tears streaking down his haggard cheeks. I was just putting my hand on his shoulder to comfort him when six soldiers thundered into the clearing, knocked me aside, and dragged Micah off like they were hunters with a fresh kill. I shouted after them and even tried to chase them down, but one of the men whipped around and shot me with some kind of dart that knocked me out before I hit the ground.

When I woke up, Render was perched on a branch above me, his head tilted to the side as if to ask if I was okay.

Micah was long gone. I stayed in the woods for hours, my shoulders shaking with sobs. I'd lost my brother all over again. Render stayed with me, watching over me the entire time. Occasionally he flew down and tucked his head into the crook of my arm. When I finally managed to pull myself together, it was more for his sake than mine. I knew he could feel my pain, and I hated the thought of him suffering because of it.

That was three years ago, and I haven't heard from Micah since. I can only hope he's still alive.

"Did he say anything else?" Cardyn asks.

"Nothing more than what I've already told you and the others. He wasn't himself. He mostly rambled on about the Eastern Order and how the Executives had all these new special military training plans for us to fight them. He seemed really excited, like he thought we were on the verge of winning the war, but…he was scared, too. Like he knew something, but he couldn't say what. The last thing he said was about how Special Ops was the best-kept secret in the military. He did say it's really hard to get in."

"Well, in that case you're in for sure," Card tells me, his tone oddly sincere. "Besides, it sounds secret, and secret things are usually the most fun."

A shudder claws its way down my spine. "I'm not so sure that's true, Card," I tell him, casting my gaze toward the distant mountain peaks. "Everything in the outside world is secret now, and something tells me it's not so great. Some days I want to know what's out there, but other days I'm not sure I want to know any of it. We may have it hard in here, but whatever's down the road and beyond the mountains may be a lot worse. The war's still raging."

"Oh, come on," Card protests. "You've seen the broadcasts. We're winning."

"I'm not so sure about that," I tell him, though I can't offer him a real reason for my skepticism.

"The Execs are rebuilding the cities that were bombed out," he protests. "Stronger and better than before. If the reports about those Arcology things are true, we'll be living it up high in the sky before you know it."

I roll my eyes. I've seen the same broadcasts about the Arcologies— massive skyscrapers that contain entire cities within their walls. But I'll believe it when I see it. "They may be rebuilding giant structures in the cities, but they sure as hell haven't gotten around to fixing anything here in the Valta or opening up the roads, have they?"

Card opens his mouth and shuts it again when he realizes he doesn't have a leg to stand on. "Okay, you have a point there."

There can't be more than four or five buildings still standing fully upright in our town, and we have to rig what we can just to survive the wild weather patterns that constantly whip through here and change practically by the hour.

The Casters make a lot of noise about how great things are going on the outside. I'll believe it when I find myself living somewhere other than our rat-infested, hollowed out shell of a school building.

Card's right about one thing, though. The Casters are good at making things look sunny out there in the world. Day in and day out, we hear how the Eastern Order has been pushed back another few miles. How the grid is protected. That soon, law and order will be restored to our great nation, and we'll all be free again. We've heard it all ten thousand times. As my dad used to say, it's like a broken record.

The thing is, no one has come to liberate us. No one's reunited us with our families. We still don't have access to the Internet, television, or even old-fashioned phone lines.

Not to mention that there are only two ways to get out of town: Hiking through the dead forest and over the jagged mountains to nowhere. Or, of course, getting recruited.

Then again, most of us aren't in a huge hurry to leave. We

may have to scrounge for food, but at least we haven't been targeted in a while.

"It's possible that they keep the grid down because they want this town to look dead," Card says pensively. "The Order won't bother bombing a place that's got nothing in it, right?"

"All I know is that this war has been going on for what...fourteen, fifteen years now?" I say quietly. "Practically our whole lives."

"Wars take a long time," Card sighs. "I'm not worried. The Execs still send soldiers up every year to bring us back down for Recruitment. They're rebuilding. Obviously, things out there must be going okay, or we wouldn't hear from them at all." The words come out of his mouth, but he doesn't look entirely convinced by them. "Anyhow," he says, letting out another nervous breath, "tell me some more about your stupid bird's amazing abilities."

"Hey! My bird is a genius," I tell him, punching him on the arm. "And you'd do well to remember it." I'm feeling extra affectionate today. Maybe it's the fear of an unknown future that's driving my need for human contact.

"I'll believe he's a genius when I see it," Cardyn says.

A laugh bubbles up in my chest. "I think Render and I should probably keep his brilliance a secret for now. You said yourself that you don't want the Recruiters knowing that you're friends with a bird-training weirdo. I hate to say it, but I don't want to put a target on his back, let alone mine."

"Well, that's very boring of you."

"I'm fine with boring. It's way better than dead."

"Fine, then," Card says with a smile, glancing up one more time at Render and then back toward the school. "I'll catch up with you later." He turns to jog away before spinning back to me. "Hey. You're coming to Final Feast tonight, right?" he asks, blasting his index fingers at me like revolvers in a boyish attempt at coolness.

"Wouldn't miss it," I tell him, even though part of me is dreading going to a gathering that includes every person in town. The limit of my desire for human companionship tends to be one or two people around me at the most. The only time I'm around more people than that is when we're sleeping in the gym, and even then, I have a hard time relaxing.

Card says, "Great! See you tonight!" and runs off, sprinting up the school's steps and through the door.

Pulling my chin up, I look toward the top of the building where Render is still perched, his head bobbing as he scans the world around him. I give a low whistle, and he takes off into the sky, soaring out over the mountains until he's barely a dot in the distance. I push my jacket sleeve up again and glide my finger along my forearm. When I close my eyes, a vision flashes into my mind. As the raven's wings stretch wide, I can see the world below, Render's shadow slipping over row upon row of pine and cedar trees scattered around big patches of scorched forest.

He sweeps down toward the makeshift shed I built in the woods a few years back, tucked away on the far side of one of the old ski slopes. It's way past the hunting line, in a zone where few of the Juvens or Neos are likely to wander. Even the other Sixteens don't go down that way. There's nothing there but black trees and charred earth, dead and dying reminders of what used to be.

As I watch Render's destination grow in my mind's eye, my thoughts shift to the war, to the Recruiters. To my future.

"I can't believe they're coming tomorrow," I say softly, knowing the raven can hear me and can sense my mood, even if he can't understand what I'm saying. "I wish you and I could just fly off and live in the woods," I sigh. "I'm not exactly excited about taking part in an unwinnable war. And I don't know what I'm going to do without you."

In the distance, I hear a high-pitched *Kraa! Kraa!*

Apparently Render feels the same way.

2

AT SUNSET, AFTER A QUICK HIKE THROUGH THE WOODS, I MAKE MY way down the dirt path toward the small beach that sits along the bone-dry ravine that was once the Kokanee River.

Seating myself on an ancient tree trunk in the shadows, I pull my long brown hair back into a sloppy bun and surreptitiously watch the others gather around the bonfire. I've heard through the grapevine that Brohn, the town's most impressive Sixteen, killed a deer earlier today, and a couple of the others have already prepped it for cooking. If that's true, Final Feast will live up to its name for once.

Some years, the celebratory meal consists of little more than a rabbit or a raccoon, usually not nearly enough to feed everyone who's gathered around. Other times, when the weather's been unpleasant enough to drive the birds and the game animals down the surrounding mountains and away from us, we've been content to gorge ourselves on yucca buds, wild strawberries, stonecrop soup, and slightly bitter dandelion wine. It doesn't sound like much, but it keeps us alive, so who cares if it's not the tastiest food in the world?

Right now, I can't really bring myself to care too much about food. The tangle of nerves in my belly has replaced any thoughts of hunger with a growing sense of dread.

Up above, Render is soaring in overlapping circles. Ravens don't normally fly at night, but this evening he's making an exception, and I'm glad. He banks right then left in a giant swooping arc, letting out the odd cry to remind me that he's close by.

"I know you're there," I mutter under my breath. "We're literally connected, silly."

Render flies down and perches on the log next to me. When I reach over to stroke my fingers along his back, he presses his head into my arm, his beak pointed at the ground. It's something he used to do when he was little and in need of comfort.

"I could use a little comfort myself," I say. "I'm scared, too."

As I attempt to stop focusing on my uncertain future, my mind veers to the past, to a memory of sitting here exactly one year ago, watching in silence as every Sixteen who awaited their fate paced tensely around the fire. No one ate. No one spoke. The Recruits were all too nervous, so the rest of us ended up joining them in some kind of sympathetic, silent freak-out. Anxiety, it turns out, is as contagious as the common cold.

On the other hand, the Recruits from *two* years ago were gung-ho and totally military-minded. All they cared about was getting out of the Valta and taking down the Eastern Order as quickly and as violently as possible. "We're going to win this war for all of you!" they chanted, just before the transport trucks took them away.

Given that the Casters remind us every day that the war is still raging, I guess the plan didn't work out so great.

That's how it goes. Each Cohort has its own temperament. My class is a strange, mixed-up bunch. We're not as worried about dying as some have been, and we're not as obsessed with jumping head-first into war as some of the others. We're a herd of walking personalities, each different from the next.

My eyes move to a bunch of my fellow Sixteens who are probably talking about tomorrow. It's funny. We've all known this day was coming, but no one really talks much about it until it's actually here. It's like talking about will bring it here sooner. Or worse. That talking about it will jinx it, and what's left of our pile of broken-down buildings we call home will be blasted from rubble into total and unrecognizable dust. Tonight, though, the flood-gates open, and tomorrow's Recruitment is all that's on anybody's mind. I scan the other Sixteens, quietly assessing them, trying to figure out what they'll do, how they'll react.

Karmine is faster and better at hunting than the rest of us, a fact he's never too shy to remind us about. He's super competitive, too. It probably bothers him to know that Brohn supplied tonight's meal. Cardyn is generally quiet, like me. He's turned into a pretty handsome guy, full lips, freckles, and all. Kella is all about following the rules. Like Karmine, she's eager to jump into the war. She may look like one of those old Barbie dolls on the outside, but inside, she's a Rottweiler. Terk is as big as a cement-mixer and twice as strong. I like him a lot, although we have absolutely nothing in common. Plus, he's tall, so it hurts my neck to try to talk to him. Rain is brilliant, gorgeous, super flirty with the guys, and oozes confidence from every pore despite being barely five feet tall. I don't like her as much as the others. Amaranthine is paranoid and slightly psycho, a long-haired and constantly disheveled wild card who I kind of like anyway without knowing why. Like me, she's not big on social gatherings and will probably slip away from Final Feast long before the night's over.

Last, but never least, of course, is Brohn. He's a natural leader. Textbook handsome. Eyes that manage to be scary and pretty at the same time. They're so blue they're practically silver. Everyone looks up to him, even though he constantly tells them not to. As the dominant member of the group, though, he's ended up being a reluctant commander to the rest of us.

Our group has spent so much time teaching and training the Neos and Juvens over the last couple of years that we haven't even particularly gotten to know each other. Maybe it's because we're the last class that remembers what life was like before the first attacks. And we're the first ones who have really started to wonder if the war will ever end, or if it will just swallow us up like it has everyone who's gone before us.

As I skulk in the shadows, I can't help but notice the atmosphere on the beach has begun to settle into the same nervous, frightened energy that I'm feeling. Not at all festive like it's supposed to be. True, we're about to eat better than we have in months, but I know without asking that almost every Sixteen is feeling the same sense of profound dread that I am. What's supposed to be a celebration—a coming of age ceremony of sorts—is injecting a heavy dose of anxiety and fear into our bloodstreams.

Well, not quite all of us. Karmine and Kella have been talking non-stop for the last year about how much they're looking forward to getting uniforms, weapons, and training. In the high school's underground cafeteria, they strategize like generals about how they'd take out the Order's bombers, snipers, and drones. While the rest of us are on assignment, cleaning up debris or gathering building materials, they're off reading about battle tactics in old library books, high-fiving each other, and bragging about all the enemy kills they're planning to rack up.

To hear them tell it, they're going to make it into Special Ops and save the world all on their own. The two of them spend half their day fantasizing about a glorious future and the other half watching the viz-screens, hoping for new footage of the war zones to see what carnage our side has wrought.

I've never been able to stand the broadcasts. I've always despised the Casters, with those gleaming grins plastered on their faces despite the chaos they report on all day long. It's like they're oblivious, unfeeling constructs, numb to death and destruction.

Then there are the weekly addresses by President Krug, who's always dressed in grey suits with a bright red tie. Always with the same slicked back hair and ice-cold expression in his eyes as he announces both sides' casualty numbers for the week.

He follows that up with a cheery declaration, made through chapped lips and crooked yellow teeth, about all the enemies we've managed to take out. We can see all those numbers on the scroll at the bottom of the viz-screen, but President Krug takes special pride in announcing them as part of his regular address. Images of the dead flash on the screen for a second here and there, but they're quickly replaced with footage of happy Recruits training, shooting at targets, saluting, marching.

It's no wonder we're all so confused. We have no idea if we should look forward to a bright future or be terrified of certain death.

Over by the bonfire, some of the younger boys are fussing over Brohn's skinned deer, which they're rotating slowly on a spit-skewer. Tiny orange sparks dance up into the air like a swarm of fireflies that flicker, rise, and die. It's one of the prettiest things I've seen in a long time. The mountains surrounding the Valta used to seem pretty, too, but now all I see when I look at them are the imposing walls of a penitentiary.

It seems ironic, but I think I'm going to miss these little moments of light in the monotonous fight for survival that defines the rest of the year in this place. A life that's all about routine and the pressure to just stay alive can be a double-edged sword. There's comfort in routine, but that comfort comes with boredom and with frequent anxiety about what might happen when that routine is finally broken.

The air along the beach begins to fill with the smell of meat, along with the mountain sage, juniper berries, and wild fennel we sometimes use for seasoning. The pleasant aroma mingles briefly with a foul stench of decay rising up from somewhere in the woods behind me. The two scents fight for dominance as I inhale, and I take in as much of the good smell as I can and try to exhale the bad, filtering it from my body and mind.

I don't want to recall rot and decay when I think back to my last night in the Valta.

A couple dozen kids are talking about the Order and the war while I sit quietly, listening, aware that I blend into the long shadows cast along the beach by the rising fire. Some others are jostling and joking around, churning up contemptuous laughs at the concept of an army of violent psychopaths that would kill them as soon as look at them. We all have ways of trying to cover up our fear.

Of course, most of the laughing kids have nothing to worry about. Most are Juvens, the younger kids who will be around the Valta for a few years yet. As long as there are no more drone attacks, all they have to look forward to is Recruitment in a few years and the possibility of peace.

From my quiet perch on the periphery of our small society, I've memorized the back of every kid in town. Not just the Sixteens, either. I know the Juvens just as well: Sophie's wavy black ponytail. Vella's impossibly tiny waist and curvy hips that signal how close she is to growing up. The long, rubbery scar behind Spence's ear from when he fell into the ravine when we were kids. Cici's weird sense of humor and her long, tapered calves like sculpted ivory. Justin's clumsiness and prematurely thinning hair. Talia's ballerina neck. By this time tomorrow, I'll be gone, and they'll be the ones running things.

The Juvens technically start at age thirteen. They're the ones who will follow in our footsteps over the next couple of years. The Neos, of course, are too young to worry about anything, so they spend their time bouncing around, asking dumb questions, and getting underfoot while the older members of the town's population try to get things done. The Neos don't remember anything about the world as it was before the Valta was attacked. Most of them would have been babies or toddlers when the first of the raids happened, so this is the only life—the only *world*—they've ever known.

Our town's history is pretty simple. The Valta started out as a trading post a long time ago. It was a hub of activity between settlers, people passing through, and the small pockets of native people who called this area home. Then it became a mining town, before bigger and better silver and mineral ore deposits were discovered over on the other side of the western mountains.

Eventually, it turned into the tucked-away town we all knew as kids. Four traffic lights, one gas station, the bandshell, two cafés, the Anasazi Heritage Center, and a white and blue sign welcoming visitors to *The Best Kept Secret of the West*. The businesses and homes run by our parents were long since bombed out. The Fisherman's Market. The Vonn Family Ski and Snowboard Repair Room. Keith's Bike and Hike Equipment Rental. The Valta Souvenir Shop. Andrea's Tea Room. The Backpackers' Bar and Grill. The Fresh Company grocery store. The small chalets and bed and breakfasts along Center Street. They all lie in ruin.

Now only their foundations remain. We've cleared away the rest over the years. After the Invasion, the older teenagers pulled together, organized the younger kids, and somehow managed to keep things running. After the government locked us in, they airdropped supplies from time to time, but eventually even those dried up, and we quickly learned that we were going to have to fend for ourselves.

Every year, when the newest group of Sixteens gets recruited and becomes Seventeens, the next batch steps up to take their place. They arrange hunting and wood-gathering squads, cooking schedules, and clean-up patrols. They take over the teaching duties and run the lessons and hands-on activities we keep building on with each passing year. We're like a colony of ants. We do what we need to do. We learn to cooperate, all just so we can survive another day.

I give Render's head one last stroke and bid him a silent *Goodnight.* He flies up to perch on a tree limb where he'll entertain himself watching the gathering below before tucking himself in for the night.

I miss him already. But I need to get used to being on my own, and so does he.

I tell myself to try to enjoy this moment of relative calm while I can. The deer meat roasting over the fire smells amazing. It could definitely be one of the best meals we've ever had.

For some of us, it could also be the last.

3

"KRESS!"

Cardyn's voice startles me out of my reverie. I turn my head and narrow my eyes into the darkness until I spot him plodding toward me through the soft sand.

"Hey," I say as he drops down next to me, adjusting himself until he finds a comfortable position on the log.

"What are you doing over here by yourself?"

"I'm not by myself," I say, hugging my arms around my shoulders to ward off the chilly evening air. "You're here."

He puffs out his chest and drops his voice to his most manly baritone. "You're right, little lady. As long as I'm around, you'll never have to be by yourself."

I resist the urge to gag. Barely. "Hey, thanks. But I like being alone, in case you hadn't noticed."

Card slides a hand through his mop of reddish-blond hair. "Okay. Then as long I'm around, you'll never have to be *lonely*. How's that?" His voice betrays embarrassment, and I feel a little bad about being snarky to him.

"Good enough," I reply.

For a few seconds, Card kicks at the sand. I can't quite tell if he's still feeling awkward, or if he's just nervous about what tomorrow will bring. "The meat smells good, doesn't it?" he asks, pulling us out of an uncomfortable silence. "I heard the town hero caught a big one."

My eyes scan the crowd until they land on Brohn, standing over on the far side of the fire with his little sister, Wisp, who's practically attached to his hip. She's had that nickname for as long as I can remember. Even though she's thirteen now and officially one of the Juvens, she's only the size of most Neos. Thin as a twig, she looks like a gentle breeze might blow her over.

Tonight, she's clinging to her brother like a lifeline, as though she's terrified he'll disappear. I can't help but feel sympathetic. I was in her position a few years back, when the Recruiters came for Micah. Knowing I'd lose him was awful. But at least I got to say goodbye, and she will, too.

Wisp will turn fourteen tomorrow, which means she has three more years before the Recruiters come for her. That's three more years of trying to survive here while we're off trying to find a way to end the war once and for all. With any luck, she'll never be recruited.

Right now, though, I don't think she cares too much about any of that. It looks to me like all she can think about is her big brother, who's standing over her like a protective sentinel. All six-foot-two of him. For all the girls in town who have a thing for Brohn, I've always suspected that only one is remotely important to him, and that's Wisp.

So a bolt of shock hits me when he leaves her by the fire and starts to make his way over to the part of the beach where Card and I are sitting.

"Hey, Kress!" he calls out, holding up a hand in greeting. I swallow hard, fighting off the urge to look around like I'm trying to make sure he's actually talking to *me*. It's not like Brohn and I have ever sat around for any length of time and had a meaningful conversation. At most, we exchange the usual greetings about the weather and what food we've managed to collect for the other kids. Occasionally, he'll ask how Render's doing. But he's never actually approached me to socialize.

As Brohn strides over, a torch in his right hand, Card stands up, his body suddenly tense. "I'm gonna go hang out by the fire for a bit," he mumbles, "and see what the others are up to."

"You don't have to—" I start to say, but he's already gone, his head tucked down into the collar of his beat-up old jean jacket as he plods past Brohn, who gives him an unrequited nod.

Brohn buries the end of his torch in the sand, far enough from the patches of dry grass so it won't start any forest fires. The woods are dense but mostly dead, which is great for gathering building material or making weapons and tools, but terrible for how easily one act of carelessness could burn them—and us—down. We've had some close calls in the past, and through every crisis, Brohn was out there on the front lines, cleaning up after somebody else's stupidity. To be honest, I'm not sure how this town will function after he's gone. It's no wonder Wisp looks so distraught. She's losing a brother *and* a savior.

As I stare at the flickering flame on his torch, Brohn plants himself in Card's former spot next to me.

"Hey," I say, trying to sound casual, like I'm not remotely excited that the most interesting guy in town has singled me out for a one-on-one chat. "How are things?"

He shrugs and reaches down to the sand to grab a long twig, which he proceeds to snap absently into tiny pieces. "Fine, I guess. Why did Card take off like that?"

"I don't know. He probably just wants to check things out."

Brohn snickers. "He's not my biggest fan, is he?"

"He likes you just fine."

"I'm not so sure. Anyhow, it doesn't matter. I don't have time to care about who likes me and who doesn't. I've spent the last year trying to make sure everyone's okay, that Wisp and the others will be able to look after themselves for the next year. And now…"

"And now?"

Brohn turns to look at me, his eyes alive with the reflections of the distant flame. "That's the big question, isn't it?" he says. "Nobody knows. We don't know where we'll be sleeping tomorrow night, you and I. We have no control over anything in our lives anymore, as of tomorrow morning. After the transport trucks takes us to…wherever, we don't really even know if we'll ever see each other again."

It's so strange to think that for the past ten years, I've slept in the same building as Brohn. For a long time, his room in the school was just down the hall from the one Dad, Micah, and I shared up until our father's disappearance. But for the last year, most of the Sixteens have slept on rows of cots in the big gymnasium, despite the fact that there are still holes in its roof thanks to residual damage from the Eastern Order's lethal drone strikes.

The current sleeping arrangement is a tradition started by the Sixteens of the 2035 Cohort. It's supposed to be a kind of bonding thing for each Cohort, a way to become a team in our final year as we prepare for Recruitment. I spend the occasional night in my Cohort's company, but most of the time I use the excuse that I want to stay upstairs in the room that holds memories of my family.

Over the last year, I've managed to stay as far away from Brohn and most of the others as possible, and they haven't particularly made any effort to get close to me. But now, for some reason, the thought of separation from Brohn has begun to feel almost as acute as being separated from Render. I suppose it's a matter of comfort. Brohn's presence, however lacking it's been in intimacy, has always soothed me and made me feel safe. I always knew that as long as he was around, I'd be okay.

If we get split up tomorrow, I'll no longer have the promise of a strong ally nearby.

"The unknown makes me nervous," I confess.

"Me too," Brohn says, his voice gentle and even. "Always has."

A lump forms in my throat as I realize that by this time tomorrow, our entire world will be overflowing with unknowns.

"They say we're winning the war," I add, my words intended to reassure us both. "Maybe it'll be over soon."

"Maybe. But unfortunately, probably not by tomorrow morning."

We both chuckle, and I feel myself blush when we share a brief moment of eye contact.

"Still," he says, "the Casters keep saying things are going well for our side." Now Brohn's got a crooked smile on his lips—a trademark that's been known to charm some of the girls. The expression gives him the look of someone who's got every thought in the world churning through his mind at once. "So we must totally be winning," he adds. "For now, at least."

"For now, at least," I repeat.

The four words long ago became a mantra for those of us in the Valta. It's the reply to every greeting, every piece of small talk.

"The weather's nice."

For now, at least.

"Doing well?"

For now, at least.

"No Recruiters are banging down the door today."

For now...at least.

Everything in our world is temporary. We know how vulnerable we are, that we're just playing a waiting game until life gets very complicated very fast.

Brohn gestures toward a ceramic jug that's sitting on a stump several feet away. "Oh, hey, I made strawberry juice. You want some?"

A grin spreads its way across my lips. "You killed a deer *and* strawberries? Impressive."

Laughing, he takes my reply as a *yes* and strides over to grab it, handing it to me when he's back. I take a swig from the jug, and the sweet juice slides down my throat like liquid candy.

"So, listen. How are you really doing with all this?" he asks as we shift around on the log like two people who aren't sure if it's okay for any of their body parts to touch.

"I'm…good," I say. I don't want to reveal my concerns about tomorrow. "I mean, I'm not *totally* good." I swallow hard with the realization that I'm about to divulge something personal. "Okay, I'm kind of terrified."

"We all are," Brohn says without hesitation. "Even the ones who pretend they're not."

I shake my head, and my hair tumbles down over my shoulders as it escapes its knot. I push it back self-consciously, but Brohn reaches out and draws a wavy strand down in front of my shoulder. "You always wear your hair up," he says, his eyes on mine. "It's really nice down."

"I...thanks," I say, staring for a moment at his lips.

Wait—what am I doing?

"It gets in my way when it's down," I add in an attempt to sound casual and hide the fact that I'm feeling completely flustered.

"Sure, *that's* why you don't do it," he says with a renewed crooked grin.

"What are you trying to say?"

"I'm saying I think you don't want the world knowing how pretty you are, Kress."

Okay, what's going on today? First Card, now Brohn? Apparently being faced with your own mortality makes young men say insane things.

Not that I'm complaining about Brohn's compliment.

I pull my eyes away from his and stare into the distance. "Do you care?" I ask.

"About what?"

"Whether or not people think you're handsome."

He shakes his head. "Not most people," he says in a cryptic way. "Present company excepted, however."

I can't help smiling. "You know you're good-looking, Mr. Hotshot. You hardly need to worry about my opinion."

"I didn't say I was worried."

I narrow my eyes at him before letting out a laugh. "What I wouldn't give for your confidence," I say.

"Seriously? Little miss mysterious bird trainer is telling me she's not confident? You and Render are the talk of this town. Everyone thinks you're amazing."

"Yeah, well, I won't have Render anymore as of tomorrow," I tell him through an awful tightness in my throat. "Which means you'll realize pretty quickly that I'm not all that great."

"I doubt that. You seem to be the only person around here who doesn't know you're pretty cool."

"I...don't think about it that much," I tell him.

"I know. That's what makes you so attractive," he replies.

"I really don't know how to respond to that," I say, my body leaning a little toward his.

He nods silently. "Well, you are. You're mysterious—you and that bird of yours. I've never known what's going in your head, but I've always wondered. That makes you...I don't know, alluring."

"Well, if you want to know what's going on in my head," I tell him, pulling my eyes away, "right now I'm scared that we'll be separated." My voice has gone thin with some emotion I've never quite encountered. "I mean...all of us. I feel like we're some kind of weird, dysfunctional family, and even though we might not be that close, it feels strange to think of suddenly being alone. I've already lost one family. I don't want to lose another one."

"Which is why you've avoided getting close to any of us," he observes.

"You've noticed that, huh?"

He nods, a smirk stretching his lips. "I can't help but notice. Most of the other girls are around all the time. But you...you keep to yourself. It's like you don't need anyone."

If he only knew the truth. I need *everyone*. I'm scared out of my mind about tomorrow. I'm devastated. I haven't been comforted by anyone in years, and part of me craves it like a thirsty person craves water.

But saying it out loud would make me feel weak. And I can't afford to be weak right now.

"Tell me something about your dad," Brohn says in a gentle tone, kindly changing the subject. "He seemed like a good guy, from what I knew of him."

The thought of my father makes me smile. It's been six years since I last saw him. In that time, I've talked with Card a million times about my family, but never once with Brohn. "Dad used to be a geneticist," I say. "That was his thing back when we lived out east. But when the Execs tried to recruit him for a bunch of the government's techno-human development programs, he said no. That's when he and my mother packed me and Micah up and moved us to the Valta."

"But he didn't work as a geneticist *here,* did he? There aren't facilities for that kind of thing."

"No. He was more like a tinkerer. He was always building things or showing me the ins and outs of code and micro-circuitry. We used to forage in the old stores that had been bombed out or looted, on the off chance there might still be some decent scraps. I would have been really little back then—only about six or seven. I remember scurrying along behind him, trying desperately to keep up with his long strides. We managed to recover copper wire, fiber optic cable, you name it."

I clam up, realizing I've just said way too much. I shouldn't be telling Brohn any of this. I always promised my father not to talk to anyone about our projects—especially the most secret one of all: Render.

He was the last project my father and I worked on together. Dad called the experiment *TOBI,* which stands for *Trans-species Organic Bio-tech Integration*. My father built certain surveillance capabilities into the raven's body, gave him knowledge and skills no other animal has—including a direct link to me.

But the connection between us goes beyond micro-circuitry. The implants function beyond a visual level. Sometimes I can feel what Render feels: hunger, fear, pain, loss. I've even felt the freedom of flight when he takes off over the trees.

I peer up into the tree limbs above us, wondering where he is right now. I know perfectly well that with one tap of my inner wrist, I could figure it out. But I'm not about to give away that particular secret to Brohn.

"So, wire and cables, huh?" Brohn says with one of his perfect crooked grins. "Should I even ask what you and your dad did with those?"

"Probably not," I reply with a chuckle. I'm relieved to realize how laid back he is about it all. He's probably got his own secrets, anyhow. Everyone does. Even in a place this small. *Especially* in a place this small.

It's the only way to maintain any semblance of sanity.

"My dad and I never got a chance to say goodbye," I add quietly. "I still think about that every day."

"I'm sorry." Brohn moves his hand toward mine then pulls it back, like he's realized it's a bad idea to touch me.

"One night," I continue, trying to put his gesture out of my mind, "I was lying on the sleeping pad in our room while Dad played around with some old electronics in his lab just down the hall. The next morning when I got up, he and a bunch of the other adults were gone. No one saw anything. At least, if they did, they didn't talk about it."

"I remember that night," Brohn says. "We were Neos. We would have been…what? Ten years old?"

"Eleven."

"Right," he says. "Still…so young to lose, you know…"

"What happened to your parents?" I ask, realizing I've been selfishly behaving like I'm the only one who's lost family. Brohn and Wisp have been on their own as long as I can remember, but I've never actually sat down and talked with either of them about it.

"I lost both my parents a few years before that in the first sweep. I barely remember them. Shadows mostly. I've always wondered how they were taken so quietly. For months I couldn't sleep. I was convinced that someone was going to come for us, too."

"You were right. They are. Tomorrow."

"True."

"I can only hope my dad's somewhere peaceful and quiet," I say with a sigh. "Toward the end, he seemed tired all the time. Part of me feels like he gave so much to me that he lost some pretty important parts of himself. He taught me everything I know, how to read, to write, and how to build…stuff." I avoid telling Brohn about the time my father let me help him with Render's ocular implants, or how he taught me to create a solar-powered EMT pulse-emitter small enough to fit into my palm.

"Maybe he knew he wasn't going to be around forever, and he wanted to give you every tool at his disposal," Brohn says, his voice soft and sympathetic. I'm not sure if it's my imagination or if he's leaning in a little closer now. Part of me wants to push my shoulder in his direction, to feel the warmth from his body, if only so I can remind myself that we're both still alive.

"What about you?" I ask, my body going rigid as I order myself to keep my distance. "How are you doing with all this?"

"Me? I'm doing okay. But I'd be lying if I said I'm not worried about Wisp," he says with a sigh. "I worry about you, too." For another long moment we stare into each other's eyes. This time it's him who pulls his gaze away. "I worry about all of us Sixteens. Life's about to change a lot for the seven of us."

"Eight," I correct him. "There are eight of us who are turning seventeen this year."

"Right. I forget about Amaranthine. I guess I figured the Recruiters would..."

Brohn trails off. There's no polite way to describe the people the Recruiters skip and leave behind, discarding those of us who are too odd or undesirable to train. The kids who don't see the world the way the rest of us do.

Most of the new Seventeens get recruited, but a few have been rejected over the years, all of whom are young adults now. They usually live out in the thin strip of woods on the edge of town, or else hide out in their own small rooms at the school. Some of them lurch around town, talking nonsense to invisible people and getting in the way of the visible ones. Sometimes they disappear in the middle of the night, never to be seen or heard from again.

"Nothing's ever predictable around here, is it?" I say, breaking the awkward silence. "We live in the most boring place on earth, but we never know what's going to happen."

"Except for President Krug's weekly addresses." Brohn reaches down, picks up a little stone, and tosses it toward the crusted-over black riverbed. It skitters across the lumpy earth and lands somewhere in the dark with a thunk.

"Oh, yes. The greatest of all presidents is so inspiring," I reply in my best dramatic voice. "*So* presidential."

In 2028, President Krug declared martial law after the Eastern Order invaded. Four years after that, the war found its way to the Valta. Word spread from place to place after the phones and Internet went down. People drove through towns, using the last of their fuel as they shouted the news. Some came through in jeeps or on ATVs or even on horseback to give us updates.

The only sign of power now comes from the smiling Casters and the constant reports scrolling along on the flashy viz-screens. For some reason, the Execs are more than happy to provide enough electricity to run the news feed, but none to power refrigerators or appliances to help us cook our food.

"Krug's been in charge for the better part of two decades, while our country wallows in a state of war," Brohn says in a bitter tone, before muttering, "Don't tell Karmine and Kella I said that, by the way."

"I won't."

"Good. Those two are so patriotic, I think they probably piss red, white, and blue."

That makes me laugh, but a glimpse of Brohn's sister standing quietly over by the bonfire brings me back down to earth.

Brohn and I go quiet for a minute before I speak again. "So, who's going to take care of Wisp?"

"There are some responsible Juvens around," he says, his shoulders slumping a little. I detect a faint quiver in his voice, but I don't say anything. "Sophie's been really good to her. She's a natural leader. And I know Trent can be a jerk sometimes, but he's got a good protective instinct. Anyway, she'll be fine."

"Yeah, she will," I assure him. I pull my eyes into the distance. "Truth is, it's us I'm worried about."

Brohn nudges his shoulder against mine. It's the most contact we've ever had, and it feels a little better than it probably should. "Of course you are," he says. "You were always the worrier of our Cohort."

Okay, *that* doesn't feel so good.

"I'm not a worrier. I'm just cautious," I growl through a pout. "Besides, you said *you're* worried, too. It's not like I'm the only one."

"Oh, I didn't mean it like that..." he says, chuckling. "Jeez, you're a sensitive one, aren't you?"

That just cheeses me off even more. I hate being called sensitive. Which I suppose only proves his point.

"I guess I am," I announce, thrusting my shoulders back to yank my body away from his. Okay. Yes, I'm sensitive. Who can blame me? My entire world is going to come crashing down around me in less than twenty-four hours. *Sensitive* should definitely be considered the new sane.

Brohn leans over and elbows me gently in the ribs, which melts the ice a little. "Lighten up," he says. "We're supposed to be having a good time tonight." He nods toward the fire, where some of the Sixteens and a bunch of the Juvens are quibbling over how long to leave the deer over the hot coals.

"It's hard to have a good time when you don't really know what's about to happen to you," I say. I look over and study his profile. I don't remember exactly when it happened but one day, a couple of years ago, Brohn magically transformed from a gangly boy into an athletic man—all shoulders, stubble, and testosterone. He looks like he could lead an army right now, a strange, determined expression setting itself on his face.

A sudden pang of regret hits me square in the chest. I wish I hadn't avoided him all these years. If I hadn't been so shy or intimidated or embarrassed, I could have gotten to know him. Hung out, like teenagers used to do in the days before the attacks and the blackout. Instead, I withdrew and told myself there was no point in getting close to anyone since we all knew death could be advancing on us from over the horizon at any time.

"I don't want to go. I want to stay here and do the things I'm supposed to do," he murmurs, as if he's reading my thoughts. Once again, he looks over at me. "I'd want you to stay, too. I would have liked to spend more time with you. Maybe if we'd just—"

A shriek in the distance cuts him off. Great. The Juvens' argument about how to properly roast a deer has heated up to a fever pitch.

"Oh, crap," Brohn grumbles, jerking himself to his feet and striding through the shallow dunes of dry sand toward the fire. "Guys, that's not how I showed you!" he yells at two inept Juvens who are struggling to re-position our dinner, which has started sliding off the skewer.

Brohn pulls off his black hoodie and wraps it around his hand as an impromptu oven-mitt. He grabs hold of the steel bar that's impaling the animal and heaves it up to reset the skewer. With the help of Talia and Cici, he manages to reposition the carcass over the flame. Someone clever has rigged a foot-pedal to the crank on one end of the spit so they can more easily turn the meat for an even roast. Brohn assigns Cici the job of pumping the crank while he slices off a piece of meat and samples it.

Since it looks like he's lost interest in our conversation, I debate whether to disappear back up to the school or join the others at the fire. On any other evening, I'd probably opt for the former and go out to explore some of the more dangerous parts of the mountains with an old crank flashlight my father gave me.

Instead, I take a deep breath and walk through the sand toward Brohn and the others.

"Maybe they won't come this year," Terk is saying when I walk up. He towers over the rest of us, but his voice has gone uncharacteristically high, and even I can tell he's holding back a flood of fear.

"They'll be here," Brohn replies. "Trust me."

I can't help but notice how many sets of eyes are trained on Brohn. His calm sense of authority has always garnered him respect, but it's not just that. It's also the *way* he speaks. It's his confidence, the rich, round baritone of his voice.

"The Militia still has a war to fight," Kella says in support of him. "They're building an army. They won't stop until they've achieved their goal."

Brohn nods. "She's right. The Execs say we're winning the war, but they're worried about something. That's why they..." He stops talking, his gaze shifting toward the woods.

"Why they what?" I ask, my voice piercing through the silence.

Our eyes meet for a moment. "Okay. Here's the thing. They re-jigged their whole training protocol," he says. It sounds like a confession.

"Wait, what?" Card asks. "How do you know that?"

Brohn lets out a sigh and looks around at each of us in turn. "Look, I wasn't going to tell you guys any of this, but I guess it doesn't matter. There's not much we can do about it now anyway."

"You weren't going to tell us *what*?" I ask. So, it turns out I was right about him keeping secrets.

"I ran into some military guys a while back," he says. "Last year, just a few months after the last batch of Recruits got taken away. Remember that time I told you guys how I nearly caught that huge rabbit in the woods down by the old ski hill?"

"Sure," Card says. "The one that none of us ever actually saw, you mean?"

A few of the others laugh.

"Well, I actually *did* catch it. I ran into two soldiers who'd gotten lost out on patrol way over on the south ridge, that part with the big drop-off. They were hungry, so I offered to cook the rabbit for them in exchange for information about the outside. They told me a bit about what happens to the people they take."

"Marvie!" Karmine exclaims. "So tell us! What happens?" He's bubbling over with excitement. He's always looked forward to Recruitment, always spoken about it like it would be the day when he comes into his own. For him, any news gets him one step closer to combat.

"Now, remember," Brohn says. "These guys could have been lying or just repeating what they think they heard. They didn't seem a hundred percent right in the head. Which is partly why I didn't say anything before."

"We get it," Karmine says. "So...?"

"Okay. So, according to the soldiers, the Recruits were originally taken to a special facility for training, like a kind of boot camp. They learned to shoot, drive transport rigs, whatever they were needed for. Some of them were selected to go around and collect fuel. Others were trusted with weapons, guard duty, things like that. But now they've changed things. With no end to the war in sight, the testing and training have gotten much harder. At least, that's what the two soldiers told me. They said the Recruits get put through a series of tests. Physical, mental, you name it. It's become this really specific selection process."

"Tests? What kinds of tests?" I ask. My mind goes to Render, and all I can think is that if they'd just let me bring him, he could help me work my way to the top. Maybe if I got into Special Ops, I could find my way to Micah, to my father. Maybe I could have a family again.

"Not sure," Brohn says, a sympathetic look on his face. "They just said they were glad they never had to do it themselves. They told me it breaks some of the Recruits."

"It won't break me," Karmine says, seemingly oblivious to the portentous tone in Brohn's voice. "I'm so ready for this." With that, he high-fives Kella, who's standing close by.

"Don't be so sure. From the sounds of it, the testing facilities aren't something any of us can prepare for."

"Do any of the Recruits ever try to leave?" Rain asks.

Brohn shakes his head. "The one thing the men told me, the one thing I find it easy to believe, is that they hunt down deserters."

"What happens to them?"

Brohn stares at Rain, grinding his jaw. "I don't know," he says. He turns my way and our eyes meet again. Like everyone else, he knows about Micah's forbidden visit, about how he got away from the Recruitment Center and found his way back to the woods just outside of town. I have no idea if my brother was considered a deserter or not, but I can tell that Brohn doesn't want to destroy any shred any hope I have of seeing him again.

All I can do is hope Micah found his way back to his training facility, apologized to his commanding officers, and was spared any harsh punishment.

"I don't like the sounds of any of this," Sophie says, her voice quivering. She's a Juven, safe for another year, but she looks terrified. "We should leave this place tonight and not look back. If we go somewhere they can't find us…"

Brohn shuts her down. "There's nowhere to go and nowhere they can't find us. Besides, even if any of us managed to make it over the mountains, I'm sure we'd discover there are far worse things out there than the Recruiters."

"The Order, you mean," Karmine says, holding up his hands like he's grasping and aiming a rifle.

Brohn nods. "Our choices are get killed, or get trained to kill," he reminds us. "Face it, those are the only two options. All I know is that we have to win this war. We need to make this world a better place. Because right now, it pretty much sucks."

He looks over at his little sister, who's talking to a bunch of Neos and younger Juvens on the far side of the big fire.

She's safe in the Valta, I think. *Way safer than we are.*

For now, at least.

4

THE MORNING AFTER FINAL FEAST, I WAKE UP ANXIOUS, EDGY, AND sad.

I'm disoriented at first. I usually sleep upstairs. But in the time leading up to Recruitment, I've given in to Cardyn's badgering and have joined the others in the gym. Even Amaranthine, usually squirreled away in some broken-down corner of the school, has joined us these past few nights.

I swing my legs down from my cot and pad over to the Bunker, which is the cave of concrete blocks that used to serve as the girls' locker room in the high school's basement. It's filled with chipped and bent lockers, their metal doors slanted and warped from the old drone raids and rusty from disuse. A decade ago, this room would have been filled with girls jostling around, plodding in and out of gym class, getting ready for some big soccer or basketball game, sneaking a smoke, talking trash about a teacher, or giggling over some boy they all liked.

Now it's a quiet chamber where all the Sixteens hang our clothes and start our days. Chipped porcelain sinks offer us apologetic trickles of rusty water, which we use in a vain effort to wash the night's sleep out of our eyes. The old cracked benches still invite us to sit and pull on a dry pair of socks at the end of a sweaty day.

In addition to acting as our makeshift dressing room, the Bunker doubles as a bomb-shelter. It's the best place in town to be if and when the drones ever strike again.

This morning I seem to be the first one up. It wasn't exactly a hard feat to accomplish. I just never really fell asleep. Instead, I spent the night listening to the thrum of my fellow Sixteens breathing deeply into the cold night air while I stared up at the broken and stained acoustical tiles of the ceiling high above and wondered if I'd miss quiet moments like this, if I'd ever even *have* another quiet moment like this.

In the Bunker I shed my oversized t-shirt and shorts and slide into a pair of too-big khaki cargo pants, a clean white shirt, and my age-softened jean jacket. After rinsing my mouth with the concoction of baking soda and essential peppermint oils we keep in a plastic jug by the sink, I start to feel slightly refreshed. I head back into the gym, where the light of morning is just beginning to shine down through the small windows way up on the walls and through the various holes in the ceiling that reappear as fast as we can patch them.

Brohn kicks his tattered wool blanket to the floor and swings his muscular legs around. He smacks his hands to his knees and thrusts himself to his feet before declaring, "Well, no sense prolonging the inevitable."

I find myself avoiding his eyes this morning. I had a dream about him last night and am slightly embarrassed at the impossible idea that he might somehow find out. I don't know if our conversation last night at Final Feast actually meant anything to him. It was strange to open up to him like that—both good and bad at once. I can't help hoping we'll find ourselves staying together, regardless of where the Recruiters take us. Maybe we'll train together, and we can finally get to know each other better after years of avoiding each other's company.

But part of me knows it's probably a bad idea. If I really want to make it into Special Ops, I'll have to focus. And not on the king of our Cohort, either. I'll need to keep my mind on the prize, which will mean keeping to myself for a little while longer.

Of course, all of this depends on where we are when the sun goes down tonight. For all I know, Brohn will be taken to some special training camp exclusively for boys, while I'm led off to culinary school.

Kella yawns, stretches her hands to the sky, and pulls herself off her cot. "Brohn's right. Sitting here isn't going to change anything or stop the world from spinning. I say we head out and show the Recruiters and all those hot-shot Execs what the new Seventeens of 2042 are made of!"

While I don't exactly share Brohn's composure or Kella's rah-rah enthusiasm, I nod my meager agreement and do some morning stretches while the others plod into the Bunker to change. Cardyn, the first one back out, joins me in some yoga moves in the center of the room.

"I don't know about you," he says, his back curved into a smooth arc as he touches his fingertips to his toes, "but I'm suddenly super excited."

"Then you're also suddenly super crazy," I mutter. My stomach's in knots right now, and I have zero idea how anyone can be looking forward to a bunch of strangers herding us into trucks.

"Hardly!" Card protests. "Like Brohn said, it's inevitable now. There's something comforting and energizing about that. Like once you don't have a choice anymore, the stars kind of align, you know? Your mission, your future, everything becomes focused and clear."

"I'm happy for you and your new clarity," I say with a snide grunt as I shift positions and roll onto my back to stretch out my hamstrings. "But there's nothing good about not having a choice."

Card answers me with a smirk as the rest of the new Seventeens file one by one out of the Bunker. As soon as everyone's up and about, we head upstairs to the front door and take our final steps out of Shoshone High School. When we're clear of the building I spin around to take in a last glance of the beaten down, blasted out husk of a structure we've called home for so many years.

I can't help but feel a pang of affection for the school. It may be ugly and decrepit, but it's been home. We set up our mock school house on the second floor, where the Sixteens taught the Juvens who in turn taught the Neos. Shoshone's where we developed our simple educational philosophy: share your talents, teach others what you know, learn from others what you don't know, and ask as many questions as you can. Those words kind of became the school's unfortunately-long slogan over time. Simple enough in theory, but it could be challenging in practice.

There was so much to know, so many half-burned books gathered from ruined houses throughout the town to be sorted through and salvaged. So many personalities, abilities, and talents to figure out. But somehow, we made it work.

I look up at the broken building's windows one last time and give it a mental *Thanks*.

Today, we graduate from the place where we grew up. More than once, it was the place that saved our lives. I owe it a lot.

As I take my last steps away from the building, I see Render waiting for me on the black handrail leading to the path that will take us to the square in the center of town for our official Recruitment. As I walk out onto the concrete landing, Render flicks his head around and flaps over to perch on my shoulder. The other Seventeens take a step back amid the flurry of black feathers and the cloud of dust and debris Render kicks up into the chilly morning air with his powerful wings.

"You need to teach that bird of yours about personal space," Rain jokes. The truth is, she likes Render nearly as much as I do, although she sometimes seems a bit scared of him.

"I've been trying," I assure her. "But what can I say? He has a mind of his own."

The irony of that statement amuses me, given that Render and I more or less share one mind. Not that anyone else knows the extent of our rapport. To tell the truth, even I don't fully know the extent of it. The connection is strong at times, weak at others. Sometimes I feel like I've become a bird psychic, but occasionally he just seems to disappear, and I'm left inside my own head with nowhere to go.

Of course, after today, none of it will matter. I'm sure when I'm taken far from the Valta, we won't feel each other's presence anymore. For a time, he'll think I've deserted him...and I'll be left with a hole inside my chest that I won't be able to tell anyone about, because there's no way they'd ever understand. Even Card can't possibly fathom how devastating it's going to feel to lose Render. To him and to the rest of our Cohort, Render is just an amusing mascot, a wild animal I managed to tame for a time.

They can't possibly know that losing him will be like losing a limb.

As the Seventeens trudge the rest of the way down the walkway ahead of me, I give my wrist a quick tap, and Render's mysterious mind overlaps with my own.

Despite what the Neos, the Juvens, and most of my fellow Seventeens think, his mind is more than just a tunnel-visioned quest for food or an empty void that shuts down as he soars effortlessly through the sky. Right now, he's afraid. He may not understand why, but he knows I'm scared too, and he knows how much I'm going to miss him.

At least I know he won't starve. As dependent as he is on me, he's always been a phenomenal hunter. After I'm gone, he'll fly off to track down deer mice or pick at some carcass he's found. But he also enjoys being hand-fed his morning grubs, so I reach into the plastic pocket inside my satchel and toss one to him. He snatches it out of the air with a lightning fast snap of his beak and a *kraa* of thanks. His claws dig into my shoulder, but I don't care. I'm used to it. In fact, I've grown to like it. Just one more thing I'm going to miss.

"This is where we need to go our separate ways, old friend," I whisper, hoping none of the others can hear me trying not to cry as I say good-bye for the last time. A sympathetic look from any of them would be enough to make me break down, and that's the last thing I want to do before coming face to face with the Recruiters.

No sense prolonging the inevitable seems to have become the theme for the day. With a last stroke of my finger over his feathered head, I tell him to fly away one final time.

Pushing off from my shoulder, Render launches himself into the air and soars in big circles, scoping the ground below for a proper breakfast as I walk down the sidewalk and give him a quiet whisper of goodbye, tears welling in my eyes.

I can't help but imagine what my dad would think if he could see me now, crying over a bird. Actually, it would probably make him happy to know there was something in my life I'd miss. Something that was actually worth crying over.

The walk down to the square is short. Too short. I wish we had a proper hike ahead of us, a chance to enjoy these last moments a little longer. Even so, as usual, Amaranthine is straggling behind, and I hold back to make sure she keeps up. I try to tell myself that I'm just looking out for her, making sure she doesn't try to bolt. She'd only get tracked down and killed.

But the truth is, I'm not really all that interested in her safety. Despite her weird quietness and roughed up appearance, she's an oddly tough girl who's always been just fine on her own. I'm the one who's being a coward, using her as an excuse to hang back. To have just one more minute before I enter the square and say goodbye to the Valta forever.

"We'd better not fall too far behind," I advise her with what I hope is a friendly smile. "The Recruiters don't have a sense of humor about slowpokes." I put out my hand as if to help her along.

Amaranthine glares at me through her tangle of dark, partially-dreadlocked hair.

I drop my hand, lose my cheery smile, and stare as she shoulders past me, leaving me to take her place as the straggler bringing up the rear.

As has become tradition, the Juvens and Neos are already gathered together in the square, ready to salute us and see us off. The crowd parts for us as we walk to the center of the large open space and watch as the cloud of dust in the distance whirls away to reveal the Recruiters' small military convoy.

When the three vehicles grumble up as one, Karmine explains that the big cargo truck is for us. "The other two are escorts," he says out of the side of his mouth. "For show. I can't imagine they think a handful of teenagers living on their own in a burned-out nothing of a town is going to present any kind of threat."

It's not just that we've seen similar caravans on this date every year. Karmine knows these things from his books. Not many books survived the raids over the years, but among the ones that did is a three-volume set of hardcovers called *Combat Regs and the Protocols of War*. Karmine has practically memorized them, and he's fond of tossing out random bits of military trivia. In the past, he's regaled us with everything from the importance of objective to the best techniques for effective guerilla warfare to how best to conduct a strategic flanking operation. It can get pretty annoying, but I have to admit, the Juvens and Neos have really taken a liking to him over the years. He's the go-to person whenever anyone wants to learn about all things military, and, from what I've seen, he's a really good teacher.

Brohn gives a gracious nod of thanks to Karmine for the info, and we all take a step back as the trucks grind to a stop, kicking up a cloud of thin brown dust that causes a lot of us to cough and cover our mouths and eyes.

A soldier with the name "Kellerson" embroidered in yellow thread on the left pocket of his combat military jacket hops down from the open back of the larger transport truck. He's almost as tall as Brohn, but thinner, with bugged-out eyes and a snaggle tooth that makes him look like some kind of mutated wild boar. He scans us all and starts jotting something down on an old-style wooden clipboard.

A second soldier, this one with the name "Chucker" printed on his beige and spinach-green button-up shirt, drops down from the truck behind Kellerson. This guy is nearly as thick around as Terk, but he's shorter, which gives him a kind of squarish appearance, like he's a cement block someone decided to deck out in military fatigues. His sleeves are cuffed above his elbows, and his exposed forearms are as big around as one of my legs.

The ground seems to rumble as he jumps down from the truck and clomps toward us.

A knot forms in my throat, and a trickle of sweat snakes its way down my spine. I'm not going to last long if our military training involves sparring against full grown men three times my size.

Facing us, but staring into the sky as if he's reciting reluctantly from a memorized statement, Chucker announces, "Per the pleasure and discretion of President Krug, the Cohort of the Seventeens of the Class of 2042 has been invited to aid in the noble effort against the Eastern Order, which has violated the sanctity of our borders and seeks to destroy our way of life and our very existence. With your aid, and by the grace of God and with the gratitude of President Krug as your companions in battle, our nation shall not perish from this earth but will forever prevail, and our military might shall reign time immemorial."

Chucker continues to stand ram-rod straight and turns his gaze to us. His voice is as husky and intimidating as his body.

"Your loyalty to your nation and your undying allegiance to your president are appreciated and will not go unrewarded."

It's the same speech they give every year. Sometimes I've found it funny. Other times, it's seemed inspirational. Occasionally it's sounded like nothing more than a desperate call to arms.

It used to at least hold the potential to give me tingles of patriotism.

Now it just gives me tingles of dread.

A half-dozen Recruiters jump out of one of the smaller escort trucks to march into the crowd of Juvens and Neos, passing over each set of features with a clunky facial-recog scanner that looks like it's been recently assembled out of spare parts. It's nothing like the old, smooth tech we used to have, but still, it looks like Card was right about the Execs starting to get things back on line. Every year, their scanners get a little more sophisticated.

That fact gives me hope, but it also makes me a little jealous. Who knows how much we could have accomplished over the last few years in the Valta with some better tech at our disposal?

Satisfied that there are no unregistered Seventeens hiding out with the younger Cohorts, the six men are joined by six more. They all trudge into town to start their door-to-door sweep for anyone hiding out or for any signs of resistance or evidence that someone might be planning to leave the Valta without authorization.

In the meantime, Kellerson double-checks his clipboard and nods his approval to Chucker, who proceeds to order the eight Seventeens to line up single-file in front of him. We shuffle into as straight a line as we can manage, with Brohn in front and Amaranthine, as usual, in the back.

Kellerson is just starting to tell us about the long trip we have ahead of us when Wisp bursts from the shuffling crowd of Juvens and runs full speed toward her brother. She latches onto his waist with a vice-like grip, tears running in little streams down her puffy red cheeks. Brohn kneels down in front of her. He's just brushing the stray blond hair away from her face and telling her not to worry when Chucker thunders over and grabs her by the back of her jacket. He yanks her away from Brohn in one sweeping motion and holds her dangling a few inches off the ground as she kicks and screams. When he flings her back toward the advancing crowd of Juvens, she slides to a stop in the dirt at their feet.

Brohn takes a step toward Chucker, his fists balled up, suddenly as big as boulders. Kella and Karmine each grab him by an arm to hold him back.

"Smart move," Chucker grunts at them. "No sense letting your buddy get ended just when he's getting ready to begin."

Brohn bites his lip as he watches some of the older Juvens help his sister to her feet, comforting her as best they can. Wisp tucks her face into Cici's shoulder, as Cici wraps her arms around her and spits on the ground in Chucker's direction. He's already turned back to her, which is good. There's no telling how he might react to such a disrespectful move. Cici is pretty tough, but this guy looks like he eats her weight every day for breakfast.

Brohn's jaw is locked tight, and I can tell he's fighting back tears, which isn't exactly unusual on November 1st. I've seen new Seventeens break down and cry. I've seen others whoop it up and practically dance their way onto the transport trucks. Three years ago, there were twins—Dani and Michella—who were so eager to fight, they kept bouncing around, asking the Recruiters when they'd get a chance to use guns. The Recruiters rolled their eyes and told the twins to *just get in the damn truck.*

Everyone reacts according to their fears. Two years ago, a boy named Arven swore he wasn't a Seventeen. "I was born in '25," he kept screaming as he backed slowly away from the Recruiters. "Check the records!"

But no one checked anything. Instead, the driver of the transport truck bashed Arven's head in with the butt of his rifle, and two other soldiers tossed his limp body into the back of the truck like he was nothing more than a giant sack of birdseed.

The best we can hope for today is to avoid a repeat of that drama.

Seeing that Wisp is okay, Brohn takes a deep breath and steadies himself. Karmine and Kella are energized and strangely enthusiastic. Cardyn is nervous but trying to resign himself to his fate. Terk is a bundle of nerves. Rain is quietly assessing the situation. Amaranthine is her usual oddly stoic and mysterious self.

I already miss Render.

Brohn already misses Wisp.

We all miss who we were and wonder what we're about to become.

Brohn takes a last look over at Wisp and raises his hand in a half-wave. From under Cici's protective arm, Wisp sobs and raises her hand back. Then she buries her face back into Cici's shoulder, unable to watch as her brother gets led away.

As we step forward toward the truck, I'm a lot closer to crying myself than I am to celebrating, but I know perfectly well that neither will prepare me for where we're going or for what's about to happen. Neither will keep me safe or get me any closer to finding out what happened to my father and my brother.

Shielding myself from view behind Terk's wide body, I tap the black implant pattern on my forearm and try to concentrate. The dust, the Recruiters, and the green and beige camouflage of the truck are replaced by a sudden flash of white and an expansive field of blue that I immediately recognize as the sky.

I'm in Render's head, and he's in mine…for one last goodbye.

I don't know if it's my nervousness, or if I'm feeling Render's own fear feeding back to me through our implants. What I'm sure of is that another important connection in my life is breaking, and it hurts. I can feel how much he wants to follow us, to come with me. But now, more than ever, I know it's impossible.

These men have no problem tossing a little girl around. They'd shoot a raven dead just for sport.

I'm now trying and failing to hold back the tears that I've held back since last night.

I'm sorry, Render. This is the way it has to be. You'll be safe here.

I try to console him, even as I fail to console myself. I'm about to lose the last member of my family, and the thought of it feels like a massive weight hanging around my neck.

The eight Seventeens of the Class of 2042 climb one at a time up the rear fender and into the transport truck. Kellerson and Chucker leap up behind us. Chucker pulls up the lift-gate, drops a thick canvas curtain down over the rear doors, and we begin the long ride out of town, leaving Render, Wisp, the school, our memories, and everything else behind.

5

The man called Chucker seats himself on the rear bench with a huge black gun across his lap. It's a terrifying beast of a rifle, clunky and decked out with scopes, stocks, and some kind of long sliding bolt. I know it's just one gun, but it looks like someone broke into an armory somewhere and glued four or five guns together to create one enormous weapon.

Chucker scowls at us as we duck our heads and shuffle around to take our places on the green steel benches on either side of the truck's interior. When we're all as settled as we're going to get, the stuffy, windowless vehicle kicks into gear and begins to grind its way out of the Valta, on its way to an undisclosed location.

Which is probably why my anxiety is through the roof.

I can't stop thinking about Render, wondering if he's feeling the severing of our bond as acutely as I am. I can't help but think of the new Sixteens, of how much weight has just been thrust onto their shoulders.

All I want right now is comfort, but there's nothing here that can give it to me. Brohn has retreated into a quiet rage. Card looks even more nervous than I feel.

The only thing left to do is breathe and hope.

Up until now, we've always known how close the Valta was to the ongoing war. It's never been pleasant, but at least we knew how to deal with the constancy of that dread. Now, a fear of the unknown has begun drifting through the inside of the truck like a tangible fog.

This is literally the scariest moment of my life. And Chucker and his stink-eye aren't helping.

"Don't mind my grumpy buddy here," Kellerson says with a thin smile. He's sitting on the rear bench next to Chucker, his legs spread in a relaxed pose that totally contradicts the stiff young bodies all around him. "Recruitment duty isn't one of his favorites." He gives his partner a playful shove that reminds me of my rapport with Card. "You'd rather be out killing the Eastern Order's guys, wouldn't ya, Chucky-boy?"

Chucker glares at Kellerson and then turns his squinty laser-eyes back on us in the dusky light of the truck, grimacing like he's doing everything in his power not to shoot us all dead.

Kellerson shrugs his shoulders and turns toward Brohn to call out over the roar of the rumbling engine. "So, eight of you this year, huh?"

"Eight of us. Yes sir," Brohn says evenly. He interlocks his fingers, his elbows on his knees, and stares at a spot on the floor. There's no doubt in my mind that he's thinking about Wisp, and I can tell that he's struggling to maintain some small morsel of self-control.

What I don't know is if his love for his sister is going to motivate him to excel as a Recruit. Right now, I get the feeling that it could just as easily break his spirit, or at the very least, inspire him to leap across the short distance between him and Chucker and try to kill the man who roughed up his younger sibling.

But for now, Brohn, unblinking and a bit scary, just clenches his jaw, keeping his head and eyes down like an irritated bull who's about to turn homicidal.

"I'm no 'sir,' Seventeen," Kellerson says with a flash of his snaggle-toothed smile. "Corporal Kellerson'll do just fine. Or just 'Kellerson.' Not much need for ranks where we're going. We're all in the same leaky boat."

Karmine leans forward from his bench and extends his hand toward Kellerson. "Karmine," he says. "Good to know you, Corporal."

Kellerson rejects the hand shake and instead folds his arms and leans back against the truck's steel wall. "No sense getting to know you, Seventeen. In a couple months, you'll be a drone, out there killing off the Order so the Execs can keep building their vertical cities. If you live through the training, that is!" With that, he laughs and turns toward Chucker for some kind of confirmation of his cleverness. But the other man just stares straight ahead, apparently still resisting the urge to slaughter us all.

"What do you mean, live through the training?" Terk asks, his tree-trunk arms around his thick legs as if to bundle up his big frame to make more room in the truck for the rest of us. "It doesn't do the Execs any good if we get hurt, does it? I mean, they're not out to kill us, right?" He looks over to Brohn for support, but Brohn doesn't look up.

Kellerson shakes his head and shrugs one shoulder. "Don't ask me what's good for the Execs and what isn't. They decide that. Our job is to get you to the Western Recruitment Processor. After that, you aren't our business any more. A bunch of us will be assigned to guard duty over you, but that'll be the extent of it. You'll see once we get there. Eight buildings. Eight guards. Eight of you." He sucks in air through his teeth like he's thinking, then says, "Makes for a kind of a nice symmetry, doesn't it?"

"But no one gets…I mean, they don't…do they?" Terk looks to me next, but I have no support to offer him. For all I know, we'll all be dead by this time tomorrow. Besides, I don't want to think about it. It's hard enough trying to keep my mind off my sadness at losing Render.

Kellerson raps his knuckles against his clipboard. "Look here, Seventeen. I got a program roster here with a lotta names and numbers on it. Let's just say there's more numbers going into most of the Processors than there are coming out." His friendly wink doesn't make his words any less terrifying.

"The Execs need us, though," Terk says, his voice almost a whine as he looks across at Rain next. As small as she is and as big as Terk is, she's always had the ability to talk him out of his fears. I've seen her do it more than once, and despite the fact that I'm not her biggest fan I have to admit that it's impressive. "Why recruit us if they're just going to kill us?" he whimpers.

Rain starts to lean across the truck to put a reassuring hand on Terk's knee, but Chucker barks at her to sit back. Startled, she obeys. "Don't worry," she tells Terk quietly, "No one's getting hurt or killed. We're being trained to keep ourselves alive and our nation safe. You'll see. When this is all over, life will be so much better. We'll take the Order down, drive them out, and we'll all get the freedom back that they tried so hard to take away."

Terk gets ready to say something else, but I lay a stealthy hand on his forearm. I've got a feeling that he's about to turn this thing into an interrogation that wouldn't end well for him or for any of us.

He gets my unsubtle hint, closes his mouth, and leans back against the truck's rattling wall.

Kellerson flicks a thumb toward Amaranthine, who's slouching in the corner by the rear lift-gate, her hair falling around her face in its usual mess of dark brown tangles. She's wrapped in silence and in her own arms—not to mention in an invisible cloak of pure attitude. "So, what's her deal?"

"She's just a little off," Kella says with a laugh and a dismissive wave of her hand.

"She doesn't have a 'deal,'" I say, sounding more snarky than I mean to. "Her name is Amaranthine, and she—"

But I'm quickly interrupted by Chucker, who barks at me to

sit back. Which is impossible, since I've already got my spine pressed against the cold steel of the truck's wall. The guy has a thing about sudden or unauthorized movements, and I'm beginning to wonder how many past Recruits he's killed in this very truck.

Kellerson holds up his hand again and shakes his head at me. "I told you before, Seventeen. Don't bother. You don't need to give me details, and I don't need to know. At the Processor, you'll just be another number anyway. Just another cog in the machine."

Grumbling along the twisting, pitted road down the mountain, the jostling truck pitches us back and forth against each other. It's a strange sensation, being in a motorized vehicle for the first time in so many years. Along with all the old tech going down, the accompanying EMP drone raids of ten years ago also knocked out all the ion cells, lithium batteries, and the capacitors in all the vehicles in the Valta—from cars and trucks to motorcycles and snowmobiles. Even the little grav-scooters the older kids used to fly around on became useless lumps of carbon fiber and synth-steel. We still rode bicycles from time to time, but the rugged, cratered terrain after the raids and the fact that there wasn't really anywhere to go made our feet the most sensible means of transportation.

The thrum of the truck's engine is both aggressive and surprisingly pleasant. Motorized things have always fascinated me, from the cogs in Dad's little gizmos to the micro-processors of Render's ocular implants. Not just artificial machines, either. I used to love reading about the inner workings of the most complex machine of all: the human body. There's even an old anatomy book we used to read as part of our lessons in the Valta. Out in the woods, with Render keeping us company, Card used to quiz me. Over the years, I learned the name of practically every muscle, ligament, and tendon. I learned the nine regions of the abdomen, the layers and types of skin cells, and the functions of the central nervous system. I even memorized the six types of synovial joints: Pivot. Hinge. Saddle. Plane. Condyloid. Ball and Socket. For some reason, that one always impressed Card the most. I tried teaching some of it to the younger Neos and Juvens as part of my required teacher-rotation, but I wasn't as good at teaching stuff as I was at learning it, and most of my lessons kind of fizzled.

Along the way, really just to challenge myself, I did extra reading from old high school textbooks on math, biology, and physics. A few years ago, with the help of a Sixteen named Nadia, I tried to get through a chemistry book, but I didn't understand most of it and eventually got frustrated and gave up.

The truth is, I liked the detective novels the best, but most of those got burned up in the third wave of drone attacks that hit the town's only library five years ago. To this day, everyone wonders knows what our little town did to deserve such a fate.

"Who goes out of their way to slaughter anyone as helpless and innocent as us?" one of the Sixteens of 2037 asked the day after that raid. Her name was Harlan. She was a strange blend of whiny helplessness and random cruelty. Brohn, only eleven years old at the time and very much a Juven, pointed out the irony of her asking the question while she was absently crushing tiny black ants with her thumb.

At the end of the road, the truck grinds to a clanging, mechanical halt, but the doors don't open. Instead, we hear voices from outside and a series of pings from some sort of electronic device.

Kellerson informs us that we're about to cross the desert.

"Just a checkpoint," he assures us. "Gotta make sure we are who we say we are. Believe it or not, you Seventeens always rate V.I.P. treatment."

"What is it about us anyway," Rain asks. "Why us? Why do they want the Seventeens?" It's a question we've all asked ourselves many times over the years.

Kellerson drops his friendly smile and gives her an acidic

stare. "Careful, little girl. Look around you, see where you're at. You think me and Chucky-boy here are alive 'cause we asked a lot of questions? Questions lead to answers. Answers lead to knowing too much. Knowing too much is the first shovelful of dirt on your open grave. Catchin' my drift?"

Rain nods, shocked by his hostility, but I can see the gears turning in her head. She's always been a problem-solver. An unsolved riddle is a cancer in her bones. Now her curiosity is clearly piqued, and I don't doubt that she's going to find the answers she's looking for one way or another. I just hope Kellerson was exaggerating about the open grave part. Rain and I will probably never be close, but I respect her mind, and I admire the way she never lets anyone sidetrack her from whatever mission she's on at the moment.

The truck starts up again and we continue on our way. I'm not sure how long we've been on the road now. Three hours? Six? Without windows—and with a flickering overhead bulb as our only light—it's pretty much impossible to keep track of time. The disorienting sensation is compounded by the stiffness that's set into my shoulders and the narrow rivers of sweat I've got meandering down my neck and back. It's a strange combination of sensory deprivation and sensory overload. I wonder if that's by design.

At various times I try to sleep, but of course it's impossible. Too much is happening. Has happened. Is *going* to happen. Only Amaranthine, down at the end of the bench, seems to have drifted off. The rest of us try to close our eyes from time to time, but we always snap back to attention at the slightest jolt of the truck. Jolts that are coming harder and more often now. The road feels like it's going from nicely paved to more and more deeply cratered every half mile or so. Are we in the war zone? Is this the Eastern Order's doing? Is this the devastation we're expected to help stop? I can't see anything beyond the interior walls of the truck, but in my mind, the outside world around us is littered with obliterated buildings, overturned cars and grav-trams, huge cities in fiery ruins, and stacks of burned bodies. The casualties of war.

I shake the images from my head, afraid they'll make me go crazy.

After what feels like a week of bumping over dunes and dipping through craters, the truck screeches to another stop. More pings. I'm bracing myself for the driver to take off again, but this time, the engine clicks off and huffs a deep sigh before going still. The little noises I couldn't hear before over the rumble of the truck—the shifting of our bodies, our breathing—suddenly sound awkwardly loud.

Kellerson explains to us that the drive is finally over.

"We walk you down the rest of the way," Chucker adds curtly, part explanation, part order.

We pile out of the truck, our hands over our eyes against the blazing sun that pounds down in streaks through thick red clouds. It's like we've traveled to another planet entirely. Up in the Valta the air was clean, at least. We lived in the bright white light of the unfiltered sun. Here, the air tastes grainy and toxic. It feels like sand on my teeth.

Kellerson takes the lead, and we follow him down an abandoned highway with Chucker, his monstrous rifle slung on his shoulder, keeping an eye on us from behind. The pitted road winds through a small forest of dead and dying trees until the rough pavement thins out, and we're walking on hardpacked soil.

From the worn footpath leading to the Western Recruitment Processor, we can see an array of eight huge cube-shaped buildings, all black, set up in an octagon with what looks like a giant lawn between them. At first, the trees obscure most of the view, and I'm not sure what I'm looking at. But as the woods thin out, I guess out loud that what we're seeing is one of the "Arcologies" Card was talking about from the viz-screens.

Kellerson laughs. "You guys really have been in isolation, haven't you?"

"We've been living the way we live," Brohn says in a surly voice. The cryptic answer to an impossible question is the first thing he's said in hours. There's no sign left of the friendly, warm young man I was sitting with last night.

He's right to divulge the bare minimum, of course. We don't know these men or anything about their politics, let alone any orders they might have to shoot anyone they think isn't toeing the party line.

"Those are the Cubes and the Agora," Kellerson explains with a laugh, ignoring Brohn's icy glare. "Also known by us guards as 'Trials and Tribulations.' That'll be home for you for the next eight weeks." He keeps walking but points out past the tree-line to a tall building that's under construction way off in the distance. "The Arcologies are giant towers like that one, that will rise thousands of feet up into the sky. They're whole cities in one convenient location," he proclaims proudly, as if he was the actual designer and architect. "People live in them. Work in them, too. They never have to leave. Never have to worry about getting bombed out by the Order. Total independence. Total isolation."

"Sounds a lot like where we just came from," I say but immediately wish I hadn't. I'm not one to put my neck voluntarily into a noose.

As if to confirm my fear, Chucker gives me a menacing growl from the back of our little procession and barks at me to keep my mouth shut. I'm not used to being yelled at, and I feel like I might start crying. I know that would be the kiss of death, so I clench my jaw, bite down on my cheek, and try to remember to keep my opinions to myself.

The long hike is exhausting, partly because we're all tired, hungry, disoriented, and dehydrated. But also because we don't know what to expect when we reach our mysterious destination. I can't speak for the other Seventeens, but that fact alone has given me non-stop heart palpitations and an annoying eye twitch.

At the top of some of the hills, I'm able to catch a few more glimpses of the Western Recruitment Processor. The eight onyx-colored buildings look identical, but out of place with their polished black luster among the groves of trees, many of which are cracked in half and dying, and the scorched brown earth of the surrounding areas. At one point, Card tugs my sleeve and gestures with his head toward a small clearing between a patch of dead trees. I'm not quick enough to get a full look, but what I think I see is enough to frighten me: It looks like a dust covered ghost town filled with hollowed out buildings leaning over, crumbling, ready to collapse. The shattered remains of what was probably a city, now flattened and dead.

Like a much bigger version of the Valta.

We're forced to keep walking so the image disappears quickly enough. Still, I can feel it burning its horrible reality into my memory. If that's what the Order's managed to do to the big cities, what hope does the Valta have? What hope does any of us have? Those half-built Arcologies Kellerson was describing are small consolation. I can't imagine the self-contained cities-in-a-building being finished in the middle of a war, and even if they are, who's to say the Order won't just bomb them into oblivion?

I never thought I'd be grateful for sore and blistered feet, but I am. The sharp pain is taking my mind off of the horrors all around us—horrors we're about to be trained to face head-on.

We walk for what feels like forever, until we arrive at last at a massive chain-link fence, twenty feet high and topped with coils of dangerous-looking razor wire. Kellerson scans an input panel that unlocks a section of the fence, and we step through a cut-out door. "Don't brush against the fence," he warns as we walk through. "It's still live. Touch it, and you won't be."

There are a few feet between us and the fence as we file past, but I hug my arms around myself, just to be on the safe side.

It's another hundred yards or so up to the front door of one of the giant cube-shaped buildings that tower up, casting long shadows over the wrecked and partially-wooded land. The building is windowless, its surface glistening black, casting our reflections back at us. I don't know what it's made of, but it's not like anything I've ever seen before, except maybe the viz-screens back home. Kind of shimmery like glass, but way stronger looking. Like shiny black steel.

Kellerson beckons us forward with a regal wave. "Welcome to the Alpha Cube of the Western Recruitment Processor."

"What happens now?" Kella asks. Somehow, she doesn't look quite as enthusiastic right now as she has for the last several months.

"The Execs will take you through their training program," Kellerson replies with a ton of snark, as if it's the most obvious answer to the dumbest question he's ever heard.

"And then?"

"I'm sorry," he says with a gentle shrug and a slightly cruel smirk. "But 'and then' is a little beyond my pay-grade. Don't worry your pretty little self, Seventeen. I'm sure I'll see you around."

Before Kella can follow her questions with an impolite comment, a huge set of steel double-doors, each at least fifteen feet tall and lurchy as a battleship, start to grind slowly open with a metallic whir.

I step back involuntarily. I can't seem to fight off the feeling that something huge is going to lumber out and eat us.

But instead, the big doors open at last to reveal a tall, stern woman with stylish silver-framed glasses and her white hair pulled back in an immaculate ponytail. She's wearing khaki cargo pants with a green military shirt and a starched white lab coat like she's half soldier, half scientist.

She's flanked on one side by a surprisingly handsome military guy, maybe twenty years old or so, who introduces himself as

Sergeant Granden and on the other side by a thin young man, maybe even younger, who introduces himself as Trench. He's angular and pretty good-looking too, despite, or maybe *because* of the long, thick scars on his face. Kellerson and Chucker stand behind us and herd us forward into a small semi-circle on the worn patch of grass as the woman and her two military escorts stand in the big doorway in front of us.

"We're your training team," the woman says. "I'm Captain Grace Hiller. Each unit of the training program consists of a Cube like this one with an indoor challenge, and the Agora that you'll see out back, where you'll undergo a series of outdoor training sessions. You'll be here for eight weeks. That's two weeks per session in the Agora plus at least one day in the Cube —though you will not be training in the last two Cubes. Those are the medical and control facilities. You'll sleep in barracks at the end of each day. You'll eat what we give you, when we give it to you."

Her words sound threatening, but her voice is as pleasant as can be. She sounds like a kind aunt, rather than the woman who apparently holds our lives and futures in her hands.

With a wide sweep of her hand, Hiller gestures toward the big buildings. "These facilities and this program are designed to train you to fight the Eastern Order and push you to your physical and mental limits. You will be graded along the way. Everything you do, what you say, how you react…is subject to assessment."

She looks around, appraising each Seventeen in turn. "You will receive points for a job well done. You'll be deducted points for everything else. Your marks overall, broken down by each of the four deployments, will be posted on a viz-screen in the Silo, which is the name of your underground barracks. It's where you'll eat, sleep, and shower. Keep a close eye on your assessment numbers as they will determine where you'll end up after your time in the Processor."

Hiller points to a panel on the wall of the building where a display lights up to reveal five letters: T.I.C.S.O. Beneath the letters, a flow of holographic text and schematics scrolls in a constant stream. "The T.I.C.S.O. program represents the four possible deployments. *Tech* represents your ability to think like a machine, in ones and zeros. It's for fiddlers and tinkerers, those of you who can make something useful out of a bunch of useless parts."

Cardyn glances at me out of the corner of his eye and gives me an encouraging thumbs-up, though I'm not feeling particularly excited at the moment.

"*Intel* is for those who are the best at figuring things out, solving puzzles, unraveling mysteries," Hiller continues. "Those are the detectives in our army. *Combat* is for warriors. Fearless. Loyal. Dedicated to the cause and to the protection of others. Finally, *Special Ops* is the 'harmonious expertise' deployment. It means your skills are in balance. You're versatile in mind and body. A free-thinker. An intellect with empathy. Special Ops is reserved not just for the best and brightest, but for those who surpass their own limits, who are better than the sum of their parts, and who demonstrate extraordinary abilities, even beyond known human limits."

All of a sudden, I'm beginning to regret that I didn't at least ask about bringing Render. Maybe I was right all along, that he would have helped me get into Special Ops. If Hiller could see me work with him, she might be impressed.

Then again, she might have him put to sleep. She doesn't exactly strike me as the kind of person who loves animals. Actually, she doesn't seem like she's especially fond of people, either. I think she'd get along great with a computer.

"You will be assessed and graded at every step of the way," she announces in her oddly charming lilt. "At the end of the program, if you pass it, your final scores will determine your deployment."

I nudge Cardyn in the ribs with my elbow. "See?" I whisper through the side of my mouth. "I *knew* Special Ops was real."

Speaking of extraordinary abilities, Hiller must have some kind of super-hearing, because she turns and shoots Card and me a quick, unreadable look. "I guarantee you," she says with a pleasant smile, "Special Ops is as real as it gets."

I feel myself blush, embarrassed at being overheard. Thankfully, Terk pulls the attention off me by thrusting his muscular arm into the air. "Excuse me. But what if someone...?"

"Doesn't pass?" Hiller interrupts, reading his mind. "Then that person has nothing to offer us against our enemy and will be reassigned to the place where they can do the least damage to the cause."

I look around at my fellow Seventeens only to see expressions of fear and shock on their faces. The word "reassigned" might as well have had finger-quotes around it. It's a lot to take in, but the gist of Hiller's introduction to the Processor is crystal clear: if you're not part of the solution, you're part of the problem.

This woman, the two heavily-armed men standing behind us, and the other two standing next to her seem like they'd happily get rid of any and all problems without losing a second of sleep.

6

Part of me has been hoping for what feels like ages that Hiller will direct us to a place where we can take a shower and get a bite to eat. But instead she leads us, along with Granden and Trench, into the imposing building. Like a herd of bleary-eyed sleepwalkers, we make our way down a long hall, through a door, and into a large open room. The room's walls are as black as the building, but the floor is sterile and white. Eight treadmills, glistening silver, white, and blue, sit lined up side-by-side in the middle of the strange chamber.

Each of us Seventeen is assigned to one of the sleek machines. As we step up, Granden and Trench apply circular adhesive pads to our temples and forearms. Each pad is translucent with a thin coil of wire wrapped up inside of it like a tiny snake. As he applies more of the cold pads to my neck and hands, Granden lingers over the dark black pattern of the implants encircling my forearms. He traces the thick bands, the small black dots, and the gentle curves of the tapering black tails with his fingertips. I'm used to people in the Valta asking about the markings, the Neos, especially. I usually just call them my "tattoos" and that tends to be the end of it. If one of the younger kids pressed me on it, I'd joke about the patterns being a set of amazingly intricate birthmarks. Or a design plan for my next batch of crop circles. Or an elaborate stamp that my dad pressed into my skin, so he could identify me in case my zombie double appeared one day and tried to take my place.

Granden doesn't ask anything, though. He lifts his finger off of my forearm and glances up at me, embarrassed for a split-second, I think. He smiles a little and moves on to Card.

After he and Trench finish applying the sensor pads to us, they go about fitting us with clear oxygen masks that they attach to our faces with white elastic straps. I turn to my left to see how the others are doing. I can barely see Brohn way down at the far end of our line. He's still got that angry, determined look on his face that tells me he's not anywhere near over the incident with Wisp.

In between us are Karmine, Kella, Terk, and Rain. Card is on my left with Amaranthine as the last in our line over on my right.

It occurs to me that none of us have really had a single chance to talk, compare notes, or commiserate about our fate as new Seventeens since we were first piled onto the transport truck back in the Valta.

Back home, I was never particularly sociable. But at least we could talk whenever we wanted about whatever we wanted. We may have been prisoners, slaves, or innocent victims of war, but when it came to expressing ourselves, we were at least free. Looking down the line of treadmills, I suddenly want nothing more than to joke around with Cardyn or to sit on a beach again and get to know Brohn better. I'd even settle for getting a math lesson from Rain or listen to Karmine blather on about military strategy.

But instead, we all just exchange a set of helpless, silent looks.

In the meantime, Trench goes back down our line. He's taken

what looks like a fat magic marker from a holster on his belt. He flips the bottom of it open with his thumb and inserts a thin metal clip. He snaps the device shut and spins it on his finger.

"I'll be administering your Biscuit now," Trench says with a maniacal grin.

Hiller advises us to ignore him. "What Mr. Trench is inserting under your right shoulder-blade is actually just a tracking chip. Won't hurt a bit. You won't even know it's there, and it'll help us keep you safe in case of an emergency. It will also help your commanding officer to locate you in the event you get lost on a mission once you're out of here and off on your deployment."

She says "lost," but the crystal-clear implication is "wounded or killed."

One by one, Trench sidles up behind us. He slips his marker device under our raised shirts and injects the chip under our skin. Hiller was wrong. It hurts a lot. I wince at the sharp pinch and try not to move my shoulder around too much while the pain slowly fades.

Satisfied that we're all sufficiently prepped, Hiller gives us instructions that we're now ready to begin what she calls a baseline cardio test. "We need to see where your endurance limits are, so we can properly elevate our expectations of you. I know you're probably still reeling, and you just had a long drive and a bit of a hike getting here. But these stationary running tracks are low-impact grav-pads, so this should be smooth sailing. Just keep up with the pace of the pad, and you'll be fine."

"How long are we supposed to run?" Cardyn asks. His voice is muffled by the plastic mask over his face that fills with steam as he speaks. "There's no timer."

Hiller smiles at him and then gazes down the line at all of us. "You're the timer," she says. "There's no clock and no countdown. You run until *you* hit zero."

She turns around and heads for the door on the far side of the room with Granden and Trench still flanking her on either side. As the door slides shut behind them, sealing with a breathy whoosh, our puzzled looks are rudely interrupted by the whir of the treadmills that start zipping along under our feet. Simultaneously, we all break into a light jog. I've got my hands on the thin silver grip-bar in front of me, but the others are running without any support, their arms dangling or else pumping in slow rhythm at their sides.

After I feel like we've settled in, I decide I want to try to talk to Cardyn, who's jogging alongside me, but the oxygen mask makes it next to impossible for me to call out to him. I try to get his attention with a quick hand-wave, but he's either too focused or too tired to notice me. I almost lose my balance and decide to keep my hands on the bar and my focus on not slipping off and killing myself.

As we jog along, I begin to lose my sense of time. There are no clocks on the walls or timers on the treadmills. There are no windows either this deep in the bowels of the building. It's like being in the Recruiters' transport truck all over again, and not knowing where I am in space or time twists my brain. At first, it's kind of a nice feeling. To be alone with my own thoughts and in the company of my own breathing and heartbeat. I think back to Render. I know he can't sense me from this distance, but I send him a mental message anyway. I tell him I'm okay and that I hope he's feeling full and flying free. Normally, I'd feel something in return. Kind of a soft tingle in my temple and a warm sensation like a liquid blanket around my heart. But now...nothing. I know it sounds silly to think of a bird leaving a hole in my heart, but that's how it feels. I glance down the line at Brohn and wonder if it'll ever be filled again.

Then I think back to the fun times Card and I had, goofing around in the woods as we were growing up. Gathering berries and digging up edible roots, reading from whatever scraps of books were left, being taught about grammar and math by the Sixteens and the older Juvens, performing dangerous experiments to determine which leaves on which trees and which colorful plants were edible and which ones would make us violently ill. We all learned the hard way, after a series of intense asthma attacks and some muscle paralysis, to avoid the two pretty purple plants we later discovered were called "Larkspur" and "Lupine." I remember all my training sessions over the years with Render. The meandering explorations into the woods. The hunt for the fat grubs he loved so much. The verbal and hand signals we eventually perfected to go along with the strange mental connection we were slowly cultivating. The times when I started to realize that the connection between us wasn't just in my imagination. When I could feel the feedback of his mind in mine and the realization that, in a way, he was training me, too.

They're nice memories to have, bright spots in a life that was often bleak and filled with danger and uncertainty.

I'm getting distracted. I haven't run this much for this long in...well, ever. I feel my feet starting to drag a little on the treadmill's grav-pad, so I turn my thoughts to the task at hand: chugging along, trying to stay focused, trying not to be the first one to stop. At least I'm not as hyper-competitive as Karmine or Kella. They've been known to get into rivalries that could last for days. I'm sure they'll each try to outlast each other on the treadmills.

There isn't much to the machine, just the thin silver handrail in front of me and the constant zip of the shiny white track beneath my feet. Back in the Valta, Keith's Bike and Hike Equipment Rental had an old treadmill in the basement storage room. Rain's family owned the place. Keith was her uncle. He brought a bunch of us downstairs once when we were maybe five or six years old. It was like a museum down there. He showed us the old equipment he said he couldn't bear to part with. There were solar-powered flex machines, rubber-covered steel plates from before they came out with the mag-resistance system for weight-lifting, a frayed heavy bag for boxing, and a stationary bicycle with broken handlebars and a missing seat. And there was a big clunker of a treadmill, all faux-wood and black plastic around a heavy steel frame, with a complex panel of numbers and settings that looked like an airplane flight console.

We all scampered around down there, ducking back and forth between the aisles of dusty old equipment. We made up pretend games where the treadmill and broken bike were monsters, and we had to sneak around behind them to avoid being spotted and gobbled up.

Three months after that, Keith's Hike and Bike was a pile of rubble with exposed pipes and wires and bent lengths of rebar snaking out from under jagged blocks of concrete and twisted steel cross-beams. Keith died in that first attack along with his wife, Rain's parents, and two of her cousins. Years later, I saw two of the Sixteens dragging that same treadmill, smashed nearly beyond recognition, out of the broken building and over to the Discard Field in one of our many clean-up projects.

Pulling myself back to the present, I look over past Card to where Rain is and wonder if she's having the same kind of memories. If the treadmill she's running on reminds her of that tour of her uncle's basement and of the family she lost at the hands of the Eastern Order and their cowardly drone attacks. For a second, I consider trying to signal her somehow, but she seems so focused that I decide to leave her alone. Besides, I'm getting tired, and I think if I tried to raise my hand or turn my body toward her, I'd go flying off this thing and make a total idiot of myself. So I keep chugging along, one foot after the other. The pace seems to quicken over time and has now settled into a relentless whoosh under my feet. I lengthen my strides to keep up. Then lengthen them again when the speed increases even more.

I'm sure hours have passed. At least six or seven if I had to guess. I'm soaked with sweat. My leg muscles are locked up like vice-grips. My throat is a scorched desert. I can't focus my eyes anymore. It's like I'm underwater, looking through wet glass in the middle of the night.

But we're not supposed to quit, right? So am I supposed to run myself to death on this thing? Is someone watching us? There are no windows in this room. But that doesn't mean they don't have micro-cams or pocket drones or some other kind of hidden surveillance system set up. I doubt they'd go to the trouble of monitoring our vital signs without being able to see us as well. Is this part of some psychological test to see how well we follow orders, how long our minds and bodies will hold up under the weight of sheer exhaustion?

All I know is I don't want to be the first person to quit. And I'm not.

I look down the line and see Terk, trembling and sweat-soaked, peeling the sensor pads from his body. He rips off the face mask and leaps down from his treadmill. His feet give out as he hits the floor and all six-and-a-half feet of his massive body slams to the ground. His long sandy-brown hair splays out as he falls. He rolls onto his back, sucking in air while his stomach rises up and down. He's panting like a freight train, which is a horrifying sound, but at least it means he's still alive. On either side of his now-empty treadmill, Kella and Rain whip their heads around and look like they're preparing to hop down and help him. They hesitate, though, exchange a look, and face forward again, still running. I can't see either one of them very clearly with Cardyn in between us, but I think Rain might be crying.

Down at the far end of our line, Brohn and Karmine exchange similar looks. Karmine keeps running, but Brohn doesn't. Instead, he tears off his own mask and leaps down from his treadmill. Like Terk, he stumbles, but he doesn't fall. He staggers over on shaky legs to kneel down beside Terk. I catch Karmine gazing in my direction from down the line. He shrugs and detaches the mask and defiantly peels off the sensor pads on either temple. Leaping from his treadmill, he lands awkwardly and lurches over to help Brohn tend to Terk. To my left, Cardyn does the same.

Looking over my shoulder to see how they're all doing has thrown me into a wobble. My left foot clips against my right heel, and in a split-second, the world goes upside down. I spin off the treadmill, fall down, and roll for ten feet before sliding to a painful stop on the cold hard floor.

Maybe out of boredom, or maybe because she wants to help me, Kella detaches herself and hops down from her treadmill. She's breathing almost as hard as the rest of us and looks relieved to still be alive. She asks through a pant if I'm okay, and I tell her I am. She's bent over with her hands on her knees and smiling up at us through sweaty strands of blond hair.

Amaranthine is the last of us to quit. In fact, she doesn't quit. Instead, her body gives out.

While the rest of us are on the floor, gasping for air, and nursing our wrecked muscles, Amaranthine continues to slog along, one desperate and exhausted foot after the other. We all call out to her, but she ignores us. And then, after a few more minutes of trying to keep up with the rapid whoosh of the white track, she collapses. The track-pad whips along, kicking her feet out from under her. Her head cracks against the hand-rail, and she crashes in a heap at the foot of the machine. I leave Terk and the others and rush over to her, sliding to a stop by her unmoving body.

"Manthy!" I call out. I give her shoulder a shake, and her eyes flutter open. I try to help her to a sitting position, but she shrugs me off and climbs slowly to her feet.

"Leave me alone," she mutters. "I'm fine."

Her faint voice and a reddish bruise forming above her eye say otherwise.

Leaving Terk on the floor to catch his breath and leaving Amaranthine alone as she's asked, the rest of us mill around for a while. Still panting, we investigate the area where Hiller and the others left, but the door has either blended seamlessly into the wall or else disappeared completely. We pace the large open room and look for other doors or a hidden panel, anything that might help us get out of what's become a nightmare of a situation. Then the lights go out, and we're in total and absolute darkness with only the sound of the still-moving treadmill tracks to keep us company. It's an eerie sound, the rhythmic hum of the tracks in this totally light-less room.

I'm trying to stay calm, but I'm physically wiped. My brain feels fuzzy, and I can't think straight. Out of the pitch black, Brohn's quaking voice calls out for us to take a breath and not move.

"It's just dark," he says. "That's all. Other than tripping over the treadmills or each other, there's nothing in here that can hurt us."

"Not yet, anyway," Karmine says through a wheezy cough.

"We really need to find that doorway," Kella says. She sounds out of breath but in better shape than the rest of us, especially Terk, who's still on the ground, now gently moaning somewhere near my feet.

"I'll stay with Terk," I say as I kneel down and try to locate his head in the dark.

"I'll stay with you," Card's voice offers.

On what I'm sure must be shaky legs, Brohn, Karmine, Kella, and Rain start to spread out, sliding their hands along the walls and around the seamless area where Hiller, Granden, and Trench walked out who knows how long ago. They call out to each other to get their bearings. I'm just starting to despair. What if this is it? What if we're just locked in here forever? No food. No water. No way out. Will we die slowly in the dark? Or maybe go crazy and try to kill each other? Is this a fluke or part of some twisted test? Or, even worse, is it a deliberate attempt to drive us insane to make it easier to kill us off?

No. Get a hold of yourself, Kress. If they wanted us dead, they've already had a million opportunities. Everything from leaving us out in the desert to die to just shooting us all in the head the moment we boarded the transport truck.

The others are still calling out, but their voices are so weak from fear and fatigue that I doubt anyone outside of this room could hear them. With Amaranthine sitting somewhere nearby, I'm holding Terk's head in my hands. His hair is soaked with sweat. He's mumbling something about not being able to see, and I explain to him about the lights going out and that we're all going to get out of here soon, and everything will be just fine. Card backs me up, promising we'll be out of here any second now.

The others follow the sound of Brohn's voice and make their way back to Terk and me. Still struggling to catch their breath, they all plop down heavily around us on the cold floor.

We must be sitting for an hour, maybe longer, still trying to catch our breath and collect our thoughts. We talk back and forth without being able to see each other. Brohn's voice reminds us that panic isn't going to get us out of here any sooner. "Once we're all relaxed and have caught our breath, we'll start looking for a way out again."

"Maybe we can pick some parts out of the treadmills to make a flashlight or something," Kella's voice suggests.

"Right," Karmine's voice chimes in. "Or maybe we can use part of the frame to smash a wall out."

Before anyone has a chance to come up with any more plans, a thin rectangle of light appears out of the gloom and expands to reveal an open doorway. The shock of the light on my eyes sends a wave of pain through my brain.

The shadow in the doorway enters the room. Hiller's voice calls for us to stand up, which we do with great effort. I'm not strong enough to help Terk up, so Brohn and Karmine each take him by an arm and get him to his feet. He's caught his breath, but his legs are still wobbly. Hiller leads the eight of us out of the treadmill room, down a short hallway, and up two flights of stairs to another room.

All I can think is, *Please, let there be some water!*

My wish is answered. Kind of.

7

"WHAT HAPPENED TO THE LIGHTS BACK THERE?" BROHN ASKS.

Instead of answering, Hiller escorts us into the next room, which is pure white. It's empty except for an old-style picnic table, the kind you might find in a playground or a park. The long boards of the table are riveted to the steel frame, and two cinder blocks on chains hold the whole thing in place, although I have no idea why. I can't imagine who would try to walk off with a picnic table.

It hits me that we've moved from a black room filled with sleek, high-tech treadmills to this odd, barren white space, and I can't help thinking that if a town like the Valta had a polar opposite, this is about as close as it gets.

When we've gathered around the table, Hiller stands at its head to give us instructions.

"Sit," she commands, and we obey.

"You haven't had anything to eat or drink, correct?" she asks when we've each found our place on the two benches that flank the table.

We all nod, too exhausted and dehydrated to summon the anger we know we should feel right now.

"Not since you left the Valta?"

We all nod again. For some reason, Karmine whispers a barely audible "Yes ma'am."

It's not the first time any of us has had to go for a long stretch without food or water. Every Seventeen in this room has grown accustomed to rough conditions over the years. But with the long drive, the running in place, the sensory deprivation, and the general mystery of the recruitment experience so far, I'm starting to wonder whether these people are testing us or just plain torturing us.

Biding her time, Hiller calls out, "Sergeant Granden. Mr. Trench."

The two men appear, each carrying a tray that holds four glasses. They walk around the picnic table and set a glass of cloudy water in front of each of us. There's no doubt in my mind that every Seventeen in the room is tempted to dump the liquid down their throat, but we also know better by now than to make a move without permission.

That is, most of us do.

Terk, who apparently doesn't share our sense of caution, reaches out for the glass in front of him.

"Uh-uh," Trench says, clicking his tongue. "Don't touch."

Terk draws his hand back like it's been slapped by a ruler-wielding nun.

Hiller speaks up again, her voice cold and authoritative. "Here are your instructions: You can each have the glass of water in front of you now." Out of the corner of my eye, I see a few hands reach out, ready to grab their drinks. "Or—" Hiller interrupts, "you can wait one hour, and get your own personal pitcher of nice, clean ice water instead." The hands disappear again. "You can talk during the hour, but no getting up. If you move from your seat, you're out. Also, no sharing. If you drink, you drink alone."

"What does that mean, 'out'?" Kella asks.

"It means exactly what you think it means," Hiller says with a smile that's part threat, with a bit of mocking sneer thrown in for good measure. "Keep in mind that your decisions are all part of the assessment that will ultimately determine your deployment. This isn't some clichéd boot camp like you might have seen in old movies. We aren't just here to make you crawl under barbed-wire or march around in straight lines, although there will definitely be some of that later on." Granden and Trench let out a knowing laugh. "Your minds need as much training and evaluation as your bodies." Hiller gestures toward the water glasses "You all passed the treadmill test. Now it's time for test number two. This one is about intellect. Will-power. Teamwork."

I eye my glass. Grayish streaks sift around in the liquid like little party streamers.

"Is there anything wrong with this water?" I ask.

"If you're thirsty enough," Hiller says as she heads toward the door, "there's nothing wrong with anything that might keep you alive."

As Granden turns to follow her, I catch him staring at my arms again. I can't help but wonder if he's curious about my markings or suspicious. Either way, I tell myself I'm going to have to be careful. I have a long history of blending in and not attracting attention. It's a streak I'm not eager to end.

"So what do we do now?" Cardyn asks when Hiller and the two men have left the room. Like Karmine's, his voice is little more than a rasping whisper.

Brohn shrugs. "I guess we wait. It's only an hour." He and I exchange a quick glance, and I can't help but think he's still hurting after the day's painful events.

It's insane to think that it was just this morning that Wisp was torn away from him or that I said my final good-bye to Render. It feels like weeks ago now. Yet the memories hang in my head as clear as anything.

I have no doubt that Brohn feels them, too.

"An hour? Easy for you to say," Rain protests, drawing his attention away. "There are a lot of different levels of tolerance at this table, and not everyone here can make it through another hour of deprivation."

Terk looks offended. He stammers a weak, "What's *that* supposed to mean?" He's trying to maintain his composure, but his glazed-over eyes and parched lips betray the true depth of his suffering. I can't blame him. I'm using whatever reserves I've got left to keep the room from spinning, not to mention trying to keep myself from passing out.

"No offense," Rain assures Terk. "But Brohn might not know what's best for everyone. Look, this is just a test. So I suggest we try to work out an optimal solution. You heard Hiller. It doesn't even matter if we know the problem's purpose or not. The only way forward is to think it through."

"It could be a test of our will power," Kella says with a slight nod. "You know, to see who can resist, and who gives in to temptation."

"Who's to say that delayed gratification is the be-all and end-all, though?" Card asks, running a hand over the patchy reddish stubble coming in on his face. "Isn't there something to be said for indulging in something good when you have the chance? Especially if that something can save your life?"

Rain shakes her head. "Nope. That's called giving in to temptation."

"So? Just because something's tempting doesn't mean you shouldn't have it. In fact, I'd say it's the opposite."

"How do you mean?"

Cardyn looks like he's struggling for words. "Something tempts you because it's good. If it's dangerous, or toxic or whatever, it won't tempt you. But if we're tempted by the water, doesn't that mean it's good for us?" His voice quivers and breaks, but he manages to make his point.

"Sure," Rain says. "All food is tempting when you're hungry."

Brohn nods. “It’s not a bad point. If you knew you were going to die in an hour anyway, it would be stupid not to drink the only glass of water you have in front of you.”

“That’s what I’m saying,” Card says, managing a weak smile. “Life’s short. Eat dessert first.”

Maybe it’s just my weakness talking, but I offer a gasping, half-hearted laugh and say, “Agreed!”

“Wait a minute,” Brohn says. “This could be a teamwork test. Which means they want to see if we’ll all stick together and drink or delay.”

“I’m sorry, I don’t care what kind of test it is. I’m tapping out,” Terk mumbles with a shake of his head. “I need water now, or I’m going to drop dead right here on the spot.”

“You’re not going to die,” Brohn assures him.

“Says you. My vision’s been blurry since the treadmill. My head’s pounding, and my throat’s on fire.”

I don’t think he’s exaggerating. His eyes are starting to roll back, and he’s clearly unable to focus. His voice is barely a scratchy whisper, like his throat is full of dry sand. Being the biggest of us has advantages in certain situations, but endurance tests followed by water deprivation clearly aren’t among them.

“I can’t feel my legs,” I announce, trying to take his mind off his own suffering as I rub the feeling back into my numb calf muscles.

But my well intentioned words don’t work.

Terk, who’s sitting on the end of the bench just across from me, suddenly jerks over to the side and spews a thin spray of white vomit on the floor. His eyes roll back all the way, and he slumps over.

Brohn starts to get up, but Kella interrupts him. “We can’t leave our seats!” she calls out, as if Hiller’s rules are concerning her more than the fact that our gentle giant of a friend is about to die in front of our eyes.

"Screw the rules," Brohn says. "I might fail their test of willpower, but no way am I failing at basic humanity."

"No, wait," Card says from his seat next to Terk. "Let me check on him." He reaches over to feel Terk's forehead and neck, then holds a hand under Terk's nose. "He's breathing. And he's got a pulse. But it's weak."

That's enough to set everyone into a panic. Card's eyes are darting back and forth, looking for some sort of guidance. Kella has turned red, and Brohn is biting his lower lip in helpless frustration at the other end of the table. He keeps pressing his hands into the table top, ready to push himself up. But he hesitates each time and sits back down. His dilemma is written all over his face: *Do I lose if I get up, or does Terk lose if I don't?* It's the first time I've ever known him to seem indecisive, not that I can blame him. No one's sure what to do right now, how severe the punishment might be if we fail. Hiller mentioned points and assessments, that we were being watched all the time. Without any other details we're all kind of frozen in place, an unfortunate but also pretty understandable precaution in any minefield.

"You've got to get him to drink his water!" Brohn finally shouts down to us from his end of the table. "The only thing I know is this little game of theirs isn't worth dying over."

"Wait," Karmine says. "This could ruin the challenge. He might get punished, or we all could." When I shoot him my glare of death, he adds, "Terk's my friend as much as he is yours. He's not going to die from waiting an hour for water."

"We don't know that," says Brohn.

"He's right," Kella says. "At some point, everyone crosses the line when dehydration becomes death."

"But how do we know where that line is?" I ask.

"We don't," Kella says. "That's the test."

"In that case, it's a horrible test."

"Wait. There are eight of us," Rain says. She's the only one whose voice is even close to normal and controlled. The rest of us sound like panting, hyperactive puppies in a sack on the verge of getting tossed into a river by a psychopath. "We can't share our water now, but they didn't say anything about not sharing our pitchers with each other later."

"So?"

"So the four of us who need it most will drink the water. That includes Terk. If it's poisoned or toxic or whatever, at least we'll know."

Kella starts to object to using Terk as a guinea pig, but Rain stops her with a raised hand. "I know it sounds cold, but it's a necessary step in the act of self-preservation. After the hour's up, the rest of us will drink our own water, then share our pitchers with the table." Rain interrupts herself with a hoarse, hacking cough that she quickly suppresses. "That way, we take care of the neediest first, and share with everyone once we get through the rough patch."

"I get it," I say. "We can consider it a kind of triage situation, assigning levels of treatment based on need and urgency." Although I'm not a fan of potentially being called one of the "needy" ones, I see Rain's point, and it does seem like a good way to help some of us while the rest muscle through, until we can do something that will benefit all of us.

"Hold on," Brohn calls out to Rain. "It's a good idea, but I'm not sold on the part where Terk might get poisoned."

"It's a chance we need to take. It's a chance I know Terk would take for any of us." Rain draws in a shallow breath. "Now the big question: which of the four of us are the most in need?"

"Terk, obviously," Brohn says. Though from here, his weakened voice tells me he's not doing much better. But instead of asking for help, he says, "And Amaranthine."

"Are you okay, Manthy?" I ask. She has her head down, her chin in her chest. Her arms are dangling loosely at her sides. I can't tell if she's unconscious, annoyed, sleeping, or dead. "Manthy?"

"She needs our help," Brohn says. "No question."

"Agreed," Karmine says as he looks us all up and down as if to assess our level of fatigue and dehydration. "And Kress, you're not looking so good. And…I…think…" His voice trails off as his eyelids flutter, and he droops heavily against Kella, who's sitting to his left.

Kella braces herself to stop from falling over and helps guide Karmine's head gently to the table top. "And Karmine," she says.

Rain checks with the rest of us to make sure we're all in agreement. Through a dizzy haze, I feel myself nod in the hopes that enough of the hour has already gone by so I can survive what's turned into a dangerous game of life or death.

One by one, Brohn, Kella, Cardyn, and Rain help me, Terk, Karmine, and Amaranthine to drink. My hands are shaking either from fatigue or terror, so Cardyn helps me tip the glass to my mouth. I'm almost too dried out to part my chapped lips, but I manage to take in a tiny sip.

The water is tepid and slightly brackish, like the Kokanee River back in the Valta during the summer before it finally dried up. But I don't care. The first sip loosens my lips, so I take another. Card is leaning toward me, watching like a hawk to make sure I don't faint or choke to death.

The next sip goes down, but not without a fight. At first, my parched throat tries to reject it. I try again and manage to get down a sizeable gulp. After that, it becomes easier, and I finally drain the small glass to the bottom. I no longer care about how bad it tastes or how cloudy it looks. After what we've been through already since leaving the Valta, I'd drink down battery acid if I thought it would keep me alive for another minute or two.

Tipping my head back, I breathe a monstrously large sigh of contentment and thank Cardyn for looking out for me. "No problem," he says, but looking over at him, at his flushed complexion and dry lips, there very definitely *is* a problem.

Down the length of the table, Kella is helping Terk, Rain is taking care of Karmine, and Brohn is assisting Amaranthine, who looks like she doesn't really want to be helped. I don't think she's even fully conscious, but she still manages to thrash her head away from Brohn out of some instinct of pure defiance. Eventually, he's able to steady her long enough to get some water into her.

While we're busy trying to keep each other alive, no one seems to notice that Hiller and her two bodyguards have come back into the room. Hiller alerts us to her presence with a condescending, "Well, well, well. It looks like our brave little band of Seventeens has figured out a way to keep themselves alive for a little while longer." Maybe she's trying to sound surprised or proud, but it just comes out as mocking.

"We followed the rules," Brohn says. "You promised us water." It's a statement of fact, but coming from him, it sounds more like an order. Hiller raises an eyebrow. She seems skeptical but nods to Granden and Trench, who walk back into the hall and return seconds later with pitchers of crystal-clear water.

Before they even hit the table, we've got the pitchers in our hands. The mood around the table shifts immediately, like a deflated balloon suddenly filled with helium. Instead of feeling wiped out and ready for death, I'm suddenly light and tight, like I can handle anything else Hiller and her gang want to throw my way.

"It's time for the Agora," Hiller announces, gesturing for us to get up and follow her out of the room.

My feeling of renewed confidence takes a hit when I try to stand and realize my legs don't want to cooperate. I'm relieved when I realize that we're all going through the same transition, groaning to our feet and rubbing life back into our tired limbs.

As he takes his first steps toward the door, Terk thanks everyone for the help and apologizes for needing it.

"Nothing to be sorry for, Big Guy," Brohn says with a friendly clap on Terk's burly shoulder. "Needing help isn't weakness. Weakness is not helping someone who needs it."

Out of the corner of my eye, I notice Granden nodding his approval.

8

ONCE WE'RE OUT IN THE LARGE, HIGH-CEILINGED HALL, WE SUCK IN air like we drank down the water, with big, greedy gulps. It's true that we didn't know what to expect after Recruitment. What I definitely didn't expect was to have my lungs empty, my head spinning, and my muscles in tight knots this early in the game.

Before we get a chance to gather ourselves, Granden and Trench order us into a line. In her white lab coat and slim khaki pants, Hiller positions herself in front of the doorway like she's royalty appearing before her loyal subjects.

"I'm very pleased to inform you that you've all passed the Orientation Test and can move on."

"More like *dis*orientation test," Cardyn whispers to me through the side of his mouth.

I nudge him to be quiet.

"Yesterday, you were Sixteens," Hiller proclaims. "Today, you're Seventeens. You're Recruits. What you do with this honor is entirely up to you. But if you succeed, you will serve President Krug and join in the fight against the Eastern Order, who have invaded our nation and slaughtered our children in the name of a false, violent, and unforgiving god. With your help, we will take back our world and return things to the way they were."

Karmine pumps his fist and high-fives Kella. Rain nods silently. Terk manages a weak but genuine smile. Amaranthine is busy looking intently at her feet, and Brohn stares straight ahead, refusing to react on impulse. He doesn't need military training. He's already the most self-controlled and disciplined person I know.

As for me, my head's still a bit foggy from the treadmill and sensory deprivation torture, but I manage to focus just enough to hear Hiller announce that she'll be the one coordinating our psych and reflex training inside the Cubes.

"At the moment, we're in Alpha Cube," she says. "From here, Granden and Trench will be taking the lead in the Agora. After a two-week training session, you'll graduate to the Beta Cube for another psych evaluation." Her voice echoes in the wide, empty hall as she explains the next few weeks and prepares to escort us outside. "You'll see your scores reflected on the viz-screen in the Silo, which is where you'll find your living and sleeping quarters. Don't get too comfortable, though. There are more mental training protocols to go in the other Cubes. But right now, it's time to introduce you to the Agora."

Card inches his hand up. "What exactly is an 'Agora'?"

"I'm about to show you," Hiller replies. "Come with me." She pivots, and the black door slides open in front of her. She leads us outside, down a caged-off walkway, through a chain-link fence, under a turret with an armed guard, and out to an enormous, manicured field. The grass stretches out in a clean, expansive octagon at least three times as big as our soccer field behind the school back home. Unlike ours, though, this field's octagonal perimeter is lined on all eight sides with a high chain-link fence with coils of razor wire along the top.

I've seen fences like this. We all have. Back in the Valta when we were first quarantined, they used them to keep us safe from the Order. I was just a Neo at the time, but I remember hearing about the early Sixteens who tested the fences out, or even tried to escape. A boy named Stance had to be treated for horrific burns from the electrified fence way down the mountain at the foot of the road. I watched a few of the Sixteens carry him back up to town, where some of the remaining adults applied some kind of cream to his hands and arms.

He died the next day.

They buried him in what was left of the bombed-out cemetery next to the pile of bricks and wood that used to be our church.

The fences that run around the perimeter of the Agora remind me of the prison that our town turned into. The difference is that these fences are punctuated at each of the eight corners with tall turrets, like watchtowers. At the top of the turret to our left, peering down at us from behind a metal guardrail, is a familiar face: Chucker, the huge Recruiter who looked like he was going to kill us all before we even got out of the transport truck.

He's got to be fifty feet away and twenty feet in the air, but I can practically feel his scowl searing deep holes into my forehead. He's still cradling his huge gun like it's a newborn baby.

To our right is another watchtower. From behind the railing of his station, Kellerson, a pistol in his hand, gives us a big, friendly wave. Scanning the entire Agora, I can see that each of the other six corners has an identical turret, each with an armed guard monitoring the large, open space. One of the guards looks like he might be one of the men who led that team into the Valta to check for stragglers. I didn't think we'd see any of those Recruiters again, but in a weird way, it's comforting. At least it's proof that people around here don't necessarily just appear and then vanish.

Which means there's hope that we'll be able to stick around.

For now, at least.

Between each of the eight massive cubes and stretching out for miles beyond them, we can see a dense black forest of dead and dying trees. Some of their gnarled limbs are still reaching toward the sky, looming up even higher than the black Cubes. Others are cracked in half or leaning at every precarious and crisscrossed angle imaginable. Clearly, this place was once attacked, just like the Valta. The earth beyond the buildings is cratered in the same way that our town was. The angled trees have the same charred look to them, black, scarred, and hanging on to whatever shreds of life they can.

But unlike the Valta, the air here is thick and hazy. Instead of rolling white clouds and thin, breathable air, a red fog hangs around like an annoying swarm of insects.

"The Cubes are where I'll train your minds," Hiller announces nonchalantly. "But the Agora is where my partners here will train your bodies. As you can see, there are Recruiters stationed at each of the eight watch-points. That's for your own protection. As you can imagine, we can't risk having the Order find this place."

She's trying to be reassuring, but there's no doubt in my mind that those stations are designed to keep us in just as much as they might be designed to keep the Order out.

"Does our training include weapons instruction?" Karmine asks. He's practically licking his lips just thinking about it.

"That it does," Hiller says. "We'll be monitoring you from up there." With a nod of her head, she directs our gaze straight up. Fifty or so feet up in the air, at an even level with the top floor of the Cubes and hovering above the Agora, is a massive, gleaming silver ring. It rotates slowly, its surface polished to a mirror shine.

It seems to defy gravity, suspended in the air. An enormous, slowly-revolving chrome donut. Nothing seems to power it, and as far as we can see, nothing is holding it up.

"That's the O.A.H. The Observation and Assessment Halo,"

Hiller explains. "We call it the Halo, although technically, it's a Torus."

"A *what*?" Cardyn asks in a voice that reminds me that he's still a kid in a lot of ways. We all are.

Hiller laughs. "A torus is basically a ring. In this case, a huge hollow tube. It's suspended above us by a controlled magnetic wave vortex. That's where the science and tech offices of our training are located."

"Is that kind of the place where you'll be spying on us?" Terk asks with a nervous tremble.

"Not 'kind of,'" Hiller says evenly. "That's *exactly* where we'll be spying on you. The Halo gives us an overhead, 360-degree, 24-7 view of your training in the Agora. The so-called 'Biscuit' we implanted under your shoulder blades links us to your vital signs and lets us know how you're standing up to the mental and physical rigors you've only just started to experience. As I said, it also lets us keep track of you at all times." Hiller points up, a strangely proud look on her face. "It's from up there that you'll be assessed for one of your military deployments, and it's from there that we'll determine if you have what it takes to help us win this war."

"How do you even *get* up there?" Cardyn asks. It's a good question. I don't see a set of stairs, a pulley-rig, an elevator, or anything.

Hiller gives him an approving nod and praises him for his inquisitiveness. "There are retractable sky-bridges that run from the top floor of each Cube across to the Halo. But that needn't concern you at the moment. For now, your top priority needs to be focusing on your assessments. Based on your performance in the Alpha Cube, you've each been assigned a grade." She taps the comm-link on her wrist, and a holo-display appears beside her showing a series of names and numbers.

She steps to the side as we rush up to see our scores.

I can't speak for the others, but I'm weirdly excited. We're the last Cohort from our town that ever attended a proper school. Valta Elementary. But that was only until we were six. After that, of course, our "proper" school became just one of the many casualties of the drone attacks.

The idea of classes and studying had always appealed to me, though. My brother used to come home with tales of his prowess on the basketball court, or about how some kid got in trouble for this or that grave sin.

I always thought Micah was kind of spoiled for complaining about homework. He made it sound like a punishment, but it sounded more like a gift to me. Of course, he was more interested in being popular than in grades and learning. I wouldn't have liked being the center of attention like he was, but I did fantasize in my young mind about having assignments to take home and work on in the quiet of my bedroom.

		TECH	OPS	INTEL	COMBAT	OVERALL
		mechanical expertise	harmonious expertise	languages & puzzles	physical ability & military strategy	
		(1-5)	(1-5)	(1-5)	(1-5)	
1	Rain	5	4	5	3	17
2	Brohn	4	4	3	5	16
3	Kella	2	3	4	5	14
4	Karmine	3	2	2	5	12
5	Terk	1	4	1	5	11
6	Kress	5	1	2	2	10
7	Cardyn	2	2	3	3	10
8	Amaranthine	0	0	0	0	0

Hiller explains the assessment chart to us as eight pairs of eyes lock on its contents. "You'll see your score broken down by potential deployment," she tells us. "This will give you and us an idea of which area of service suits you best."

Before she leaves, Hiller points over to the next black building in the octagonal field. It has the letter "B" stamped on its face above the door. "I'll rendezvous with you in two weeks at the

Beta Cube. Meanwhile, Granden and Trench will take it from here."

With that, she heads back under the guard tower, through the fenced-in entryway, and into the Alpha Cube, where the black door glides shut behind her.

"Time to get to work," Granden says.

Trench steps in front of him, a giant grin stretching his lips wide. "More like time to get to play!"

He tells us to stand back as he pulls a small black device from a holster in his belt. He taps in a code with his thumb, and before our eyes, a panel in the grass slides back, and a large rectangular box rises up out of the ground. It looks like Trench has just summoned a coffin from the underworld, and we all take a cautious second step back. I can't speak for the other Recruits, but after our experiences with the treadmill and water tests, I'm not ready to trust anyone or anything.

Trench laughs at our reaction and tells us not to worry. "Trust me. We'll have a lot more fun out here than you'll have in the Cube tests with that mind-bender, Hiller." He taps another few keys on his little black controller. The segmented top of the large container rolls back on round metallic hinges.

Inside are clips of ammo and neat rows of handguns and rifles in assorted shapes and sizes. Most of the weapons are sleek and silver or glossy-black. Some have scopes, laser sights, or other stuck-on attachments. A few of the pistols are gold-plated. There's a bunch of old wooden-stocked rifles that are chipped and dented like they've been backed over by a truck. One of the weapons is in three pieces and packed into a half-block of foam.

Combined, there must be at least fifty assorted guns and rifles laid out in the display in front of us.

"That's a lot of fire-power," Card says.

I nod agreement. "Shouldn't these guns be used by the soldiers who are out there fighting the Order?"

Trench shakes his head. "Don't worry about it. These are

decommissioned. Some have already been used in the war. Others are just old. Anyway, they're not combat-ready anymore, just for training purposes now. Most are retrofitted to fire flat-headed wadcutters or alloy pellets."

"That doesn't mean they can't still hurt you. Or even kill," Granden adds as a caution. "Your training will include how to protect yourselves, as much as it will be about how to kill the Order."

I shoot another glance at the weapons. Other than apparently being decommissioned, the only thing they have in common is that every one of them was designed for one purpose: to kill.

The realization hits me with a violent force.

I've lived in a world at war since I was six years old. I was one of the first Neos. I grew older, outlived my mother, and for all I know, my father and brother. I've survived air strikes and drone attacks. And now, as part of the most recent Cohort of Seventeens, I've been recruited specifically to help save our nation from an army of ruthless invaders.

So why should the sight of a couple dozen weapons chill my soul?

"Are you okay?" a voice asks from behind me. I turn around to meet Brohn's eyes. The anger that had settled into him for so many hours seems to have been replaced by something calmer, like he's returned to his reassuring leader mode at last.

I shake my head. "You'll think I'm an idiot."

"No I won't. What's going on?" He reaches out like he's going to put a hand on my shoulder, but he pulls back, like he did on the beach at Final Fest. I wish he wouldn't. For the first time in a long time, I need the reassurance of someone's touch. I need to feel calm, or at least vaguely human.

"The guns," I say, pulling my gaze over to the weapons. "They're freaking me out. Maybe it's because we're closer to the front lines now, or maybe it's because we're about to head into battle, instead of waiting for it to come to us."

"*Or* maybe it's because they remind you that our enemy has weapons of their own," Brohn says softly, taking a step toward me. "It's hard to avoid thinking about it, Kress. It's on my mind, too."

I nod, chewing on my lip. "Some girl from the Order could be out there right now, getting trained how to kill *me*. I don't like thinking about it."

"Just...do yourself a favor," he says, looking over his shoulder toward Granden and Trench. "Try to find a way to play the game, even if you're not into it. The last thing you want is to let on that this isn't the place for you."

"You think they'll kick me out," I say. It's not a question.

"Let's just say that I think we need to be careful," Brohn mutters softly. I'm biting my lip again, shifting my weight uncomfortably. "Hey," he adds, slipping his fingers under my chin and lifting my face so my eyes meet his again, "it's going to be okay. You're one of the strongest people I know."

"I'm pretty sure you're mistaking me for someone else," I counter, but a strange warmth is filling me, reinvigorating my insides. Maybe, just maybe...he's right.

He looks around for a second, pulls his hand away and says quietly, "Listen, I've been wanting to ask you—how are you doing without Render?"

"Seriously?" I ask. "You had to say good-bye to your sister today, and you're asking about how *I'm* feeling?"

"Well, yeah. I mean, I get that sometimes we have to leave pets behind, but I know he was more to you than a pet. You've never really talked about him much, but I saw your eyes this morning, Kress. You looked...I don't know. You looked like I felt when they pulled Wisp away from me."

"I'm okay," I reply, trying to maintain control over my trembling voice. "But you're right, it's hard. I'm worried about—"

"Get over here, Recruits!" Trench calls out. I slam my mouth shut, afraid of being reprimanded for disobedience.

As we make our way over, Brohn grins at me and repeats, "Remember to play the game. For me, if not for yourself."

I nod and throw him a withering smile.

Apparently, most of my fellow Recruits don't share my reservations about digging into a trunk full of guns. When Trench invites us to have a closer look, they charge forward. I join them, trying to follow Brohn's advice and look excited about the new toys.

"Now this is more like it!" Kella exclaims with a squeal of genuine glee. She pushes past me with Karmine hot on her heels. Except for Amaranthine, the others are quick to join them. Our exhaustion has been replaced by adrenaline, and now it's like we're all little kids, scrambling and jostling over each other for a peek at some rare, exotic animal.

Granden and Trench stand beaming on the other side of the long display case. They're clearly proud of their collection of weapons and seem genuinely happy to see joy on the faces before them.

Trench steps closer to the Seventeens, gesturing toward the weapons like they're prizes to be won. "Welcome to the fun stuff, Recruits. Let me introduce you to our little family."

One by one, he points to the weapons and calls out their names, adding little details as he goes.

"This chunky fellow is an FN F2020 Assault Rifle. Then there's this whole family of Sig Sauers. A 2020, a 2032, and this 2040 with the longer barrel, expanded clip, silencer-fitting, and ergo-handgrip. You can see how they kept the gold-plating over the years. This lanky lady here is a Bolt-Action .338 Gen 2030 rifle. The scope, barrel, and stock snap together like this."

With a couple of deft motions, Trench assembles the rifle and clicks its stand into place. He sets it on the grass next to the case before moving on.

"This classic is a Golan Corner-shot. Great for alleyways and corridors. Nice way to kill the enemy before he even knows he's got company. Here's a Magpul FMG-9 folding submachine gun. Here we have a gas-powered 12-gauge. This little white one is a plastic and carbon-fiber composite. Nice and light but blow-your-face-off deadly."

He goes on for several more minutes, giving us an abundance of details about each weapon. For some of the guns, he gives their military history. For others, he tells us about the engineering that went into them, or recounts in graphic detail the mess they can make of an enemy's body when fired.

Trench's knowledge is impressive, but it's a total information overload. I'm hungry and tired and way too out of it to pay much attention. The last thing I want to think about right now is blood and guts and the dead bodies of war.

After a few minutes, Granden catches Kella eyeing the corner of the case that holds the gold-plated handguns.

"I can tell you've got good taste," he says. He hands her one of the weapons and encourages her to fiddle around with it. "Go ahead. See how it feels in your hands."

As if she's been doing it all her life, Kella slaps a magazine in, slides the bolt back, and squints down the length of the gun's barrel.

"Impressive," Granden says with a charming smile. He's not much older than us, maybe twenty or so. I can see Kella blush at being on the receiving end of his attention. He steps around behind her to show her how to extend her arm and keep both shoulders lined up. "See. Square, like this," he says with one hand on her elbow, the other making its way from her shoulder down to the small of her back.

Kella is smiling from ear to ear now, although I'm not sure if it's from the feel of the gun in her hand or the feel of Granden pressed up against her while he demonstrates proper form. Kella is fashion-magazine gorgeous and accustomed to getting what she wants based on how she looks, but she didn't have a lot of romantic options back in the Valta. Here, with Granden, she's found a whole new opportunity to do her annoying flirty thing.

I roll my eyes and leave Kella and Granden to their lesson. I join the others in sorting through the weapons, telling myself not to panic as I feel the weight of the guns in my hands.

"Each of you, grab any one of them you want," Trench says, "and follow me."

After we've each taken our weapon of choice, we follow Granden and Trench out into the middle of the Agora. As we walk, Trench punches in a code on his little electronic device. "You'll love this," he promises, waggling the cell phone-sized piece of equipment.

"What is it?" Card asks.

"With this little guy here, we can transform the Agora into pretty much anything we want."

In the distance, a line of human-shaped targets rises up from the ground like magic.

"Time for your first lesson," Trench announces gleefully.

Beside me, Amaranthine stops in her tracks.

"Come on," I say with an encouraging smile and a tug on her elbow. "This is what we're here for. We don't have a choice."

With her head down, she mumbles something about moral objections. "The Eastern Order never did anything to me. Why should I learn how to kill them?" She tosses her rifle onto the ground behind her.

Rain is walking just a few steps ahead, and she spins around when she hears those words. "Never did anything to you?" she shouts, instantly nose-to-nose with Manthy. "Show me our town! Show me your family! Show me mine!"

Amaranthine raises her head and looks into Rain's eyes, but only for a second. "I just don't think it's right to kill people. Why does the Order have to be our enemy?"

"You can be their best friend, then," Rain shouts, "but trust me

—you just made an enemy!" She shoves Amaranthine's shoulder, causing her to stumble back two steps.

Cardyn rushes over and tries to jump between the two girls, but Rain doesn't seem particularly interested in a truce. Her anger is ramped up in a way I've never seen out of her before. Reaching over Cardyn's outstretched arm, she steps forward and throws a wicked right-cross that catches Amaranthine just under her left eye.

Amaranthine's head snaps sideways. Her long, dark hair splays out, and she stumbles back another two steps. Her eyes go wide as Rain pushes her way through Cardyn and continues her assault. Rain's small, not much more than five feet tall. But she's going after Amaranthine with a ferocity Card can't contain, and I'm not brave enough to try to stop her.

Rain storms toward Amaranthine again with Brohn and the others running over at the commotion. Amaranthine clips her heel over the rifle she dropped a second before and hits the ground with a heavy thud. Rain leaps on top of her, her fists flying in a wild flurry. Brohn shoulders past me and catches Rain's wrist just as she's getting ready to strike again. He yanks her to her feet and drags her away from Amaranthine as Rain kicks and screams at Brohn to let her go.

"Knock it off!" Brohn thunders, as he tosses Rain harder and farther than he probably intended. She staggers several steps back, but somehow manages to stay upright.

"You didn't hear her, Brohn!" she shouts, still glaring past him at Amaranthine, who's on the ground with red eyes and a thin trickle of dark blood flowing from her lip. "She doesn't care about what's happened. She doesn't care about all the other towns like ours that the Order's blown to hell. She never lost anyone except her psycho mother, who was almost as psycho as her!"

Amaranthine has her arms folded across her knees, head down, eyes closed.

I kneel down next to her and beg her to get up and join us. Granden and Trench are on the move, heading in our direction us with quick strides. "If you don't do this," I say, "they'll…"

She lifts her head for a second and looks into my eyes. "They'll what? *Kill* me?"

"I don't know, Manthy. Just please..."

She looks over my shoulder to where Granden and Trench have just pushed their way past Brohn and Rain to position themselves over us.

"Do we have a problem already?" Trench growls. His friendly demeanor has been replaced by a scary intensity. I don't know him well enough to test the limits, so I muster a meek "Not at all" as Manthy finally lets me help her to her feet.

"It's okay," I tell her quietly. "Everything's going to be okay."

She pulls her hair away from her face and dabs at her bloody lip with the cuff of her sleeve. "For now, at least," she says. "For now."

9

With Amaranthine on board for now, we follow Granden and Trench halfway across the Agora to the firing range they've set up with the gizmos on their belts. With a whir of gears, this part of the giant field magically transforms before our eyes from a clean carpet of short grass to a full-on shooting range. There are concrete bunkers, synth-steel barriers, and rows of paper targets floating in the air on invisible mag-beams that run the length of long shooting alleys.

Trench explains that a station to our right contains a trap for pigeon-shooting. I don't mind the thought of killing birds. We've had to do it for years just to survive in the Valta. But the idea of it still brings images of Render to mind, and a little knot of anxiety expands slowly in my chest. Karmine catches my distress and explains that "pigeons" are just clay targets and the "trap" is just the machine that launches them into the air. "It'll be fun," he assures me. I nod gratefully and step forward with the others.

Lagging behind, Rain is still fuming. Brohn puts his arm around her to comfort her, and I expect her to shrug him off, but she doesn't. That's the kind of guy Brohn is. He's not always a peace-maker or a pacifist. I've seen him get rough sometimes—

even with Sixteens when we were just Juvens screwing around in the Valta. He lost as many scrapes back then as he won. But what he won, more than fights, was respect. He always stood up for the Juvens against the Sixteens and for the Neos against the Juvens. He was good at getting even the strongest kids through the roughest of times. It's an ability he's had for as long as I've known him. He's less about making peace and more about weathering the storm.

The calming effect he's having on Rain right now might save our lives.

Or at least our grades.

Still, I can't help feeling a pang of something close to envy to see them huddled so close together. It makes me wonder, if I were more like Rain—prettier, more confident—if Brohn and I would be closer.

"We'll start basic," Trench says, pulling me out of my thoughts. He's the weapons expert while Granden seems to be in charge of keeping us calm and organized, which has begun to seem like the tougher job.

Hiller is clearly the one who'll be running the mind-games, not to mention watching us from on high in her creepy floating laboratory that hovers over the Agora like an alien mother ship.

Trench leads us up to the shooting range, and I'm sorry when we get there. It's not that I'm afraid of the guns so much as the fact that the grass feels amazing under my feet, and I want to rip off my shoes and socks and sprint around barefoot for an hour or two. Something about the feeling of soft grass is so soothing, such a simple pleasure...

But Trench's voice snaps me out of my reverie. "We'll start with a static use of the handguns," he barks out so everyone, including Rain and Brohn in the back of our little group, can hear him. "That's the easy one. After that, we'll get into mobile firing, firing from cover, and then some assault tactics starting today and continuing over the next two weeks."

First, he demonstrates proper loading, aiming, and firing techniques. He goes over gun safety and maintenance, flying through each lesson and not taking any questions along the way. There's a robotic calmness to his voice, like he's given this same spiel a hundred times, which he probably has. But there's also an urgency to the whole thing, and I'm reminded that this may be educational and interesting and even fun, but there's a war waiting for us outside of this Processor.

After his demonstration, Trench puts us through our paces, one by one. We fire down range at the targets floating twenty, then fifty, then one hundred feet away.

My gun is heavy in my hand. The kick-back jars my elbow, hot discarded cartridges fly out of the gun, and I have to cough away puffs of white smoke that explode from the chamber every time it fires. There used to be a hunting store in the Valta, but it was destroyed in the early attacks. A few personal rifles, bows and arrows, and other hunting equipment were scavenged from some of the wrecked houses and businesses in those days, but ammo quickly ran out and over time, broken weapons just couldn't be repaired anymore.

By the time I was old enough to handle a weapon, we didn't have more than a few good hunting knives, an old cross-bow, two long bows, and maybe a few dozen arrows left. So this is my first time ever handling an actual, working firearm.

It turns out that what I thought were paper targets are actually sims, holograms that replicate the look of shooting ranges. Granden announces, "The Agora is a chameleon of holographic projections, matter-manipulators, and endless bins of training equipment stored underground. You'll see what I mean," he adds with a wink. "This place will have mock-combat scenarios, mazes for war games, and you'll see every landscape from desert to arctic, and everything in between."

I don't doubt him. I'm impressed by the tech they have here, though it makes me wonder why the Valta is still cut off. I mean, if the Processor can rig holo-sims, run mag-grav and electro systems, and have a huge field that transforms into all the things Granden claims, why can't the Valta at least have a couple of working light bulbs?

I don't dare ask, of course, but quietly I've griped about it to Card a bunch of times. Finally, during a break from the target practice, he asks Granden, partly because he wants to know too, but I'm pretty sure it's mostly because he wants to shut me up about it.

Granden is more gracious about answering the question than I would have thought. I expected him to tell us to mind our own business or to keep our minds on the task at hand. "The Eastern Order is enemy number one," he says. "Distraction is enemy number two." But he leans on his silver, high-tech rifle and tells us not to worry. "Power is being restored everywhere. It's just a matter of time before either it gets up to the Valta or else the kids left in the Valta get recruited and have a chance to live out here in peace with the rest of us."

"What about the Arcologies?" Cardyn asks. "Do you know anything about those?"

"I've never been in one. Not yet anyway. But they're being built throughout the country. I'm sure you saw one of them on your way in. Not finished yet, that one. But soon, though. The idea is to centralize, keep everyone and all the power in one place. They're saying just three or four of those per major city. Once that's done, the Order will have no one left to fight, and we can wipe them out once and for all."

"Sounds kind of like genocide," I say.

Granden laughs and waves me off with a flick of his hand. "It's not genocide to protect your country, your people, from extinction. Our survival depends on the best and most well-trained we have to offer. And that means all of you. Provided you get through the training." He slings his rifle over his shoulder and leads us back to where Trench is preparing us for our next lesson in the shooting range.

We practice for hours. Trench is relentless in his pursuit of excellence from us. He's an odd guy, thin and kind of insecure with that patchwork of thick scars on his face that he never talks about. During breaks, he jokes around with us, asks us about the Valta. But on the firing range, he's all business. He drills us in everything from weapon-selection to proper stance to the most effective breathing techniques to enhance our composure and improve our accuracy.

A full two weeks pass like that.

Each night after our training, Granden does his trick with the gizmo on his belt—he calls the device a "Catalyst"—and eight clear Capsules rise to the surface from underground in the middle of the Agora. Every night, we step into the Capsules, which lower us down into the "Silo," our barracks, which consist of lockers around the perimeter of the main Dormitory, the Shower Room, and its attached Changing Room through a doorway on one side. A small Mess Hall sits on the other side, which is where we eat our meals together. The food is mostly synthetic but still pretty good. Better than I expected anyway, at least from a military training program. Dinner, which is our only real meal of the day, appears from chutes in the Mess Hall wall.

At meal time, we sit together at a long table with four seats on either side. It always feels like we should be comparing notes and decompressing after another long day of training, but most of the time, we're too tired to talk much.

On our first night in the Dormitory, we slept on cots laid out for us in two rows of four. But on our third night down there, Brohn suggested that we rearrange the cots so we could talk better. "Our own little debriefing at the end of the day," he said. So we rearranged the cots to form a spoked pattern in the middle of the room. Now, we all sleep with our heads at the center. That way, we can discuss the day's events, guess at what the future holds, and keep each other company as we fall asleep. Well, we all do that except for Amaranthine. She sleeps the opposite way, with her feet in the center and her head out at the perimeter of our circle of cots. Always has to be different.

I wouldn't mind so much except that no matter how many showers she takes, her feet always smell like death.

We train all day. We move from target practice with handguns to clay pigeon-shooting with a modified version of the Beretta DT33 series rifle. "This sleek beauty, Trench explains, "has a laser-crafted burnished forcing-cone for greater accuracy and less recoil." Karmine drinks every bit of that kind of stuff in like it's the last glass of water in the desert. Terk and Kella, too. Terk's not as good at shooting as Karmine and Kella, but he enjoys it almost as much. Karmine and Kella are focused with tunnel-vision on killing the Order. Rain just cares about getting the highest scores.

Brohn's good at shooting, too, although he says he doesn't enjoy it. I find that hard to believe. I'm pretty sure I'd enjoy anything I was that good at.

I'm not the only one who's noticed his skill. Granden and Trench both compliment him all the time, and even assign him to give the rest of us pointers. Rain's noticed, too. Of course, that's not exactly surprising. She's been spending almost all her time with Brohn these past few days. They stand next to each other at the shooting ranges. They sleep in adjacent cots down in the Dormitory and keep up their whispering conversations, even after they think the rest of us have fallen asleep.

Whenever I find myself thinking about their budding relationship, I try to force the thoughts from my mind. It's good that Brohn's found someone. He's a nice guy, and he deserves some happiness.

I also like to tell myself I'm not jealous.

Out on the range, I tease him, saying it's cute how chummy he and Rain are getting.

"We're not chummy," he protests.

"That hand on her hip during the sniper lesson wasn't exactly standard military protocol," I tell him, trying to hide the slight tinge of bitterness that wants to take over my voice.

"It was just to help center her weight while she tried that decked-out M900 Squad Level Assault Rifle." he says. "The one with the big Zeiss scope."

"Sure," I say, nodding my head. "That *incredibly* specific explanation makes perfect sense to me." I don't bother pointing out that he wasn't nearly as eager to put that hand on *my* hip when I was stumbling around under the weight of the exact same gun.

But I tell myself for the hundredth time that I'm not jealous.

Okay.

Maybe I'm a little jealous.

Meanwhile, Cardyn has been his usual great company, and he's the best at getting me out of my own head. His new favorite hobby is teasing me about my scores, which are posted at the end of each day on a viz-screen down in the Silo.

"I didn't know the target shooting scores could get as low as yours," he says, scanning our names and ranks on the floating holographic chart next to the lockers.

"I didn't know I.Q. scores could get as low as yours," I snap back.

"I may not be the smartest guy in the world—"

"You don't need to finish that sentence," I say.

Card laughs and gives me a playful nudge. "Nice to see you drop all that seriousness."

"I haven't been that serious, have I?"

"You haven't exactly been a pile of laughs lately."

"There's not much to laugh about around here."

"I could say the same about the Valta. But we had fun back home."

"Yeah. But back then it was just you, me, and Render. Now it's...this." I nod over to where Brohn and Rain are sitting side by side on her cot and then over to where Kella, Karmine, and Terk are off to the side comparing notes about which service pistol has the best weight-to-recoil ratio per caliber of ammo or some such tactical talk that I still don't totally get.

Card gives a nod over to the cot where Amaranthine is lying face down with her blanket covering all but her smelly, bare feet. "Well, at least Manthy is still her usual sociable self," Card whispers.

I elbow him to knock it off, and we sit in silence for a minute. Then we reminisce for a while. We talk about Render, about Brohn's sister Wisp, about the other Neos and Juvens we left behind. We talk about the new Cohort of Sixteens and laugh about how there's no way the Valta can survive in their hands. Eventually, we start talking about the serious stuff, the things that will change our lives, or maybe end them, like who's going to get which deployment. What will happen with the war. What we'll find once we're out there in it.

At some point, we stop talking and find our cots. I lie down and stare up at the gray ceiling, thinking about how far I've come from the Valta, but how far I still have to go to live anything resembling the normal life I used to dream about as a little girl, before the drone attacks ever began.

In the morning, it's more of the same. We get up. We put on our government issued training uniform: green cargo pants, form-fitting black tank-tops, and black combat boots. We head up to the Agora for more training, which, for me, means more watching Brohn and Rain, deeply immersed in quiet conversations away from the rest of us.

At the end of each day, we step into the Capsules and drop down into the Silo for food and water. After that, we scrub ourselves off in the communal showers. Girls first, then the boys.

We sleep for maybe three or four hours—it's hard to tell since there are no clocks, and the strange sifting of light through the red sky and constantly shifting cloud-cover up in the Agora makes it hard to determine time by the position of the sun. Even the temperature is unreliable. On any given day, we'll experience radical swings from excruciating heat to biting cold. Yesterday at target practice, my fingers were so numb, I could barely pull the trigger of my Sig Sauer 2040. Later in the day, the temperature had skyrocketed, and we were forced to shed the heavy green coats they gave us on the second day and finish off our training exercises in a hellish heat.

Not that I'm complaining. Fed up with their discomfort, the guys all ripped off their soaked black t-shirts and finished the day sweaty and bare-chested. So, some good came out of it anyway.

This morning, after we step into the Capsule Pads and rise up to the Agora, Granden and Trench greet us for what they tell us will be our final outdoor challenge before we're assigned back to Hiller in the Beta Cube.

"You'll be in two teams," Granden announces. "Based on a random draw and to keep this a fair fight, Brohn, Karmine, Kella, and Rain will be on Team One. Kress, Cardyn, Terk, and Amaranthine will be on Team Two."

Even as he says this, I know there's no way these teams were chosen at random. I've been keeping track, and I know that Brohn and everyone on his team have scores right up at the top. Cardyn, Terk, and I are at the bottom. Amaranthine is dead last. This isn't a fair fight. It's a set up for a slaughter. I look one by one at the Recruits on my team. Not one of them seems to notice or care who's on which team. Cardyn is happy that he and I get to be together. Terk is just happy to have a war game to fight in. And Amaranthine wouldn't care if it was her against the world.

"This drill will be like capture the flag," Trench explains. "Except no flag. The objective will be to take out the members of the other team before they take you out first."

We're each given three weapons: a knife, a handgun, and a rifle. Granden explains that this exercise will teach us which weapon to use and when. "You still won't be using live explosive artillery in the field, but just like the shooting range, these weapons will fire real projectiles. You won't be 'shot,' just 'tagged.'"

"We're going to be shooting at each other with live rounds?" Terk asks.

"Not just yet," Trench smiles. And I can't tell if he's joking about the "yet" part. "No. Each magazine contains small cartridges of paint. The cartridges are a plasto-gelatin compound, but if you get hit, it'll sting. A lot. This will be a real fire-fight, so you won't be targeting dummies anymore."

"I guess that means we can't target you anymore, Terk," Karmine teases. Terk gives him a "Hey!" and a half-hearted shove that still manages to knock Karmine off balance.

We're outfitted with a belt that holds a sheath for the knife and a holster for the handgun. We're shown how to sling the rifle across our backs and adjust the strap for optimal comfort and movement.

"The knives aren't sharp," Granden explains. "Instead, they have a thin strip of red paint stored along the edge and a small pocket of paint in the tip. Contact with the knife on the edge from a slash or in the point from a thrust will cause the compartment to open up and release the paint. If you get tagged, we'll know it."

Karmine says, "Marvie" and fondles the knife, holding it up to the light like he's inspecting a precious jewel.

The weapons are heavy. The knife alone weighs enough to slow me down. I'm sure the weight of the gun is going to pull my cargo pants down, and I have a brief panic attack as I imagine myself standing there in my black tank-top with a 20-lb. gun on my back and my pants in a bunch down around my ankles.

On Granden's instructions, our teams retreat to opposite ends of the Agora. Once there, with Trench on our side and Granden over on the other, Trench inputs some codes into his Catalyst. As we watch, the Agora morphs into a maze of half-walls, mini-bunkers, concrete barriers, and deep trenches. There's even an empty transport truck and a collection of overturned cars. The sound of gears and hydraulics hums through the air as all the necessary props of war nestle into place throughout the expansive Agora. It's an impressive sight with all its transforming objects rising up and folding out from underground. It's also a depressing sight. The scarred and battered mess of a re-created war-zone reproduction reminds me way too much of home.

With a quick flurry of his fingers on his Catalyst, Trench calls up another set of walls—this time at least six or seven feet high and all white synth steel—rises up to complete the maze and cut off our view of the other team across the way.

As Granden makes his way to the far side of the arena, Trench steps up onto an observation platform and calls up three holo-screens that glisten to life in shimmering full-color around him. "I'll be standing here," he explains and gestures to the screens. "I'll be monitoring your performance, assessing how you apply pressure, and how you react under it. You've spent the last two weeks learning how to take aim and shoot. We've talked about strategies and battle conditions. Well, the talk and practice are over. This challenge is simple. Same as life. It's kill or be killed."

With that, Trench sends us into battle.

10

The battle arena is a chaotic mess of obstacles, barriers, concrete tunnels, drainage ditches, and even piles of smashed up furniture. Everything from old construction equipment and heaps of building materials to car frames and old appliances.

"Which way should we go first?" Terk asks. It takes me a second to realize he's talking to me.

Wait—how did I become the leader of this team?

Just to be sure, I look over at Cardyn and Amaranthine. They're both gawking at me, wide-eyed. This is insane. I'm used to being the one stepping back while others take the lead. It's not that I'm not confident. I am, in certain ways and in certain situations. If I have a job to do, I'll always put my best effort in and do it well. I just do it quietly. And alone. But assigning jobs to other people, well, that's Brohn's area of expertise.

Unfortunately, for today he's the enemy, so I don't think I'll be looking to him for guidance.

Swallowing hard, I glance around at what has bizarrely become "my" team.

Terk has the potential to be a great soldier. He's big, strong and fearless. But like me, he'd rather follow orders than give them. Cardyn is smart and a real team-player. He asks all the right questions and has great intuition for what needs to be done. But he's always had trouble getting outside his own head, and he has a long history of second guessing himself.

Amaranthine is, well, insane.

That makes me the odd one out and the only logical choice to lead our group toward what will probably end up being an absolute slaughter.

"Okay, there's no way Brohn will try a direct frontal assault," I say after a brief pause, trying to make my voice sound controlled and authoritative. As I speak, I glance around at our surroundings. "They'll try to outflank us." I point over to a row of battered aluminum sheds tucked behind a line of low concrete barriers. "We can use those for shelter while we move."

"Move to where?" Cardyn asks. We're thirty seconds into the battle simulation, and he's already got a seed of terror germinating in his voice.

"Don't worry," I reassure him with a hand on his shoulder. "The 'where' doesn't matter. It's the 'how' that counts. We're bound by the borders of the arena. There's no objective to this battle, other than survival."

Card nods nervously. "So it's like Trench said. Kill or be killed, right?"

"Right, which means we have two choices: stay where we are, or else move. We either play offense or play defense. It won't matter what we do, who wins, or who loses. The only thing we can't do is sit still. They want to see how we react under pressure."

"I can answer that for them right now," Card stammers. "I freak out and wet myself under pressure."

Terk and I both laugh at what I secretly hope was a joke. I've never seen Card so nervous, and it's not helping my own mental state to watch his silent freak-out. "This way," I say with a confidence I don't actually feel.

The others follow me, heads turning left and right as we crouch down, weaving through the jungle of junk in our way. I'm not sure how Brohn always falls into a leadership role so naturally. It feels like way too much responsibility. I know this is just a simulation and no one will really get hurt, let alone killed, but the thought of making a wrong turn, of letting my team down, weighs on me like an oppressive force of nature. I can feel it pushing me down, and it takes all my strength to lock my uncertainties and insecurities away for the sake of the team.

Still ducking low, Card and Terk follow me, with Amaranthine dragging along behind. We keep zigging and zagging around obstacles, down into shallow trenches dug into the earth, and in and out of small, barren rooms formed by the walls of the maze. The entire arena is a marvel of technology.

For a second, I get caught up in imagining all the work that must have gone into creating this huge Agora, which can apparently transform into nearly any environment. In the Valta, it took us years to clear away rubble from bombed out buildings and to shore up the houses and businesses in danger of collapsing on any of us who happened to be walking by. Meanwhile, here in the Agora, they accomplish in a minute what it took years for us to do…and they do it with the simple touch of a button.

Snapping myself out of my thoughts of home, I lead my team down a small embankment and up the other side, where we enter into a large open area.

My team. It has a strange sound to it, one I'm not sure I'll ever get used to or even like.

Brohn's team.

That makes sense.

Rain's team. I can see that. Those two are leaders. They're the ones Card, Terk, Amaranthine and I should be following into battle. The current arrangement feels more dubious with each step I take.

"This might not be the best place to set up camp," Cardyn says with a look around, noting the absence of shelter. I nod my silent agreement. Card's sensible and cautious nature makes him a perfect second-in-command. When I tell him so, he thanks me with a blush and wide smile. I feel like I've just told a golden retriever he's a good boy. If he had a tail, I'm sure it'd be wagging at top speed right now.

We skitter out of the open area, pleased to have avoided an easy ambush. I keep thinking I'm catching glimpses of movement through the spaces between barriers and along the far walls. It's never occurred to me before how much my imagination ramps up my fear. But here they are, feeding off each other with total disregard for my sanity.

"Hey," Cardyn says to me as we continue along, "this is way more fun than fighting for survival back home, huh?"

I put a finger to my lips. "I'd hardly call this fun," I whisper.

"You manage to make everything fun," he whispers back. "I think because you don't try to. Anyway, I'm really glad we're on the same team."

"You might not be, if I wind up getting us all killed."

"Just 'tagged,'" Terk reminds me from over Cardyn's shoulder. "No one's getting killed in here."

I thank him for the reminder and allow myself a little internal chuckle. I'm not sure which is bigger, Terk's body, his heart, or his uncanny ability to keep everything grounded in reality as a means of self-preservation.

As if to remind us that we're not alone, a voice calls out from somewhere behind us. "They're not in the drainage ditch!"

It's Karmine.

"Or under here," Kella's voice replies.

"Over in the clearing by the piles of lumber! We'll corner them there," Brohn's deep voice declares. *That's* what a leader should sound like. Decisive and strong, rather than uncertain and vaguely terrified.

"I'm heading there now," Rain calls back.

Uh oh. My team looks around at the piles of wood lying in uneven stacks around us. We have a matter of seconds before they jump us.

"We'd better get out of here," Terk says, and I couldn't agree more.

"This way," I urge. "There's a narrow alleyway between an arena wall and a line of metal crates up ahead." My team follows, unquestioning. We hustle down the alley, anxious to get as far away from the wood pile and the ominous voices as possible.

Since we know where they're headed, I'm hoping maybe we can slip away and circle around behind the enemy somehow. Maybe we can even turn this thing to our advantage.

I cross my fingers, then cross my arms across my body—our old tradition from back in the Valta for warding off bad luck. I'm already imagining our success.

But seconds later, I discover that I allowed hope to settle in prematurely. I should have seen this coming. A few days ago, Trench led us in an exercise called the "Pincer Envelopment Movement." The idea is to draw the enemy into a straight-line formation while flanking them on either side. You disorient them, disrupt their ability to communicate, and cut off their escape route, all at the same time. It turned out to be pretty simple, not much more than a hinged, two-jawed animal trap.

Brohn, Rain, Karmine, and Kella set the trap for us.

And my team, I realize too late, has just stepped right into it.

"Got 'em!" Brohn's voice calls out triumphantly.

For a second, I wonder how he got ahead of us, but my heart begins to sink as I realize that all their shouting and calling out to each other back there was a trick, a way to get us moving to exactly where they wanted us.

In a flash, the quiet of the arena explodes in a frenzy of screams and gunfire. With paint slugs whizzing in the air around us from every angle, we retreat back into the alley, stumbling over each other in our haste to find some kind of shelter.

Card shoves me ahead of him. I crash into Amaranthine, bounce off of Terk's back, and hit the ground hard. Terk spins around, picks me up by my jacket collar and belt, and tosses me almost ten feet toward a crooked aluminum tool shed. I roll into the dark of the shelter as Amaranthine dives in after me.

Through the small doorway, I see Card take a hail of hits to his neck and chest. He drops like he's been hit by a fast-moving cannon ball, his face and most of his upper body covered in dripping red paint. It would be a hysterical sight, and I'd probably tease him mercilessly about it if it—weren't so realistic and utterly terrifying.

Outflanked, outmaneuvered, and heavily outgunned, Terk goes down hard under a second barrage of paint pellets. Like Card, he looks like he's been through a blender. Karmine and Kella laugh as they watch him squirm on the ground, but I can't bring myself to find any of it amusing. Terk's cries of pain at the impact of the pellets are all too real. I don't care how simulated it all is or what kind of projectiles are being used. There's nothing artificial about being shot.

The fear is just as real as the pain.

Even though I'm sickened at the thought of leaving two of my team behind, I realize I've got no choice. Scrambling out the back door of the dark shed, Amaranthine and I duck under some twisted fencing, squeeze through a wooden gate with missing boards, and slide for cover under the rusted hulk of an old army jeep.

Leaving behind the sound of Brohn's team laughing over Cardyn's and Terk's moaning bodies, we decide to put some more distance between us. It should give us time to regroup and maybe salvage what's left of this strategic debacle.

In the dark shadows under the jeep, Amaranthine and I exchange a look and then make a run for it. We sprint as fast as we can through more makeshift alleyways, past a row of old refrigerators, around a wall of car tires, and on a breathless winding run through a maze of synth-steel walls.

Finally, we hit a dead end. Amaranthine stops with her back pressed against a wall. Its pristine silver-white shimmer makes her look even more grim and haggard than I feel.

"Okay," I pant, my chest heaving, "that was exciting." My hands are on my knees, my heart in my throat. "We may have bought some time. Maybe we can get around behind them." I point up to the top of a pyramid of large wooden crates. "Maybe we can even make it to higher ground."

"Nice thinking!" a voice calls out.

That's when we both freeze.

It's Brohn again. His voice seems to be coming from all around us at once.

How does he keep doing that?

Amaranthine turns to face me, her eyes wide with a combination of confusion and terror. I shrug my tight shoulders, as mystified as she is about where Brohn's voice is coming from or how he could have tracked us down so fast. I'm just turning to peer down a small alleyway formed by a series of concrete barriers and one of the synth-steel walls of the maze when a glimmer of movement just behind Amaranthine catches my eye. A small panel drops down in the wall behind her, and a shadowy figure appears in the opening.

An hand thrusts through the portal and latches like a vice onto Amaranthine's neck. Her scream is choked silent by the tightness of the muscular arm that follows. The shadow leans forward to reveal Brohn, the sinister blade of a knife glinting in his hand. Across the distance, he gives me a playful wink before sliding the knife slowly across the lower part of Amaranthine's neck.

He seems to be enjoying himself. But it takes me a full two heartbeats to remember that it's not real. Amaranthine's shock, like Cardyn's and Terk's pain, however, is *definitely* real. She gasps as Brohn relaxes his arm, then she slides down the wall to slump onto the ground, puddles of red paint pooling along her collar bone and staining her shirt. She's not hurt, of course, not really. But the sudden, quiet attack, coupled by the fear of being choked to death, seems to have sapped the life out of her. Her arms are folded across her knees now in surrender, her hair in a dark waterfall cascading down her face. I look back up at Brohn, who points with two fingers to his own eyes and then at mine.

His mouth forms the words "You're next," and with a smile, he disappears back into the shadows. The portal in the wall drops shut behind him while I bolt as fast as I can in the opposite direction.

Okay, Kress. Keep it together. You're alive. You're armed. You still have a chance.

I slip my rifle off my shoulder and chuck it to the ground. It's too heavy, and it's not doing me any good in these tight quarters, with no idea where the enemy is. I slip my handgun out of its holster and hold it at the ready by my cheek. My back is to the wall now, literally.

If I can just make it to the other side of the clearing, I can regroup and re-plan. This thing isn't over. Not yet.

I'm getting ready to make my move when a hard blast strikes my Sig Sauer 2040, which flies out of my hand and skitters to a stop under the twisted body of an old solar-celled car several feet away. Instantly, I drop down and roll under a steel I-beam, slide down into a shallow trench and scramble along its length until I'm convinced that I'm clear. Squatting down, I scuttle through a long concrete pipe, through a maze of half-walls, and into a small brick shed not much bigger than a dog house.

Breathing hard, I allow myself a split second of pride, knowing that I'm the last one standing from Team Two. That's small consolation, though. I know perfectly well that my team was hand-picked and set up to get wiped out. Still, I have no intention of going down without a fight. Forget Hiller's points and assessments. I owe it to my team to salvage something out of this total and absolute fiasco.

The day's drawing close to dusk, but it's still way too bright out to risk making a run for better cover. I can't hide in this tiny shack forever, but I don't know where else to go. I should have taken more time to memorize the layout of the training arena. I bet that was supposed to be part of the training—and I blew it.

On my hands and knees now, I crawl back out of the brick shed. No sense making it easier for the others by cornering myself. Now I'm crouched in a shadow behind a low concrete barrier. I know it's just a matter of time—maybe mere seconds—before I get tracked down and shot to death. I know that what will hit me won't be real bullets, but the thought of getting hit at all—by *anything*—makes my eye twitch. I'm pretty sure my heart's about to thump its way out of my chest.

For a moment I wonder who will deliver the kill shot. Brohn would probably go easy on me, at least I would have thought so before I saw the terrifying way he took down Amaranthine. I'm going to have to yell at him for that. That whole moment is going to give me more than a few nightmares.

Maybe I'll get lucky since I'm the last of my team, and he'll just shoot me in the leg. Better still, maybe he'll just let me surrender. If that's even an option, that is.

Karmine would be less merciful. He'll want to send a signal to me and to the Trainers: He's all business, and he'll do what it takes to win, friendship be damned. Kella would do the same, only she might add an extra shot or two just to prove that a pretty blond girl from a tiny mountain town can still be a ruthless animal on the battlefield.

Rain scares me the most. She's a five-foot tall genius with a chip on her shoulder and an obsession with winning. She's your best friend when she's on your side, but your worst enemy when she's not.

My head is throbbing from exhaustion, fear, and from the

anticipation of getting caught. I may still have a knife and a shred of a chance of eluding Team One, but let's face it, I've become a prey animal. My heart rate is jacked up, and I can't remember the last time I took two even breaths.

I can hear Brohn call out "Clear!" every time he rounds a corner or investigates another possible hiding place and doesn't find me. I take a chance and peer around the corner of the chipped and pitted barrier just outside the small opening of the shed. With my head close to the ground, I duck back quickly when I see Rain, not more than twenty feet away. Her back is to me for the moment, but she's way too close for comfort.

"I'm seeing her boot prints!" she calls out, and Karmine and Kella reply in unison that they're on their way over.

With my gun long gone, I withdraw my knife from its leather sheath, careful not to make too much noise in the process. This will be my last hope, though I can't begin to imagine how I could possibly take out all four of the others before they blast me to pieces. I figure if I can just get one of them, I'll still qualify for a few points from this challenge. Maybe I won't be *totally* excluded from consideration for Special Ops.

If Hiller and her crew really are watching our every move, they'll be pleased to see that I refused to go down without a fight.

My pulse goes crazy at the sound of the others jogging right toward me. I'm somewhere between crying, hyperventilating, and throwing up in my mouth when I slip out the back of the shed and scurry down a pathway behind a low wall.

That's when things go deadly quiet. Forget about calm before the storm. This is quiet before the kill.

I avoid the temptation to squint my eyes shut. Just on the edge of the battle scenario, Trench is not more than thirty or forty feet away, watching me watching him. He's standing on his little platform surrounded by his screens. If only he'd tell me where the others are. But when we make eye contact, he just shrugs his shoulders.

I can't help you, Kress. You're on your own.

I can't believe there was ever a time when I actually looked forward to being assessed, marked, and graded. Now more than ever, I'm sure Hiller and her brain-gang are up there in their silver Observation and Assessment Halo, watching every move I make. Every mistake, every little flinch in the face of danger. I can picture them in front of their monitoring screens, pointing and laughing at my total incompetence.

My cheeks burn and my brain throbs at the thought of it when all of a sudden, the pain in my head and the liquid fear churning through my veins stops, only to be replaced with a strange feeling of euphoria. I feel like someone's just pumped some kind of narcotic into my blood stream.

Setting my knife on the ground, I ease up to peer over the low wall, half expecting to see the barrel of a gun jammed between my eyes.

But instead, I spot a small black dot in the distance just above the tree-line between buildings seven and eight, the Eta and Theta Cubes. Even before the dot has moved close enough for me to make out any detail, I know exactly what it is that I'm looking at.

Render. You've found me.

He comes to a landing on a high branch of a tree between the two large buildings overlooking the fenced-in Agora. Squatting back down to avoid detection, I stroke a pattern on my forearm tattoos to call for him to come to me. But strangely, he doesn't move.

It doesn't occur to me at first that summoning him into the middle of a battlefield, even if it's just a war game, might not be the best idea in the world. But my overwhelming surprise and joy at seeing my friend overrides my common sense. All I feel right now is a deep desire to stroke his feathers and make sure he's okay.

How did you find me? Why won't you come to me? What's wrong, Render?

His head jerks around, and I follow his gaze, my breath catching hard in my chest.

Over on his small platform, Trench has a long silver-barreled rifle raised up, his head on a slant as he squints into the scope.

He's got an itchy trigger finger, and his sights are locked on Render.

11

Forget the game. Forget Terk, Cardyn, and Amaranthine, who are somewhere in this maze sulking and covered in red paint. Forget Brohn, Rain, Kella, and Karmine, who have come out from their various hiding places and are now standing in front of me in a daze, wondering why their final victim suddenly decided to sprint right at them.

I don't think. I don't contemplate the repercussions. I don't hesitate.

I just dive right between the Team One Recruits, who actually lower their weapons and step back, startled, probably trying to figure out how it is that I don't even seem to see them as I dash madly forward, my eyes wild with determination.

I don't have time to worry about them, their shock, or their incredibly slow reflexes. In a flash, I'm past them in a full-speed run, covering the forty-foot distance between myself and Trench in what feels like the blink of an eye. Lowering my shoulder to turn my body into a battering ram, I dive right through his holo-screen projections and slam myself full-tilt into his ribcage, under his left arm. At the same time, I grab the barrel of his rifle with my palm.

But I'm too late.

He gets his shot off.

The bullet explodes from the gun and screams through the air.

The heat from the gun's barrel sears my hand. The pain is intense. I can smell the skin burning on my palm, but I don't have time to worry about that. Trench and I tumble to the ground in a tangle of limbs. I'm not sure if it's the explosion from the massive gun, or if it was my head hitting against Trench's, but there's a ringing in my ears that feels like it's going to blast my eyes out of their sockets.

Trench must have thought I was attacking him personally, rather than trying to stop him from killing a bird. He reacts, unlike Brohn and the others, with swift and decisive military precision. With his boot pressed into my side, he catapults me off of him. He's thin as a reed, but strong as a horse. I fly though the air and crash to the ground.

The impact knocks the wind out of me, but I don't care. I roll over and scramble to my feet, scanning the branches along the tree line, then up to the sky for any hint of Render. As Brohn and the others run up and start asking what the hell is going on, I shake my head and sprint toward the fence. The last thing I want to do is look for Render on the ground. I'm stopped in my tracks by the crack of more gunfire, this time coming right at me. The ground in front of me and on either side is riddled with bullets that kick up divots in the dirt and grass. I slide to a stop and look up to the turret where Chucker is firing off warning shots at my feet. Apparently thinking I'm trying for some sort of insane escape attempt, he's just lowering his rifle and yelling for me to stop when he's dive-bombed from the side by a feathery black missile.

Render attacks claws-first, raking at Chucker's face and giving him a sharp peck to the temple with his beak. Then he flies off before his victim knows what's hit him. Chucker swings around in his post at the top of the turret, raising his rifle again as he tracks Render, who's soaring in tight, twisting loops just over his head, preparing to renew his attack. His wings are spread wide at first, but now he clamps them tight against his body, his eyes on his target. He's in total attack mode.

I've got to stop him before he gets killed.

Tapping the black implant markings on my forearm, I enter the raven's head as he enters mine. In the weeks we've been apart, I'd all but forgotten what it feels like to fly, but it all comes back to me now in a rush. I'm puffed up by a surge of adrenaline, my body excited by this new potential.

Unfortunately, I don't have time to enjoy it. Chucker is whipping around, trying to get a bead on Render while Trench shouts and runs toward me from behind, Brohn and the others following close on his heels.

My mind is a swamp of overlapping images, and I'm having trouble sorting them out. My connection with Render has changed. It's more expansive, more three-dimensional than it was back home. I can see Chucker with his gun up above in his turret, his thick finger on the trigger. His back is to me.

No. He's *facing* me.

He's aiming at Render.

No. He's aiming at *me*.

Render and I are on opposite sides of him. *How does he have both of us in his sights at once?* Trench and the other Recruits are behind me, but I see them from Render's point of view. They're down below, running toward me. They're small. They're shouting something I don't understand. Wait. Are they behind me or in front of me? I see myself, my hair and clothes, a mess of dirt and sweat, looking up at the black bird of prey, whose sole purpose right now is to protect his friend.

Sorting through the dizzying images and concentrating as best I can, I try to explain the situation to Render:

They didn't know you were my friend. I'll explain it all to them. You'll be safe. I promise. Trust me.

What I get in return from Render isn't language—at least not in the way humans understand language. Instead, I get a flood of feelings, a stream of instinct and emotion. *He's tracked me all this way...Without a Conspiracy of his own, I'm his only family...He's protective of me...He trusts me...He loves me...He'll do as I ask...*

Render banks abruptly and disappears into the black branches of the forest while Trench comes to a screeching halt next to me, with Granden and the Recruits, all seven of them now, thundering along behind. I breathe a sigh of relief as I see Chucker lower his weapon just as Trench spins me around.

"You're in so much trouble, Kress," he shouts into my face. "You completely disrupted the battle-sim challenge, left the arena, and you just attacked a Trainer! And over what? A bird?"

"He's not just a bird," I stammer. "He's Render, he's my friend! He came all the way from the Valta to be with me!"

Trench doesn't seem to know what to say, but Card, haggard and covered in a rainbow smattering of paint, has just jogged up next to him and tries to explain. "They have some kind of special connection," he pants. "The bird's smart. Kress has had him forever. He's super-protective of her." He puts his hands on his knees and looks out over the Cubes into the dark forest. "I'm not sure how he managed to..."

Everyone has gathered around now, and suddenly I'm the center of attention. Great. I'm living my worst nightmare.

"I don't care what the hell that *thing* is," Trench hisses. "Or how the hell he got here. You're Seventeens. You're Recruits. That means you're *ours*. No distractions. No outside visitors, birds, people, or anything! You think we'd let you bring a stray puppy into this place?"

"He's right," Granden says with a sad shake of his head. "We can't have a bird flying around the Agora while you're training."

Terk, who's covered in paint, nursing a bloody lip and a gash on his thick forearm, steps forward. "Why not? It might be good to have him around. He can be like our mascot."

Standing in Terk's huge shadow, Rain agrees. "He's been with Kress in the Valta since we were Neos. She trained him. He does all sorts of stuff."

I'm standing, listening in silence, my heart warmed at the outpouring of support for Render, and, by extension, for me.

"He could give us a strategic advantage," Kella offers. "You know, like our own flying guard dog."

"Right," Karmine says. "Plus, he's got the perfect camouflage for night operations. And how marvie would that be? Having our very own battle-bird as part of our troupe?"

Even Manthy is standing in the back, quietly nodding.

Slinging his rifle across his shoulder, Brohn steps over to Granden. "So, what do you say? We'll re-do the battle sim if you want. No problem. Just maybe let Kress keep her bird. It won't hurt anything. She'll keep him under control. She's really good with him." With that, he throws me a look that tells me he's looking out for me, despite the fact that we were all-but-mortal enemies a few minutes ago.

Granden looks from one of us to the next. He's clearly out of his element on this one. In the many years of the war against the Order, I'm pretty sure this is the first time a Trainer's been surrounded by a bunch of yipping, heavily-armed Seventeens begging to adopt a telepathic bird.

"I'll need to check with Hiller," he says at last. He takes a few steps off and mutters into his comm-link. Trench tells us to wait where we are, while he walks over to the fence and calls up to check on Chucker.

"Hold off," he tells Chucker. "We've got a situation here. Granden's on link with Hiller to figure it out."

Chucker frowns, clearly disappointed that he didn't get to

take Render down. He was probably looking forward to shooting the rest of us for dessert.

Standing next to me, Cardyn is all smiles. He puts his arm around my shoulders and presses his cheek to mine. "You got your old buddy back! This is definitely a sign. You're going into Special Ops for sure! And once they find out about how you can—"

I cut him off with a vicious glare. "Not now, Card," I warn as I wriggle out from under his arm. "Don't say anything."

"Okay fine. Have it your way."

"That was a close call," Brohn says, stepping toward me. He puts a hand on my upper arm and gives it a gentle, slightly hesitant squeeze. "Nice to see you in action, Kress. If you go after the Eastern Order like you took down Trench, they don't stand a chance! Plus," he adds with a nod toward the woods on the other side of the high fence and the Cubes, "it's nice to see another friendly face around."

"Thanks," I reply with a smile and a reddening of my dirty cheeks.

"Yeah," Karmine grins. "Even if that 'friend' is some kind of giant devil-bird from Hell."

"Hey!" I object with a laugh. "Don't say mean things about Render, or I'll sic him on you, too."

Karmine takes a step back with his hands up in surrender. "Okay, okay. I wouldn't want to end up with a shredded face like poor Chucker up there."

Granden walks back over to us after about thirty seconds. "Good news and bad news," he says. "Hiller says Kress will get docked points for assaulting a Trainer and for disrupting the training sim. That puts her behind the rest of you when it comes to deployment."

"What's that mean?" Terk asks.

"It means her chances of making Special Ops just got a kick in the teeth."

Kella slides her fingers through her long blond hair and then ties it back in a tidy ponytail with the leather band she keeps on her wrist. It's a gesture I've seen a million times. It means she's about to go into attack mode.

"You can't punish her for something she doesn't have any control over," she says from behind a deep frown. "And it's not fair to single her out. She was protecting a friend—an *ally*—which is exactly what we're being trained to do."

It's not like Kella to leap to my defense, or to *anyone's* defense for that matter, so I offer her a grateful smile of thanks.

Granden shrugs and points to the glimmering chrome-colored Halo hovering high above our heads. "It's not my call. Hiller has an entire assessment team up there. They're careful about deployments, and they don't have a sense of humor about anything that causes one of you Seventeens to stray from training protocol."

Kella looks ready to engage in a counter-attack, but she's stopped by Rain, who literally has to grab her by the arm to hold her back.

"You said there was good news?" Rain asks.

"Yes," Granden says with a pleasant smile and a nod in my direction. "She can keep the bird. The guards have been ordered to leave him alone for the rest of your time here." He gives me a friendly point with his index finger. "After that, no promises."

The sigh of relief I breathe is the first real exhale I think I've taken in hours. Cardyn high-fives me, and Terk, beaming ear to ear, shakes me by my shoulders and tells me how happy he is for me.

"Looks like your friend's here to stay," Kella says.

"Thanks to you," I admit. "Thanks to all of you. Thanks for sticking up for me."

"Don't mention it," Brohn says with a wry smile and a wink. "We were all just looking out for your best interest."

"Not me," Karmine says. "I was sticking up for the devil-bird."

Brohn gives him a half-hearted punch to the shoulder, Kella rolls her eyes, and we all have a good laugh before heading back to the battle-sim site to collect our assorted weapons and get ready to drop back down into the Silo.

LATER THAT NIGHT, after refreshing and well-deserved showers, we find ourselves sitting around in the Silo on our cots. It seems gloomy down here tonight. The glass tube that runs around the entire ceiling of our round room casts its usual flickering yellow-white light, but somehow our shadows seem darker. The good news is that our spirits are a lot brighter than usual.

"How do you think Render found us?" Terk asks. "I mean, we've got to be a thousand miles from the Valta."

I shrug, feigning ignorance. "Maybe he followed the transport trucks?"

"Sure. I guess that's possible." Terk chuckles. "It doesn't matter. All I know is it's starting to feel like old times," he says. "All of us together, I mean. Plus, you and your bird. Only we're not worrying about surviving or getting taken away by the Recruiters."

"Well, that's because we've *already* been taken away by the Recruiters," Rain sighs. "I'm with you, Terk. It's nice to be all together. But this isn't exactly the freedom we used to dream about, is it?"

Card gives Rain a sarcastic "Thanks for bringing us back to reality," which she answers with a silent sneer. "And thank you, Kress," he adds.

"For what?"

"For helping break up the boring training routine."

"I'd hardly call getting shot at by these guys 'boring,'" I tell him. I can still taste the terror of dodging gunfire and hiding behind that barrier, waiting to get caught and killed. It was an experience I don't care to repeat, war or no war.

"You know what I mean. Training is fun, I guess. But it's still routine, and we're still kind of like prisoners here. It was just nice of your bird to remind us that there's still a speck of freedom out there in the world."

Card's right. Amid all the excitement of shooting guns, throwing knives, target practice, and simulated combat conditions, there is something mind-numbingly dreary about knowing you're not really free.

"And seriously?" Card adds. "'Team One' and 'Team Two'? How boring is that?"

"Not just boring," I say. "It's about trying to divide us. They split us up so they could assess us better."

Karmine scratches his head. "Isn't that their job? The whole reason we're here?"

"No," Brohn says in a weirdly hostile tone. "We're here because we were forced to be. Let's not kid ourselves, guys. We had no choice but to come to this place. This isn't about being trained or assessed for our own good. This is for *them*. We were kidnapped, as sure as if they'd snuck into the Valta in the middle of the night, bound us, gagged us, and tossed us into the back of that transport truck."

"Which they've done to Recruits in the past," I remind him.

"Exactly. Their job is to weed us out. *Our* job is to stick together. It's how we survived as long as we did in the Valta, and it's how we'll survive now. Whatever conflicts, problems, worries, or whatever else we had back home, none of it matters here. This may not exactly be the paradise we were hoping for after Recruitment Day, but it's a fresh start, and we need to make the most of it. Keep climbing. Keep surviving. Keep together. It's how we'll win in the end." With those words he throws me a knowing look.

"What if they keep splitting us up, like for war games and stuff?" Terk asks.

"Let them. They can divide us into as many teams as they want. But we'll never let them split us up. We're family. All of us. Render, too."

Everyone nods. Even Amaranthine.

"Then it's settled," I say quietly. "We're a Conspiracy."

12

The next day, when we rise up in our Capsules, the Agora seems to have magically opened up. It's uncluttered, calm, and green again. There's not a trace of the chaos from yesterday's battle, which I'm sure I failed.

Granden and Trench greet us and lead us into the shadow of the next giant black building. "Congratulations on your two weeks of weapons training!" Granden calls out. "You've now advanced to Beta Cube."

With Trench at his side, he leads us over to the second of the eight large buildings. I'm still bleary-eyed and exhausted from the slaughter the day before, but thinking about Render, knowing he's safe out there somewhere, gives me a boost of energy.

I scan the treetops for a sign of him, but I can't see anything. I don't dare try to connect with him directly, not with this many people around. Besides, after what happened yesterday, I'm not sure if I could handle another bout of sensory overload. My feeling of internal emptiness hasn't come back, though, so I know he's okay.

I find myself craving privacy. Just a few minutes to be truly alone, to breathe, to think. I still don't want anyone to know just how powerful my connection to Render has grown. The other Seventeens still see him as my pet. To most of them, he's nothing more than a familiar of some kind. Some sort of cute, loyal mascot. Brohn and Cardyn seem to understand that our bond goes deeper than that, but for now I don't want them knowing the full extent of our link. It would only put the two most important people in my life in danger.

At the Beta Cube, a wide black door slides open to reveal Hiller. Wearing the same form-fitting top and billowing white lab coat she had on the last time we saw her, she throws Granden and Trench an undisguised look of condescension before turning to face us.

"As you know from your daily scores, we've been monitoring your progress. But now playtime's over. Welcome to Beta Cube."

I have no idea what she means. If what we've experienced up until now is *playtime,* she must be planning to outright torture us. I exchange a quick glance with Brohn, who looks concerned. His jaw's tight, his body rigid, fists balled up.

By now I know that look. He's preparing for the worst.

Hiller leads us up a flight of stairs, down a hallway, and into a conference room with four desk-like tables in each corner. On either side of every table sits a black office chair on round silver wheels.

"You've done some good work...but also some very *poor* work," Hiller says, turning her gaze to me. "But before I get into the specifics, I think we need to get to the bottom of our little bird situation."

"What's to get to the bottom of? You said Kress could keep him," Brohn interrupts defiantly, and I immediately want to hug him for it. I only wish I could.

"That's true," Hiller says. "But that doesn't mean she doesn't deserve a penalty for straying from training protocol, attacking a Trainer. Or for losing the battle-sim, for that matter."

"I didn't lose," I protest. "They never actually tagged me."

Hiller ignores me at first as she shifts her eyes from Terk to Cardyn to Amaranthine. She seems to be sizing up my team, looking for weaknesses. "No, I suppose they didn't," she says at last. "But that's a technicality. The fact is, you left the arena. Team One shot each of your teammates. That makes you a deserter. And the bad news?"

Oh, great, I think. *There's bad news?*

"Team One's failure to finish the job—no matter what the distraction was—makes *them* subject to punishment as well."

"What? How is that fair?" Rain asks. Her voice is high-pitched, bordering on a yell. The heels of her fists are pressed firmly into the top of her desk. "Shouldn't we get credit for sparing our friend?"

"Absolutely not!" Hiller thunders, a look of rage flashing across her face for a second before she regains control. She raises her hand and starts ticking off facts on her fingers. "As I see it, you sparing her means three things: she allowed herself to get so distracted by the bird that she became reckless. You got distracted by her. And you *also* forgot that, for purposes of this challenge, she was the enemy." With a judgmental frown, she glances around at all of us. When Cardyn opens his mouth to talk, she immediately cuts him off. "I'm not asking if you think you deserve punishment. I'm *telling* you there is a penalty for your actions. There is too much at stake here to risk compromising your training. I know you're having fun. You like being challenged, not to mention running around blasting each other with paint pellets. But never forget, there's a real war out there with real people, many of them your age and younger, who are dying."

Hiller's words hang in the air for a second like a dense cloud. Before any of us can react, she taps the comm-link on her wrist, and we hear the sound of heavy footsteps in the hallway. The door swings open, and Chucker and Kellerson stride ominously into the room. I've seen them as Recruiters in the back of the transport truck and as guards up in their turrets. But seeing them like this, flanking Hiller like stone sculptures, is a different, scarier sensation. Their height, thickness, and solidity seem to fill the room entirely. As tough as I tell myself we Seventeens are, part of me feels like these two men could break most of us down just by virtue of their presence.

"Stand up," Hiller orders. The eight of us rise to our feet as she commands. "Now you will each be taken to separate rooms, where your punishments will be handed out."

Tentatively, we look around at each other. For a moment I make contact with Cardyn, whose bugged-out eyes make him look like he might drop dead from a panic attack. I'm pretty sure I've got the same look on my own face. For that matter, we've probably got the same questions spinning through our minds. *Are we getting docked points on our grades? Or are they taking us somewhere to kill us?*

Right now, the latter seems like a pretty realistic end result.

As if we've turned into a herd of hypnotized zombies, we line up and follow Chucker and Kellerson, who take us through a series of long, twisting halls. We walk up two flights of stairs, down a corridor, around a few turns, back down two flights, and then up another set of stairs. I'm thinking, *there better be a nice big block of cheese at the end of this maze,* but there's no way I'm saying that out loud. While I don't always share Terk's paranoia that we might be killed at any time, I have no interest in testing the two men who've already made it abundantly clear that my sense of humor stops where the barrels of their guns begin.

Our dour group navigates several more disorienting twists and turns until we enter a final wide hallway. Chucker and Kellerson deposit each Seventeen into one of the eight rooms—four on either side—along the way. They close the doors behind each of us.

Surprise, surprise. I'm the last one.

"Get in!" Chucker growls as I stare at the open door and the desk beyond. When I make my way in, the door slides shut behind me. The metallic click of a lock tells me in no uncertain terms that I'm now a prisoner.

Stop it, Kress. This is just another test. It's not like the powers that be have suddenly become totally evil.

Cursing myself for my paranoia, I spin back to realize there's no doorknob or handle.

Resigned, I seat myself in the chair in front of the small desk, where I remain until what feels like half an hour has passed. Eventually, I find myself getting fidgety, desperate to stand up and walk around. The room really *is* a cell, with no windows, no vents or overhead pipes. No features of any kind, really. The sliding door nestles so seamlessly into the wall that not even a groove or a gap indicates it was ever even there.

I tell myself I'm not going insane, that I really did walk in here like a perfectly normal person. But with every minute that passes, I become more convinced that I'll go crazy, stuck in this pointless little room.

I'm on the verge of screaming when the door finally slides open and Hiller comes striding in. I wonder if she can see the fury in my eyes.

"You have two choices, Kress," she says, dropping a writing stylus and a sensor projection pad onto the table. They hit with a hollow clatter that doesn't faze her, but it makes me flinch. "You can confess that your distraction interfered with the battle-sim… or you can say nothing. Just so you know, your friend Cardyn has the same choices."

I glance up at her with what I hope is a look of casual indifference, but I know it's probably a lot closer to confusion bordering on terror.

"There are four possible results," she continues. "First, if you confess to your distraction but Cardyn stays silent, you will not be penalized. He will be given a five-hundred-point penalty. Second, if you stay silent but Cardyn confesses, *you'll* be penalized the five-hundred points. He'll get no penalty but will be thanked for his honesty. Third, if you confess, and he *also* confesses, you'll both be deducted three-hundred points. Fourth, if you both refuse to confess, we'll have no choice but to deduct one hundred points from each of you."

Reeling now, I'm trying to get my mind around my options.

"What about the others?" I ask.

I don't want to say it out loud, but I can't help wondering if Brohn is going to lose points too. I hate the thought of him losing his chance at Special Ops because of me.

"The others are not your concern. We know you and Cardyn are close. We know he knew about your raven. That makes the two of you complicit, so now you need to choose. I've told you your options. Cardyn has the exact same ones. You have five minutes, starting now. I'll be back to receive your answer."

Without another word, Hiller leaves the room. The door disappears again, and I'm left alone with the small aluminum desk, the writing stylus, the sensor projection pad, my thoughts, and absolutely no way out.

MY HEAD IS A CHAOTIC MESS. I wish I could press pause on the world for two minutes, so I could catch my breath and pretend I'm a regular human being for a change. But the world isn't listening, and the clock's ticking.

What were the choices again? She threw everything at me so fast. Even at my best and most focused, there's no way I could have retained it all.

"I need to see the options written out," I mutter to myself.

Grabbing the stylus, I start scrawling on the sensor pad. The words hover before me, glowing faintly gray in the air above the table. I start by jotting down Hiller's four rules, but they're too long and hard to remember, so I wave my hand over the screen like I used to see Dad do on a similar piece of equipment back home before we lost power.

My hovering notes disappear.

Think like Dad, I tell myself. *Think visually.*

I haven't used tech like this since I was six, but it comes back to me in a rush, along with what Dad called my "natural ability to think like a techno-organism." When I was little, I thought it was an insult. Only later, after my bond with Render started to solidify, did I start to see it as my father's greatest compliment.

I quickly sketch out a diagram of Hiller's dilemma:

Hiller's Dilemma			
		Me	
		Stay Silent	Confess
Cardyn	Stay silent	100, 100	500, 0
	Confess	0, 500	300, 300

Some quick taps to a tool palette on the projection pad allow me to color-code it. I feel myself blushing, embarrassed at my meticulous nature, even if no one's around to make note of it.

Finally, I can see all my choices laid out for me. Okay, so Cardyn and I each have two options, which end up as four pairs of numbers. For each pair, Cardyn's payoffs are on the left and mine are on the right.

It's confusing at first, and suddenly I wish I were as good at puzzles as Rain is. She'd have this figured out in two seconds. Back in the Valta, she was queen of games and puzzles, even as a Neo. When she was five years old, she taught herself how to play chess from a book and an old set in her uncle's basement. She tried to teach the rest of us years later, but no one other than Karmine and Kella ever really took to it.

When the Sixteens from that year found a half-burned copy of a book called *Mind-Benders* in the rubble of the local library, Rain easily solved what puzzles she could salvage and then spent the next three months creating her own brain-teasers, then making everyone else—even the Sixteens and Juvens—feel dumb when they couldn't figure them out.

At first, Hiller's dilemma seems like an easy choice. All Card and I have to do is both stay silent, and we'll each get a pretty mild penalty of one-hundred points.

But then those "five-hundreds" catch my eye, and I see the problem. If I refuse to cooperate, but Cardyn decides to be honest, he'll avoid *any* penalty, while I'll be stuck with a five-hundred-point deduction and probably be out of the running for Special Ops.

Unfortunately, Cardyn is the most honest person in the world. He'd also hate to see me suffer.

So, does he hold true to his values of honesty and confess, or does he stay silent and refuse to cooperate, so I won't have to suffer quite so much?

Do I do the same? If I'm honest and confess, but Card decides to look out for me by staying silent, I get no penalty, but Card gets nailed with a five-hundred-point deduction and will definitely hate me for the rest of our lives.

My mind is swirling almost as much as when Rain tried to teach me chess. She told me every move relied on the one before. That I had to try to anticipate dozens, maybe hundreds, of possible responses. Back then, I didn't toss the board over and throw the pieces at her, but now I kind of wish I had.

Things designed to turn your brain into a churning tapioca vortex should be banned on principle alone.

Honesty or loyalty.

That's what it comes down to. I can protect myself at the expense of my friend. Or, I can help my friend and hurt myself.

What is Cardyn thinking right now? What will he do? And how will what he thinks I'll do affect whatever he decides to do?

This is exactly why chess made my head hurt.

After analyzing the choices and staring for a full minute at my beautiful full-color rendering of the problem, I make my decision and sit back in my chair as the sound of footsteps approaches from the other side of the door.

"So?" Hiller asks as the door slides open and she steps into the room. "We have Cardyn's answer. What's yours?"

"I'll tell you," I say, swallowing hard past the lump in my throat. "Listen carefully."

I stare right into her mean little eyes, cross my arms, and clamp my mouth shut.

Hiller looks tense for a second, like she's expecting me either to talk or leap out of my seat and attack her. When she realizes that she has my answer—*silence*—her shoulders slump and her face relaxes. "Then I take it you're willing to risk losing five-hundred points just to protect someone—even a friend—who might be right across the hall admitting that your bird was, in fact, a distraction?"

I feel a quiver in my lip, but I clench my jaw to stop it in its tracks. There's no way I'm giving her the satisfaction of knowing how scared I am.

Hiller squints daggers at me. "And you're prepared to accept full punishment while Cardyn goes back to training, and very possibly earns enough points to qualify for Special Ops. While you're left with what? Combat duty and its high mortality rate?"

I still don't answer.

"I'm giving you a chance here, Kress. An opportunity to change your mind for the sake of your friend and, frankly, for your own sake."

I answer her with a snarky stare that oozes a confidence I'm nowhere close to feeling.

"Very well," Hiller sighs. "But remember this: you have to live with your decision."

"I understand."

"Okay, then. Come with me."

I stand and follow Hiller out of the room, down a series of hallways, and finally back to the conference room with its four islands of tables. Brohn and Rain are back to sitting across from each other at one table. *So, Hiller and her people decided to pair them together.* I try to push away the ugly feeling of envy that's surging its way through my chest. I'm not the only one who sees how close the two of them have become.

Terk and Amaranthine are sitting together at another table. Karmine and Kella are at their own. Only Card is sitting by himself, so I slip into the empty seat opposite him.

Hiller leaves, closing the door behind her.

As we start discussing what just happened, we realize that each pair of us just had the same experience. The same scenario. The same choices. Amaranthine, as usual, doesn't talk. But Terk is a total chatterbox.

"At first, I didn't understand the rules," he says. "I thought we were going to get court-martialed or lashed or killed or something. I didn't want to get Manthy in trouble, but I didn't want to get in trouble either. And then I remembered what you said, Kress. About us being a Conspiracy. That means we're a team, with a common enemy."

"Enemy?" Karmine asks.

Terk gives him a vigorous nod. "Yes. But it's not the Processor or the Recruiters or the Trainers. And it's definitely not Manthy."

"So who's the enemy?" Karmine asks, clearly intrigued by Terk's rambling thought process.

"Fear," Terk says after a pause. He folds his hands behind his head, leans back, and smiles broadly enough to split his face.

"Fear?"

"Yes. Fear of getting the worst punishment possible. Isn't that everyone's fear? So I tried to get past that and do what was best for Manthy, no matter how scared I was about what she might be doing or thinking, or what punishments either of us might get."

Brohn gets up and walks over to stand behind him, laying his hands on Terk's enormous shoulders. "You did good, Big Guy. Real good."

Terk's proud smile somehow gets even bigger, and we all have a good laugh over his description of what turned out to be the way we were all thinking.

I watch as Brohn weaves through the jumble of desks and chairs to get back to his seat.

"This is ridiculous," he says, staring at the four desks' linear layout. "We can't talk like this. Let's move the desks into the middle of the room—just like our cots are arranged in the Silo."

We each grab a chair, slide it up to the new circular cluster of desks, and sit down facing each other to finish our conversation.

"This is better," Rain sighs.

Kella agrees. "No sense shouting around at one another when can just be face to face."

"Besides," Card observes cheerfully, "we're obviously better together than apart."

I find myself occasionally looking at Brohn as the discussion shifts to the two Cubes we've seen so far. But he's focused, his eyes on his hands as he speculates about what we might experience next out in the Agora.

"I'm hoping it's more gun training," Karmine says.

"Me too," Kella agrees.

"Not me," I tell them, pulling my eyes away from Brohn. "I'd be happy not to get shot at, for a change."

After a while, Hiller returns to the room. She steps in and takes one long look around, her mouth open. But she doesn't say anything about our new circular arrangement of desks and chairs. Instead, she tells us that the Beta Cube challenge is over. "You have all agreed in your respective pairs to remain silent. Without cooperation from any of you, we have no choice but to penalize each of you the one-hundred points, as promised."

She means it to sound like some sort of harsh disciplinary action, but I don't care. I'd rather take a one-hundred-point penalty for Cardyn's sake than get no penalty for my own sake. I won't be intimidated into doing what's best for myself at the expense of my friend. I look around the room, and I can guarantee that my fellow Seventeens are each thinking the exact same thing.

Once all of us have made it clear that we've accepted our fate, Hiller escorts us out of the room, down another series of halls, and out of the building to the Agora.

Out in the open air, we all walk together through the Agora and over to the Silo, where Trench is waiting for us. He taps a code into his Catalyst, and the Capsule Pads appear from underground to deliver us down into our barracks.

With all of us mentally wiped out, everyone seems to fall asleep within five minutes. That is, everyone except me. I've got too many things on my mind to drift off peacefully.

As quietly as I can, I swing my feet around and tip-toe into the Shower Room. Squatting down in one of the shower stalls with my back to the cold concrete wall, I tap a pattern onto my forearm implant and concentrate.

A moment later, even though I'm deep underground, I begin to see the outside through Render's eyes. He's full from picking at a deer carcass he found in the blackened woods, and now he's perched in a dying tree that leans up against the Beta Cube. It's not quite night-time, but the air is growing gray as the last threads of the day's light start to fade.

Things are blurry at first. The sounds of the world above crash against my eardrums in thick, thunderous waves, reminding me how strong our connection has grown since we both left the Valta. I recoil and clench my hands into tight fists at my sides.

As things begin to focus, I can suddenly make out the forms of Hiller, Granden, and Trench, standing near the door of the Beta Cube.

They're talking, but at first it doesn't sound like any language I've ever heard. It's mostly just gibberish; a mixture of caw-ing and grumbling. But after a minute or two, I begin to identify words, then full sentences. The language is choppy, the words crunching together, but I find that I can make most of it out.

Hiller's voice is mechanical, like an angry robot who's trying to sound like a happy flight attendant. "This is the first time in my experience with Recruits that no one has broken. No one defected—not one of them. It's not uncommon for someone to sacrifice themselves for the other person, even if they know the penalty will be real and severe. But for *everyone* to risk the possibility of getting the worst punishment? That's unheard of."

"Maybe it's just a coincidence," Granden offers. "Or maybe luck."

"Maybe they're masochists," Trench offers. "Or geniuses."

Hiller shakes her head. "There's no such thing as one hundred percent cooperation in the real world. It's like they suddenly have some kind of group mind."

Trench answers her, his voice full of static and brittle in my head, like someone walking on dead leaves. "But that's good, isn't it? I mean, we want them to think like a team."

What happens next is crystal clear.

With a sharp *thwak* that makes me flinch, Hiller smacks Trench hard across the face. "No, you idiot!" she says. "That's the *opposite* of what we want."

My connection disappears a few seconds later, and I'm almost glad. I feel like I've just had a weird nightmare that doesn't entirely make sense. I try to tell myself it wasn't real, or that I just misheard what Hiller was saying.

As I get into bed and press my head into my thin pillow, I promise myself not to tell anyone about it. At least not for now. I need to figure some things out first, especially the part about being able to see and hear so much more detail through Render than I ever could before.

13

In the morning, we wake up to eight sets of white martial arts uniforms hanging on pegs along the perimeter of our barracks. The pegs are next to our lockers, our names displayed above each, so it doesn't take a genius to figure out who belongs to which uniform. Besides, Terk's locker is next to mine, and his pants alone are the size of a sleeping bag, so I'm not too worried about grabbing the wrong clothes.

I slip into the white pants and white canvas jacket assigned to me, pushing thoughts of last night's strange events away from my mind. Fortunately, Karmine provides a distraction by offering to show us all how to tie the long black belts around our waists.

"Just one of the many practical skills one can pick up from doing a little combat reading," he boasts.

"Great," I reply sarcastically. "Knowing how to tie a belt should come in real handy against the Order."

"You joke," Karmine says, pointing with his thumb to the world up above, "but we've got to impress Hiller and her bunch before we even get a shot at the Order. Every point counts. And no way am I getting Combat deployment. Granden says those guys don't usually even last as long as your team did yesterday."

I give him the dual reaction of a shrug and a smirk before he moves on to help Kella tie her belt. I hate to say it, but he's right. I should be more focused on what I can do to earn the points I'll need to make Special Ops. Otherwise, I'm going to wind up on the front lines with no skills, no friends, and eventually, no life. Literally. If what I heard last night was true—if Hiller wants us to think like individuals—that means she'll reward independent thinking. I need to prove I'm up to the task.

Now that we're all dressed and looking like an eight-person team of black-belted ghosts, we stand on the Capsule Pads and wait to be lifted up. Once we're in place, the clear pods close up around us and whoosh us up to the surface. We step out of the Capsules, which seal up behind us and whoosh back down. This is becoming a familiar routine.

Train until our bodies ache.

Drop down into the Silo.

Sleep.

Return to the surface for more training.

Repeat.

For the two weeks before Hiller's test in the Beta Cube, we were greeted by weapons, target ranges, and combat simulations. We've learned how to handle a wide variety of guns and occasionally got to practice with some old-style cross-bows, as well as some of the more high-tech volters, stun-guns, and other non-lethal weapons.

Trench and Granden have even given us lessons in the inner workings of nuclear, hydrogen, and neutron bombs—not that we're likely ever to use them. Through it all, we've been overseen, assessed, and graded. The updated grades always show up on the viz-screen down in our barracks. Karmine, Brohn, and Kella continue to jockey for position at the top of the list. No surprise there. Kella has better vision than any of us and can track moving targets as well as Render can. Karmine is obsessed with weapons and keeps hoping out loud that we'll get to handle even more.

Brohn is amazing at everything.

Meanwhile, I'm nowhere near the top.

When we step out of our Capsules this time, the Agora has been converted into a field of mats, blocking-dummies, and heavy punching bags suspended on thick metal stands throughout the wide, open space. There are training stations scattered all around. An old-style boxing ring sits off in one corner. There's also a smaller ring of some kind, surrounded by a steel cage.

Another area houses a bunch of wooden stands, maybe six feet tall, with smaller wooden spokes sticking out like arms from their cylindrical bodies. Everything's changed. Even Granden and Trench are dressed differently than before. Instead of the drab military camouflage outfits they've been wearing, both are dressed exactly like us, in white, loose-fitting jacket-and-pants combinations that Trench describes as "keikogi." The only difference is that their belts are red instead of black.

Everything else in the Processor remains the same. The guards are still posted up in their turrets. The huge black buildings still glisten around the eight sides of the octagonal Agora. The Halo still rotates silently overhead, casting its shadow over all of us down below.

Granden smiles and gives us a slight bow as we approach. "Welcome to hand-to-hand combat training." Trench bows to us as well and explains that today, we'll begin our unarmed martial arts training.

Looking out over the magically-transformed Agora, I greet Render from across the open space. As if for my exclusive entertainment, he launches himself from his perch just above the turret on top of the Delta Cube and skims over Chucker's head.

Chucker swats at him but misses, and Render goes into a steep climb. I follow his flight path with my hand above my eyes to block out the harsh rays of red morning sunlight just materializing over the horizon. Glancing around to make sure no one's looking, I give my forearm a quick tap. It takes a few seconds, but eventually I get glimpses of the raven's point of view. For some reason, though, the images quickly fade. I try again, but this time, I'm rewarded only with a sudden throbbing headache.

"What's wrong, Render?" I mutter into the morning air. But even as I say it, I start wondering if the problem is with me. Did something cause an overload? Or, even worse, could Render be blocking me out, tired of seeing the world through my eyes? Maybe human vision and feelings aren't as interesting as we think they are. It's terrible, but kind of funny, to imagine a bird finds me too boring to bother with.

Whatever the case, I don't have time to delve into the mystery right now.

"You have exactly five minutes to meet me in front of Gamma Cube!" Granden calls out. Kellerson is stationed high up in the turret, looking out over us, his rifle hanging from his shoulder.

As we approach, the building looms over us like a shadowy guard. The symbol "Γ" is stamped on its face just above the door. "It's the Greek symbol for Gamma," Trench explains, although I'd already figured that out.

The day begins with Granden sitting us all in a circle and talking about "chi," which he describes as the life force that flows through our bodies. He then leads us in hours of breathing exercises and meditation techniques. It all seems simple at first, but pretty soon, I find myself getting light-headed and kind of bored. My mind begins to wander despite my earlier resolution to get my head in the game.

Out the corner of my eye, I can see the other Recruits. They're stone still and seem to be far more at peace than I am. How come I can't get myself out of my head? Am I just too easily distracted?

As if in answer to my question, my eyes wander over to Brohn, who's sitting on his knees, his feet tucked neatly under him. His hands are palm-down on his thighs, and his back is ram-rod straight, his head tipped ever so slightly forward. His lips are parted just the tiniest bit.

His lips are perfect. Full, but not as thick as Card's. *How did I never notice them before? Have his shoulders always been that broad? Has his jaw always been that chiseled?*

Wait—why am I thinking about his jaw when I'm supposed to be concentrating on improving my breathing so I don't pass out in the field?

Keep it together, Kress. You're not here to lose your mind over a boy.

Not even a ridiculously handsome one.

Finally, Granden instructs us to open our eyes and stand up. "Follow me," he says before leading the eight of us over to a different training station.

As we're walking, Card taps me on the shoulder and nods toward Brohn. "You like him, don't you?"

Damn. He caught me.

"What makes you say that?" I ask.

"I saw you staring at him when we were supposed to be meditating."

Damn again. "Then you were looking at *me* when you were supposed to be meditating," I snap back.

"Guilty," Card says. "Just making sure you were okay." He glances up ahead in Brohn's direction. "Looks like you were maybe more than okay."

"It's nothing," I tell him curtly. "We're…family. That's all."

"Ha. If my sister had ever looked at me that way, it would've been pretty weird."

I know he means it as a joke, a way to needle me. But it's also backfired. His older sister Angie was a Recruit from the Class of 2037. That was five years ago. For Card, that's five years of trying to figure out why she did what she did. Why she resisted the Recruiters. Why she didn't just go along with the other new Seventeens or listen when they shouted at her not to run. There were twenty-two in her Cohort that year. Four of them preferred to be shot dead and buried behind the church than to be taken away in the Recruiters' transport trucks.

Card clears his throat and tries to laugh off what I know must be excruciatingly painful memories. "Maybe you should just tell him how you feel," he says. "You know, like, more than friends."

"Don't be ridiculous. I admire him just like everyone does. He's cool under pressure. Someone we can rely on."

"Uh-huh," Card says, hitting my shoulder with his. "Just be careful. You tell yourself that for long enough, and you'll start to believe it."

With that, he heads over to the new training station where Granden and Trench are starting to gather us up to continue with the day's session. I wait for a minute and then follow him. There's no way I'm taking his advice to talk to Brohn, not that there's even anything to say. I'm sure his mind is on his little sister back in the Valta. He doesn't need me complicating his life. Besides, he's been spending so much time with Rain, I'm not sure if he even remembers my name.

"We'll be doing some simple sparring exercises first," Trench announces, pulling me out of my own head. I'm grateful for the distraction. He proceeds to lead us in all kinds of grappling and throwing lessons. We learn how to shift our weight, keep our balance while under attack, and deliver counter-attacks to our enemy.

Despite his size, Terk quickly falls behind. The moves are tricky, and his body can't quite keep up with what his mind is telling it to do.

Despite *her* lack of size, Rain is great. She proves to be a quick learner, which doesn't surprise anyone. But she's also turned out to be a lot stronger than any of us suspected. During throwing drills, she's able to grab me by the jacket, lean her hip into mine, and toss me halfway across the ring like I'm a small sack of potatoes. After she's dazzled us over and over again with her prowess, Trench explains that her strength comes not from muscle, but from her ability to channel her chi to when and where she needs it for any given parry or attack.

"We all have this in us," he explains. "We all have a strength and an ability to regulate it. We can alter our weight, amplify our power."

Kella looks skeptical. "You're saying we can control how much we weigh? How's that possible?"

Trench rubs his chin and looks at her. "Ever try to pick up a baby or a puppy that doesn't want to get picked up?"

Kella nods.

"And how'd that go?"

"Harder than it should be," she admits.

Trench says, "Exactly. You have more control over yourself than you think. It's a matter of finding and developing your inner energy like Rain's been doing."

No wonder Brohn likes her. Not only is she perfect on the outside. Apparently, her inner energy is off the charts, too.

Rain is the best at this stuff, but it's Karmine who really loves to fight. Over the course of the next few days, he practically drools every time Granden or Trench asks for a volunteer to demonstrate a move. Even so, he's stiff and constantly relies on his instincts, instead of on the lessons we've been learning. I'm open to the lessons, which is why I keep beating him.

That drives him batty.

I think I'm starting to learn how to access my inner energy. I'm no Rain yet, but I'm finding all kinds of ways to be stronger than I thought I was, and it feels really good.

After nearly two weeks of prep, Granden and Trench tell us we're finally going to push ourselves to the limit. Today, we're getting a chance to show what we've learned from all the Close-Quarters training.

Clicking his Catalyst, Granden calls up a cylindrical cage the size of a boxing ring from the bowels of the Agora. Trench climbs in and invites me to the do the same.

"Me?" I ask, shocked to be the first.

"Yes, Kress. Time to fight."

I climb in.

We spar.

I hold back because I can tell he's holding back. As he baits me, I start to ramp up my attack. But the harder I swing, the faster he moves. I attempt the front leg kick he taught us a few days ago. The sweep. The elbow strike. The reverse punch. Even the knife-hand. He seems to anticipate my every move and counters with quick feints and half-powered punches to my shoulders and light tap-kicks to the outsides of my legs.

In such close quarters, I'm amazed I can't make contact with him. It isn't long before frustration overcomes me, and I'm lunging at him like a drunk maniac. When I still can't hit him, but he seems able to hit me at will, my frustration levels go through the roof, and it isn't long before my anger follows. My arms and legs are burning from the acid build-up in my muscles, and I'm weak from exertion. I don't know if it's the sweat in my eyes or the blindness of fury, but I can barely see anymore. The blurry figure that Trench has become puts me out of my misery with a reverse-elbow to my solar plexus that sends me crashing backwards into the steel mesh and then head-first to the floor, the last bits of breath fleeing from my body in one last massive whoosh.

I can hear the others rushing toward the cage, calling out my name, asking if I'm okay. I'd answer them if I could, but my ability to form sounds is long gone—as is my grip on consciousness. I drift off into a murky blackness.

When the first bits of fuzzy light appear, I think I must be dead. But the shadowy figures eventually take shape, and I realize I'm just on the floor outside of the cage with Brohn and Cardyn both kneeling over me. Brohn's hand is on my cheek like he's feeling my temperature. When I make eye contact with him, he offers me a reassuring smile and strokes his fingers over my skin, which I have to admit feels pretty good.

"She's awake," he calls out to Trench, who I can now see standing over by the entrance to the cage. He's leaning against it, inspecting his knuckles without a care in the world.

"Too bad," Trench says. "A little more time asleep, and maybe the lesson would take better."

"What's the lesson?" Cardyn mutters. "How to knock out someone half your size?"

Trench overhears him and storms over. He grabs Card by the back of his white workout jacket and hauls him to his feet. "It's not about size, Recruit. It's about speeding yourself up by slowing yourself down." He tosses Card aside and turns to the others. "Once that makes sense to you, you'll be better able to avoid *that*." He points to me and spits in my direction before storming off to join Granden over by the fence.

When I'm feeling strong enough, Brohn puts a guiding hand on my back and helps me push myself up to a sitting position. Either my head is spinning or else the world is. Either way, I try to grip the ground beneath me and hope I don't throw up.

"You okay?" Brohn asks.

I nod, pressing my hand to my forehead. "I think so," I tell him, letting my body sag against his. I can feel the hard beats of his heart now, fast and furious. I can't tell if it's from rage or something else. All I know is that as usual, I'm grateful to be close to him.

I just wish I could get closer without losing myself.

"Don't worry," Terk says as he kneels down next to Brohn. "I'm sure this is as bad as it'll get."

The next day—one of our final days before moving on to the Delta Cube—we discover that it's not.

After learning the bare-bones basics of judo, aikido, and jeet kune do from Granden and Trench over the past two weeks, they declare us ready for a final few days of hand-to-hand combat training. This time, Granden has summoned a small mock grocery store to serve as our sparring arena. The space has a cashier's counter, glass-doored refrigerators, and four rows of shelves lined with all kinds of cans, cartons, and food props. It reminds me of how our own grocery store back home looked in the days before the attacks.

"This will simulate one of the many locations where you may encounter the Order," Trench tells us. "Not every site in a war zone will be a battlefield. Not every fight will take place in the pristine comfort of an open-air gym. The fights you'll face will be in real places. Apartment buildings. Alleyways. Restaurants. Parks. And yes, even small convenience stores. I'll take the part of the Eastern Order terrorist. I need two of you to try to take me down."

We stand in a little group to watch as Karmine and Kella step across the threshold and into the simulated store. Trench looks only too pleased to square off against the toughest most gung-ho members of our little Conspiracy.

I'm next to Brohn, who's standing protectively next to me, close enough that I can press my shoulder into his if necessary. As usual I'm trying not to let myself touch him. Trying to convince myself to focus on my end goal of Special Ops. But right now, my head is throbbing, and all I want is the reassurance of his strong body against mine.

Karmine and Kella start slow, shifting into their places on either side of Trench. They quickly outflank him, just as we've been taught. Trench retreats a bit between two of the aisles, but Karmine and Kella reposition themselves to keep him between them. Kella is the first to attack, covering the space between them in an instant and delivering a side kick that Trench easily deflects. Keeping her balance, she resumes her fight stance as she and Karmine advance.

This time, it's Karmine who initiates the attack. He lunges forward with a straight fist punch, but Trench deftly steps into his attack, and Karmine's fist sails harmlessly by Trench's face.

Trench delivers a close-in elbow strike to Kella's face. It's not a full-contact blow, but it's strong enough so her head snaps back, and she staggers against one of the display shelves before slumping to the floor. Karmine snaps into an instant fury and lunges at Trench, who deflects his punch with one hand while delivering an open-hand strike to Karmine's exposed forearm with the other.

The sickening sound of a bone snapping in two horrifies me to the point of nausea. Instinctively, I lunge forward, not sure if I'm supposed to leap to my friends' defense, attack Trench myself, or just hold back and be grateful it wasn't me. Brohn has the same idea and leaps in front of me, looking like he's ready to beat Trench senseless, but Granden puts an immediate stop to any thoughts either of us might be having by stepping between us and the mock store.

"Lesson's over," he says with his hand up. "The medics are already on their way."

He's barely finished announcing this when Kellerson arrives with two other guys who he introduces as part of a Med-Team. They confirm that Karmine has a fractured ulna before scanning Kella's face with a small device and announcing that she has a broken occipital bone.

While we look on, horrified, they apply a gel-filled splint to Karmine's arm and what looks like a blue, half-filled water balloon to Kella's eye.

For the next two days of training and sparring, those two sit on the sidelines, brooding and recovering. Their injuries are bad but not crippling, which means they get to stay with us in the Silo instead of being transferred to a med lab in the Eta Cube.

Karmine says the gel cast on his arm actually feels pretty comfortable. "Doesn't itch or anything," he announces with a glint in his eye. "Besides, it's just a fracture. Nothing I can't handle."

Kella doesn't exhibit the same bravado, but she gets through the next two days without too much trouble. The day after the accident, one of the medical guys gives her a shot of something in her arm. I don't know what it is, but it seems effective. The swelling in her eye goes down right away and is nearly completely gone by the next day. She and Karmine are still excused from the training, of course. Still, they insist on watching and cheering us on.

We get through our last day of Close-Quarters training in a simulated real-world environment without any more incidents. Brohn and Rain both do especially well, which is only reinforced when Trench and Granden commend them for it. Terk lumbers through the sparring but manages to get a few good shots in to Trench before Trench redoubles his efforts and takes him down.

When my turn comes, I get taken down in about two seconds flat and am rewarded with disappointed stares from the two Trainers. Even Amaranthine manages to last longer than me, although she kind of cheats by running away over and over until Trench is finally able to drag her back to the simulation set-up and forces her to defend herself. She dodges his first strike, but then he hits her with a lightning-fast leg sweep, and that's it for Manthy.

"Hey," Brohn says after the day's events. I give him a look that says I don't feel like receiving any tips on how not to be a weakling, but he just smiles and says, "You okay?"

I nod, but there are tears in my eyes. I want to tell him it's frustrating to feel so helpless, but something holds me back. "I'm fine," I say. "Just fine."

After a solid night's sleep, we step out of our Capsule Pads to be greeted by Granden, who announces that it's time to move on to the Gamma Cube.

Grateful to know I won't get thrown to the ground this morning, I turn to look back at Karmine and Kella, who are usually up front but are now lagging behind.

"Do you think they'll be okay?" I ask Brohn as we follow Granden over to the third of the eight black buildings.

"Physically?" he says. "Definitely."

"And Emotionally? Psychologically?"

"Sure," he says without looking at me. "Absolutely."

"You don't sound so sure."

"Well, that's because I'm not."

As I stare at him, I realize his jaw is clenching so hard that I can see the tension in his face.

"Why not?" I ask. "Karmine and Kella are tough. They've been talking about fighting the Order forever. Why would you think they'd back down now?"

He gives me a sideways glance. "Because this is starting to get real, Kress. All that stuff we talked about on our last night in the Valta? When you and I admitted we were worried?" I nod, surprised he even remembers that conversation. "It turns out that all those worries were justified, and now we're finding out exactly why."

He picks up his pace and walks ahead with Rain, Granden, and Trench, leaving me behind, where I suddenly feel more alone than ever.

14

"Welcome to Gamma Cube."

Hiller is all smiles, but I'm starting to get a sense there's more going on here than meets the eye. Training isn't supposed to result in serious injuries. Up until Karmine, Kella, and I got hurt, I thought Trench was deliberately going pretty hard on us.

Afterwards, though, there was a look in his eyes, one that I didn't expect to see. It was almost pleasure, like he was finally getting a chance to stop being nice.

Hiller walks us through a few corridors and finally to a door where she instructs us to stop.

"Your job is simple," she says. "You will enter this room. I'll lock it behind you. You just need to get back out. In order to do so, you'll have to gather clues. You'll try to solve some puzzles. If you're successful, you'll find the key that unlocks the door. Your goal is to get out in thirty minutes or less. If you manage that, you'll be rewarded with points. If you fail, you'll either get punished or else you'll get off with...a stern warning."

She pushes down on the two large gold handles and pulls. The big double-doors swing out with a gentle sigh. One at a time, we enter the room. As Amaranthine and I step in, Hiller reaches over and closes each of the big double doors behind us. They click shut, and we all take in the large room.

Through the gloom, we can see that it's a mess of random objects. A large silver table sits in the middle of the room, surrounded by four silver chairs. The walls are dark, crumbling brick. A tall cabinet leans against one wall, its shelves lined with books and various knick-knacks. Paintings hang on two of the walls. A piano sits off in one corner, hollowed out down to its frame and looking ready to collapse.

"It's an Escape Room!" Rain blurts out after a few seconds.

"A what?"

"My dad told me about them. He always liked solving puzzles and such. He told me about these rooms he and his friends used to play in when they were in college. They were designed to be fun, challenge your mind, and improve your teamwork abilities. Stuff like that."

"So what do we have to do?" Terk asks.

"I was wondering the same," Kella says. "Hiller didn't exactly give us a giant list of detailed instructions."

"Well, I think we're supposed to look around and find clues," Rain says, "track down a key, and get out of here."

"In thirty minutes?"

"Don't worry, Terk," Rain says, reaching up to put her small hand on his bowling-ball sized shoulder. "We can do this."

Cardyn isn't so optimistic. It's dark in here but there's still enough light for me to see the wrinkles in his forehead and the deep stress lines spreading through his face. "But where do we even start?" he whines. "Anything in here could be a clue. Or it could all just be a big time-wasting trick to see how gullible we are and how much dumb stuff we're willing to do just to pass another one of their weird tests."

"Relax, Card," Brohn says. "What happened to Karmine and Kella was a fluke."

"Hey," I protest with a smirk. "I got hurt, too."

Karmine gives me a good-natured snort. “Kress, you got the wind knocked out of you. We got cracks in our skeletons. There’s no comparison. Either way, it’s all part of our exercises. We’re being trained to fight the most important battle ever with everything in the world at stake. It’s totally normal that there will be some glitches along the way.”

“You call that a glitch?” I ask, gesturing to the blue gel cast still on his healing arm.

“How’s it feeling, anyway?” Brohn asks.

Karmine flexes his fingers and rotates his arm slowly at the elbow. “Better than I would’ve thought. Stiff, but not crazy pain like before. This cast is actually pretty amazing. Wish we’d had something like this in the med kits back in the Valta. We could have fixed up a lot of injuries.”

“Good to know,” Brohn replies. “We’re going to need you for this challenge.”

“So how do we start this thing?” Cardyn asks, panic in his voice.

“How about over there?” I say, hoping to calm him by directing his attention somewhere specific. “That could be where we’re supposed to start.”

Everyone turns to see where I’m pointing. Next to the cabinet is a large painting that looks like an up-close tangle of black, white, and yellow threads.

“I know this painting,” I tell the group. One just like it used to hang above the couch in my living room back in the Valta. I always thought it looked like the fibers of a carpet through one of Dad’s microscopes. Micah swore he could see patterns and figures of people and such hidden among all the random lines. Dad told us that it was an example of abstract expressionism. “It’s called Jackson Pollack’s *Number One*. And the one over there,” I add, pointing to the opposite wall where a painting of black lines and blotches on a cream-colored background is hanging on an angle, "is Franz Kline's *Painting Number 2.* I think they must be steps one and two in the puzzle."

Kella looks impressed, and I can't hold back my pride or my smile. I give her a shrug. "What can I say? We had a bunch of paintings in our house before, you know…the attacks. I only liked the weird ones that didn't look like actual things. Dad taught me about some of the artists from a big book we had on the coffee table. He said this kind of art was spontaneous and instinctive, like me."

"And pretty clever, too," Kella adds. "We've got a one and a two. That's a good sign we're on the right track."

"So what are we waiting for?" Card calls out, already on the move. "Let's get this thing solved and get out of here. This room is too creepy to hang around in."

We all follow him over to the first painting, which hangs next to the cabinet. On one of the cabinet shelves is a small box sealed with a combination lock. Instead of numbers, though, the four dials on the lock contain just letters.

"What are we supposed to do with this?"

"Open it, obviously."

"But how?"

"There's got to be a clue, right?"

"Here," I say. "Try this." I lift the Pollack painting down from the wall and flip it around. Sure enough, on the back is a riddle written in black marker in small, tidy handwriting.

WHO IS THE YOUNGEST OF THREE SISTERS IF ANNA IS THE OLDEST, BARB IS NOT THE OLDEST, AND CARA IS NOT THE YOUNGEST?

(I OPEN ONLY FOR THE YOUNGEST OF THE THREE. NO RANDOM GUESSING. YOU GET ONE TRY TO GET IT RIGHT. FAIL THE RIDDLE, FAIL THE ROOM.)

"I guess we can't just guess, then."

"Why not?" Card asks. "We have a one in three shot at getting it right."

"This isn't meant to test our gambling skills," I say with a sideways glare. "We're supposed to figure out the clue."

"Well, it can't be Cara, by definition," Rain says. "It tells us right there that she's not the youngest."

"And it can't be Anna. Also, by definition. She's the oldest."

"So it's Barb. Do we all agree?"

We all chime in with a nod, a "Yes," or an "I think so."

Brohn invites Rain to step forward and spin the dials on the lock. She clicks each dial around until they all line up to spell "B-A-R-B."

"Fingers crossed," she says and tugs on the lock. To our combined relief, it clicks open. Rain lifts the lid to reveal a scroll of parchment paper. When she unrolls it we all peer over her shoulder in the dim light. On one side is a huge red "N," which we quickly realize matches the large red "N" on the wall with the Kline painting. "So, we go over to step number two," she says.

We cross the room and stand in front of the Kline painting. As we do, the "N" on the parchment lights up, and we're able to make out the faint text on the reverse side of the scroll:

The next three numbers in the pattern will turn you the right way to earn your degree:

149162536496481_ _ _

"It's a bunch of random numbers," Terk moans with a hang-dog look. "How are we supposed to know what numbers are supposed to come next?"

"Try adding each number with the one before," Karmine suggests.

Rain does some quick calculations. "No. That's not a pattern."

Kella suggests seeing if there's a pattern in the difference *between* numbers. We all do some more calculations in our heads, but nobody comes up with anything.

"What if each number represents a letter of the alphabet?" Kella asks.

"Yes!" Brohn says. "Great idea! So if one equals 'A,' four equals 'D.' Nine equals 'I.' One equals 'A' again. Six equals 'F.' Two equals 'B.'" Brohn's voice trails off. "*Adiafb*? I don't think that's a word."

"Too bad," Karmine says to Kella. "I thought you had something there."

"Wait!" Rain shouts with a bounce and a clap of her hands. "It's squares!"

"What?"

"See. One squared is one. Two squared is four. Three squared is nine. Four squared is sixteen. That gets us up to nine squared, which is eighty-one. So the next number to be squared is ten, which makes the last three numbers one, zero, zero."

"You're a genius!" Cardyn says.

"What does the other part of the riddle mean?" I ask. "The 'turning the right way' and the 'degree'?"

Rain nods and asks us to give her a minute. "Well," she says at last, "the arrow on the wall with the 'N' above it must be a compass. 'N' is due north. If we turn one-hundred degrees to the right from here..." Rain pivots around until she's facing the wall behind us. We all turn with her and see what she sees: On the wall, there are nine apple-sized blue dots that we can see only from a certain angle. Underneath, a faint caption reads:

Connect the dots with four straight lines.

No lifting your finger.

No backtracking.

Surrounding the dot in the lower right-hand corner are the letters: RTHERESTA.

"I guess we're supposed to connect the dots by tracing with our finger," I say.

"Don't worry, my fellow Conspirators," Cardyn announces grandly. "I've got this!"

He begins by reading the letters at the bottom of the puzzle. "Wait. What does 'Rest Art He' mean?" he asks.

"No," Karmine calls out. "It says, 'He Restart.'"

"No," Brohn offers. "It says 'The Rest Ar.'"

"The rest are what?" Terk asks.

"You're such dopes," Kella says, shouldering past the boys. "It says, 'Start Here.'"

Brohn, Terk, Cardyn, and Karmine exchange sheepish grins and step back.

Starting at the blue dot in the lower right-hand corner, Kella begins to draw lines on the wall with her finger. She drags her fingertip along the wall, connecting the dots left to right and up and down. As she goes, the lines light up bright yellow.

When she lifts her finger, the lines she's already drawn disappear, and she's forced to start again. When she tries to backtrack over lines she's already made, the other lines disappear, and she's forced to start yet again.

"Let me try," I say. But I don't have any more luck than Kella did.

The others try as well, and we waste ten minutes on failed attempt after failed attempt. We draw squares. Rectangles. We try vertical, horizontal, and back and forth in every combination until we finally give up.

"It's impossible," Terk complains.

"Maybe we should focus on a different clue," I suggest.

"Yeah," Brohn sighs. "Maybe."

We turn to follow him across the room to where three marble sculptures of horses sit on a shelf. Brohn, Rain, and Kella each grab a statue and start turning them over in their hands. They poke and prod the statues, pull at the legs and heads, but...nothing.

"Nothing," Kella announces. "This is hopeless."

I get startled when I'm suddenly tapped on the shoulder from behind. I whip around to see Amaranthine standing in front of me, pointing back to the wall with the nine blue dots that she has apparently just connected on her own:

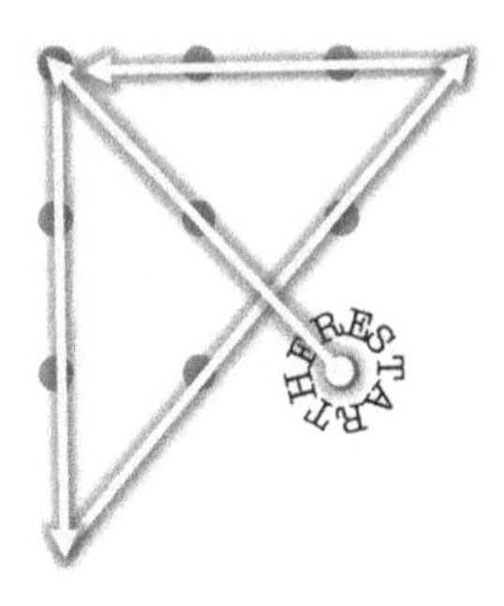

The lines she's traced with her finger on the wall are lit up in bright yellow.

"Hey!" I call out to the others. "Manthy solved it!"

They all turn to see Amaranthine standing off to one side, her head down, her hands crossed in front of her.

Card charges forward to give her a hard clap on the shoulder. "Good ol' Manthy," he beams. "Always thinking outside the box."

Amaranthine scowls at Card before taking a step back and brushing off her shoulder where he touched her.

"It's an arrow!" I say.

"And it's pointing up and to the left," Card adds.

Everyone follows my finger to the top of the brick wall where we see that one of the bricks high up by the ceiling now has a faint yellow glow around its edges. It's too high for any of us to reach—even Terk, who stretches up as high as he can before giving up.

We have a quick look around for something to stand on, but the chairs and the table are fixed to the floor.

"How about giving me a boost?" I ask.

Terk grins. "Sure thing."

I step into his cupped hands, and he slings me up and around until I'm on his back. Pressing my hands to his head, I climb up onto his shoulders and stand nearly all the way up on shaky legs. Reaching up, I'm able to wiggle the brick and eventually slide it out completely.

When Terk's helped guide me down from his shoulders, I hand the brick to Brohn, who flips it over in his hands to reveal a false bottom. He slides it open, and a thick golden key in the shape of a boat clunks to the ground.

The timer on the wall above the big wooden door has ticked down to less than a minute. We rush over as one, and Brohn slips the key into the keyhole. He tries to turn it, but nothing happens. He tries again. Nothing.

"Let me," Terk says and grabs the key with both hands and starts to strain it one way then the other.

"Stop!" Rain calls out. "You'll snap it, you big dope."

"Wait!" I say, jumping between them. "I just figured out why Hiller said we'd get 'a stern' warning."

"What do you mean?"

"I mean, what if she didn't mean 'stern' like strict, but 'astern?'"

"What the heck's 'astern'?"

"It's the back of a boat. Here. Let me." I take the key from Terk and, holding it by the toothed side, I insert it backwards, head first, into the lock. Before I have time to doubt myself and wonder how wrong I might be, I give the shaft of the key a quick turn. It rotates easily, and the lock disengages just as the clock above our heads stops with twenty seconds to spare.

The wooden double doors open to reveal Hiller on the other side. She's nodding, clearly impressed. But Chucker and Kellerson, who are positioned on either side of her, seem disappointed.

"Well done," Hiller says.

"What's with them?" Cardyn asks, pointing one at a time to her burly bodyguards.

"Oh, they're just mad. If you hadn't made it out, they were going to get to administer the punishment."

She turns and starts walking away down the long hallway. "Don't worry. You made it out."

Terk leans down to me. "Did she say *punishment?*"

"Yes. Yes, she did."

Without another word, Chucker and Kellerson lead us from the building, out to the middle of the Agora, where we take our places on the Capsule Pads for our nightly descent into the Silo.

15

WHEN WE'RE BACK IN THE SILO, THE BOYS SHOWER FIRST WHILE Rain, Kella, Amaranthine, and I collapse on the cots to wait for our turn. The rhythmic thump of the water in the next room is music to my ears. For some reason, it sounds like applause.

Steam from the Shower Room billows out into the Dormitory in a thick cloud of underground fog. The Silo is always humid, but tonight, it seems especially sticky. Stray strands of hair keep clinging to my face, and my body keeps churning out perspiration whether I'm standing, walking, or sitting perfectly still. Even so, I'm feeling unusually content.

While the boys chatter in echoing fragments in the next room twenty feet away, I stretch out on my cot and take deep, sighing breaths. I'm just hoping I don't fall asleep before I have the chance to shower. Waking up this sticky would mean a full day of physical training while tugging at my clothes and getting distracted into all kinds of mistakes I can't afford to make.

Training has been a daily challenge, but some days—like today—are actually kind of fun. With the structured days, the set routine of lessons and instruction, and the feeling that I'm actually improving over time, it's the closest I've come to feeling like

I'm in school. My childhood was derailed by war, loss, and fear. But now that the terror's subsided over being recruited, I'm finally getting a taste of what a normal life could have been like if the war had never begun. I even like the fact that we're being graded. It fills me with a weird sense of purpose, kind of an assurance that everything we're doing here is happening for a reason and that a prize awaits us on the other side.

Of course, technically that "prize" is war. But at least I'm beginning to feel like an active participant in my own life now, instead of slogging around in the Valta waiting to die.

Of all of us, Rain seems to share my enthusiasm the most. She's even gotten into blathery speculations about the personal lives of the guards, the Trainers, and Hiller. She's good at acting like a regular teenager instead of a mentally and physically tough warrior-in-the-making, and I'm grateful for it.

Today, she's set her gossipy sights on Kella.

"So what's with you two?" she asks her, perching on the edge of her cot.

"What's with what two?" Kella replies, a thread of suspicion in her voice.

"Oh, you know," Rain replies with a melodious lilt. "You and Karmine. Pairing up all the time for shooting drills in the Agora. Hanging out together while we did the Escape Room puzzles. Always finding a way to get matched up as sparring partners for combat training."

"I don't know what you're talking about," Kella says, trying to hold eye contact with Rain but failing. She glances over toward the Shower Room, then at Rain, and then quickly back at the ground. "You're crazy. Karmine and I don't have anything going on."

Rain turns to me. "The lady doth protest too much, methinks."

"*Hamlet*," I blurt out, enjoying the game a little too much. "Act three. Scene two."

Rain raises her eyebrows at me and smiles. "Very good."

She presses on while Kella pretends to be engrossed with a loose thread on her gray blanket. "It's just that you've always been close. We all have. We've had to be. But you two…well, let's just say that it's nice to see you…"

Kella looks up, waiting for Rain to finish, but Rain just leans back on her elbows and smiles.

"Nice to see me what?" Kella asks with more urgency than I'm sure she intended, her blue eyes flashing.

"You know. Loosening up. Not quite so cold as you used to be."

"I'm plenty loose."

"Says the girl who was all business back in the Valta. What did last year's Sixteens used to call you? 'Cool as Cream Kella'?"

"Cool's not the same thing as cold," Kella says defensively.

"Fair enough," Rain says with her hands up in a gesture of partial surrender.

"Besides, who made it your business to assess my personality?"

I look back and forth from Kella to Rain, not sure if this mild teasing is about to turn into a full-on brawl. Whatever it is, Rain defuses it with a smile and a sudden shift from lying back on her elbows to scooching up to the end of her cot to sit cross-legged in front of Kella, who's sitting on her own cot with her head sagging down and her feet flat on the floor, her toes wiggling like nervous little newborn mice.

"C'mon, Kella. You have a better personality than anyone I've ever met," Rain says. "Seriously. That's why it's nice to see you two together. It's nice to see you coming out of your shell, and I think…I mean, I'm just saying, that there's something about Karmine that seems to be helping."

Kella finally looks up and gives Rain a half smile. She says, "He's okay, I guess," then starts undoing the long blond French braid she's been wearing for the past couple of days.

"So do you think you two might be an…item?"

Kella blushes and laughs, and I'm thankful to feel the rest of the tension flit out of the room. "Maybe," she says. "We do have a lot in common. The way we think…the way we just *are*. But I guess I always thought of him as more like my twin brother. At least I used to."

"Until he got tall and cool-looking with those muscles and those shapely legs, right?"

Now Kella's cheeks really do go full red, but she also looks happier than I've seen her in a long time. She sits up now, with her shoulders relaxed and a sparkle of silver in her blue eyes.

"I don't care how he looks," she says with a glance over to the Shower Room to make sure we're not being overheard. "But you're right. I admit it. We have a connection. I don't know what to call it. It's not really the gushy romantic stuff our parents used to talk about. And it's definitely not like with Cleo and Martin."

Rain holds up her hands and says, "Whoa. That's a whole other situation."

Everyone knows the Cleo and Martin story. It was as big a scandal as you could have in a town made up mostly of kids. On November 1st, eight years ago, the Recruiters showed up to take away the Cohort of new Seventeens as usual. While we all gathered in the square to watch, they scanned the Recruits, stopping at Cleo, who was visibly nervous. One of the Recruiters called out to his buddy, "This one's pregnant." Our jaws hit the ground. Martin grabbed Cleo's hand, they both blushed, and Cleo started to cry. The Recruiters pulled her away from Martin, loaded him and the other Seventeens into one transport truck and flung Cleo, who was screaming and clawing at them to let her go, into another.

We never heard from either of them again.

"Don't worry," Kella says. "It's not like that. It's…different." She turns to me with a smile. "You know what I mean, Kress. About a strange connection, one you can't explain, but it seems to mean so much anyway?"

At first, my chest tightens because I think she's talking about Brohn. I didn't think anyone but Cardyn had ever noticed that I was attracted to him. It's not like we spend much time together—if anything, we avoid contact like we're both afraid of what might happen if we ever get too close. Not to mention the fact that I'm pretty sure Rain likes him a lot, too. Nothing like an awkward love triangle to make our living situation utterly horrible.

So I let out a choking cough when Kella says, "You know, like with you and Cardyn."

"Wait!" I blurt out. "What *about* Card and me?"

Kella seems relieved to have Rain's attention turn my way. With a seriously impish smile, Rain reaches across the space between our cots and puts a hand on my knee. "You're kidding, right, Kress?"

"Kidding about what?"

"You know. How you and Cardyn would sneak off all the time back home, just the two of you, romping away to your little secret hiding places in the woods. We've all known about you two for years."

"First of all, I've never 'romped' in my life. And if I ever do decide to 'romp,' I doubt it will be with Cardyn. There's no *us,* so you can put that out of your minds right now."

"But you have to admit, you two have something special," Rain says.

"Yes. It's called friendship. You should try it sometime."

She laughs, and I'm glad she realizes I was joking. She's not someone I want mad at me.

"You don't want to be...what's that term again?" Rain asks as she thrums her fingers on her leg and stares up at the ceiling.

"Just friends," Amaranthine says quietly.

We all stare at her as she drops her eyes and lowers her head. When she retreats back into Amaranthine turtle-mode, Rain shrugs her shoulders and nods.

"She's right. There are only a finite number of possible relationships that can exist between any two people. You can be friends. Related. Partners. Teammates. Lovers. Guess which one Cardyn wants the two of you to be?"

I can't get my head around Rain's question. Card's my best friend. No, he's more than that. After losing my father and brother, in a lot of ways, Cardyn has been *everything* to me. He's been with me through so much—even the secret stuff, like my training with Render. What Rain might think were amorous stolen moments between us in the woods in the Valta were actually some of the most special times in my life. Card and I talked about our hopes, our feelings, our fears. We supported each other when we were down and reveled in each other's happiness when things were going great. We had an intimacy then, a bond beyond Rain's limited ideas of what two people can mean to each other. Besides, when did "just friends" get to be such a bad thing? Cardyn isn't "just" anything to me. There's no way I'll let someone that close, that special, that indispensable in my life, be demoted to a "just" anything.

"Maybe there's more kinds of relationships than you think," I say to Rain as I stand up. The showers are off now, and our voices will be easily audible to the boys. I'm grateful for an excuse to finish the conversation, which has veered into some pretty weird and slightly awkward territory.

When the boys come out of the Shower Room, they're dressed in the same outfits we wear every night for sleeping in the Silo: black gym shorts over army green compression pants, with charcoal gray t-shirts. Everything's tight and form-fitting but still breathable and as comfortable as a second skin.

"Quite a day," Brohn says with his hands gripping the ends of the damp towel resting around his neck. He runs his fingers through his smooth, wet hair. The move makes him look tidy, elegant even. I stare at him for a moment, wondering if he has any idea how often I think about him. If Kella and Rain haven't clued in, maybe he hasn't either. Maybe...

"You ladies ready for your turn to get clean?" he says, interrupting my thoughts. It's his trademark phrase. He says it every time they get the shower first.

"We'll shower," Rain says with a wink as she stands up and leads Kella, Amaranthine, and me toward the Shower Room. "But that doesn't mean we have to get clean." She runs her hand along Brohn's face before giving him a wink and a light slap.

He laughs and puts a hand to the red splotch on his cheek. The boys are clearly amused and respond with laughs of their own and with playful punches to each other's arms and shoulders as they make their way to their cots.

I can't help but feel a rush of envy at how easily Rain touches Brohn. She's comfortable in her own skin in ways I may never be.

I think back to the conversation Brohn and I had in our last night in the Valta, when he told me I was attractive and mysterious. I wonder sometimes if he still thinks so. We've been sleeping in the same room for what feels like years now, so it's not like there's much about me that he hasn't figured out.

Or is there?

In the Shower Room, the girls and I step into the individual stalls, disrobe, and scan our hands over the green input pads that have been programmed to provide the exact optimal water temperature and pressure for each of us. At first, we thought it was just a coincidence, but about five or six days into our training, Granden confessed to me out in the Agora that yes, the showers were calibrated to meet our personal needs. "You're far too important to this war for us to risk throwing you into uncomfortable water pressure," he'd said to me with the blankest expression and best poker face I'd ever seen. To this day, I have no idea if he was joking or dead serious.

Right now, I really don't care. The conversation with the girls has my head in a dizzying spin. I can't tell if I'm more mortified about what they think is happening between me and Card or about what I wish might happen between me and Brohn. It's enough to make me queasy. The shower is the perfect antidote. Soft beads of water, just this side of hot. My muscles relax. I draw my fingers through my slicked-back hair. The water swirls down the small drain at my feet, taking my tension and embarrassment away with it.

16

EVERY MORNING FOR THE NEXT TWO WEEKS, WE RISE UP ON THE Capsule Pads and start a tough day of weapons and combat training. The mind-numbing repetition of it is somehow both comforting and infuriating. During all this time, I find myself avoiding eye contact with Cardyn and Brohn. The conversation with the girls has thrown me into some sort of vortex of shame, and I'm worried that anything I say or do will be construed as proof of my attraction to one or both of the boys. I remind myself that I'm here to work my way into Special Ops, as unlikely as that seems at this point.

Fortunately, Card seems oblivious to my attempt to retreat from any kind of closeness. He still chats with me, asks about Render, speculates about the future. I'm grateful for his company, though I frequently glance around to see if Rain and Kella are raising their eyebrows knowingly at each other.

Brohn spends the days in a quiet state, too. Maybe he's reading my body language. Or maybe it's something else. If I were Rain, I'd just run up and ask him while bouncing off the walls happily. But bouncing has never been my thing, so I just watch him from a distance, wishing things could have been different in this world of ours.

After a final week of combat training, we're finally told that it's time for our next Cube challenge. I'm hoping that means more escape rooms and puzzles, which I find far more enjoyable than pretending I'm blowing people's heads off.

Granden and Trench lead us across the Agora to the Delta Cube. Other than the symbol "Δ" that appears just above the door, it looks exactly like the other seven buildings: glistening black, imposing, and as uninviting as a giant tombstone. Inside, Hiller is waiting for us as usual. She greets us with a big smile and an enthusiastic "Good morning!" like she's about to send us off to our first day of school. I half expect her to hand each of us a paper bag with our lunch in it, then pat our heads and tell us what good children we are.

Instead, we climb three flights of stairs together until we reach a landing leading out to a hallway. At the end of the hall is a single door, which Hiller opens for us with a wave of her hand.

"Welcome to your second Escape Room. Or should I say, *rooms*."

We follow her into a windowless chamber which feels more ominous, somehow, than the last one we were in.

A tall iron box, about six or seven feet tall and a few feet wide sits in the middle of the room. It's thick, solid, and about the size and shape of an old-time phone booth. Some sort of pulley is attached to the top of the box toward the front with a thick braid of black cable rising up and disappearing into the ceiling.

On the near side of the room is a line of six heavy-looking pedestals shaped like fluted columns, each about four feet tall, each with a large smooth boulder perched on top. The boulders are all different sizes, ranging from one the size of a bowling ball to one that's as big around as good-sized tree trunk. Each of the rocks looks like it's made of marble, and even the smallest one looks like it must weigh a ton.

On the far side of the room is a line of six matching pedestals, although they don't have anything on them.

"There are three levels to this challenge," Hiller explains. "Your mission is to escape from this room through that door on the far side. Walk down one level to the next room. Escape from that one. Walk down one more level. Escape from the final room, and your mission will be completed. I will meet you at the end... if you make it. I must warn you: the stakes are higher now. But the good news is that because of the three separate levels, your allotted time has been increased. You have exactly one hour. A holo-clock will appear above each exit door on each level to let you know how much time you have remaining. Any questions?"

"Yeah," Karmine says. "I don't see the Order attacking us with too many brain-teasers. When do we get to go back out to the Agora and shoot stuff?"

"Shooting stuff," Hiller says, "as you so eloquently put it, won't do you much good if your mind isn't trained and operating at peak efficiency. Believe me, the Order is out there right now trying to prove they can not only outshoot us, but also outsmart us. Your job is to prove them wrong. Now, if there are no other equally pointless questions...?" She looks around with the judgmental gleam in her eye we all know so well by now. "Good."

Hiller gestures us inside and closes the door behind us.

"Okay," Rain says, hopping up and down like she's just won a prize. "This should be fun."

"You have a strange definition of 'fun,'" Karmine grumbles.

"Says the guy who enjoys shooting and stabbing stuff way too much."

Kella laughs and comes to Karmine's defense. "At least that'll get us combat ready. Kar's right. You can keep your riddles and puzzles. Give me one of those big FN F2020 assault rifles any day of the week."

Rain looks over and gives me a little eye roll. I respond with a quiet laugh as she surveys the room.

I walk over to the big metal box. I run my hands along its surface and discover a seam running along its sides toward the front, forming a door of some kind. But there are no hinges, knobs, dials, levers, or anything else we might use to open what appears to be the door. The metal is blue and cold to the touch.

"There's not much to this," I tell the group, "other than the pulley on top of what seems to be the box's front panel."

Just to be sure, Rain tells us to check out the rest of the room as well. We tap the walls with our knuckles and look around for any hidden panels or unusual surfaces. But other than the tall box and the two sets of pedestals on either side of the room, it looks like there's nothing here.

"I'm going to go out on a limb here," Brohn says, his palms resting flat on the top of the box, "and guess that the key to the exit door is inside this thing."

"The pulley must lift the door to the box," Cardyn suggests, and everyone seems to agree.

"I'll buy that," Rain says. She seems to be taking charge, which is fine by me. "The pedestals and rocks have got to be the key to opening the box," she announces. "So it's just a matter of figuring out what they mean."

The columns without the rocks on top are numbered one through six.

"I get the numbers on this set of pedestals," I call out to Rain. "But what are the markings on the other ones?" I walk over to where Cardyn is kneeling at the base of one of the pedestals with the odd markings.

Sure enough, each of the pedestals with a large rock on top has a strange symbol on it:

One of the pedestals has what looks like the number one. Another has a three. The rest of the marks don't look like anything. Just dashes, almost like Braille, or maybe a computer code. Terk suggests that it could be some kind of alien language.

"Let's not get carried away," Karmine laughs. "I don't think we're here to translate alien to English."

Terk blushes and hangs his head as Kella joins in to tease him about his suggestion, which is too bad, because I was thinking the same thing.

Before we have a chance to do any more guessing, Rain lets out a laugh and says she has it.

"Very clever!" she says. "It's a digital read-out, only in reverse.

Well, not reverse, exactly. More like *in*verse. Or contrapositive. It's the accentuation of negative space."

"It's the what of the *what now*?" Karmine asks. I can't help but snicker. I have no idea what she's talking about, either.

Rain narrows her eyes in thought as she tries to explain. "See, old clocks used to use seven lines in combination to make the numbers zero through nine. They were digital, so they could only operate in horizontal or vertical lines. Either a line could be on, or it could be off. For the number zero, the horizontal middle line is off. The other six lines are on. So this is just a set of numbers. The first is missing the upper-left line, the middle line, and both of the lines on the right-hand side."

Rain traces the invisible spaces on each of six numbers. "We just need to ignore the markings and focus on the negative space. That makes the first number a four. Then two. Three. Six. One. Five."

Kella nods. "Okay. That's pretty smart. How about if we need to match the two pedestals up?"

"Yes!" Rain squeals. We must have to match one rock from this set of pedestals to the numbers on the other set.

"Right," Brohn says. "The pedestals must be weight-activated. We put the right rock from these pedestals on the right pedestal from over there, and the pulley should activate and lift the door to the box."

"Exactly. Now we just need to move the giant, insanely heavy rocks from one side of the room to the other."

Brohn pushes against one of the rocks, but it doesn't move. He pushes against it again, harder this time, with both hands and with all his weight behind the shove. The rock shifts about half an inch.

"This one looks like it's going to require some special skills," Karmine says with an undisguised look and a flick of his thumb in Terk's direction.

"Terk," Brohn says. "You're the only one of us strong enough to lift those things, so I guess you're up."

Terk beams at the prospect of being useful. Brohn and Kella give him directions for which rock to move across the room to which pedestal. Terk spits dramatically into each of his palms and rubs them together. He approaches the first pedestal, gripping the large rock between his forearms with his chest pressed against it. With a grunt, he heaves the rock off the pedestal. Guided by Cardyn and me, he does a half-walk, half-stagger across the room to the corresponding pedestal and pushes the big rock up onto it. The pedestal drops a bit, and, just as Brohn predicted, the door to the big box lifts up a few inches.

Kella drops down to the floor to peer inside of the small space at the bottom of the door.

"It's too dark," she says. "I don't see anything."

Brohn directs Terk to move the next rock. *Easier said than done,* I think.

But Terk is up to the task. He practically bounces with glee over to the next pedestal, which has an even bigger rock, practically a boulder, perched on top. Like before, he somehow heaves the rock to his chest, half-stumbles across the room, and pushes it up onto the proper pedestal as directed by Cardyn and me. The pedestal drops a bit, and the door raises a few more inches.

"I can see something!" Kella calls out. Her face is nearly inside the big box.

I call out for her to be careful. "If that thing comes down, it's going to cut your head off."

She scuttles back a bit and says, "Thanks. I do like my head. I'd rather keep it."

"What did you see?" Karmine asks, kneeling down next to her and peering up into the tall box.

"I think it's a key. Yes. Definitely a key of some kind. It's hanging from a hook at the top. If we can get the door up a few more feet, I can slip in and grab it."

"Your wish is my command," Terk says with breathy enthusiasm. One at a time, he lifts the remaining rocks up onto the proper pedestals. A small puff of smoke and debris explodes into the air as each rock lands on the pedestal's top. Each time, the door lifts up a little more until Kella declares there's enough room for her to get inside and reach the key.

"Just be careful," I warn again. The steel cable looks strong, but the metal door also looks insanely heavy. "Remember, we're a Conspiracy now. We can't afford to lose members to hideous box accidents."

Kella beams at me and promises to be quick. She ducks down under the door and disappears into the dark space. It takes just a split-second that feels like an hour, then she's back in flash with a big golden key in her hand.

Brohn inserts the key into the lock on the exit door, which swings open with a gentle creak. We charge through and down a flight of stairs to another door.

"Room Number Two," Brohn announces. "I think we're making good time."

This second room isn't all that big, and there doesn't seem to be much to it. Two of the walls are made of concrete blocks. The other two are brick. There are three puzzles laid out on stiff card-stock standing up on a long table in the middle of the room. On the end of the table is a locked box with four numbered dials.

I examine the box. "It's a four-digit code," I say. "I think the numbers for the code must come from the answers to the three puzzles."

"That makes sense," Rain says. She gives me an *I'm-proud-of-you* look, which I return with a grateful grin.

"So we solve the puzzles, open the box, and find...what? Another key?"

"Yes. I think so."

"Marvie," Karmine says, rubbing his hands together with glee.

Apparently, he no longer misses his guns and stabby things. "Let's get started!"

We gather together at the head of the long table and examine the first card. Under a simplistic set of pictures, an old-style kind of type reads:

It takes five machines five minutes to make five cupcakes. How long will it take for 100 machines to make 100 cupcakes?

"Easy," Terk says. "A hundred minutes."

Rain gives Terk a condescending look. "No, Terk. The hundred machines are working at the same rate as the five machines were. It'll take five minutes."

"Oh."

"Don't worry, Big Guy," Kella says with a laugh. "I was thinking the same thing."

Rain calls down the length of the table for me to input the number into the lock, and Cardyn stands next to me at the locked box as I turn the first dial to 5.

The others move on to the next card on the table, which displays another picture and another riddle, which Kella reads out loud:

***

Four prisoners are standing in the formation shown. Each is wearing either a black hat or a white hat. They are told that there are two black hats and two white hats in total.

Prisoner #1 can see the hat color of Prisoner #2 and Prisoner #3.

Prisoner #2 can see the hat color of Prisoner #3.

Neither Prisoner #3 nor Prisoner #4 can see the color of anyone else's hat.

They're not allowed to turn around or take off their hats.

Whichever prisoner is the first to correctly call out his own hat color will be set free.

Ten seconds go by before someone finally shouts out the correct answer.

. . .

Who was the first person to shout out his own hat color and be freed?

***

Rain taps her temple and her foot a few times in unison, which means she's concentrating. "I've got it," she exclaims. "It can't be Number Three or Four. They can't see anyone else anyway. If Number Two and Three had the same hat color as each other, Number One would've known and shouted out his own hat color right away. Since ten seconds have passed, he doesn't know. That means that Two and Three have different hat colors. Prisoner Two just has to shout out the opposite color of the hat of Prisoner Three. So the answer is 'two.'"

Down at my end of the long table, I turn the second dial to "2." The mechanism gives a satisfying click.

That leaves just puzzle number three. The stiff card contains a diagram of a parking lot, kind of like the one outside the school and at the grocery store back in the Valta. There are six numbered parking spaces with one of the numbers covered up by a parked car. Under the image is a single question:

What's the missing parking spot number?

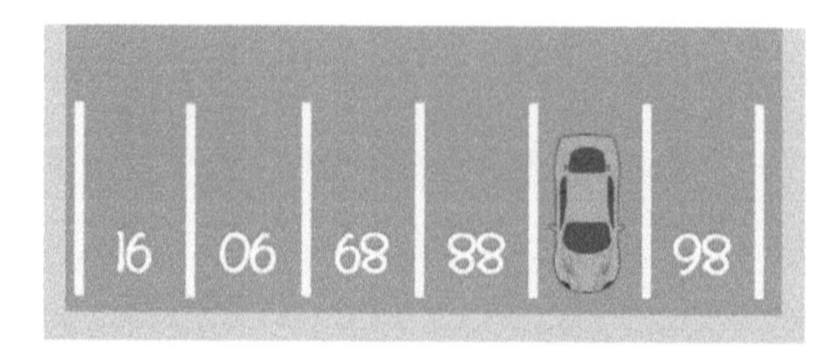

"What?" Kella whines. "It's impossible. It could be any number in the universe."

I have to agree. Other than the fact that they're all even numbers, I don't see any pattern.

"You're the math expert," Karmine says to Rain. "Can't you work something out?"

"I'm thinking!" Rain protests. "Just give me a minute."

Brohn looks up at the digital clock read-out above the door. "We don't exactly have a ton of minutes. Remember, we still have one more floor after this one."

"Okay," Rain says, her eyes on the ceiling, her fingers tapping out numbers on her thigh. "Sixteen mins six is ten. That's half the difference between sixty-eight and eighty-eight and exactly the difference between eight-eight and ninety-eight. And..."

"And?" Kella asks after Rain's long pause.

"And...I have no idea." Rain shakes her head, murmuring more to herself than to us. "Unless it's a matter of square roots. Or factorials. Maybe some sort of closed-line integral equation."

We all learned some math back in the Valta, but I have no idea how Rain remembers or even understands a lot of it. It's like she's half-human, half-computer. Still, she's got an edge to her voice, and her long black hair is already getting clumpy with sweat. She doesn't like not knowing the answers to things. She starts mumbling to herself as we look on helplessly. "Map coordinates? Degrees of a circle? Some sort of Pythagorean equation?"

I glance at the clock and back at Rain. I don't want to pressure her, but Brohn's right. The clock is ticking.

Rain stomps her foot. "It's not fair. There should be a clue or a key or an index, something more to go on that just a list of random numbers!"

"It's eight-seven," Amaranthine says.

"What?"

"The answer. It's eighty-seven."

We all stare at her. "How do you figure…?" Rain asks, her eyes in an angry squint.

Amaranthine spreads her fingers out over the card and spins it around so it's now upside down:

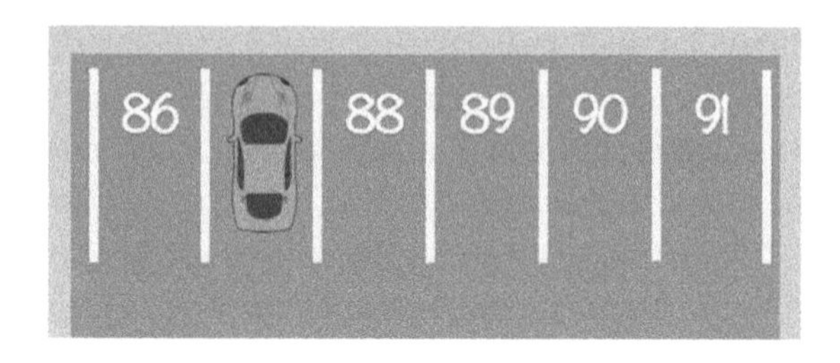

"SEE. EIGHTY-SEVEN."

"Manthy," Cardyn says with a beaming smile and a shake of his head, "sometimes I wish I knew how your brain works."

Amaranthine shrugs and walks over to the wall next to the exit door. She leans back with her arms folded and her head down like she's done and ready for an upright nap.

Rain tells me to go ahead with the locked box. I input "8" on the third dial and "7" on the last dial. The lock clicks, and the lid pops open.

Inside, as expected, is a key. Thankfully, there are no more tricks to figure out. The key slips easily into the lock on the exit door, and the eight of us file out one by one. We walk down a narrow set of steps that ends at another door. Like the last one, this one is unlocked and opens easily. Brohn leads us through into our final room.

The holo-clock above the exit door on the far side of the room is at fifty-two minutes. That leaves eight minutes to solve the final puzzle, get the last key, and get out of this room before we fail this test. I'm sure Hiller is out there on the other side of the door, probably jotting down notes on her little holo-pad and waiting for us to fail.

On the far side of the room from us are three large silver boxes sitting on top of another long metal table. Each box has a round red button in its upper left-hand corner. The box on the left has a statue of an obese gnome lying on its back, his hands folded on his swollen stomach. The middle box has seven versions of the same statue. The last box has four of them. The gnomes are chubby and cute. They remind me of pictures in the fairy tale books my dad used to read to me at night. Except these poor guys look like they're in serious discomfort with their round cheeks puffed out, their bellies distended, and their eyes clamped shut in a painful grimace.

Cardyn steps up to the statues and tries to lift them up. "Maybe there's a clue underneath one of them," he suggests with a shoulder shrug. But the pieces are attached to the top of the boxes and won't budge.

"Worth a try," I say.

"Wait. Look over here," Brohn calls out from over on the far side of the room. Hanging on the wall is a small framed photograph of the three silver boxes with the gnome statutes we were just standing in front of.

"Try turning it over," Kella suggests.

Brohn takes the picture down from the wall and turns it over in his hands. Sure enough, there's writing on the back, which Brohn shows us.

"It's a picture with another riddle," Terk says.

Rain steps forward and reads it out loud:

Four babies are sitting on each corner of a big square drawn on the ground.
At random, they each start crawling either clockwise or counter-clockwise along the lines of the square to a new corner.

What are the chances that at least two of the babies crash into each other before they each reach the next corner?

The final key is in the box with the answer. Choose correctly, exit the room. Choose wrong, lose more than just the game.

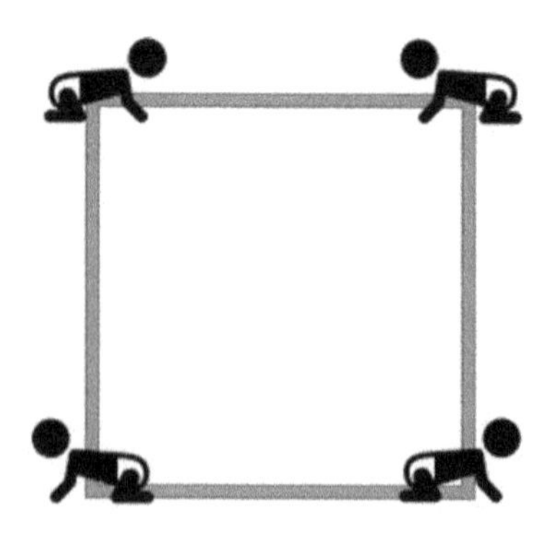

"That sounds pretty ominous," Karmine says. "Do you think 'lose more than just the game' is like some kind of a death threat or something?"

Brohn looks from the photo and back over to the actual silver boxes on the table. "Let's just worry about getting out of here. This place is starting to creep me out. The final key is in one of those boxes. We've got one shot at it." He calls for Amaranthine to join us, but she seems attached to the wall. "Come on," Brohn urges. "You're good at this stuff."

Amaranthine lowers her chin to her chest, looks up at him, and shakes her head. "I can't do it," she mumbles. "I don't know the answer."

"Wait. I can do it," Rain says. She puts her fingertips to her forehead. "Just let me think it through."

We step back, and it doesn't take long for Rain to announce that she has indeed figured it out.

"From the start, each kid can only go in one of two directions, right? That means the total possibilities are two times two times two times two, which is sixteen. Since there are two directions, their chances are two out of sixteen. That means the answer is reduced to one-eighth."

"Okay," Kella says slowly. "So how do we get from one-eighth to being able to open one of the boxes? And how do we know which box to open anyway?"

"That's what I'm still trying to figure out."

"Oh! I get it!" Cardyn says, pointing over to the box with the overfed gnome lying on top. One over eight. One *over-ate*. The box with the one bloated gnome. That's our box!"

Despite our tension, we can't help but laugh at the silly pun. We rush over to the table and gather around the left-hand box.

Cardyn presses the red button on the box with his palm, and a round panel on the face of the big metal container slides open. "Now what?"

"Maybe the key's inside?" Kella suggests.

I lean down and peer into the box. "I don't see anything. Too dark."

"Here," Terk says stepping forward. "Let me." Rolling up his sleeve, he gives us a big, crooked-toothed smile. "See?" he beams. "I'm good for more than just lifting heavy stuff."

Terk inserts his left arm until it's shoulder-deep inside the shiny box.

"Can you feel anything?"

"Yes. Not a key, though. Feels like…I don't know. Maybe a metal plate. It's cold, whatever it is."

"The far side of the box?" Brohn asks.

"No," Terk says as he leans further in. "I can't get my arm in deep enough to reach the far side."

"Can you move the plate or whatever it is you're feeling?"

Terk grimaces with effort. "I don't think so."

Suddenly, the words "INCORRECT INPUT" appear in glowing red on the box above the opening where Terk just inserted his arm.

We hear a loud thunk from inside the box, and Terk winces in pain.

"What is it?"

"Something just clamped onto my wrist."

Brohn lunges forward. "Can you pull loose?"

"Not sure. Probably."

Terk winces again as he tugs against whatever is in there holding on to him. Then he tugs harder, and his wince transforms into a grimace of pain. He tugs again, and the pain turns into agony.

"I'm stuck," he manages to murmur through clenched teeth.

Brohn and Karmine circle around behind the table and start running their hands along the edges of the box and feeling around under the table. "Maybe there's a release or a latch or something," Brohn says. He's trying to sound calm as he and Karmine circle back around to join us, but it's not working. "I think we're just going to have to—"

He's interrupted by the angry hum of something springing to life from inside the box.

Terk screams at the top of his lungs. It's a horrifying sound, one I haven't heard since the days of the bombings in the Valta.

"Get him out of there!" Kella shouts.

Brohn and Karmine each grab him by a shoulder and pull back with all their might.

The three of them tumble back to the floor in a heap. The rest of us jump out of the way so we don't get crushed. But the fear of being caught up in their fall quickly takes a back seat to the horror before us.

Terk's left arm has been severed right through his bicep, just below his shoulder.

The tissue and muscle at the base of what's left of his arm are blistered red and fused in an angry-looking patch. Whatever cut him seems to have cauterized the wound.

Terk is barely hanging on to consciousness. In a flash, Rain slings off her jacket and wraps it around the stump where Terk's arm used to be. She moves fast, but not fast enough to get the wound covered up before Terk manages to get a good look. His mouth hangs open. His eyes roll back, and he slumps down into Brohn's arms.

At the same time, a whoosh of gas fills the room, and a putrid cloud of yellow smoke begins to billow from a row of vents up by the ceiling.

Amaranthine is closest to where the smoke starts settling, and she turns around, startled. She covers her mouth with both hands and takes two steps back, but the smoke or gas or whatever it is acts fast. Manthy's eyelids flutter, and she stumbles down next to where Brohn and Rain are trying to tend to Terk. Brohn's able to catch her before she crashes to the ground. She leans in his arms, limp and unmoving.

"Everyone get down!" he cries out.

"We've got to get out of this room," Rain screams. "We need to find that last key!"

"The puzzle!" I shout. "I think I know what we did wrong!"

Without waiting for anyone to respond, I dash over and grab the photograph from Rain and drop to one knee. Card kneels down next to me, and we scan the puzzle together.

"See. That's what I was thinking, but I didn't say anything before. We're supposed to find out the chances of the kids crashing into each other, not *avoiding* a collision. We need to subtract one-eighth from one. That means *seven*-eighths. Seven over eight. Seven over-ate. It's the middle box."

Without stopping to think, I sprint back over and press the button on the middle box. Just like with the first box, a round panel slides open. I thrust my hand inside and feel around until I grab onto a lever. I pull it, and it gives a satisfying click. Behind us, the clock stops at three seconds, a vent kicks on and sucks the yellow smoke back up, and the big double doors swing open.

Hiller is standing there with Granden, Trench, Chucker, Kellerson and the two men from the medical crew.

Before we even have a chance to react, Kellerson and the med crew guys whisk Terk away, while Granden, Trench, Chucker, and Kellerson join forces to herd us out of the Delta Cube and out to the middle of the Agora. Still reeling from shock and coughing violently from inhaling traces of that yellow smoke, we're in a daze as the four guards position us onto the Capsule Pads and transport us down into the Silo. We stumble off the pads, trip across the room, and drop down onto our cots, the weight of what we've just witnessed pressing down on us like a tangible force.

Trying to choke down their coughing fits, Brohn and Rain tend to Amaranthine, who is coming to but still groggy. Karmine and Kella and I dash to the Shower Room where we kneel in front of toilets in separate stalls and vomit in unison. Three stalls down, I can hear Cardyn throwing up into another toilet.

When we've cleaned up, gotten our bearings, and are finally able to take a decent breath, we gather together on our cots in the Dormitory.

Rain is choking on her words. “It’s all my fault. I thought for sure I had the answer. I was so damn sure of myself, and really I was just being a cocky idiot.”

“I pressed the button,” Card says. His eyes are as red as Rain’s. He puts his fist to his forehead and drops his head down. “I practically told him to stick his hand into that thing.”

Kella has collapsed into Karmine’s arms. Her face is buried in his shoulder. Her voice is muffled, her body wracked with sobs. “I suggested there might be a key in that thing. It’s my fault as much as anybody’s.” Karmine’s face is wet with tears, but he holds his head up and looks at the ceiling as he strokes Kella’s hair.

“It’s my fault,” I mutter through my hands. Brohn gets up from his cot and comes over to sit next to me. For the first time, he wraps his strong arms around me and holds on tight. “I had a feeling…,” I mumble. “I knew there was something about the riddle…about the wording…but I didn’t react. I didn’t say anything.”

I never thought I could feel this miserable with Brohn’s arms around me. “It’s not your fault,” he says.

I’m sobbing now. I can barely get the words out. “I think Terk might say different,” I finally manage.

17

Our night in the Silo is different this time. There's no laughter. No chatter. No fun guessing games about what our next training assignment might be. No nursing our sore muscles and rehashing the events of the day.

I spend my time standing up and pacing around the room, then collapsing back down on my cot. The other six all perform some variation of my pattern, alternating between their cots and moving around the space like emotionally-exhausted zombies. The springs groan under us as if they're sympathetic to our pain.

I don't know why I bother wiping away my tears when they just keep coming back.

After hours of agonizing, I realize I have no idea how much time has passed, but I feel like I've been losing my mind for days now.

Brohn, who's still awake just like the rest of us, announces he's going to take a shower to clear his head. But he comes back a minute later to tell us the water's not working.

"Nothing?" I ask, thankful for a chance to think about something else. Anything other than Terk and his horrific injury is a blessing at this point. Each time I think of it, I feel an awful mix of nausea and guilt.

"Barely a trickle," Brohn says. He plops down next to me on my cot, lays a welcome hand on my knee, and asks how I'm holding up.

"I've been better," I confess. "I just can't get it out of my head. That image…"

"Me neither," he replies with a tensing of his jaw. "But maybe that's for the best. Keeping our thoughts on Terk, I mean. Maybe he'll recover faster if we keep sending him positive mental energy."

"Recover?" I ask, leaning away from him in disbelief. "You're assuming he's even still alive. Even if he is, he's not going to 'recover.' He didn't stub his toe or catch a cold. That box took his arm. Not even that. *Hiller* took his arm. She set us all up. And did you see how fast they took him away and hustled us all out of there?" I'm breathing hard now, trying not to start crying again. "Listen, Brohn," I say at last, "I've got a bad feeling about the way things have been going."

"How do you mean?"

Before I get a chance to explain, Cardyn and Rain, who have both headed into the Shower Room to try and figure out what's going on with our plumbing, come back out and sit together on Rain's cot. It's just as well, because I don't have all my theories sorted out in my head, and I wouldn't be surprised if Brohn thought I was just being a paranoid psycho.

"I heard what you said," Rain says. "And I think I know what you mean. Terk said something weeks ago, back when we were first recruited. Remember?"

"Back on the Transport Truck, right?" Card asks. "I was thinking the same thing."

Rain nods, but I shake my head. "I don't remember. What did he say?"

"He asked why we'd have to worry about getting hurt or killed if this was just training."

"So?"

"So, Kellerson never answered that question."

"Well, to be fair," I reply, "he didn't really answer any of our questions."

"That's exactly my point. Why build this massive facility, this 'Processor,' and dedicate all this time and resources into training us, but then be all hush-hush about certain parts of it? It doesn't make sense."

Karmine and Kella have been off in the Mess Hall having their own quiet conversation, but now they walk out and join us on the cots. Kella sits cross-legged at the head of hers, with Karmine next to her, his arm around her shoulders. She still seems shaken by the day's events. Although Karmine seems to want to comfort her, his red eyes and the way he keeps biting his bottom lip tell me he's barely holding things together himself. Our resident warrior's always talked a good game when it comes to the war against the Order. He all but reveled in his own injury.

But this is his first time getting an up-close look at the toll it can take. It's the first time for any of us.

"We heard what you were saying about Terk," Kella says after taking a deep breath. "Do you think...do think we're in real danger?"

At first, I assume she's asking Brohn. He's the guy everyone turns to when they have concerns and questions, after all. But when he doesn't say anything, I look up and realize everyone's looking at me.

"I don't know," I reply, trying to hide my shock. "But maybe that's not the question we should be asking."

"Then what is?" Karmine asks sullenly.

"Why does it seem like they *want* to hurt us?"

The room goes quiet for a few seconds, then Rain nods. "I agree. Whether what happened to Terk was a simple training accident, a sick lesson of some kind, or a deliberate attempt to weed one of us out…none of that matters. Kress has been knocked unconscious. Kar's had his arm fractured. Kella's got a broken bone under her eye. And now Terk. There have been *way* too many injuries for this to be a coincidence."

"Hurt is one thing," Kella says, nodding in agreement. "Having your arm literally cut off in some stupid training game is something else. Especially when we're supposed to be getting trained to fight the Order. Why subject us to something so dangerous? Especially Terk. He was the biggest and strongest of all of us. What good does it do to send him into combat with one arm?"

"I think we need to consider changing our approach," Brohn suggests quietly, looking around like he's afraid someone will overhear us. "We need to do a better job of keeping tabs on Hiller and her crew. See if we can figure out what's really going on. You know, watch the watchers."

"But how?" Kella asks. "They keep us down here half the time, and the other half, they've got men in towers with guns ready to take us out."

Raising his eyebrows, Cardyn shoots me a look that screams *Tell them.*

"Fine," I sigh. "Maybe I can help."

"How's that?" Brohn asks.

"You know about my connection with Render."

"I know you've had him for a long time."

"What's this about, Kress?" asks Rain.

I swallow hard, knowing that for the first time in my life, I'm about to betray my father by giving away his secret. "Our connection goes deeper than you might realize." I glance over at Cardyn. "Deeper than *any* of you realize." For a second, he looks surprised, even hurt by the revelation. "Sorry, Card. I told you there were some things I wanted to keep to myself."

I take off my jacket and extend my arms, wrists up. Wearing

just my black t-shirt, the markings on my forearms are clearly visible to the others.

"Your tattoos?" Kella asks. "We've seen them a million times. What about them?"

"That's the thing. They're not tattoos." I bite my lip, knowing I'm about to pass the point of no return. "They're a type of implant. My dad was working on this technology long before we even moved to the Valta." I turn to look at Brohn, recalling what I told him on the beach at Final Feast. "When the war started a few years before the first Recruitment, my dad was working with a bio-tech team. They were trying to come up with ways to bridge the Digital Divide."

"What's that?" Karmine asks.

"Honestly, I don't really know. Something about getting past the use of digital technology to understand itself. That's what Dad said, anyway. The idea was to see if digital technology could be blended with our human neuro networks. So instead of prosthetics and artificial body parts, where the tech is integrated with the body but still kind of different from it, the bio-tech would have merged them somehow. Instead of just A.I. where computers become more human, we humans would become more like computers, or something like that. Remember, Dad told me this stuff when I was still pretty little, so my memories might not be exactly crystal clear. Anyway," I say as I run my hands along the pattern of dots, curves, and lines embedded in my forearms, "these are kind of a prototype. I can input certain commands by tapping and tracing patterns that only I know into the array. They don't even need an external energy source since, technically, they're powered by my brain."

"And they let you communicate with your bird?" Rain asks. By now, Amaranthine, who was lying down on her cot, is sitting up, listening attentively.

"Not exactly," I reply, frustrated that I'm doing such a terrible job of explaining how it all works.

"What then?"

"They *enhance* my ability to communicate with my bird. No. That's not exactly it, either. They enable us to communicate with each other. It's not exactly that we talk to each other—more like we can kind of see through each other's eyes or minds. We can tap into each other's feelings. Honestly, I'm not sure how it all works, myself. And it kind of comes and goes. It's not like some super power I can control."

"Yet," Cardyn says.

I give him a *thank you* shrug for his optimism.

Brohn leans forward and takes my forearm in his hand. For a second, his fingers hover over the black array of lines and curves. He looks at me, questioning, and I tell him it's okay. "You can touch them."

He traces the curved lines and gently taps at the black dots with his fingers. I know he's just being curious. He's anxious to get to the bottom of our situation, to figure out a way to figure out what's going on in the Processor. He's not being intimate or anything...at least, I don't think he is until I look into his eyes, which are fixed on my own, rather than at the design on my arm.

It feels nice to have my arm in his hand, his finger dragging lightly across my skin. It feels calming after the events with Terk. It just feels...good.

Finally, he lets go and abruptly rises to his feet to move over and sit on his own cot. "So you think you can use this thing...this bio-tech whatever connection to help us out?" His tone is all business, and just like that, Brohn is back to keeping his distance.

"I'm not sure," I reply. "I can try to connect with Render again. I've done it before. But there's no guarantee it'll work."

"Maybe not. But there's a definite guarantee that it's our only chance, so I think I can guarantee that it's definitely worth a shot."

"Okay," I say. "I'll do it."

Everyone gathers around, scrunching in closer on their cots

to get next to me. Even Amaranthine has moved over to watch. But being the center of attention is making me tense. I don't know if I'll be able to access Render when I'm a bundle of nerves and perspiration.

I tap out the pattern on my array that opens up the connection. Back in the Valta, I learned early on that if I don't keep the access closed most of the time, I get filled with a kind of feedback sensory overload. It happened for the first time when I was a Neo. I was off in the woods experimenting with my connection to Render, and I must have left the connection open too long because the overload hit me like a wrecking ball. I wound up passed out on the forest floor until I woke up the next morning with a massive migraine and a lesson painfully learned.

With the connection now open, I close my eyes and reach out with my mind for Render.

Where are you?

At first, I think I'm the one asking him the question.

But then I realize it's Render who's asking me.

I'm underground. I'm with our friends. Our family. Our Conspiracy. I'm safe.

Images of the darkening red of the sky flash in my mind. Clusters of tree leaves and wild tangles of branches. There's a flurry of motion. The black tips of Render's wings. More flashes of sky mixed in with the charred ground. The images weave in and out of each other like a braid, and I get lightheaded and dizzy.

Then it all disappears.

"So what happened?" Brohn asks when I've opened my eyes again. "Were you able to connect?"

I shake my head. "Not much. At least not well. It could be because it's getting dark up there. Ravens don't usually fly at night. They roost. Render needs to sleep like the rest of us."

"You don't sound convinced that the problem is the time of day, though."

"That's because I'm not." I can feel the weight of sadness overtaking me all over again, but I swallow hard and push it away. "The connection hasn't been the same for a while now. I might be...I mean, it could be that I'm...losing it."

"So what should we do?" Cardyn asks.

"We wait until tomorrow," Brohn says, sounding slightly annoyed that Cardyn's so nonchalant about my obvious pain. "When we get up to the Agora, we're going to have to deal with this situation with Terk."

Everyone in the room knows what he's talking about, and we all agree. We need to head this thing off now, get some real answers, before things get out of hand and we all wind up like Terk.

Or worse.

BUT "TOMORROW" never comes. Not really.

When we get up the next morning, we do what we've done every morning for the past several weeks: Change into our Agora clothes. Check for updates to our scores on the viz-screen. Eat a small meal of a dry biscuit, some protein cakes, and a bottle of powdered energy drink, all served on a metal tray that slides out from a chute in the Mess Hall wall.

When we're done, we head over to the Capsule Pads to get lifted up to ground level

But not today.

The Capsules don't activate when we step onto the pads.

"Maybe the system's down?" Card suggests.

An immediate sense of foreboding tenses my muscles up. This place works like a well-oiled machine. It makes no sense that suddenly the Capsules would break down.

"Maybe," Brohn says. "But then why no contact? Why hasn't

anyone sent us a message through the viz-screen telling us to sit tight while they fix whatever it is that's broken?"

"Screw this!" Kella says angrily. "After yesterday, maybe they realize we need a day off. Anyway, I'm taking it." She steps off her Capsule Pad and heads back to her cot, where she drops down heavily on her back, one arm slung over her eyes. I don't know if it's to keep out the light, or so we don't see that she's started crying tears of rage again.

"I'm with her," Karmine says. He follows Kella over and plops down next to her. He stretches out on his side with his elbow on a pillow and his head propped up on his hand. "If they want us, let them come get us."

Not that I agree with his bluster, but we don't exactly have any other choice. We have no way to communicate with Granden and Trench, which means we're stuck here until something happens.

Following Kella and Karmine's lead, we all return to our cots, where we sit and consider our options.

As it turns out, there aren't any.

"Maybe try your Render connection?" Card suggests.

"I'll try, but I can't promise anything."

I do, but this time there's absolutely nothing. I know it's not just a matter of me being underground. I've communicated with him from down here before.

The connection is just gone.

So we do the only thing we can: we wait. Time passes...and passes.

I HAVE no real idea how long we've been down here. It's been at least six days now, based on the number of meal trays that have come down the chute. But it feels like a lifetime. We've all lived through drama before, here *and* back in the Valta. But there was always something to do. Somewhere to go. Trapped like this in an underground bunker, everything seems magnified. Every second feels like an hour. I can feel the tension around me, and at times I'm not sure if it's my own rage heating the air, or everyone else's.

To my dismay, Brohn and Rain seem to be using the time to get closer. They sit together in the Mess Hall, heads together, talking quietly. I try not to pay attention, but the truth is that when Brohn's out of the room, I miss him. I don't know what they talk about. All I know is that I'm back to envying Rain for her easy ability to be so friendly with him.

Like a loyal Golden Retriever, Cardyn's been keeping me company. To be honest, at first I found his constant chatting annoying, but now it helps keep my mind off the fact that we're imprisoned below the earth, serving a sentence that for all we know may last the rest of our lives.

Karmine and Kella are almost fully recovered from their injuries, and they seem reenergized from our forced rest period. They seem even more determined than ever to complete the training and head out into the world to slaughter the Order.

Amaranthine hasn't moved in I don't know how long. I check on her from time to time to make sure she's not dead. Occasionally, I peel back a corner of the covers from over her head. She always shouts at me to leave her alone before covering herself back up again.

From time to time, I climb out of my cot and lumber over to the viz-screen. I don't know why I bother checking. The scores haven't moved in days. Not that we've done anything to make them move one way or the other.

Everyone is desperate to know what happened to Terk. We all agree that we're sure he's fine, that the medics are taking great care of him, and he'll be back with our Conspiracy in no time. No one says anything about his arm. At first, no one expresses doubt that everything will be fine. Eventually, though, any optimism we've been cultivating dries up.

At one point, Card finally asks the questions I suspect we've all been thinking.

"Do you think there's anyone left up there? Or...maybe they forgot we're down here?"

"They didn't forget about us," Kella replies. "We're still getting our meals through the chutes every day."

"That could be automated, though," I point out. "We've never been told how they decide what to feed us, or how the serving system works."

"Maybe this is part of our training," Brohn suggests. "To see how we react in stressful, confined conditions."

"Great," I reply. "They probably want to see if we'll all murder each other. Hiller's probably up there taking bets on who will get eaten first when the killings begin."

Almost everyone laughs, for the first time in days.

Everyone except for Karmine.

"What if the Order's taken over?" he asks. "What if they found the Processor, invaded it, and everyone up there is dead, and it's only a matter of time before they find us down here and kill us—or else they don't even realize we're down here, and we're left to die?"

"Let's not go crazy, Kar," Brohn says. "Yes. All that's possible. But I doubt it's *probable*."

"Right," Rain says. "It's like Occam's Razor, remember?"

I do remember. Rain taught it to us back when she and Karmine teamed up with some of the Sixteens of the 2040 Cohort for a few months to teach us about game theory and strategy. "When facing an uncertain situation or a complex problem," they taught us, "the simplest answer tends to be the right one."

"So what's the simplest answer?" Amaranthine mumbles from under the covers of her cot.

We all stare at each other for a second, stunned to hear her voice. Other than yelling at me to leave her alone, it's the first time Amaranthine's spoken since we've been locked down here.

"It has to be a test, like Brohn said," Rain says finally. "Everything we've faced so far has been a test. Why should this be any different?"

Cardyn breathes a huge sigh of relief. "A test I can handle," he says. "I just don't want to die down here."

"You think dying up there is going to be that much better?" Brohn barks. All of a sudden, he sounds angry, but I'm not sure why.

Even Cardyn looks surprised. "I don't know. I guess not. I just thought..."

"What? That we'd slaughter the Order and live happily ever after?" Brohn stands up now and starts pacing at the foot of his cot. "Don't you see? Kress. Karmine. Kella. Terk. Their injuries. This is more than just training. Hiller and her goons are ramping things up. They're trying to break us down, not build us up."

"If it's not training, then what is it?"

"It's war games," Kella says.

Brohn shakes his head. "No. This is something else. It's like... like we're being weeded out. It's an elimination game. And if we don't do something, it's going to turn into an extermination game."

I lie back on my cot with that gloomy possibility rattling around in my head. Absently, I run my fingers along my wrists and forearms. The thick black bands and graceful curves of the pattern feel warm to the touch. Maybe it's a trick of the dim light in the Silo, but they almost seem to glow.

To my pleasant surprise, my connection with Render seems to be coming back. It's faint, but I definitely feel something. Card starts to say something to me, but I tell him I need to concentrate for a minute.

"Your Render connection?" he asks. "It's working?"

I nod and close my eyes, trying to make out what I'm seeing and feeling. The images are fuzzy. I can make out the flat green Agora and the silver Halo hovering high overhead. The eight black buildings are also easy to identify. There are flashes of movement here and there. I think it's Chucker and Kellerson and the other guards in the turrets in front of each building. But then everything fades again, and I'm left back in the bunker with the others staring at me, asking me what's happening.

"I'm not sure," I say. "But I think Render knows we're stuck down here. He knows we're angry about Terk and afraid we might be trapped forever. I know it probably sounds insane, but I think he's telling us we're not alone. He's telling us not to worry."

Normally, that would be small consolation, but these are extreme times, and we're all neck-deep in extreme emotions. As I pass along Render's message, I'm answered with six deep sighs of relief.

We all sleep that night. Still angry and afraid, but also hopeful, for the first time in days.

Maybe it's a coincidence. Maybe not. But when we wake up, we check the viz-screen, and our numbers have finally changed. Not by much—mine have gone up only slightly—but they're definitely different. Like a flock of birds moving in unison we dash over to the Capsule Pads. This time, they light up like they're supposed to and whoosh us to the surface.

The second the Capsules open, Brohn leaps out at Granden, to the surprise of the rest of us. Caught off guard, Granden gets slammed down, his head bouncing hard on the ground.

Trench darts over before Brohn can land another punch. He flies at Brohn, knocking them both off of Granden and onto the ground just by my feet.

Karmine and Kella shove me out of the way and leap into the fray. Karmine grabs Trench around the throat and starts dragging him off Brohn while Kella jumps in front of Brohn and squares off against Granden who is just rising to his feet, startled and furious.

Granden drives his forearm into the side of Kella's head, and she stumbles ten feet before dropping to her hands and knees. A few feet away, freed now from Karmine's grip, Trench leaps to his feet and strikes out at Karmine with a powerful side kick. Karmine manages to partially block the strike. He staggers but keeps his balance enough to land a straight counter-punch to Trench's abdomen. Trench doubles over as Karmine and Brohn both close in on him.

Before Card, Amaranthine, or I can react, the crack of gunfire rings out. The air around us is peppered with bullets, and the three of us hit the ground.

Chucker, Kellerson, and two other guards whose names I don't know thunder up to where Kella is just getting to her feet. They point their guns at all of us and order us to step back.

Trench grabs Brohn by one arm. Granden grabs him by the other.

"How could you do that to Terk?" Brohn shouts up at the Observation and Assessment Halo. There's no answer, of course. The huge silver ring just keeps spinning.

18

All seven of us drop to the ground. It's an act of exhaustion and surrender, but also one of defiance. Forget standing at attention. Forget military obedience. Hiller and her crew broke the rules. Training us to fight the Order means training us to survive. When they compromised that, they compromised the entire training program and our trust in them. In the one place in the world we should feel safe, we now feel danger lurking around every corner. But we can't quit. We can't just walk out of the Processor, through the woods, and out into the war. There's nothing for us to do, but they can't stop us from doing that nothing together. So we plop down on the Agora grass, exhausted, down, but not yet defeated.

Granden and Trench stand over us, guns drawn, ready to meet any more resistance with deadly force if necessary.

In the distance, we see Hiller in her white lab coat storming toward us. Her ponytail is pulled back so tight I can count the comb marks in her hair from here. I'm used to seeing her flanked by guards, but now she's alone. She also doesn't look as angry as I would have expected considering we just attacked our Trainers. She obviously takes her job seriously, but maybe she's prepared to be reasonable. Maybe she's got a heart buried under that starched lab coat somewhere after all.

Granden and Trench step to the side to let her pass. Unlike Hiller, they look unreasonable, heartless, and still pretty angry. The one thing they don't look is surprised. Makes sense. After seeing what happened to Terk and then being trapped underground for nearly a week, no one could blame us for being belligerent, fed up, and totally on edge.

Next to me, Brohn tenses up like he's going to leap to his feet and attack Hiller. His face is a twisted knot of frustration, vengeance, and rage. He presses his palms to the ground and starts to gather his legs under him. A forceful hand, palm out, from Chucker stops him before he can get going.

"I think we all need to take a breath and get some perspective here," Hiller says. She's not exactly happy about this situation, but her face and voice are calm.

Now Brohn does stand up. Chucker steps forward, but this time Brohn ignores him. The rest of us follow suit and stand in solidarity with him as he points an accusing finger at Hiller. "I think you can take your perspective and shove it up your—"

Rain cuts him off with sharp look and an even sharper elbow to the side of his arm.

"What I think Brohn means," she says, "is that we'd like, no—we demand some answers. About Terk. About being trapped down in the Silo for days."

Trench's lip curls into a snarl. "We don't care what you'd like, Recruit. You're here for us, not the other way around."

Hiller gives Trench a gentle "down, boy" look. He's instinctively put his hand on his gun, but Hiller covers his hand with hers before stepping forward.

"We're not the enemy here," she says. "We're as human as you. And with many of our resources limited by the war, we're as subject to problems as anyone else. I know we're supposed to be this big, flawless machine that churns out soldiers for the nation without any glitches or hiccups. But we've been as affected by the war as anyone else. Even the big Arcos being built are in limbo temporarily while we try to repel some of the latest incursions by the Order. I assure you, those people are pure killers, and they won't stop until we're all dead. We needed to devote some of our resources to one of the other Processors that just barely survived one of their drone strikes."

"But why Terk?" Brohn asks, pointing back to the round seam in the Agora where the Capsule Pads rise and fall. "Why not let us see him? Why keep us trapped down there?" His voice is insistent rather than pleading. It's the voice of a leader, of a full-grown man. These aren't rhetorical questions. Brohn is demanding real answers.

"We lost power," Hiller assures him. "You're kept isolated here in the Processor and down in the Silo for your own protection. But I admit it: That protection backfired on us. The same protocols we have in place to keep you safe also kept you isolated while we worked out some kinks in the system."

"And you couldn't contact us?" Karmine asks, his voice an undisguised sneer of rage. "Let us know what was going on so we weren't freaking out? We didn't know if everyone up here was gone or dead or what."

"Again, my apologies. Our communication and security systems are linked. We've argued over whether or not they should be. There are advantages and disadvantages. The big disadvantage, as we've all just discovered, is that if one system goes down, the other goes down with it."

I look over at Brohn for a clue about where to go from here. He gives me a quick glance and shakes his head. We all pick up on his "stand down for now" signal. The tension drops a level, and we shuffle toward each other into a slightly tighter group.

Granden's comm-link buzzes. He holds his wrist to his ear and then leans over to say something to Hiller. As she returns his whisper, Cardyn tugs at my sleeve. "Are you buying this twaddle?"

I shrug. "I guess," I say out of the side of my mouth. "What choice do we have?"

Cardyn starts to say something to me about making our own choices for a change when Hiller and Granden finish their little side conversation. Turning back to us, Hiller tells us that the systems are all back up and running. "Communication. Security. The Agora. The Catalysts. The Cubes. Everything should be smooth sailing from here," she says. "And Sergeant Granden here has just informed me that updates to the Agora have been completed. If things keep progressing, you're on your way to being the best class we've ever seen. There's even been word that President Krug himself has taken a special interest in your Cohort. Seems some of you have talents we've never seen before, talents that might just help us turn this war around."

For a second, I'm terrified that she's talking to me, that she knows about Render. But she doesn't single me out or give me a second look. In fact, her gaze lingers over Brohn and then Amaranthine before turning back to Granden and Trench.

"Gentlemen, our Recruits have suffered a loss. But we need to continue with their training. The survival of our nation depends on it. We lost over three thousand men, women, and children in the Order's latest drone attack. It was a coordinated effort designed to cripple our Southern Processor, derail our rebuilding efforts, and destroy our morale. They have failed. And with the help of this Cohort, they will continue to fail until they are finally defeated once and for all."

"What about Terk?" Karmine asks. The rest of us have followed Brohn's unspoken message to stand down, but Kar is still giving off some pretty serious attack-mode vibes. The knuckles on his right hand are red from where he hit Trench, and both of his fists are balled up tight and aching for action.

"I assure you, we take this as seriously as you do." Hiller's voice is soft and soothing. She's practically cooing. She points to the last of the eight black buildings. "Terk is in the Theta Cube's med-lab, being given the absolute best care. We're even arranging for him to be fitted with a prosthetic arm. Top of the line. He won't just be good as new. He'll be better."

"When can we see him?" Brohn asks.

"Soon. He needs to rest and rehab first. In the meantime, you need to get on with your training. There's not much time."

"What do you mean?"

Hiller sighs and looks genuinely distressed. She exchanges a look with Granden and Trench before dropping her head. She starts to pace in front of us, her eyes alternating between us and the lush grass of the Agora. "Okay. Look. I'll level with you. You might be the last batch of Recruits. The war against the Order isn't going as well as we'd like. They've cut off many of our supply chains and transport routes. That includes our access to the remaining free towns like the Valta where we'd be able to recruit more soldiers for our army. Intel suggests that the Order is getting ready to make a final push to invade all four of our Select Processor facilities at once, including this one."

"Four?"

"Yes. There are actually twenty-five Processors like this. But they're much bigger. Soldier-factories. Four of the Processors have been designated as 'Select.' They're built for special cases." She gives us a long look and a sweep of her hand. "Basically, for you."

"We're honored," Brohn says, his voice an unmistakable blend of challenge and contempt. "Why would they go after the smaller Processors? Why come after us at all?"

"Killing you helps them kill the rest of us. They're preparing to end the war. In their favor."

Rain steps forward, her head even with Brohn's shoulder. "But President Krug always talked about how well things were going."

"They were going well. For a while. But we may have overestimated our own strength and underestimated our enemy's resolve. So you see, we don't have the luxury of wasting time or resources."

"So the fate of the war rests on our shoulders?" I ask, half incredulous, half terrified.

"Not just yours. There are still the other three Select Processors. But yes, you represent what could be our last chance to turn things around. As our training has gotten more sophisticated, we've been able to turn our best and brightest even better and brighter. Every minute of your day, every movement, challenge, puzzle, and physical test is carefully calibrated to ensure that when the time comes, you'll be able to unlock talents you never knew you had. Your Cohort is the culmination of decades of research and experimentation. I'm sorry that your friend Terk had to suffer his injury as a result of all that. I really am. I like Terk. I like all of you. But now is not the time for emotions, especially mourning or regret."

Hiller backs off for a minute, gesturing to one of the large, dark buildings looming in the background.

"Now it's time for building number five. Epsilon Cube. Believe it or not, you might just enjoy it. If nothing else, it'll take your minds off of Terk. He's in good hands. So you need to re-focus on the larger picture. The next training is for hostage rescue. It'll teach you a bit about how the Eastern Order operates, how they move and strategize. It'll give you a tiny taste of how ruthless they can be as well. But maybe more important, it'll show you and us how you operate under real pressure. I'm heading over to Eta Cube to attend to Terk right after I get you set up for your next challenge. Let me take care of your friend. You take care of showing us what you can do in this exercise. And don't worry. You can't get hurt. It's a Virtual Reality sim."

"Really?" Karmine asks with a small, restrained smile. He

seems to regret dropping his guard, though, and his old sneer quickly returns to his face.

Granden steps forward. He looks as tired as I feel, but he manages a perky smile of his own. “The revamped VR-sim is the newest and best tool in our training arsenal. The sim will give you combat conditions and full sensory experiences but with virtual bodies in a virtual space. You’ll look and sound like yourself. You may even experience sensory perceptions similar to the ones you experience in the real world. But you’ll be safe. Basically immortal.”

“Follow me,” Hiller says grandly as she leads the way to the Epsilon Cube. “Time for you to experience some Virtual Reality.”

Sounds good to me.

I’ve had enough *real* reality to last a lifetime.

19

As we've done with the previous Cubes, we pass under the watchtower turret, walk through the fenced-in path up to the large black building with "ε," the Epsilon symbol, posted above the door.

Hiller leads the way, Granden and Trench following along behind. We walk up a flight of stairs and over to sliding steel door that leads into a small room with viz-screens and holographic input panels hovering in front of the walls. In the center of the room are eight partially reclining console chairs facing each other in a circle. The chairs look oddly comfortable considering how cold and mechanical the rest of the room looks.

After telling us she'll be in a monitoring station just down the hall, Hiller turns us over to Granden and Trench who invite us to sit in the chairs. We nestle in, but any sense of comfort we might have had quickly vanishes as we all look at the empty chair Terk would normally occupy.

I swallow hard. A Conspiracy doesn't work if everyone's not on board. And right now, there's a big hole in our little family.

Granden and Trench walk around the perimeter of our circle of chairs. They have us lean forward one at time as they scan some kind of device over the Biscuits in our right shoulder blades. After that, they tell us to lean back and relax.

A moment later, Hiller's voice comes at us from every direction at once with instructions for our VR mission. "The Eastern Order has taken hostages. They're holding President Krug, his son, and a four-man security detail in an office at the top floor of an abandoned auto-parts warehouse. Your job is a simple search and rescue mission. Make your way to the top of the warehouse. Overcome enemy resistance along the way. Save the hostages. Get out alive. The sim won't stop until the mission is completed. Which means you could be plugged in for a short time or for a very long time. If you fail, the mission resets, and you start again. Understood?"

Except for Amaranthine, who's preoccupied and fidgeting with a small bundle of wires on the side of her chair, we all say, "Yes" into the air.

"Sergeant Granden will now prepare you for the VR-sim."

Granden taps a code into a holographic input panel in the air in front of him. In front of us, eight thin metal arms descend from a compartment in the ceiling. They're shiny like polished steel but supple as a rubber garden hose. They seem almost alive, like the flexing arms of a robot octopus. Octobot? Roboctopus? I think for a second we're about to be shot or blasted with some kind of acid. Granden makes his voice gentle when he sees the shocked expression on our faces. "They're optic-arm scanners," he explains. "They'll scan VR contact modules directly onto your eyes. They'll interface with your sensory synapses. You'll see and feel and sense in the sim almost like you do in the real world. Don't worry. It's just a trick we play on your brain. Nothing permanent, and we'll remove the modules after the sim with no harm done."

Cardyn isn't pacified. "That thing's not sticking anything into my eyes!" he protests, shrinking into his chair. He squints hard and turns his head.

"Don't be such a baby," Kella calls out with a teasing laugh from her reclining console just across from him.

"I'm not a baby," Cardyn insists.

"Then why do you look like you're refusing to eat your peas?"

Cardyn sticks his tongue out at her, grips his console's armrests, and sits up—wide eyed and clamp-jawed—to face the oncoming octopus arm. It draws in close and fires a pair of thin blue lights right into Cardyn's eyes. He blinks a few times and turns to me. "That wasn't so bad," he admits.

I'm surprisingly not nervous about it, and I open my eyes wide to receive the modules. After what we've been through the past few days, I'm anxious to do some serious escaping from the real world.

Kella leans back in her chair, her eyes wide open as the optic-arm in front of her scans the VR contact lenses onto her eyes. "Doesn't feel right without Terk, does it?"

"No," Karmine agrees. "That big oaf better be all right, or..."

Brohn reaches over and gives Karmine's shoulder a comforting shake. "We all feel the same way, Kar. Let's get through this, get Terk back, get our deployments, and get the hell out of this place."

The optic-arms scan the VR modules onto Rain next and then Amaranthine before slithering back into the ceiling.

Granden skims his fingers on the holographic input panel and tells us he's activating the sim. "You'll be inside in about five seconds," he says.

As he passes behind my console chair, he leans down and whispers, "You need to be part of the sim to win it. And be careful. Recruits have died in these chairs."

"Wait. What?"

I must have misheard. But I don't have time to follow up. Granden turns away and doesn't look back. I repeat his words in my head. His tone. The look on his face. But nothing implies he was joking. Before I have a chance to call out to him or consult with the others, the world disappears in a flash of white. A single eye-blink later, and I'm standing with the other Recruits just outside the front lobby of a giant steel-walled and windowless warehouse. The place is as tall as the Cubes, about four or five stories high, but it's a ragged structure, streaked with dirt and rust. The rest of the world around the warehouse is pure white. No. Not even white. More like an absence of white. An absence of everything. Like whoever designed this program didn't worry about any details of the world other than the warehouse. The warehouse is realistically solid down to every grimy detail. Everything else around it is...non-existent. If "blank" were a crayon color, this would be it.

We turn back to the warehouse where the outer doors have just opened on their own. We step into the lobby and stop to have a good look around at ourselves and at each other.

It's us. But it's also not us at all. We all walk around in the warehouse lobby, swinging our arms and marveling at this virtual version of ourselves. On the surface, our digital avatars look almost exactly like us. Almost. There's something not quite right, though. Maybe it's the way we move. So smooth, like we're strutting. Like we don't have a care in the world. It never occurred to me before how much of our feelings are projected in something as simple as the way we walk. Or the weirdness could be the odd sensation of weightlessness. I feel the lobby floor under my feet, but it feels distant and softer than it should. Or maybe it's our clothes. Eight-inch, lightweight black leather combat boots. Charcoal-gray cargo pants embedded with a black and green camo design. Black military tactical vests with multiple pockets, pulled on tight with side grip tab-closures. The clothes all move as we do, kind of like real clothes. Only the wrinkles and creases don't move exactly the way I'd expect them to. It's like they respond a split-second too slow or even too fast, like they're anticipating our movements instead of just moving in accordance with the physical rules of the real world. Our looks are a bit off, too, although I can't quite put my finger on what it is. Everything's there. My forearm "tattoos" in exact detail. Cardyn's full lips and the small constellation of freckles on his cheeks. Karmine's chipped tooth. Kella's long blonde hair and high cheekbones. Rain's jet-black hair and olive skin. Brohn's stubble and arched eyebrows. Amaranthine's brooding eyes and messy shoals of hair.

Cardyn says, "Marvie" and stretches his arms out in front of himself, wiggling his fingers to make sure they work. His voice sounds right. Maybe a little tinny. Or is that just my imagination at work? Am I seeing what I'm seeing or only what I expect to see and hearing what I expect to hear?

I think that what's wrong is that everything about us is a little too…perfect. Where is my insecurity? Or Rain's genius? Or Karmine's never-say-die attitude? Where is Kella's steely determination? Or Brohn's enviable blend of confidence and kindness? Where is Cardyn's friendship and defensiveness of his friends? I didn't used to think of such things as visible, but looking around at our avatars, I feel like I'm looking at us, just minus the souls.

"Guys. Before we got…zapped into here or whatever, Granden said something to me I'm sure I must have misheard."

"What'd he say?" Card asks.

"Something about being part of the sim and other Recruits dying."

"That sounds ominous," Rain says with a pensive squint.

"More like creepy as hell," Karmine pipes in.

Kella shakes her head. Her digitally-created blond hair falls in waves on her shoulders and catches the light almost like it does in the real world. "It could just be a motivational thing. You know, 'get your head in the game' and all."

"What about the part about dying?" I ask.

Kella shrugs and glances down at her perfect digital body.

"Our avatars can probably die. Doesn't mean anything bad will happen to the real us."

"I guess."

"Hey troops," Brohn calls out, pointing to a rack of weapons and a digital count-down chronometer that's just materialized into the wall next to us. "Looks like we need to get armed and on our way."

The clock starts counting down from fifteen minutes.

The seven of us approach the rack in a line to collect our weapons. Sig Sauers. Magpuls. And two Bolt-Action .338 Gen 2030 rifles. We attach suppressors to each weapon to act as silencers and to contain muzzle flashes like we've been taught. Then we check our ammo like we've also been taught to do.

The guns look and feel just like the weapons we trained on back in the Agora. I know it's just artificial sensory inputs, but with my eyes closed, I wouldn't be able to tell the difference between this and the real thing.

Karmine and Kella take the rifles. The rest of us take a combination of the other weapons, tucking them into our holsters and waistbands.

"Follow me," Brohn says, as he leads us to the main doors.

Follow me. He doesn't even really have to say it. Avatar or not, leadership is built right into his character.

Flanked by Karmine and Kella and their two big rifles, Brohn leads us through the metal double-doors from the lobby into the warehouse.

The place is huge, empty and cluttered at the same time. Orange-colored racks of old auto and airplane parts tower up in the expansive space. The shelves are stocked full of crates, overflowing metal bins, and palettes of parts and tools covered in clear plastic bags. Appliance-lifters, trolleys, grav transport skids, and all sorts of assorted warehouse equipment litter the aisles. Thick spools of copper-colored cable sit just inside the warehouse entrance as we step in. The ground is cold concrete, pitted in places and with long, jagged cracks running through its surface. On the far side of the warehouse, leading up to the mezzanine level and barely visible from this far away, is a rickety-looking and rusted out metal staircase. Painted red, it rises high up into the warehouse, stops at a landing, and then continues up to a bank of offices. The office windows seem to be covered with thick curtains or boarded up from the inside. It's hard to tell from here. Thin bits of light shine through the cracks around the edges. The light is interrupted by the shadows of figures passing by on the other side.

"They must be in there," Brohn says.

"We'd better be careful," Rain warns. She points around at the racks and at the large wooden crates and heavy moving-equipment cluttering the spaces between rows. "Lots of places for bad guys to hide."

"Good guys, too. We'll use the crates and storage racks for cover. We can bounce from one safe spot to the next. We'll head over to the far side of the warehouse. See if we can get to those stairs. If we do this right, we can get up to the office and rescue the hostages before anyone knows we're here."

"The stealthy approach. Not nearly as much fun as a good ol' frontal assault," Karmine says.

"Consider this silent but deadly."

Brohn leads us in a jogging crouch down one row of storage racks and up another. We get to the end of the next row before we encounter our first resistance. We catch one of the Order off guard. He's got his back to us and is fiddling with his weapon. He's got it in pieces on top of one of the big wooden crates. One at a time, he holds parts of his gun up to his eye and then up to the light. Something in his program alerts him to our presence. He whips around, drawing a small pistol from inside his jacket.

Kella drops him with a single "silent but deadly" shot to the head. He slumps down against the crate and slides silently to the floor before pixilating out of existence.

Kella walks over and taps her toe against the ground where the man just was. "See how real he looked?"

"Marvie," Karmine says. "Real or not, that was a terrific kill shot."

Kella beams. She and Karmine exchange a high-five, and we continue along toward the red metal staircase.

"Hold it," Brohn hisses. We all stop and automatically drop into a recon-cover formation with me, Card, and Amaranthine ducking behind some auto equipment on the bottom shelf while Brohn drops down to the right with his back to a broken-down appliance-lifter. Karmine drops to a knee behind Kella. Both of them raise their rifles to the ready position, careful not to expose too much of themselves or their weapons to an enemy's potential line of sight.

I hate to say it, but Granden and Trench trained us well. We move as a team, fluidly and totally in synch. Like we're reading each other's minds.

Up ahead, I count ten guards on patrol. Their uniforms are standard military issue like ours, only orange and brown instead of black and green. The men's faces are dark and angry, mouths contorted in menacing and permanent scowls. Their faces look creased and tough as old leather. The squad walks toward us in standard two-by-two formation from the end of the aisle. In about five seconds, they're going to be right on top of us. Brohn doesn't wait even half that long. He gives Cardyn a look from his hiding place across the aisle. Cardyn confirms with me and Amaranthine. I nod. Manthy just stares at him. Still, we get the idea.

Cardyn takes careful aim, not at the advancing guards but at the flickering light hanging from the ceiling high above their heads. He checks his silencer, fires once, and the bullet finds its target. The bulb explodes in a hot blast of glass. The guards whip around and look up in unison.

That's when the rest of us make our move.

Karmine and Kella lay down a cover fire for us, tagging two of the guards in the process. Brohn advances in a flash, firing his gun and taking down two more guards as the rest realize what's happening and turn around to face us. Card and I dodge their first volley of gunfire, roll to either side of the aisle, and come up firing. We each take down a guard, but we're all in close now, which means hand-to-hand combat. The four guards left standing aren't standing for long.

Shoulder-to-shoulder, Card and I lunge at them. We dispatch two with quick jabs to the solar plexus followed by interior elbow strikes that pixilate the guards clean out of the simulation. Brohn takes down one of the two remaining guards with a leg sweep followed by a devastating heel-stomp to the chest once he's down. The last guard whips out a knife and lunges at Amaranthine. For a second, I think she's going to get killed. Then I remember that, one, this is a simulation. And two, there's more to Amaranthine than meets the eye. Sure enough, she dodges the knife strike like she's been doing it all her life. When the man's arm comes around again, she steps right into his space, nose to nose, and fires the heel of her hand upward into his chin. His head snaps back, and he disintegrates away into colorful little cubes before he hits the floor.

"Nice move," Karmine says, clearly impressed.

Manthy shrugs and ties her tangle of hair back in a messy ponytail.

So far, we've been either very skilled or very lucky. Either way, that's eleven members of the Eastern Order we've taken out in under five minutes, all without making a sound.

In a quick jog now, we hustle the remaining distance to the red staircase and begin to make our way up. Karmine and Kella walk up backwards behind us, their eyes and rifles trained back into the warehouse in case we're spotted or followed.

A bank of metal garbage bins sits against a rail on the wide landing halfway up. A hint of motion behind one of them alerts us to the presence of an enemy. This time, it's Rain who holds up her hand to tell us to stop. With a dash and a shoulder-roll, she crosses the distance between us and the last garbage bin. She comes up on one knee, her gun at the ready, and blasts three silent shots into the enemy combatant who drops face-first to the floor and then disappears.

"Nice," Cardyn says.

Rain gives him a wink. "Felt good."

We continue up the stairs to the top landing, down the metal walkway, and over to the office. That's when our streak of luck or skill or whatever it is comes to an excruciating end. With no other way in, we try the doorknob. Brohn turns it and eases the door quietly open a few inches. The rest of us are crouched under the bank of windows lining the office. There's no sound coming from inside, so Brohn opens the door the rest of the way. He's greeted by a hail of gunfire that riddles his body with holes. At the same time, the rest of us are blasted away by a cluster of plasma grenades lobbed in our direction by the guards we didn't see hiding just beyond the office.

There's no real pain, but the expectation of it is nearly as painful as the real thing. Fortunately, it hits hard but then vanishes in an instant.

With a flash of white light, the game resets, and we're back in the warehouse lobby.

We make it back to the red staircase and up to the office only to be killed all over again the second we breach the room. We try different tactics: Karmine and Kella leading the way with a second wave of us close behind. The seven of us split up into two groups. Then split into three groups with two teams of two and one of three. Doesn't matter. We all die. We can always get past the warehouse guards, up the stairs, past the guy on the landing, but there's no way to enter the room with the hostages without getting killed. We try back ways and look for other ways to access the mezzanine level. We find a window-washer's rig but no way to get it or ourselves back outside of the building. Once we're in, we're in for good. Until we die, that is. We try other things, too. The freight elevator is off-line. We inspect every inch around it, but there's nothing. Not a seam or a hidden access panel. Nothing. It's a closed program. Just us inside a big building filled with old vehicle parts, construction and transportation equipment, and the enemy. That gets us back to the staircase, our only way up to the mezzanine level.

So we try a more strategic approach once we get to the office: me and Brohn darting in first to draw the enemy's fire with Karmine and Kella flanking us a split-second later on one side while Cardyn, Rain, and Amaranthine lay down cover fire. Doesn't work. We all die.

We all rush in together, shouting and firing to disorient the enemy. Doesn't do any good. We all die.

We try removing the silencers from our weapons and luring the Order out of the office with loud gunfire.

In some versions, they come out and kill us. In others, nothing happens, so we go in, and they kill us. We try bursting into the room in one screaming mass, but the Order kills the hostages in front of us before we die. In other versions, we're able to make it to within ten or fifteen feet of the hostages before the Order takes us all down. In at least one version, the entire top floor of the building explodes and kills us all.

Then the sim resets again. And over and over—I don't know how many times. Whatever we do, we can't get past this last batch of guards in the office. The hostages are right there. We can see them. We can even get most of the way across the room. But we can't save them, we can't defeat the Order, and we can't seem to survive.

Every time, we reset back in the front lobby of the warehouse. I don't know how long we've been living as our avatars. I have to remind myself that my body, the real me, is reclining in a chair in the middle of the Epsilon Cube. The rest of my Conspiracy, too.

Well, minus Terk. For now. The rest of us are all sitting there in a circle, our eyes staring into space at nothing, as these digital versions of us get blasted to pieces over and over and over again.

Our physical status resets each time. We never get tired. But the mental fatigue is real. I feel every bit of the frustration of failure. Hiller's warning about this sim not stopping until the mission's been completed rings in my ears. I know the others are thinking about it, too. Could we be stuck in this loop of a no-win situation forever? Brohn tries to reassure us. He tells us not to worry. "Everything will be fine. We'll figure this thing out," he promises. It doesn't matter that the words are coming from a computer-generated avatar. I can still detect the doubt in his voice from a mile away.

I pull Brohn aside after our latest reset while the others are picking out their weapons. Their heads are down. There's no joy anymore. Even Karmine and Kella have lost their gung-ho spirit. If we were soulless before, now even our avatar shells are running on empty.

"What if there's no end to this?" I whisper to Brohn. "I mean, forget training and forget the war. These are our friends. Our family. They're going to go crazy if this keeps up much longer. And I don't mean mildly crazy. I mean we're all going to lose our minds. Literally."

Brohn puts his hand on my shoulder. "Remember back in the Valta when I said you were sensitive?" I give him a pouty frown, but he stops me with a pained smile. "I just wanted you to know that I don't take it back. You really are the most sensitive person I know, and I love that about you. No matter what we've been through, your heart stays as big and as strong as ever. You really care about…us. And that means a lot to, well, me." He nods over to where our dejected friends are mindlessly selecting their newest batch of weapons for another pointless foray into another unwinnable battle. Without waiting for us, they start to make their way into the warehouse. Again. To face more failure. Again.

I start to follow them, but Brohn holds me back. "They may look to me as the leader, but you're the one keeping us all together."

"Thanks," I say, feeling myself blush pink with pride and then full-on red with embarrassment.

"Hey," he says, leaning in close. "We make a good team, don't we? You and I, I mean."

I know it's just a VR illusion, but I swear I can feel his breath on my neck.

"Seems like you and Rain have become more of a team lately." I don't mean it to sound like an accusation, but I know it kind of does.

"Rain's great. But she's all business." He puts his VR hand on my VR face, and I swear I feel it as sure as if it was real. "You and I are—"

He's cut off by Amaranthine, who practically never talks but somehow manages to have the worst timing when she does finally decide to open her mouth.

"Hey guys. I have an idea," she says. "What if the Order thought the hostages had already been rescued?"

Brohn drops his hand from my face, and we walk over to the others just as Rain is asking Manthy what she means.

"Nothing," Manthy says, pumping the brakes on her own idea. "Not really. I guess I haven't thought it through…"

Brohn and I both say, "Manthy!" at the same time. He steps toward her. "If you think you have something, if you think you may know a way out of this…"

"Okay." Her hands are folded in front of her. Her voice is barely audible, and she stares at the floor the entire time she talks. "Let's say that the Order gets distracted. Hears an explosion or has to respond to an assault. When they look back at the hostages, they just aren't there. When they leave to try to figure it out, they drop their guard. We swoop in, rescue the hostages, and we're out before they know what's going on."

"Sounds like a great plan. Only one problem. How the heck do we do all that?"

Amaranthine finally glances up and smiles. She has a strange look I've never seen in her before. It's almost…confidence. "We're plugged into a VR system, right?"

"Yes. So?"

"You really haven't been able to feel that?"

"Feel what?"

"The system. The energy. I thought I was imagining it at first. But it's real. It's not just being pumped into our synaptic systems. It goes the other way, too. The energy, I mean."

"I don't feel anything," Kella says with a frown.

"Me neither," Karmine adds. His avatar wiggles his fingers in front of his face.

Amaranthine makes an odd sound I can't place at first. But then I realize it's a laugh, something I don't think I've ever heard from her before. "You have to relax. It's like being in water. Every move you make causes a reaction. You push the water away with one hand, more water swarms back at you. The VR system is like that. It's not a closed-off, one-way road. It's a mesh, a branching highway. We're not trapped. Not really. Everything connects to everything else."

We're all just staring at her. I know we're asking ourselves the same thing: *Has Manthy gone clever or crazy?*

Cardyn is shaking his head. He's not a risk-taker or a think-outside-the-box kind of guy. But his eyes light up when I remind him about Render. "Card, you've known about me and Render longer than anyone. You didn't want to believe that at first either, but you get it. What if Manthy's on to something? What if this is the same thing?"

"How do you mean?"

"What if Manthy is tapping into Hiller's VR somehow the way I have a connection with Render?"

Now Card nods and smiles. "Right. I guess it's technically

possible. After all, the VR system *is* as plugged into us as we are into it."

Rain steps up next to Card and wags a finger approvingly at Amaranthine. "There are more things in heaven and earth, Horatio, than are dreamt of in your philosophy."

"*Hamlet*," I say. "Act one, scene five." I raise my hand, and Rain gives me a stinging high-five.

"Okay. Let's say I buy this connection thing," Brohn says. "How would it work? What do you feel, exactly? What can you actually do?"

Amaranthine pauses and squints. "Um. Watch."

Before our eyes, her high-laced combat boots and her black tank-top and vest turn bright pink. She squints again, and her cargo pants blink into a pair of weathered blue jeans, torn and shredded at the knees.

We all gasp and take a full step back.

"Marvie," Karmine says with an impressed exhalation.

"How'd you…" Kella's mouth hangs open. "I mean can anyone else…?"

"I've kind of been practicing," Amaranthine offers with a sheepish grin. "Just little changes here and there until I was pretty sure I could control it."

"And you think we can do this, too?" I ask.

Amaranthine shrugs. It's like she doesn't know and really doesn't care all that much. But she suggests we go ahead and try anyway.

We do. We concentrate like Amaranthine tells us. We try to feel the energy flowing around us like water like she says. I can't speak for anyone else, but I don't feel a thing. Up until now, we haven't really felt anything other than that sudden blast of pain every time we've died in the simulation. How many times now? Dozens? A hundred? More? I've lost count.

"Don't worry," Amaranthine says as her clothes shift back to combat black. "I know what to do. Just follow my lead."

Follow my lead? Three words I never thought I'd hear come out of anyone's mouth but Brohn's. But if she can get us out of this sim, I might even forgive her for interrupting what might have been my best moment ever with Brohn.

How far we've come since Amaranthine was quietly bringing up the rear in the Valta as we piled onto the transport truck on the day of Recruitment.

We follow Amaranthine through the warehouse. As always, we're able to dispatch the assorted guards and the roving orange-clad squads of the Eastern Order. We make our way up the staircase. As always. We huddle around the office door. As always. Only this time, Amaranthine summons us away from the door and down the metal walkway to the banister just a few feet from the top of the stairs. We look out over the railing into the giant expanse of the warehouse. From up here, it looks tidy and harmless instead of chaotic and dangerous.

"Just wait here," she says.

We do, and she clamps her hands on the railing and closes her eyes as we stand around, waiting to be discovered, shot, and reset to do it all again. But that's not what happens. Instead, five members of the Order come storming out of the office. I know their faces well. They've killed me more times than I care to count.

In a frenzy, they dash right past us like we aren't even there. Karmine and Kella draw their weapons, but Amaranthine, her eyes still closed, shakes her head at them.

The five men, guns gripped in their tight fists, storm down the stairs like they're escaping from a burning building. By the time they get to the bottom, Amaranthine has opened her eyes and led us into the office where President Krug, his son, and the security detail are tied to metal chairs with a combination of thick ropes and metal chains. As always, they plead to us to help and point over to the thin white wires running from their temples to a deadly-looking battery off to the side. We've seen this before, too. We know that if we try to free the hostages, a monstrous electric current surges through the white wires and fries them into smoldering lumps of black carbon. We lose, get reset, and have to start all over again.

Manthy says not to worry. As we watch, the ropes, chains, and wires pixilate away. The hostages stand when she tells them to. Then they follow her out the door with us in a cluster close behind. We all follow her down the stairs and back to the front lobby of the warehouse. We encounter every single member of the Order along the way. But they're frozen in place. Harmless.

In the lobby, while his son and security detail dematerialize, President Krug thanks us for our heroic efforts before disappearing as well.

The lobby walls start to fade as Rain gives Manthy an enormous hug, which she resists as best she can. While the others gather around her to celebrate the end of the sim, we all start to fade along with the walls. Brohn's avatar takes me by the sleeve. I can feel the program ending. My feet are pixilating away. Then my legs up to my knees.

Brohn looks down at me. Twists my hair around his finger. The hand on my shoulder slides up to my neck, and his hand cups the back of my head. I don't resist as he pulls me toward him. He leans down and, before I know it, our lips are together. His mouth is warm, and the kiss is soft and sweet.

I know it's not real. But I don't care.

20

"Congratulations," Hiller says as Granden and Trench scan the VR receptor's contact modules out of our eyes and disconnect us from the chairs. "Your team set an all-time record for beating the sim." The octopus arms retreat back into their ports in the ceiling leaving us to try to get our bearings after the final end of a traumatic VR experience.

I look over at Brohn to see if his face shows any sign that he's aware of what just happened between us. But he doesn't look my way. Maybe he doesn't know it happened. Maybe he'd already disconnected by the time we kissed, and I was the one controlling his avatar's actions through some fantasy conjured by my mind.

All I know is that I feel a strange combination of relief and regret. I pull my eyes away from his face, telling myself to forget it ever happened. It was probably nothing more than a dream.

Karmine rubs his eyes and groans as he stands up. "What's the record? Ten years? My entire body's numb. Feels like I haven't moved in…forever."

Kella stands as well. One at a time, she crosses her arms in front of her and stretches. "How many times did we die, anyway? A thousand? Forget ten years. Feels more like a hundred."

As we each stand and try to work feeling back into our numb bodies, Hiller walks around our circle of chairs, tapping her holo-pad and giving each of us a quick once-over inspection as she goes. "You were in the sim for just under four minutes," she says without looking up from her glowing pad.

"You're kidding," Cardyn says. And I know none of us can believe it either. It took nearly fifteen minutes just to get across the warehouse and over to the foot of the red staircase each time. And we must have done that hundreds, maybe thousands of times before Amaranthine did her amazing connection thing and broke the cycle to complete the mission.

Forget the sensory deprivation of the treadmill room or even the odd sensation of living life over and over again as an avatar. The absence of a standard measurement of time is the most disorienting feeling of them all. We've gone from time meaning everything as we counted down in dread to November 1st to time meaning nothing as Hiller and her team manipulate the very universe around us.

Hiller consults some shifting graphs and diagrams over on one of the viz-screens and inputs some data with a few waves of her hand and a quick flurry of her fingers on a long keyboard that runs the length of the console. "I assure you, you performed admirably. Up to all hopes and beyond all expectations."

"Good to know," Brohn says. He's watching her like a hawk. I don't think he trusts her even when she's in the middle of complimenting us. Or maybe it's *because* she's in the middle of complimenting us.

"What was the record before us?" Karmine asks. He's ferociously competitive, even when it's not really called for and no good can come of it. It's not like the Recruits from the other Processors are here for him to impress.

"Actually," Granden interrupts, "four minutes isn't just a

record. You're the only Cohort to ever successfully rescue the hostages."

"Really?" Karmine asks. He looks over at Hiller, who looks back over her shoulder at him. She nods before inputting some more data into her screen. "Marvie," he gushes.

The rest of us stand and continue our stretches in the space in front of the circle of eight chairs. I'm still worried about Terk and still a little freaked out at the sight of an empty eighth chair obviously meant for him. But it does feel good to have my body back along with my sense of time. I pull my knee up toward my chest, grateful at the warm flow of blood that runs through the tight muscles along the back of my leg.

Hiller finishes with her screens and walks back over to us. She slips between two of the chairs and joins us in the area between as we continue to rub feeling back into our arms and legs. She walks around behind us, nodding her approval and inspecting each of us as she goes, surveying us one at a time and taking a mental picture of each us like a mother duck looking on proudly over her growing ducklings. She continues to input notes into a holo-board as she circles us, her fingers doing a little dance over the colorful pad in her hand.

"I have to say, we've had our doubts. The other Cohorts… nobody has performed at this level before. You've conquered the Escape Room tests and now the VR test. At this rate, several of you might qualify for Special Ops after all."

Cardyn gives me playful push to the shoulder. I laugh and brush the hair back that's fallen across my face.

"How's that going to work?" Rain asks. "I mean how will you decide who gets to go into which deployment?"

"Our assessments are top of the line algorithms designed to break down and compile every move you've made, every decision. The system is flawless when it comes to helping us to determine how you can best help us, which, of course, means how you can best serve your nation. Trust me, this is a much better system than the old way."

"The old way?" I ask.

"Sure. War used to be a matter of gathering every able-bodied soul you could, rushing them through a pointless boot camp, and sending them out to, well…die." Hiller pauses behind me and makes some more notes before moving on to Amaranthine, who is standing next to me, her head down, her face covered as always by a wavy shield of her tangled hair. "Not anymore. We don't recruit at random and hope to develop the best and brightest. No. We take the best and brightest and help them to unleash something even better and brighter within themselves."

Granden and Trench are outside the circle of chairs, their arms folded across my chair and Cardyn's. They watch and listen as Hiller walks around us. Clipping her holo-board to a small hook on her belt, she puts her hands on Amaranthine's shoulders. "Amaranthine, for example, has demonstrated some very unusual abilities. We're not sure how she was able to do what she did in the VR-sim. But she has made sure that our suspicions about the special nature of this Cohort have been firmly confirmed." Manthy shrugs Hiller's hands from her shoulders and steps over to stand closer to me. Hiller doesn't seem to notice the abrupt dismissal and continues talking as she walks around us. "Karmine and Kella are total dead-shots, the best marksmen we've ever seen and with an uncanny ability to adapt themselves to any weapon they're given. You don't know this, of course, but the VR system calculated every shot you took. Every hit. Every miss. These two," she says with one hand on Karmine's shoulder and the other on Kella's, "just set an accuracy record that even your Trainers wouldn't be able to match." From their positions behind Brohn and Rain, I can see Granden smile and Trench frown. Hiller doesn't notice. She passes behind Brohn and runs her fingertips along the width of his shoulders. "A natural leader. Decisive. Clear-headed."

Brohn gives her a sarcastic "Thanks" and looks over his shoulder at her hand like it's an annoying bug.

"Cardyn," she says, moving on, "has demonstrated great curiosity, loyalty, and a fierce dedication to the welfare of his friends. He is the one pressing pause to keep you alive when everyone else is scrambling to hit fast-forward. You owe him your lives. Your virtual ones, anyway. Rain here has the most logical, incisive mind we've ever seen." Rain scowls a little, but she blushes a little, too.

Finally, Hiller has circled all the way back around to me. I've got no idea what I offer that she could possibly brag about. Other than my connection to Render, which she doesn't know about, there's nothing special about me. I'm the girl in the shadows. The middle child. The shy one who sits back and watches as others win the prizes. But Hiller lingers behind me the longest.

"No construction is complete without secure connections, someone to coordinate the moving parts, to hold the pieces together. That's Kress. She is your living, beating heart. Your skills are impressive on their own. With Kress as the hub of your Cohort, your skills may well be downright unbeatable."

Maybe it's my imagination, but it sounds like she's stressing the word "connections," and I wonder if she knows something about my single special ability after all. I hope not. The more I think about it, the more I think Cardyn was right back in the Valta: the less everyone else knows about Render, the better. Hiller was nice enough to let Render hang around without getting shot at during the last month and a half or so of training. I'd rather not push my luck with the revelation that I can, and have, used my connection with Render to do some spying of my own over the past few weeks.

"We're okay with the deployment," Brohn says. "Not that we have a choice. I get that. But we'd like to stay together if possible. We've been family for a long time. It'd be a shame to split us up now, right?"

Hiller offers him and Rain a fake-looking smile. "We'll do what we can. But we're bound by the numbers. As you know, your strengths are being carefully identified by sophisticated assessment programs that we've spent a long time perfecting. The system will tell us which deployment will be best for you in our fight against the Eastern Order. I know it's hard to get your heads around, for any of us to get our heads around, but it's the war that matters. Yes, Brohn, the bonds of family matter. A lot. But without victory in the war, there won't be any family left to bond with."

Karmine nods his agreement as Hiller tells us it's time to head back out to the Agora.

We follow her on shaky legs. The experience in the VR-sim may not have lasted long in terms of time in the real world, but in our minds, we felt every second of frustration, pain, and defeat until Amaranthine was finally able to rig the system to enable us to rescue the hostages and get out.

"Any word on Terk?" Kella asks as we make our way down the hallway toward the Cube's main exit door. "Did you talk to anyone in Eta Cube while we were in the sim? How's he doing?"

"Did he get that new arm?" Karmine asks. "I'm jealous. He's going to be a Modified, isn't he?" Karmine flexes his own arm and makes a mechanical whirring sound with his mouth.

"He's fine," Hiller assures us. "And yes, I spoke with Lindell and Martenssen, the med-techs responsible for Terk. They report absolutely no problems or complications. No infection or anything like that. Terk was a little shocked at first as you can well imagine. But we're helping him get used to his new prosthetic. He's in the middle of a recovery and rehabilitation protocol at the moment. He'll be joining you in no time. He told me personally over the comm-link to tell you not to worry. He'll see you soon, and he's looking forward to all of you being together again. He sounds good, actually. Better than I probably would anyway." Hiller shakes her head. "He's impressive, even stronger than he looks."

"Tell him we miss him, too," I say.

"Yeah," Cardyn adds. "And tell him not to let you guys cut off any more limbs."

Hiller laughs like he's joking, but I don't think he is. A training accident is one thing. Rigging a box with a laser blade in it is another. I get teaching us harsh lessons before we go off to war. But that level of harsh does nothing except set us up to fail.

Hiller stops at the door and opens it for us. "Okay, troops. Time to head back to the Silo. You've earned a good night's sleep. We'll pick up again tomorrow. Your training is nearly over, which means the final assessment is right around the corner. I know how much you've been looking forward to seeing your final scores and getting your deployment orders. And we're excited to see what you can do out there against the enemy. A lot of folks have a lot of faith in you. I know it's a lot of pressure, but if anyone can handle it, get through it, and turn the tide of this horrible war in our favor, it's you."

As she says this, I'm thinking that she doesn't look so much like a mother duck with her ducklings anymore. More like a mother duck who's getting kind of tired of her offspring taking up so much room in the nest. I know she's eager to send us on our way to fight the Order. After all, her job here is pretty close to done. But I can't tell if she's eager to see us off for our sake or for hers.

She stands just inside the doorway as we pass by. My fellow Recruits and I walk in slow, unsteady steps under the guard turret and across the Agora on our way to the Silo. I'm dragging my heels, exhausted from mental exertion and still slightly foggy-headed from transitioning back out of the VR-sim. Up ahead, Trench is guiding the others onto the Capsule Pads. In a few seconds, we'll be back underground, chatting about our experience in the sim and nervously awaiting the announcement of our final deployment.

"So what happened to the other Cohorts?" I ask Granden, who's lagging behind with me. "I mean if they didn't complete the mission, like Hiller says."

Granden shakes his head. His voice is quiet. "This place is dangerous, Kress."

He doesn't have to tell me. I've lived most of my life in the rubble left over in the wake of the war. "I know all about the dangers out there," I tell him.

"Not the ones out there," he whispers with a slight nod toward the perimeter of the expansive Processor, followed by a quick glance up toward the slowly-circling Halo above our heads. "The ones in here."

He doesn't answer when I ask what he means, just walks up ahead of me to rejoin Trench and the others. I don't know what he's up to, and I'm still too groggy from the sim to think straight. As I hurry along to catch up, I'm just grateful to be real again. Almost as grateful as I am to be alive.

21

Down in the Silo, no one can sleep. All we can talk about is the upcoming deployment and about how Amaranthine saved us in the VR-sim. Karmine must have said "Marvie!" to her about a million times by now, and Kella keeps asking her how she did what she did.

Amaranthine's having none of it, though. At first, she ignores us. Eventually, she buries herself under her blanket to block out all our questions and congratulations. When that doesn't work, she gathers her blanket up in a bunch and plods over to the Shower Room, where I can see her plop down on the floor, her eyes clamped shut, her back to the wall.

"I guess she doesn't want to be bothered," Rain says.

"Who does?" I ask.

"She does have a way of letting her feelings be known, doesn't she?" Brohn adds.

The six of us sit cross-legged in a circle at the end of our cots. For a while, we make guesses about how Amaranthine was able to infiltrate a closed digital system without tools, an access port, or digital link-ups.

Karmine guesses that it has something to do with the implants. At first, I think he's referring to my forearm tattoos, but he shakes his head and gestures over his shoulder with his thumb toward his back.

Cardyn looks worried but seems to relax when Brohn says, "I doubt that."

Kella and Rain agree with Karmine. To tell the truth, I keep forgetting about the so-called "Biscuits" Trench injected into us on our first day in the Processor. I reach my left hand around the front of my body and feel along my rib cage on my right side and as far as I can to my shoulder blade. I don't feel anything, and I certainly don't feel like some tracking device is somehow controlling me or giving me magical access to any circuitry or data that might be streaming through the walls.

"I think these really are what they say they are," I suggest. "If not, wouldn't we *all* feel something?"

We debate for a while, but eventually, we all get tired of guessing—and just get tired in general. Cardyn stretches out on his cot with one arm draped over his eyes. Karmine and Kella fall asleep facing each other on their adjacent cots.

I can't sleep, so I stand up and walk into the Mess Hall, leaving Brohn and Rain behind to carry on a conversation they're having about the latest updates to our scores that have appeared on the viz-screen on the far side of the room.

I've barely settled into my seat on the bench when I hear Brohn excuse himself. He strides in and joins me in the Mess Hall, and I can't help remembering when he took a similar stroll to join me on our last night back in the Valta. So much has happened since then...yet I feel like he and I haven't really managed to get a whole lot closer. It's like there's a wall between us that either I put up or he did. It's threatened to crumble once or twice, but maybe it's too strong for either of us to break through.

He sits down across from me and steeples his fingers on the

table between us. "Listen," he says, "about what happened in the sim..."

"I'm pretty sure Manthy isn't going to want to talk about it any time soon," I sigh. "I think it was weird for her. So all we have right now are guesses."

"I don't mean about Manthy."

I look across the table into his eyes, my heart suddenly hammering in my chest. So, he really *was* there. He knew what was happening the whole time. He really did kiss me.

Even if it was only a virtual kiss.

I pull my eyes away. It's not something I'm ready to talk about without blushing my face off.

"At the *end* of the sim...?" he says, leaning forward and prodding me to reply.

"Yes," I say, trying to look him in the eyes again but failing. "I remember."

"I think maybe we...I mean, *I*...may have gotten caught up in the moment."

"There was a moment?" I'm teasing him, and he doesn't seem to know what to do about it. I've never seen him quite this uncomfortable in quite this kind of way. It's a nice feeling to know that he can get as insecure around me as I can be—and often have been—around him.

"The point is, I don't regret it." He throws me his signature crooked smile, as though he's trying to hold it back, but his face just can't quite help it. "You know, Hiller was right. There *is* something special about you." I open my mouth to reply, but he stops me. "I don't mean the Render stuff, Kress. I mean you. Everything I said to you that night at Final Feast? I meant every word. There's so much more to you than you know, Kress."

"What are you saying?" I ask, my voice trembling slightly.

"I'm saying I kissed you because I wanted to." He pulls his eyes away to stare at the far wall. "But I know it was probably a bad idea."

"Right," I reply. "Of course." I'm not sure what I mean by that. All I know is that I'm feeling hurt right now, not to mention embarrassed.

"I mean, look where we are, Kress," he says, gesturing to the air around us. "This place is oppressive. We live in a prison. We have no privacy. A relationship down here is a terrible idea. Even if we both want it." His voice warms up with the last sentence. "Besides, I've always gotten a *stay away from me* vibe from you—which is probably smart on your part."

"It's not always a question of smart," I reply with a smirk. "Like you say, it's not like there's any privacy here. Besides, you..." I want to point out that he's always off with Rain, but it seems too much like an accusation of wrong-doing, so I clam up. "It would be hard, and it would probably make the others feel weird."

"Yeah. That's what I'm thinking."

We sit in silence for a few seconds before I add, "It's not always like a prison, you know. Everyone here is sort of incredible. In my own twisted way, I've really enjoyed getting to know all these personalities."

"True," says Brohn, leaning in again with a glint in his eye. "I mean, what Amaranthine did was off-the-charts amazing, wasn't it? I'd even say impossible if I hadn't seen it for myself. And yes, Karmine and Kella can shoot the baby toe off a flea from a hundred yards away. Rain has a mind like a computer. Cardyn has a strange calming effect on those around him. And Terk..." Brohn looks over at the far wall again and shakes his head, his jaw clenching. I can tell without asking that anger's roiling up inside him, just like it does every time he thinks of what happened in that Escape Room. "I just hope Terk's okay," he says in a voice that sounds more like a growl. His hands ball into tight fists. "What happened to him was..."

"Shocking?"

"To say the least." He unclenches his hands, inhales deeply and pulls his eyes back to mine. "It should never have happened."

"The strongest one of us lost an arm," I say quietly. "I got knocked out in a sparring drill. Our two best marksmen suffered broken bones in a training exercise. You're right—none of it should have happened."

Brohn sighs and plasters on another smile, though this one feels forced. "No one said recruitment would be easy."

"True. But no one said it would be deadly, either."

He lets out a bitter chuckle. "Well, let's not get carried away. No one's dead."

Yet, I think.

But instead of saying it, I just nod.

"Anyway," he says, "we all contribute something, and I'll confess, back in the Valta, if someone had asked me…"

"Yes?"

Brohn swallows hard and looks away. "Even though I know you're strong in so many ways, I'm not sure I could have said back then what you'd contribute, exactly."

"Thanks a lot," I reply with a pout. Well, this conversation is going south pretty fast.

I'm considering pushing myself to my feet and walking away when Brohn stands up and walks around to my side of the table. He slides onto the bench seat next to me and takes my hand in his.

"I didn't mean it like that. Not like an insult. What I meant is that I was wrong not to get to know you better back then. I was wrong not to see it."

"See what?"

"You," he says. "Everything about you. What you mean to everyone around you. The role you play in our lives. The way you let us work things out while you guide us gently from behind, always keeping an eye on us. Always protecting us in your way."

"I don't do anyth—" I start to protest, but he stops me.

"I know you don't even realize it yourself, Kress. But in the Cubes, you've been the one to nudge us in all the right directions. You're the one looking out for us, every step of the way. You're smarter than Rain and stronger than Terk, and you don't even know it. I think that's why I...did what I did in the sim. I think I wanted you to know that I see you in ways you might not even see yourself."

Brohn's stroking my hand with his thumb now. A brief, forbidden moment of intimacy.

"Thanks," I say, my cheeks heating.

"You know," he says, "you can lead a group of people just as well from the back as you can from the front."

"I guess that makes us the bookends of our little Conspiracy, then, doesn't it?" I ask with an awkward smile.

Brohn gives my hand a gentle squeeze before letting go. "I guess it does," he says with a soft, pleasant laugh before putting his fingers under my chin and lifting it, just like he did in the VR-sim.

"Hey," he all but whispers, leaning closer.

"Hmm?" I reply, too stunned to form proper words.

"If we ever get out of here in one piece..."

"Yes?"

"Would you go out on a date with me?"

The biggest smile in the world spreads its way over my mouth. "Yes," I tell him. "I definitely would."

He presses his lips to mine just long enough for my head to swim, then pulls away and rises to his feet. "I'll see you around then, Kress," he says, his voice filled with a hidden meaning that does strange and wonderful things to my chest.

"See you around, Brohn."

Without another word, he heads back into the Dormitory to re-join Rain.

I STAY at the table for a minute, enjoying the rare opportunity to be alone with my thoughts. We've all been together for so long, I can't remember the last time I sat anywhere by myself. It's a lonely feeling, but kind of a nice one as well. I'm feeling rejuvenated, re-centered. What just happened with Brohn is almost enough to make me forget we're still in this place, locked far away from any world we've ever known.

But there's one thing I can't get past: Granden. What did he mean up in the Agora? What danger could we possibly be in? I think about it for a while, but I keep circling back to the same conclusion: Other than a few injuries, which we can easily chalk up to simple and expected training mishaps, we've hardly been in grave danger. Sure, we nearly passed out from the treadmill and water challenges. The yellow smoke in the last Escape Room made us sick, but there's no indication it would have killed us. And we died a thousand times in the VR-sim but didn't suffer so much as a scratch in the real world. If they wanted to seriously hurt us, they could have done so a million times. Given the choice between a few little risks in the Processor and certain death out there in the world…well, that's an easy one.

But then there's Terk. Like Brohn said, what happened to him should never have happened in a million years. It wasn't just some accident. That box was deliberately rigged to hurt anyone who made a mistake.

Through the doorway, I see Cardyn sit up on his cot, and I gesture for him to come in and join me. The alone time has been nice. The few minutes with Brohn even nicer. But right now, I need my best friend.

Cardyn staggers in, bleary-eyed but smiling.

"Can't sleep?" I ask.

"It's times like this I wish I was more like Amaranthine. She's passed out and snoring on the floor in the Shower Room." He laughs and asks me how I'm doing.

"I've got more on my mind right now than I'd like," I admit.

Cardyn slides in next to me, right where Brohn was sitting just a couple minutes before. He leans down toward the table and drops his head down onto his crossed arms. "Tell me about it," he says. His voice is muffled.

I stare out at the far wall, thoughts churning in my mind. "Granden said something about being in danger," I tell him. "Does that strike you as weird?"

"Granden's a strange guy," Cardyn mumbles. "Something about him..."

I nod. "Do you think the Order has finally found this place? Hiller did say they were gearing up for some final assault. What if this is it? What if Granden knows there's about to be an attack?"

He sits up to face me, and I pull my eyes to his. "Well," he says, his forehead wrinkled in thought, "it would explain why they seem to be in such a hurry to complete our training."

"We should tell the others," I say. "They deserve to know. If tomorrow's going to be our last..."

I choke on the final words, realizing that despite everything that's happened, I've never actually been afraid of dying. I've survived drone attacks and so much loss. But now, with the realization that the end could be so close, I feel strangely disconnected.

"Listen," Cardyn says, gesturing back into the Dormitory with his thumb. "They're mostly asleep, which we should be, too. Why don't we wait and see how things go in the morning? No sense sending everyone into a panic after what we've just been through in the sim."

We share a long look, and I finally nod and look away. "You're right. Let's try to get some sleep."

Card stands up and reaches out a hand to help me up as well. He guides me up from the bench, and for a second, we're standing face to face, just looking into each other's eyes. We smile at the same time, but my smile quickly fades. For a second, I consider telling him about Brohn, that something's happened between us. If what the other girls said was true—if Card likes me as more than a friend—the news could hurt him. And the thought of it makes me feel terrible.

"Come on, you two!" Rain's voice calls out. "Big day tomorrow."

Whatever conversation we were about to have disappears from my mind, and we pad along into the Dormitory for some much-needed rest.

I DON'T KNOW how long I've been asleep, but when I open my eyes, I'm outside, up in the Agora. It's a strange sensation. I've never seen the Agora in the dark before. We spend every day out here or in one of the Cubes and every night in the Silo. The air is warmer than I would have suspected. Even though we still get huge temperature fluctuations during the day, I'm used to nights being cooler. Back in the Valta, nights were bathed in moonlight and frosty dew. Here, the air is dry. The grass is crisp under my feet. The turrets in front of each Cube are empty. I guess they don't keep them manned at night. We're supposed to be locked away in the Silo until morning, so they don't have to worry about us. As we already discovered the hard way, there's no way in or out of the Silo once the Capsules descend. I guess the guards must be on patrol at the outer perimeter, on the lookout for attacks by the Eastern Order.

With my head down, I jog across the expansive Agora until I reach the base of the Zeta Cube, the sixth building in the octagonal arrangement. I open the gate. Hop the fence on one side, and land in a walkway running between the Zeta and Eta Cubes. I sprint down the dark, tree-lined space between the two buildings, stopping for a quick second here or there to lean up against one of the two cold black buildings to catch my breath. Instinctively, I run in a random zigzag pattern rather than a straight line down the alleyway until I reach another fence out back. This one looks like it runs around the entire Processor, encircling all eight buildings and separating the facility from the scorched earth and woods beyond. A small red light flickers at the base of each fence-post. Electrified. But there's a spot about twenty feet down where the light is blacked out, dead. A flaw. A weakness. I tap the toe of my boot against the fence where the chain-links sag by a gap near the post. Nothing.

Bracing myself for a shock of electricity to blast through my body, I reach out and tap the fence with the back of my hand. Nothing. Dropping down to one knee, I peel back the section of fence and slither through the opening.

I make my way through the woods and hike for about ten minutes until I reach the edge of a clearing. Hearing the sound of voices, I duck behind a fallen tree and tuck myself against its cold, rough surface. A cluster of spindly branches form a protective little nook around me. With my back to the trunk of the tree, I strain to hear what the voices are saying. Although they're close enough and loud enough, I can't make out the actual words. It's three men talking, from what I can tell. But it's like they're speaking in some foreign, guttural-sounding language. Dropping down onto my stomach, I crawl along the length of the tree until I reach its end. Its root system is half-exposed, which provides me with perfect cover as I peer out through the gloom and into the clearing.

To my shock, I see ten young and three young men, all about my age from the looks of it, lined up on a platform illuminated by three dim lights on thin metal posts. They're on their knees, chained together at the neck with their hands bound behind their backs. They're trying to scream and thrash around, but they're locked up too tight and muffled by metal rods in their mouths.

Through the thicket of twisted black roots and branches in front of me, I can just make out the silhouettes of the three men whose voices I heard. The light hits the face of one of the men to reveal jagged scars running down his cheeks. The man, who I recognize with a shock is Trench, raises his rifle in the direction of the thirteen chained and gagged teenagers on the raised platform. Their eyes are wide and filled with tears. They try to scream again, but nothing comes out.

The only sound in the clearing of the dead forest is the muted zing of bullets through the air as Trench shoots each of the thirteen kids, one by one, with meticulous precision, in the center of the forehead. The dead teens slump in their restraints. Blood flows down their faces and necks and soaks their tattered clothes.

I wake up with Brohn and Rain standing on one side of my cot with Karmine, Kella, and Cardyn on the other. Manthy is still asleep under her blanket in the Shower Room.

I'm shaking and have my own blanket gripped tight in my clenched and sweaty fists. My face is wet like I've been crying in my sleep.

Trembling, I explain what I saw in as much detail as I can remember.

"Just a dream," Brohn says. "It was just a dream." He sits down next to me and puts a reassuring hand on my back as if he's trying to prove that I'm awake and that his touch is real.

I nod. The memory still burns in my brain as bright as a family holo-portrait. Only there are black ridges around the edges that I realize are feathers. One other thing occurs to me as the images of the forest, the dead people, and the black tips of Render's wings begin a slow fade from my mind's eye: each of the assassinated teenagers was wearing a black, bird-shaped insignia pinned to the lapel of their blood-soaked jackets. I look down at my arm. I can feel my implants pulsing in a way they've never done before. "I didn't activate it, but somehow I'm connected," I say to Brohn. "I'm not sure if what I saw...I mean, I'm not a hundred-percent sure what I saw was just a dream."

22

"The time table's been stepped up," Granden informs us as we step out into the Agora. "Your deployment assignments are in." He seems stressed, nervous. But I don't have time to process what's got him on edge or ask him about his weird warning from the night before.

He guides the seven of us down from the Capsule Pads to the lush grass of the Agora. Hands in front of our faces, we blink our eyes against the unusually bright morning sun. We're used to the odd climate fluctuations, but this is one of the few times the sunlight has beamed down bright and white instead of tinted with red. For a second, it reminds me of the crisp light of the Valta.

In front of us, Hiller is standing up on a small stage with her hands gripping the edges of a slick white podium. Facing her is a semi-circle of eight metal-framed folding chairs. Trench stands next to Hiller, grimacing down at us but otherwise relatively at ease.

It's a strange little makeshift set-up, but I have to admit that I'm finding it all oddly pleasing. Having heard stories from Micah about school graduation ceremonies, I never thought I'd actually be part of one myself. It's not exactly how I pictured it. I imagined an auditorium full of cheering peers and proud parents. There would be streamers and colorful banners hanging from the rafters, and there would be music playing.

I never thought I'd be graduating from a military training program on a big outdoor field in the middle of eight square buildings, with a massive silver ring rotating lazily overhead. But beggars can't be choosers, as Dad used to say.

Granden guides us to our seats and walks up to join Hiller and Trench on the improvised stage. Cardyn and I exchange a glance, and he gives me a half-smile. On my other side, Brohn is sitting with his arms folded tight against his chest and his legs stretched out in front of him, crossed at the ankle. Ever since Terk's injury, the sight of Hiller and the others sets him into an instant rage. It's not surprising. Terk suffered a horrible trauma. And Brohn takes any affront to one of us as an affront to all of us.

I know every one of us blames ourselves, but we also blame the whole, twisted training system. Brohn seems like he's going through something different, though. He and Terk were pretty close. They were the strong ones back in the Valta, yet they never competed or seemed to get in each other's way. While Karmine was always competitive with Brohn, Terk just seemed to relax into his role and take everything in stride. I think Brohn appreciated that about him, and now I get the sense that he feels betrayed.

Like he's lost a true friend instead of just a handy sidekick.

I get that. On the other hand, we've been told Terk will be fine, and I have to believe it for the sake of my own sanity.

Besides, this is our big day. It's what we've been working toward and training for over the course of about three months. So I understand Brohn's gloominess—I even share it, to a point. I've got my own swarm of stomach butterflies. Is it because I'm not sure where my spot in the rankings will land me? Is it the prospect of being sent off to war?

Or is it really the looming, inescapable presence of the empty chair where Terk should be?

I give my head a little shake before I drive myself insane. At the same time, Hiller stands regally on the dais with her chin up and her shoulders slightly back. She scans all of us and gives us little smiles and nods along the way. She clears her throat like she's about to address a million people instead of just us seven.

"I'm proud to announce that this is now officially the most gifted group of Recruits to ever come through a Processor," she says. "In your time here, you have demonstrated talents, abilities, and resourcefulness far beyond that of your peers. We set the bar high, and you cleared it each time. We pushed you, and you never stumbled. We tested you, and you never—well, *rarely*—failed. We know that you will not fail us now as you lead our nation to victory over the Eastern Order. We know you will not fail us as you restore to us what is rightfully ours: our land, our government, and our freedom. We are asking a lot. But you have shown that you have a lot to offer. When you leave here tomorrow, you will be transported to your locations throughout the nation where you will be stationed and where you can best support our cause."

Did she say "tomorrow"?

I'm hardly ready for the rest of today, let alone the thought of being plunged into war *tomorrow*.

Hiller clears her throat and gives Trench a sideways glance. "We received important declassified information just this morning that the Order may have made a critical miscalculation in their planned final assault. This gives us a small window where we have a chance to turn the tide of this horrible war once and for all and achieve the victory and the peace that has eluded us for so long. Every war comes down to one battle. Every battle comes down to a large community of dedicated people. And every community comes down to a few individuals who stand out for their talents and who stand up for what's right. I'm proud to stand before seven of those individuals here today."

"There should be eight of us here," Brohn growls up at Hiller. She stammers for a second, shocked at having been so unceremoniously interrupted. Trench takes a half-step forward, his hand going for his gun, but Granden puts his hand out to stop him.

Hiller tries again. "So proud—"

"Where's Terk?" Brohn asks through a menacing scowl. He stands up and points at the empty seat at the end of the semicircle of chairs and then out toward the Eta Cube. "You said he'd be back with us by today, right? And now you want to send us out there, and we haven't even had a chance to say…"

I know Brohn was about to say "goodbye," but he chokes on the word.

Hiller gives Trench and Granden a shake of her head and an *I've-got-this-covered look*. "I appreciate your concern, Brohn. We all do. I assure you, Terk is just finishing up some rehab training. We thought he might even make it to the ceremony this morning. But there were some last-minute tests he needed to undergo. I'm happy to report that everything went very well. He should be ready to re-join you first thing tomorrow before you leave for your assignments."

"That's not—"

"Don't worry," Hiller laughs. "We want him back with you just as much as you do. But it doesn't make sense to rush it. We want him back but at one-hundred percent. We *need* him back at one-hundred percent."

Emboldened but still a bit nervous—after all, I don't feel like getting shot—I stand up next to Brohn. "Can we see him at least?" Around the curved row of chairs, the others stand up as well, even Amaranthine way down at the end.

"Sure," Hiller says after what I think is way too long a pause. "We can arrange that. After our little ceremony here, I'll contact the rehab center in the Eta Cube, and we'll see what we can do. Maybe we can get you to him tonight before you head down for your last night in the Silo. Who knows? If his condition is good enough, maybe he can even join you for this last night. After all, you should all be together one more time, right?" She gives me an unsatisfying wink, but I have no choice but to take her at her word and wait. We all sit down, and Cardyn gives me an approving pat on the shoulder.

"I think maybe we should jump to what we came here for," Hiller says. She's got a quiver in her voice. She looks at Brohn to see if he's going to interrupt her again, but he's back to sitting with his arms crossed and staring daggers at her. The rest of us sit, too.

"Okay then," Hiller says at last. "Let's proceed. Karmine and Kella, for your uncanny abilities with weapons, you have been given the honor of serving in the field of Combat. Karmine and Kella exchange a small nod. They're looking forward to battle, but I know some of the wind's been taken out of their sails. They imagined leading all of us into battle. Knowing that we'll be split up now seems to pain them almost as much as the two of them getting to stay together seems to please them.

"Come up and receive your insignia."

Karmine and Kella stand and walk up to the single step of the raised platform. They approach Hiller who, one at a time, affixes a patch to the lapel of each of their combat jackets. It's a small black circle with two larger concentric circles around it. I think it's supposed to be crosshairs, like the ones we stared down so many times at target practice in the Agora gun-training exercises.

Hiller turns her attention to Rain, who's sitting on the other side of Brohn. "For your logical thinking, you have been given the honor as serving in the field of Tech."

Rain marches up obediently, glancing back at Brohn for some kind of signal about what to do or how to comport herself. But Brohn is still off in his own world. He's looking at Rain, but honestly, I don't think he sees her. She turns her attention back to Hiller and leans back a little as Hiller puts a different insignia on her lapel. This one is in the shape of an arrow, formed by thick black lines and open on one end.

Rain gives Hiller a half-smile and two very sarcastic thumbs' up as she steps off the stage and walks back to her seat.

Ignoring her, Hiller moves on to Cardyn. "Cardyn, for your kindness, loyalty, and for your inquisitive mind and intuition, you have been given the honor of serving in Intelligence." Cardyn takes his turn walking up to receive the key-shaped insignia with a small heart for a head that Hiller pins to his lapel as he tries without success to suppress a smile of pride.

"Great," he says to me under his breath. "I guess."

Hiller turns to the three of us remaining and points to us one at a time. "Brohn, for your leadership and strength of character... Kress, for your mental acuity and uncanny degree of empathy... Amaranthine, for your ingenuity and techno-abilities, and to all three of you for your cleverness, adaptability, and ingenuity...you have each been assigned to Special Ops, the most elite and sought-after of the four deployments!"

Brohn's frown eases, but just a bit. He nods and forces the hint of a smile. Amaranthine has been staring at the ground and doesn't even look up when her name is called. As for me, Special Ops should be a dream come true. What started out as a vague myth has become a reality that's somehow landed right in my lap.

Amaranthine and I follow Brohn up to Hiller's small stage where she gives us our insignias. Brohn and Amaranthine quietly accept their reward, but I do a double-take when I see the design:

"It's impossible," I say under my breath. It's the trinket from my dream, the one I saw pinned to the thirteen kids murdered by Trench in the woods out behind the Processor. I know Brohn thinks it was just a dream. But if this is a coincidence, it's one that's freaking me out beyond any capacity for rational thought.

Hiller puts a hand on my shoulder and says, "You deserve this, Kress."

I should be happy. After all, I'm getting exactly what I wanted. In many ways, this is a dream come true. In many other ways, it's the realization of a nightmare. I've succeeded. I've even excelled. But after all we've been through, after all the tests and training, getting exactly what I want doesn't seem all that important anymore. In fact, it seems downright terrifying.

When we're back in the Silo, the others admire their new trinkets. Even Amaranthine is lying face-up on her cot, absently stroking the image of the black bird still pinned to her jacket.

For me, though, the image of the bird on the insignia is horrific.

23

I'M LYING ON MY COT WITH A T-SHIRT OVER MY FACE AND THE beginnings of a massive headache expanding like a balloon behind my eyes. On the cots around me, the others are carrying on a conversation I can barely focus on enough to follow. The voices blend into one another, an overlapping but steady flow of thoughts, worries, and feelings.

"What do you think Granden meant by the time table being stepped up?"

"I have a feeling we're about to be attacked."

"The Order?"

"No way. Hiller said we're safe."

"That's true. But she also said the Order was making a big push and might be preparing some big final assault to win the war. What if that's the cause for all the urgency? What if Hiller knows we're sitting ducks?"

"You think they might be rushing our deployment because we could—?"

"Be attacked any minute now? Yes."

"Then we need to get out of here. If they won't give us any answers, we need to get our own."

"Even if we wanted to sneak out of here, we already know it's impossible."

"If there is an invasion about to happen, what if they lock us down here again, only this time on purpose?"

"No way. The last time was just a glitch. A stupid power-outage. You really think they'd leave us here on purpose to die? Especially when we could actually help them fight if the Order really does attack the Processor?"

"We've got to find out for sure."

"And how do you propose we do that?"

I cringe as a throb of pain blasts through my head, but it subsides quickly to be replaced by what feels like a wave of warm water.

It's Render.

He's telling me to fly.

No. That's not it exactly.

Render has more than one way to express flight. This isn't his *fly-high-reconnaissance* version of flight. It's not his *escape-from-danger* version. Or his refreshing *sun-on-my-back* version. It's closer to his *spiraling-search-for-food* version. It's like he's telling me to climb. To ascend. To circle.

It doesn't make sense at first. And then I look up at the ceiling. Up there somewhere above us is the Halo, slowly rotating and glistening silver in the reddish-black of the frosty night. And suddenly it makes perfect sense.

"What did Hiller say all those weeks ago about accessing the Halo?" I ask aloud. "Something about tunnels or conduits?"

"No," Cardyn says. "It was 'sky-bridges.' 'Retractable sky-bridges.' She said they run from each Cube across to the Halo. They must use them at night when we're down here."

"Then that's where we need to get to."

"Need to get to?" Kella asks. "For what?"

"You're right," I say. "All of you. There's something here to be worried about. But it's not what we think."

"Then what is it?" Rain asks.

"I'm not sure. It's a feeling. But it's one I need you to trust."

No one says anything at first, but then Brohn pushes himself up from his cot. "You don't need to ask us to trust you, Kress. I think I speak for all of us when I say that our trust in you is automatic."

The others nod in agreement and stand up to join Brohn.

"We need to get out of here," I say. "Out of the Silo. Tonight. Right now. We need to get up to the Cube."

"Which Cube?" Cardyn asks.

"Theta Cube is where the control center is," I say.

"And how do you…?"

"Render. I've sent him on a few missions over the past few weeks. I didn't find out a lot. But I know that much. I'm kind of connected with him right now—not a strong connection—it's almost gone, actually. But he wants us up there. I can see images of the Theta Cube and its skybridge in his mind."

Brohn paces the room, his eyes on the ceiling. "Question is, how do we get out of here?"

We've already determined that there's no way out of the Silo. We were trapped in here for nearly a week, and, in all that time, we couldn't figure out a way to escape. There are no hidden doors. No secret codes. No air vents to crawl through. Cardyn points out that we don't even know how far we are underground. "The Capsules always take us up so fast," he says. "It could be twenty or thirty feet…"

"Or a thousand," Brohn continues. "So what now?"

Moving as one, we all look over at Amaranthine at the same time.

She looks up from where she's been busily picking at a spot on her arm with her fingernail. "Um. No," she says with a determined shake of her head.

Brohn grips my elbow and nods in Manthy's direction. I guess that's my cue. He and the others quietly retreat into the Mess

Hall, leaving me alone on the cots in the Dormitory with Manthy.

I've known her for sixteen years. We all have. We've all known each other our entire lives. But none of us really *knows* Amaranthine at all. No one's close to her. Most people back in the Valta either mocked her, were afraid of her, or just ignored her. I'm not sure which was worse for her. I'm not sure why I never asked.

I'm also not sure how I got assigned to be the Manthy-whisperer.

"Listen," I begin as I sit down next to her on her cot. "This could be nothing. It could also be everything. If I could do it myself, I would. But I can't. No one can. Maybe no one on this entire planet, except you. I know that's a lot of pressure. But, Manthy, we need to get out of here. I mean we *really* need to get out of here. As in, our lives may depend on it. I feel it. I *know* it." I flick my thumb skyward. "Something's going on up there that they're not telling us about. It may be part of the training. Or it really could be an invasion about to happen. But forget about all that. Forget about the tests and the war and the Order. Forget about the deployment. For right now, we need to figure out what's happening up there. We need to know how much danger we're in and what we can do to help. We need five minutes of freedom. And you're the only one who can get it for us."

Amaranthine looks over at me and then down at the floor between her feet. Her voice creaks a little, like she's using it for the first time. "I don't know how I did that before, back in the VR-sim."

I put my hand on her knee, half-expecting her to shoo me off, but she doesn't. "I don't know how I connect with Render," I say. "But we need to do things in order. We need to survive first. After that, we can figure out *how* we survived."

Manthy gives me an unexpected smile and a very welcome nod. "I'll try."

"That's great!"

"But, Kress..."

"Yes?"

"I can't guarantee...I mean, I don't know if I can..."

"Hey. It's okay, Manthy. If it works, great. If not, we'll try something else. There's no pressure and no expectations. Just a little bit of hope and a whole lot of faith in you. Not even that you'll succeed and get us out of here...just that you'll try. Hiller may get her kicks out of grading us, but no one really cares about grades. You can't put a number on what we mean to each other." I give her knee a little shake.

Amaranthine nods. I stand up and call out to the others in the Mess Hall. "Brohn. Guys. Come on in. Manthy's going to give it a shot."

We gather around and try not to distract her as she closes her eyes and sits cross-legged on her cot. Cardyn keeps looking at me for guidance, like I'm supposed to know what she's doing or how she's doing it. I shake my head, and he turns his attention back to Amaranthine whose face is growing contorted with effort. Trickles of sweat weave down her cheeks. Of all of us, I'm the only one who knows even a little bit about what she's going through. From the outside, my connection with Render might seem effortless, like a clever parlor trick. But inside my head, it's a disorienting and sometimes painful experience. I'm thankful for the connections I make with him, but each time is also a reminder of how closed-off and limited the human mind really is.

After about two minutes that feel like twenty, Manthy opens her eyes. "I'm done," she says.

"You're done what?" Kella asks with a trace of impatience. "Were you able to connect with the system? Can you get us out of here?"

Manthy nods. "I think so. I think I was able to tap into a security override or something. I don't know the tech, though. I don't know for sure..."

"It's okay," I say. "You don't need to know it in your head. Not like you know regular things. This is a different kind of knowing."

She looks up at me. "But, Kress…it hurts."

I put my arm around her shoulder and help her to her feet. "I know," I say as we make our way over to the Capsule Pads. "It really does get better. I promise."

Manthy closes her eyes again, and the yellow lights at the base of the pads spring to life. We step on and, for the first time in months, we rise to the surface in the middle of the night instead of first thing in the morning.

Outside, the Agora is as misty and creepy as a graveyard. The guard turrets are empty, and the eight black Cubes are barely visible in the moonless night. Above us, the Halo looks especially eerie as it now sits deadly still in the night sky. Its silver surface seems to absorb light instead of reflecting it, which is fine with us. We've crossed a line now, and we know it. No more punishment or docked points. If we get caught now, it'll be military prison for us for sure. If we're lucky.

But we've reached an impasse. Our situation has become intolerable. Something has to give.

I can't see Render out there anywhere, and I'm glad. The last thing I need is for him to sense my presence and come flying out of the trees, distracting any eyes that may be watching for movement.

More out of instinct than necessity, we crouch low and scurry across the Agora towards the last two Cubes of the octagon. I stop us in front of the turret and fenced walkway that lead to the Eta Cube with a large "H," the Greek symbol for "Eta," above the door.

"Rain, you take Cardyn, Karmine, and Kella. Hiller said that Terk was being treated in the Eta Cube. You four get in there, find him, and meet us in the Theta Cube. They don't seem to lock the Cubes. Every time they've escorted us in, the door just opens.

There are no guards in the turrets, so it should be smooth sailing."

"Does it strike anyone as weird that no one's in the towers?" Kella says nervously.

"They're on patrol outside the perimeter," I say, recalling my vision from the other night.

"What? How do you know that?"

"I just know." I shoot her a glance that tells her I don't want to say anymore.

"Kress just said this would be smooth sailing. Don't jinx it!" Cardyn says to Kella in a loudish whisper. We all cross our fingers and then cross our arms over our chests: our tried and true method from the Valta for staving off bad luck.

I smile actually my thanks to Cardyn and continue doling out instructions.

"I don't know what kind of shape Terk'll be in, so be prepared to help him out. Be sure to grab any medical supplies you can get your hands on. Bandages. Gauze. Any pain-killers or antibiotics they might have lying around. And a bag to carry them in. We could be on the run for a while. I'm not about to head out into the woods without provisions. So any food you can find, too."

"What about you three?" Rain asks.

"We've got to get up there," I say, pointing up to the Halo. "There are security protocols we'll still need to override if we want to get out of here. I'll lead us up there. Hopefully, Amaranthine can work a bit more of her magic. I hate to have us split up, but we've got two jobs to do and not enough time to do them both together. Let's make this quick. In, out, and rendezvous back here."

It's only after I finish calling out my plans that I realize two things: I've somehow taken on the role of leader in our Conspiracy, and I've kept myself, Brohn, and Amaranthine together. We're the newly-crowned Special Ops group. I don't know if it's a coincidence, if it's clever, subconscious strategizing, or if Hiller got it right and the three of us are destined to be teamed up and forever in synch.

While Rain and her team head off to find Terk, the three of us slip over to the Theta Cube, the last of the eight around the Agora and one we haven't been in before. Under the "Θ" symbol, the door is unlocked. It's the first sign of carelessness, complacency, laziness, or just plain stupidity I've seen since we first walked in here months ago. I breathe a sigh of relief. It's comforting to know that even the great and powerful guardians of the Processor are less than perfect. Brohn eases the door open, but then steps back and lets Amaranthine take the lead. She doesn't seem to question his decision and walks briskly ahead with me and Brohn padding along behind her. She leads us up four long sets of concrete stairs with a landing in between each flight. Despite our best efforts at stealth, our boots echo in the empty space.

At the top of the stairs, we're stopped by a locked door. It's an old-style door, the kind with a handle and an internal lock, not like the pneumatic doors or energy portals we're mostly used to. At first, I think our luck has run out, but Brohn steps forward. From inside his jacket pocket, he produces a folded combat knife, which makes a strong metallic click as he snaps it open.

"A little something I snagged from our last training exercise," he says with a wry smile. He opens his jacket and taps the bulging interior pocket. "Got a few of them," he says. "Just in case. Gave a couple to Rain as well."

He jams the blade into the door's locking mechanism as far as it'll go. Then he takes a step back, raises his foot, and slams the heel of his boot against the end of the knife's solid black handle. The blade slices deeper into the lock, and we hear the satisfying sound of tumblers cracking. Brohn yanks the knife out with two hands, turns the silver handle, and eases the door open.

We step out into a hallway, which we follow until we hear the sound of boot-steps up ahead. Just down the hallway from us is a solidly-built guard. I can't see his face, but I'd recognize that clunky, boxy body anywhere. It's Chucker. He's got his back to us as he taps out some code on an input panel on the wall. A set of silver double-doors opens top to bottom in front of him. From here, we can see the skybridge begin its crawl from the Cube over to the Halo. Chucker begins walking along the skybridge even before it reaches the other side. We inch along, hugging the hallway wall, until we can see him disappear on the far side of the bridge through another set of horizontal double-doors. He walks to the right and disappears from view, and we follow along on the skybridge, the wind whipping at us as we cross with the Agora far below.

On the Halo side of the bridge, the corridor is as shiny silver inside as it is outside. The walls are embedded with black viz-screens and long lines of circuitry snaking through nearly every surface. Small rooms, alleyways, and shallow alcoves appear every ten or twenty yards on either side of the long, rounded hallway.

I expected more guards. More resistance. But the place has the eerie quiet of one of the bombed-out buildings back in the Valta. Like it's been denied the life and energy it was meant to have.

Finally, as we round a bend, we spot Chucker again. His back is to us as he taps in code on another input panel, this time in front of a large round door.

I signal to Brohn and Manthy to duck into one of the shallow alcoves on their side of the corridor while I duck into the opposite recess on my side. The small space looks like it must be some kind of information terminal. It's got holo-projectors and a communication input panel. There are high-tech scanner ports but also some pretty low-tech metal levers and energy outlets. But that's not what interests me.

It's the language of the digital labels for each component of the terminal. I don't know what is, but it's not English. Or

French. Or Chinese. Or any other language I can recognize on sight, even if I can't really read it. The red markings are a series of long curls, dots, and thin bands. If they were black and a little bigger, they'd look a lot like my forearm tattoos.

Across the hall, I see that Brohn and Manthy have made the same discovery. Brohn gives me a "what the hell?" look, which I have no choice but to answer with a baffled shrug.

For now, we need to focus on Chucker. He's maybe thirty yards away and clearly standing guard by the large round door. Something on the far end of the corridor has attracted his attention, but he returns his focus to his post. His head's on a swivel as he scans the corridor to his left and right. We're just far enough around a bend and deep enough in our little alcoves so that he doesn't have a clear view of us. Still, I'm not taking any chances sticking my head out just to have Chucker shoot it off.

I trace a pattern on my inner forearm. Instead of Render, though, I focus on Brohn just across the corridor. I picture his face, the line of his jaw, the cadence of his voice. I imagine him sitting across from me like he did back in the Silo. Then next to me. I can smell the gentle scent of his skin. I press my eyes tight and concentrate on how he makes me feel when I'm around him. I can feel his emotions mingling with mine and our voices as clear as day in each other's heads.

We need to see what he's guarding in that room, I tell him silently.

Even with my eyes closed, I know he's looking across at me. Confused. Startled. Pleased. His voice slips into my head:

He's too far away. He'll hear us if we charge at him.

Can you get him to look the other way?

Yes. But it'll cost me a knife.

Manthy and I have you covered. Do it.

Across the hallway, Brohn slips a knife from his inner jacket pocket and clicks it quietly open. Kneeling down and holding the weapon by its blade, he flicks his wrist with a quick snap.

The knife spins in a blur, flashing through the space behind Chucker's back in between him and the door he's guarding before skidding to a loud, metallic stop just past him on the corridor floor.

Chucker's head snaps around to identify the source of the sudden clanging reverberating throughout the Halo. By the time he gets five steps down the hall and leans down to pick up the knife, Brohn and I are on him.

Brohn hits him high, leaping up to crack him in the back of his thick neck with a vicious elbow strike. At the same time, I swipe Chucker's legs out from under him with a spinning heel-kick. He twists around but goes down hard, face-first into the corridor floor. Brohn finishes him off by grabbing him by the back of the head and smashing his face into the floor a second time. Chucker's leg twitches and then goes still as Manthy dashes up to join us. Brohn recovers Chucker's gun and slides it under his belt at the small of his back.

"Now we just need to get inside," I say. "You're up, Manthy."

Our connection is fading, but I get clear pulses of emotion from Brohn. He's worried about being here. About me. He wants me to be safe. He wants to protect me. He wants us to protect each other.

His feelings are a beautiful dance of colors, complicated and overlapping.

Retrieving his knife from the floor by Chucker, he pries off the cover of the access panel. Manthy steps forward. With a couple of deft motions, she's got the leads exposed, and she quickly disables the door's security protocols.

Brohn and I exchange a look and take simultaneous deep breaths.

"Ready for what's on the other side?" I ask.

He says, "No," and gives me a wink. "But whatever it is definitely won't be ready for us."

Manthy finishes her override and gives Brohn and me a

thumb's up. We brace our feet against the floor, and get ready to storm in.

Manthy inputs an open-door command, and the big silver door slides open with a thin, metallic whisper.

Brohn and I do a fast survey of the room. One person in a white lab coat, facing away from us and staring at a viz-screen, stands on the far side of the room. She whips around as we charge in.

Hiller.

Brohn has the barrel of Chucker's gun pressed to the center of her forehead before she knows what's happening.

"Time for a little truth," he says, his teeth clenched.

"What truth do you want?" she asks with an air of self-satisfied confidence she definitely shouldn't be feeling right now. While she's clearly startled to see us there, she covers her shock with a tense smile. "The truth about what's been happening here? Or the truth about what's about to happen? To you. To the war. To the world you thought you knew?"

"What is this place?" I ask her over Brohn's shoulder. "What is it, really?"

Hiller doesn't answer, but her eyes dart involuntarily over to the monitor just behind her.

I step over to it, but I can't read any of the figures or symbols. They're in the same style we saw out in the alcoves in the corridor and like the patterns on my arms.

"What's this say?" I ask Hiller. Even as I utter the words, I realize how strange it is to hear myself barking orders, especially at an adult who holds my fate in her hands. But I'm brimming with a new energy, a new confidence, and a new knowledge that my fate is in my own hands now more than ever. "I can't read this," I say.

"Of course not," Hiller sneers.

"*I* can read it."

It's Manthy. She steps past me and up to the monitor. She

scans her finger over the red and blue figures of the holo-screen. The lights quiver and dance at her touch. "It's us," she says. Her voice is choppy and strained. She sounds tired. "It's our deployments and outcomes. Intel: Scheduled for manual labor in hazard zones. Tech: Scheduled to be channeled into the service industry. Combat: Scheduled to be programmed to kill without question. Special Ops. Scheduled for…" She pauses like she doesn't recognize the word right away.

"Scheduled for what?" I ask.

"Termination."

I can feel my brow furrowing in confusion. None of this makes any sense.

Brohn has been in control of himself up until now. But now he's in a rage.

He presses the barrel of his gun to Hiller's forehead. "What does that mean? Termination?"

"It means what you think it means. You're as foolish as you are young, and you're as deceived as you are dead." Hiller pushes away the gun, but Brohn pulls it back and keeps it aimed a spot in the middle of her forehead. "What do you think we've been training you for all this time?" she shouts.

"To fight against the Eastern Order," Brohn says evenly.

Hiller laughs. "There is no Eastern Order!"

"What?"

"No Eastern Order. No enemy. Not like you think. There never has been."

Brohn squints and then gives a little laugh, himself. "You're crazy. We've seen the war. The Eastern Order destroyed our town. Killed our families."

"The violence was real. But the Order? That's just an invention of our own government. A way to instill fear and keep control."

Brohn shakes his head hard. "Not possible. We've seen—"

"What? Staged stories on a bunch of viz-screens? You saw

what we wanted you to see. We showed you what you needed to believe."

"You're lying!"

I put my hand on Brohn's arm. "I don't think she is."

"Why? Why us? Why the Seventeens?" Brohn's face is contorted with rage, and he's practically crying. Manthy is open-mouthed, and my brain is on a new level of overload.

Hiller leans back against the slanted wall of read-outs and input panels and looks from Brohn to me to Amaranthine. Brohn steps forward, his gun still pressed to her head and orders her to answer him.

She offers a sigh and a menacing stare. She's putting on a brave face, for someone about to die.

"Fine," Hiller says at last, "I guess it doesn't matter now anyway. Long ago, we discovered that an assemblage of genetic anomalies was causing certain people to manifest certain abilities. Always right around the age of sixteen going on seventeen. Always in the mountain towns around where you lived. Maybe because of the proximity to new kinds and amounts of radiation in the atmosphere. Maybe it's an evolutionary upheaval or some glitch in the genetic code. No one knows. No one really cares why. The Processors were set up to determine which of you could help the cause and which could hurt it. If you could be used, you lived. If you couldn't, or if you had the potential to do more harm than good, you died. All this so-called training you've been doing was just a matter of weeding out which of you was which." Hiller looks again from one of us to the other. She looks scared, but she's trying to sound brave. "Funny. The three of you here together. You were the real threat this year. The three who qualified for Special Ops."

I shake my head and lean toward her. "So Special Ops just means...?"

"That we were the biggest threat to them," Manthy whispers.

Hiller glances at her and nods. "You're the ones whose abilities were beyond our control. Amaranthine's techno-sensitivity. Kress's telepathy." She shoots me a look. "Oh, yes, Kress. We know all about it. And you, Brohn...well, you haven't even begun to discover your power yet."

I can see Brohn tensing. Like Manthy and me, he has to be wondering what exactly his mysterious hidden power is. But Hiller doesn't say.

"Terk was the one we really wanted," she continues. "Congratulations. The rest of you are all dead. We might have been able to use a few of you, but after this little stunt..."

Brohn has both hands on the gun now. Somehow, he's totally in control. His hands are way steadier than mine would be. "I'm not the one with the gun to my head," he says.

"You might as well be, Brohn," Hiller says with a menacing grin. "You were never going to get out of the Processor alive anyway. Now, you've just sealed your fate. You've tripped all kinds of alarms coming in here like this. You won't even get off the Halo."

Brohn looks back toward the door. Hiller takes advantage of his lapse in concentration. With her hands clamped on Brohn's she pushes against his trigger finger, and an explosive shot blasts her brains out onto the console behind her.

24

HILLER'S BODY SLUMPS TO THE FLOOR, HER HEAD A MESS OF WHITE hair and blood. Behind her, the console she was working at is lit up with schematics and scrolling lines of text in that strange language we've now seen a number of times.

"They're extermination orders," Manthy says.

"You can really read all that?" I ask.

She nods.

"It's a sorting protocol." Her voice is quiet, barely audible. She points to a series of dots and long, swooping symbols that are overlapping with holographic swirls of fluctuating charts and graphs. Manthy's eyes dart back and forth as she scans what we're seeing. "'Special Ops' is code. Like Hiller said, we weren't winning anything. We were being selected out for elimination. 'Special Ops' just means they didn't think they could control us well enough to actually use us. The Recruitment, the training... they were just a way to weed us out, to study us. And to help the government keep the lie going so they could maintain power, I guess forever." Her voice is even and matter-of-fact, like she's announcing the weather instead of informing us that we've spent the last three months living an impossibly deadly lie, not to mention the lie we'd been living for years before that. But as she stares at the images in front of her, I sense that she's mesmerized by the crushing waves of reality and by the enormity of the betrayal.

"So all that talk about improving us...?" Brohn asks.

"Oh, they were improving us all right," Manthy says. "Hiller was telling the truth about that much anyway. But it was for their benefit, not ours." She scans the display and gestures towards parts of it with a small wave of her hand. The symbols and images scroll and morph at her touch. "This is about us. Our Cohort. Class of 2042. And not just in the Valta either." She scans the images again to reveal a new cluster of symbols and morphing schematics. "See. There are more of us out there. More Seventeens being selected for Termination." She turns to look at us. "That must mean they have powers, too. Or at least potential."

"So it's been a big set-up," Brohn says with a heavy shake of his head. "A con. But if they're the other side, where's our side? Is there even really a war going on? If there's no Eastern Order, who bombed the Valta? Who killed our families?"

Manthy and I don't have an answer for him, but it wouldn't matter anyway. He's frozen. Stunned. He looks down at Hiller's body, slumped and lifeless on the floor. The muscles in his forearm tense, and I honestly think for a minute that he might shoot her again just for good measure.

Shaking off my own shock and remembering what Hiller said about alarms, I tug his arm. "We've got to get out of here, Brohn. Like right now!"

He shakes himself out of his daze and peers out the door with Manthy and me just behind him. Giving us an all-clear nod, he leads us out of the room. Chucker is still lying unconscious on the floor. Leaping over his prone body, we take off on a full-tilt run down the corridor and back to the skybridge only to find it drawing back into the Theta Cube. Someone must have given it the order to retract, which means two things: Brohn, Amaranthine, and I have been discovered, and we're about to be stuck on the Halo.

I don't even want to think about what happens after that. In front of us, the glistening silver bridge starts gliding away from us like some large aquatic animal slipping out into the sea.

"Come on!" Brohn shouts. "No time to second-guess ourselves!"

He explodes in another full-on sprint. His powerful legs propel him forward and out over the expanding void. His arms and legs flail with the effort as he soars across the increasing expanse of space.

He just makes it to the edge of the retreating skybridge, rolling forward as he lands to cushion the impact of the fall. Manthy's not so lucky. Running as fast as she can, she leaps a half-step behind Brohn, but her foot slips on the far edge of the skybridge, and she starts to plummet into the chasm below.

Sliding over to the edge of the bridge, Brohn snaps out his hand and catches her by the wrist. She reaches up to grab onto his forearm, and he hauls her up. They collapse together in a heap.

Brohn and Manthy are faster, stronger, and better jumpers than I am. And the space between the Halo and the Cube is just too far now. I watch with horror as the Agora appears in the darkness below. It's such a long way down.

Wind whips through my hair and chills my skin. A wave of dizziness crashes over me at the sight of the open field of green grass looming under now-still Halo. The bridge, taking Brohn and Manthy with it, has retreated beyond any distance I could ever hope to clear. There are no options. A fall from here would kill me. I've got a chasm I can't leap in front of me and the sound of men shouting and the thunder of their boots closing in behind me.

I'm trapped.

"Hurry!" Brohn screams. "You can still make it! I'll catch you!"

He slides on his stomach over to the edge of the bridge. His hand and arm are extended out over the void. Kneeling next to him, Manthy is trembling with desperation. Her eyes are pleading. Her face is a knot of urgency and worry. There is no mistaking the look of hopeless defeat on their faces. They know as well as I do that, one way or another, I'm as good as dead.

I shake my head and call across to them that it's too late. The skybridge is way too far away now. It's taking Brohn and Manthy away from me as it draws away to the far side. Brohn continues to reach his hand out to me, frantically waving me over to him, screaming at me to do what he knows is impossible.

"Go on!" I shout through my cupped hands across the distance. "I can't make it. You've got to warn the others!" I turn back to see soldiers coming around the bend, rushing toward me from down the curved silver hallway of the Halo. I consider doing something heroic like charging at them and taking out as many as I can to give Brohn and Manthy a couple of extra seconds to escape. The soldiers will have to wait for the skybridge to extend again anyway.

I'm determined to do what it takes to make it as hard as possible for them to hunt my friends down, even if it means dying.

I get ready to turn and face the armed, advancing men, my eyes already filling with tears at the thought of being shot, of falling to my death, of failing my friends.

Then, in a flash, I feel Render in my head.

Fly.

It's more of an idea than a word. A command, not a suggestion. And I know I need to obey.

Right now.

I'm suddenly filled with the ability and understanding of two minds, two souls. No time to think. No time to weigh the pros and cons. Turning back toward the impossibly wide breach between the Halo and the Theta Cube, I take a single step back, then a single step forward. I barely bend my knees as I leap out over the abyss. The deep green space below passes under me in a blur. Unlike Brohn and Manthy, I don't kick my legs or swing my arms for momentum. It's more of a glide, like I could go forever, clear any space between me and my friends.

With the wind whipping around me, I seem to coast through the air to an easy landing with both feet on the receding skybridge before stumbling forward into Brohn's and Manthy's waiting arms.

"How?" is all Brohn says, his mouth open, eyes wide. But I don't have an answer to give him, and we don't have time to figure it out. He gives me a quick, surprising kiss on the lips before we spin around, my heart racing now for more reasons than one.

The bridge has fully withdrawn, and the three of us hop up onto the landing in the Theta Cube. Across the way, five men, their guns drawn, slide to a stop on the Halo side of the expansive gap. They fire at us across the distance, but we're already around the corner and sprinting down the hall to the staircase that will take us back down to ground level. I duck anyway at the sound of bullets striking the walls behind us.

We dash through the bleak corridors of the Cube and scurry down the stairs. With Brohn leading the way, we skip half the stairs on each level, bounding to the landing below and then down the next flight of stairs. As we leap down the last steps, Cardyn, Karmine, Kella, and Rain are running up at the same time. We all practically collide into each other.

"What happened?" Karmine asks. He's as out of breath as we are.

Cardyn asks if I'm okay. "Not even close," I say. "It's the Order!"

"What about the Order?" he asks.

"All of this is a lie!" I shout, pointing back the way we came and then at the whole building around us. "The war, the training, everything. The Order doesn't exist!"

Brohn shouts, "Come on!" as he and Manthy start heading towards the main door leading back outside, but Cardyn, Karmine, Kella, and Rain don't budge.

"Are you saying they've been defeated?" Rain asks. "Has there been a breach? What do you mean?"

"There's no breach," I snap at her. "This place *is* the Order!"

"Just trust her," Brohn barks. "We've got to move!"

Rain takes a tentative step forward. "Where?"

"The woods," I say. "It's our only chance. If we stay here, we die."

"We can't leave without Terk!" Rain says. "He wasn't in the Eta Cube. We looked everywhere. There's no one in there. Not even guards." She's clearly overwhelmed and on the verge of tears.

Brohn shakes his head. "We don't have a choice. We don't know where he is. If he's even..."

He glances at Manthy and me and doesn't have to finish. The three of us know the truth: Terk belongs to the other side now. If he's even still alive, that is.

"We need to go," Brohn says. "We don't have time to look for him. Did you find any supplies?"

Rain points to a small canvas backpack she's got slung over her shoulder. "Like I said, place was empty. But we grabbed what little we could find. A few medical supplies and a bit of food." She holds up two small hand-guns. "Oh, and these might come in handy. No extra ammo, but at least they're loaded."

Brohn frowns but nods and then leads us through the Theta Cube's main door. We dart down the fenced in corridor, under the empty guard turret, and out onto the edge of the Agora.

"How do we get out of the Processor?" Kella asks. "The guards and the fences...?"

"I can get us out," I say. "There's a blind-spot over there between the Zeta and Eta Cubes. And a gap in the fence out back they don't know about. If we're careful and follow just the right path, we can slip past the cameras and motion-detectors and be out of here in two minutes."

Rain is still reeling. "How do you know all this?"

"I *don't* know," I answer honestly. "But Render does. He dreamt it for me." With that I gesture toward the sky.

Above us, Render swoops down on cue and leads the way along the edge of the Agora, past the Eta Cube. On the far side of the Agora, lights start springing to life in the other Cubes and in the guard turrets. A squad of scrambling men starts to charge across the large field in our direction.

With Render's sleek black form gliding effortlessly in front of us, we run as a group, the Halo looming ominously above. Instead of its slow rotation, it's now deadly still. Instead of pure polished chrome, it has a strip of red lights running along its underside and blinding spotlights activated around its edges. It may be night-time, but the Agora and the surrounding Cubes are suddenly lit up like the mid-afternoon sun.

With all of us packed in tight, we zip between the Zeta and Eta Cubes, out of the intense white light, and down the same dark alleyway I saw in my vision. Render darts left and right ahead of us, fluttering slowly and beating his wings hard to stay aloft as we scramble to keep up. Brohn has stepped to the side to let me take the lead.

We run single-file, careful to follow Render's path exactly until we're safely behind the Zeta Cube with nothing but a massive electrified fence and the dark woods in front of us. After a mad dash between a nearly invisible gap in the razor wire fence, we leap into the woods and skitter down an embankment. The ground is crunchy under our feet. The earth is dry and lifeless, and the black trees lean in dense clusters around us.

Ducking and running along blindly in the gloom of oncoming night, we arrive at a clearing where thirteen people—ten boys and three girls, all with Special Ops badges—lie dead in shackles along a long, raised stage. Their arms are chained into a series of pillories, their bodies are slumped over, blood pooling below them and dripping off the edge of the platform to soak the ground below.

Standing over them are Trench, Granden, and one other figure we all recognize in a sickening instant of shock: Terk. He's dressed in the same military fatigues as Granden and Trench. He's as big as ever, but his long hair is gone, and two deep scars run along either side of his shaved head. Coils of wire run from his temple and down the side of his neck before disappearing into his left arm, which is now an immense assembly of steel plates with long black metallic tubes snaking down from his shoulder like iron tendons. More braids of wire run down his wrist to a three-pronged black metal vice where his hand used to be.

Trench quickly overcomes the shock of seeing us outside the Processor. He hops down from the stage, whips his Sig Sauer from his holster, and starts blasting away at us.

We dive for cover, our arms over our heads, and huddle behind a cluster of dried tree trunks. With deafening cracks, bullets blast chunks of bark from the trees. Clouds of wood shards burst into the air around us.

In the moment it takes for Trench to reload his weapon, Brohn gives a nod to Karmine and Kella who take off in opposite directions, ducking low as bullets swarm again in the air around us like angry bees.

Outflanking the men at the foot of the stage, Karmine and Kella fire the two small guns Rain found at Granden and Trench, and both men crumple to the ground. Karmine runs over to Terk before Kella can stop him.

"Terk! It's us! We've got to get out of here!" he shouts.

He's answered by a violent swing of Terk's metal arm that strikes him hard in the chest, sending him sprawling back, confused, horrified, and grimacing in pain.

I leap over a fallen tree trunk and shout across the clearing to Karmine. "Kar! Get out of there! He's not one of us anymore!"

Karmine is crab-walking away from Terk, his feet scrambling and slipping on the dry ground. As Terk advances on him, Karmine grabs Trench's gun that's lying on the ground just beside him.

"Don't make me do this!" he shouts at Terk, training his gun on our big friend.

Terk lumbers forward, and Karmine fires.

Terk deflects the bullet with his metal arm. Karmine fires again, but the gun's bolt has slid back after the last round. The chamber is empty. Terk takes two giant steps forward and grabs Karmine by the arm. Karmine tries to pull away, but Terk has him in a vice-like grip, his metal pincers locked around Karmine's wrist.

"Terk, No!" Kella shouts as she bursts into the clearing. She lunges at Terk, leaping onto his back with her arms in a strangle-hold around his neck.

But Terk doesn't seem to register anything. It's not just his arm that's changed. It's like he's all machine now. Unfeeling. His eyes are black and unfocused. With his human arm, he slings Kella off, sending her flying across the dry glade. Even for him, his strength seems unworldly and off the charts.

He turns his attention back to Karmine and slams him hard to the ground. Stunned, Karmine is just trying to get to his knees when Terk swings the weight of his prosthetic arm up hard in a huge arc. His metal forearm smashes into the side of Karmine's head. Through a spray of blood, Karmine slides twenty feet across the clearing and lands up against a large rock, his head tilted on his neck at an impossible angle.

Terk turns his attention next to Brohn, Cardyn, and Rain, who have jumped over the fallen log and darted over to where Karmine is lying, twisted and still.

From the safety of our cover, I grab Amaranthine hard by the arm. "His circuitry—can you tap into it?"

She's shaking, her eyes wet with oncoming tears, her breath a series of uneven gasps. But she reins in the panic attack and manages a series of quick nods.

I tap my implants and connect with Render who swoops down around Terk's head. Distracted, he drops his guard, and Brohn and Cardyn are able to charge him and tackle him to the ground. He lashes out with his metal arm and sends Brohn flying through the air to the far side of the clearing. Brohn smashes back-first into a tree and slumps to the ground. It takes him a few seconds to push himself to his feet.

Cardyn delivers a straight punch to Terk's jaw, but Terk shrugs it off and lumbers to his feet. He drops Cardyn with a back-fist strike with his human arm. He raises the mechanical one, prepared to deliver a killing blow, but the arm freezes above his head. Next to me, Amaranthine has her eyes shut tight. She's trembling with the effort of connection. I know how it feels. I've felt it with Render—the feeling of being one with an energy other than your own. It's a shock to the system.

But right now, it's a shock we can't live without.

Rain has grabbed Granden's gun from the ground. I call out, "Now!" and she fires off a shot that hits Terk a glancing blow across the temple. Terk goes down in a heap just as a mass of lights and alarms explode in a chaotic storm from the woods behind us.

Amaranthine and I leap into the clearing to join Brohn, Rain, Cardyn, and Kella. We're just running out of the clearing and into the tangle of woods leading away from the Processor, the lights, and the sound of dozens of soldiers on the hunt for us, when someone latches onto my arm. The grip is tight. The voice in my ear is urgent, but gentle and weak at the same time. "Follow Render."

The voice is Granden's. A search light passes over us, and I can see his face. It's roughed up and bruised with blood seeping down his cheek from a bullet-wound above his eye. "I'll keep them off of you for as long as I can," he says. His eyes dart left and right before landing on mine. He's shaking. "If I don't see you again, Kress," he says through what sounds like a sob, "you have my apologies. It's been an honor. You'll make a fine leader." He lets go of my arm and stumbles away into the dark tangle of branches around us.

Cardyn calls back to me. "Kress! Come on!"

Catching up with the others, I spot Render perched on a branch down a small path leading between banks of black and broken trees.

Dashing past the others, I grab Manthy by the hand and call out to Brohn. "This way!"

In a mad scramble, we dash down a thin path, which quickly disappears, and we duck into the thick of the woods. We might not know where we are exactly. But we know this type of terrain. Because of our lives in the Valta, surviving in the woods has practically become second nature to us.

Now that I think about it, surviving, itself, has become second nature to us. We're survivors. What's more, we're a Conspiracy. And we have family to fight for, friends to avenge, and an enemy to take down.

To do all that, we need to live.

Flushed with adrenaline, we sprint along, dodging and weaving through a maze of black tree trunks with Render flying low just up ahead. He stops from time to time to alight on a branch so the rest of us can catch up. Then he's off again, a black glistening shadow slicing through the darkness of the devastated forest.

The thunder of the men's boots behind us grows dim until it fades away completely. We hear men's voices calling out to each other, but they're far off now, heading in the opposite direction.

Granden must have misdirected them. I don't know why he helped us, but I hope we all live long enough to find out.

The six of us slide down a ravine and navigate our way through a series of enormous root systems. The branches and vines form a tangled maze with razor sharp brambles and thorns slicing at us, cutting through our clothes and skin as we run. Arriving at another steep drop-off, I lead us down into a dried river bed. Just behind me, Brohn loses his footing and slides past me before coming to a stop at the bottom of the slope by my feet.

Render circles overhead. He cries out a series of "all clear" *kraas*.

"So we're safe?" Brohn pants as the others stand behind him. After a moment I realize that all eyes are trained on me, searching for an answer.

Nodding, I reach out a hand and help Brohn to his feet.

"For now, at least. For now."

End of Book 1

NEXT IN SERIES

If you enjoyed this book, please consider leaving a review on Amazon. Reviews help books' visibility and help authors in many, many ways.

Also:

Book Two of the Resistance Trilogy, *Render,* is out now!

Having discovered a terrible secret, Kress and Render lead the others on a dangerous journey. But nothing is ever quite as it seems, and danger lurks behind every corner...

A NEW SERIES BY K. A. RILEY: SEEKER'S WORLD

What readers are saying about K. A. Riley's Fantasy series:

"This book will keep you riveted..."

"A page turner. It stirred up memories of how I felt reading the Twilight Series..."

On her seventeenth birthday, Vega Sloane receives a strange and puzzling gift: a key in the shape of a dragon's head, along with a note that claims she's destined to save the world.

When the handsome and mysterious Callum Drake enters her life, she finds herself inextricably drawn to him, and more questions begin to arise. Who is the boy beyond the exquisite façade and charming smile?

Get the books here:

Seeker's World
Seeker's Quest
Seeker's Fate
Seeker's Promise

On her seventeenth birthday, Vega Sloane receives a series of strange and puzzling gifts. Among them is a key shaped like a dragon. The question is: What exactly is it meant to open?

All of a sudden, the peaceful town where Vega grew up is crawling with shadows, strange beings and unlikely allies.

Vega soon discovers that many of the ancient stories she once considered myths and legends are true, and that a magical world exists beyond her own...one that only the chosen few can see. It's a world where cruel beings stalk the lands and magic lives on the air, where the Blood-born prove their worth in an ancient academy that trains those born with special powers.

Get it here: Seeker's World

ALSO BY K. A. RILEY

Resistance Trilogy

Recruitment

Render

Rebellion

Emergents Trilogy

Survival

Sacrifice

Synthesis

Transcendent Trilogy

Travelers

Transfigured

Terminus

Academy of the Apocalypse Series

Emergents Academy

Seeker's World Series

Seeker's World

Seeker's Quest

Seeker's Fate

Seeker's Promise

Athena's Law Series

Book One: *Rise of the Inciters*

Book Two: *Into an Unholy Land*

Book Three: *No Man's Land*

If you're enjoying K. A. Riley's books, please consider leaving a review on Amazon or Goodreads to let your fellow book-lovers know about it. And be sure to sign up for my newsletter at www.karileywrites.org for news, quizzes, contests, behind-the-scenes peeks into the writing process, and advance info. about upcoming projects!

K.A. Riley's Bookbub Author Page

K.A. Riley on Amazon.com

K.A. Riley on Goodreads.com

Milton Keynes UK
Ingram Content Group UK Ltd.
UKHW010644031023
429856UK00004B/228